L.A. Outlaws

This Large Print Book carries the
Seal of Approval of N.A.V.H.

L.A. Outlaws

A NOVEL

T. Jefferson Parker

LARGE PRINT PRESS
A part of Gale, Cengage Learning

GALE
CENGAGE Learning

Detroit • New York • San Francisco • New Haven, Conn • Waterville, Maine • London

3|09   16.00/ 9.57

GALE
CENGAGE Learning™

Copyright © 2008 by T. Jefferson Parker.
Large Print Press, a part of Gale, Cengage Learning.

ALL RIGHTS RESERVED
This book is a work of fiction. Names, characters, places, and incidents
either are the product of the author's imagination or are used
fictitiously, and any resemblance to actual persons, living or dead,
business establishments, events or locales is entirely coincidental.
The text of this Large Print edition is unabridged.
Other aspects of the book may vary from the original edition.
Set in 16 pt. Plantin.
Printed on permanent paper.

LIBRARY OF CONGRESS CATALOGING-IN-PUBLICATION DATA

Parker, T. Jefferson.
  L. A. outlaws / by T. Jefferson Parker.
    p. cm.
  ISBN-13: 978-1-4104-0435-0 (hardcover : alk. paper)
  ISBN-10: 1-4104-0435-8 (hardcover : alk. paper)
    1. Los Angeles (Calif.) — Fiction. 2. Large type books. I. Title.
  PS3566.A6863L25 2008b
  813'.54—dc22   2007040680

ISBN 13: 978-1-59413-306-0 (pbk. : alk. paper)
ISBN 10: 1-59413-306-9 (pbk. : alk. paper)
Published in 2009 in arrangement with Dutton, a member of Penguin
Group (USA) Inc.

Printed in the United States of America
1 2 3 4 5 6 7 13 12 11 10 09

For Rick and Debra

1

Here's the deal: I am a direct descendant of the outlaw Joaquin Murrieta. He was a kickass horseman, gambler and marksman. He stole the best horses and robbed rich Anglos at gunpoint. He loved women and seduced more than a few during his twenty-three years. Some of his money he gave to the poor, but to be truthful most of it he spent on whiskey, guns, expensive tailored clothes and on the women and children he left behind.

I got Joaquin Murrieta's good looks. I got his courage and sense of justice for the poor. I got his contempt for the rich and power-ful. I got his love of seduction. Like Joaquin used to, I love a good, clean armed robbery. I steal beautiful cars instead of beautiful horses.

Right now I'm about to stick up a west-side dude for twenty-four thousand dollars in cash. He won't be happy, but he'll turn it over.

And I'll be richer and more famous than I already am.

My name is Allison Murrieta.

Here's how you get a mark to bring you that much in cash: you put an ad in the *Auto Trader* for a 2005 BMW 525, low mileage and mint condition, and you ask twenty-five thousand, which is three grand less than it's worth. You get a lot of calls on that car. They know you should be asking twenty-eight, but you're a woman and you don't sound overly bright. You've got a soft voice. You talk up the Beemer's options and upgrades. The creamy leather and all that, even though BMW leather isn't creamy. You say you're pretty sure it's worth more but you're willing to sell quick because there have been some disappointments lately and you really do need to get on with your life.

You can hear the excitement in the men's voices. The women often say they understand the disappointment part. You set up a time and a location to meet and you forget about them.

You're waiting for Greed to make its appearance. It always does. Guaranteed. In this scam it's always a dude, because they smell a chick in distress and can't pass up an opportunity to help her out and cheat her at the same time.

"Will you take twenty-four thousand in cash?" Greed asks.

You can hear the pride in his voice when he says the word. *Cash.* You try to sound firm. "I need twenty-five. I think that's a pretty good deal for a 525 with twelve thousand miles, isn't it?"

"You said LoJack and navigation?"

"Premium sound, too."

"Twenty-four, cash."

"Okay. I'm Allison."

"Rex. What's your address?"

Laurel Canyon. Dusk on an August Saturday, about eight P.M. The L.A. sky is orange and gray and the air smells like flowers and exhaust.

The lot is tree-shaded, surrounded by a wall heavy with nightshade. There's a "For Sale" sign out front on the street. It took me weeks to find this place. The right place is everything.

I park down the street and wait outside the house, a swanko glass-and-steel job with big smoked windows. Nobody can see me from the street. I've got my back to the driveway. I've got my gloves on and my mask on and my hair under a wig and the wig in a ponytail. My leather satchel sits on the ground beside me.

When I hear the car coming up the drive behind me, I hold Cañonita up next to my ear. Cañonita is a .40-caliber, two-shot, over-and-under, ivory-handled derringer that fits in the palm of my hand and from any distance at all looks like a cell phone. It will blow a big hole in you but is accurate only to about ten feet. Maybe. I continue to stand in front of the window with my back to the driveway.

In the smoked glass I watch Greed come up the drive in an old BMW 535, probably a '92; he's got it washed and waxed and the "For Sale" sign taped inside a window. He's five minutes early. I leave my back to him, and my head cocked toward Cañonita.

Greed parks and gets out. He's forty and fit, wavy gray hair. I see his reflection as he walks up, and I'm careful to keep my back to him. He smiles small, trying to keep his good luck under wraps and not tip me to my own stupidity. He approaches, checking out my butt, his smile tight and dry.

"Allison. Rex."

I impatiently wave him toward me but I don't turn around. I can't allow a mere person to interrupt a cell call.

Rex walks obediently toward me, stops, looks around. "Where's the car?"

I can't let him come any closer or he'll make me. Or at least he should.

In the window, reflected Rex looks oddly hopeful, then I turn, take a quick step up to him and place Cañonita right in front of his eyes. The two barrels must look gigantic to him at this range. Tunnels to hell.

"Fuck," he says quietly. *"You."*

Rex backpedals off-balance, falls but gets up and backpedals again. Two seconds later I've got him over the hood of his ancient sedan, gun pressed up nice and snug to his forehead. I'm physically strong, have a black belt in hapkido, and I'm swearing at him in a very calm voice. Through the windshield I see the envelope on the passenger seat and think to myself, Mother of God, people do the dumbest things, which is exactly why I do so well in my business.

"Is that my money, shithead? That better be my money I see in there."

Of course I talk like this is because I'm half terrified that something might go wrong. Terrified I'll have to shoot this guy — there's a first time for everything. The words are just weapons, something I can use to hurt and scare him.

He picks this moment to try to turn things around. Almost every guy will try to fight you. Most dudes just cannot get jacked at

11

gunpoint by a woman without putting up a fight — they're incapable of it. I feel his body tighten and hear him holding his breath, and I know he's about to explode on me, so I blast him with the full-strength pepper spray I have ready in my left hand, and he writhes away and slides down to the driveway with an agonized moan.

I get the envelope and make sure it's my money.

He's on his elbows and knees now, his face buried in his hands, breathing fast and whining quietly with each exhale. He peeks up at me, eyes flooded. I rock him over with one steel-toed construction boot and zap him again. Then I cinch his wrists and ankles with plastic ties from my pants pocket, tight but not tight enough to cut him unless he struggles.

"The car's worth thirty, dumbass," I say. "You get what you pay for."

I get my satchel and drop one of my cards beside him. He's crying. I walk away while into the satchel goes Cañonita, my mask, my money and my black wig. I shake out my own light brown hair and slide the pepper spray into its little holster on my belt.

I round the nightshade-covered wall.

Then I stride — don't hurry, don't hustle, don't trot — toward my car. It's parked one house away, facing downhill toward Sunset.

What a nice evening. Some frat boys in a ragtop Mustang check me out on their way up the hill, hoot and holler. Nice to be appreciated.

I've got a little swagger to my step, and I'm tapping the mask and envelope against my left thigh with each stride toward my Corvette Z06 — 505 big-block horses, all mine. They whinny as I get in.

2

Home for tonight is the Luxe Summit Hotel up Sunset — big rooms, you can park yourself and you're right on the freeway. I let myself in, shower off the fear, break up my cell phone on the cool bathroom tile and flush the pieces down the toilet. I've got three more cells, the ones you load with prepaid minutes and toss before the number gets hot.

I lie down on the bed and picture Rex coming toward me, checking me out. Then his eyes, bloodshot and dripping tears. I sleep hard for an hour, dream I'm riding a horse along a beach where I hold up a good-looking buck with a saddlebag full of gold bars then we make love in a sand dune on the beach and I steal both horses and ride away while he sleeps.

I eat some of the food I stocked in the fridge, shower again and put on laundered jeans, cowboy boots and a yoked C&W

blouse I shoplifted from a saddlery up in Topanga. I make the local ten o'clock news: *The armed robber who calls herself Allison Murrieta has apparently struck again, this time in the Hollywood Hills . . .*

They show the nightshade-covered wall, partially lit by roving spotlights, and the dark driveway. Then they run the popular video clip that shows a woman robbing a McDonald's. It's from last year. It's me all right. Everything on screen is yellow and red and cheery except this babe dressed in black with a gun. I had no idea somebody was shooting video, but these days somebody always is. Luckily I have my professional face on, which means my wig is back in the ponytail and I'm wearing my mask. The mask is made of thick cardboard with black satin glued over it. I cut it to shape, added the satin and one very nice Swarovski crystal for fun. It covers my nose and eyes, cheeks and mouth, ears. Then the news shows an enlarged image from the McDonald's video, and I note again that with the mask on I look stylish and dangerous. The crystal is near the mouth opening, and it draws your eye, just like Marilyn's birthmark. The network goes to a commercial for — you guessed it — McDonald's.

My next job is at midnight, a little over an hour from now. If it goes as planned, I'll leave Hollywood with forty-five thousand dollars' worth of unmounted gem-quality diamonds.

Here's the plot: a friend of a friend of a friend's boyfriend is a diamond district broker, young guy, a real go-getter and they love him at the Caesars' sports book in Las Vegas and you know how it goes — he's lucky and he's smart and then he's neither. Barry. Takes him two years to run his business into the ground, borrowing, betting, losing. Throw in lots of booze. The bottom line is that Barry is into the Asian Boyz for seventy-five grand and he's willing to give them four hundred and fifty thousand retail dollars' worth of very good and very insured diamonds because the cut will be one-tenth when the Boyz manage to fence them. You'll notice that Barry is cheating the Boyz by almost half. They don't know that. They're amateurs and they're kids. They don't know that it isn't easy to lay off that much ice to one guy, all at once.

I can. The arrangements are made. Forty-five thousand dollars won't make me rich, but I love diamonds.

I just have to hit up Barry before he makes

it to the Boyz at Miracle Auto Body in City Terrace at one A.M.

And I know something way more valuable than where he's going. I know where he'll be *leaving from,* and it's his own damned fault that I do.

See, Barry is not a good man. He's Greed, too, just like Rex. In order to pay down his debt, Barry talked his girlfriend Melissa out of ten thousand dollars. But he won't pay her back. All she gets is excuses. Barry's not only gone hostile on her, he's trying to work another girlfriend into their life. I hear that Melissa is a little brokenhearted and a lot pissed off. But Barry's careless, you know — he treats her like a moron — so it was easy for her to learn the payback plan for the Boyz. Then she sent word up the friends' ladder to see if anyone could help her get her money back. If Barry had any real stones he'd have taken care of his woman. But since he doesn't, he's going to have to deal with me. And much more important, he'll have to deal with the Asian Boyz, who will be unhappy when I steal what he owes them. Barry's going to have to get his hands on enough diamonds to buy his life not once but twice.

You make your own luck.

17

I don't leave one thing at the Luxe Summit that I can't live without.

I pull up to Barry's place just before midnight. It's a modest little stucco off Highland in Hollywood. It's got stands of giant bird-of-paradise and rhododendron for privacy. The lights are on but the shutters are closed.

Melissa said that Barry will leave from home. She guaranteed it. Barry's a homebody, she swore. Home is where he is unless he's in Las Vegas or at the office down in the diamond district; home is where he loves to be, where he drinks and cooks and watches sports on the tube hour after hour — Melissa could hardly get Barry to drive her to Philippe's for a French dip. Home also has the safe where Barry will stash the four hundred and fifty thousand retail dollars' worth of diamonds he's going to give the Boyz.

Melissa also said that Barry's gun stays up in a closet at home because he's afraid of it. Never carries it.

Good to know.

I park across the street two houses down and watch for just a minute. The street lamps are far-spaced and dim. I've cased the place, and I know the giant bird-of-paradise and the rhododendron are my friends. Nobody who carries diamonds for a living should have anything but a low hedge and floodlights out front of their house. Barry undoubtedly knows this, but an informed fool is still a fool. Barry thinks he can be invisible just by keeping a straight face. The walkway to the front door isn't even lit. From the street you can barely see the front door and that's good for me. The porch light is on. I listen to the police band radio for a minute or two, just in case some Hollywood Station PD patrol car gets a call nearby, but most of the cops talk on the mobile data terminals now to discourage people like me from listening in.

At midnight I'm walking down the sidewalk with my satchel — it's a big leather and brass-studded Hobo I shoplifted from Nordstrom — same side of the street as Barry's house. When I get to his yard, I cut across the grass in the dark and push through the rubbery rhododendrons.

I hit the ground and walk on my hands and knees below the shuttered windows, dragging the Hobo along beside me. When I get to the porch, I stand up with my back near the stucco wall, spin my hair into a ponytail and put on the wig. Next I pull the mask from the satchel and put it on, then get Cañonita ready. I've got the pepper spray on

19

my belt. I'm not expecting any fight from Barry, but sometimes the chumps surprise you. My heart is pounding like someone just mainlined me with ten cc's of pure adrenaline.

I love it.

I breathe deeply and try to clear my mind. I listen to the soft whap of the bugs against the porch light and the whirring of the air conditioner up on the roof.

Minutes. Seconds. More minutes.

By twelve-forty I'm pretty sure that something's wrong. You don't leave Hollywood for City Terrace with twenty minutes to spare and your life at stake unless you have major stones, and I know Barry does not.

I give him five more minutes then put my things back into my bag, walk to the car and stash the gun under the passenger seat.

I call Barry's cell number — courtesy of Melissa, of course. She also supplied a picture of him and the make, model and plate number of his car. No answer on the cell, just Barry's curt little message, like I shouldn't have interrupted him.

I wonder if the plans have changed. I wonder how good Melissa's information really was. I wonder if she might have mixed up one A.M. with one P.M. And I wonder if Barry might have just cut and run.

I'm outside Miracle Auto Body at eleven minutes after one.

3

The shop sits under the paths of both Interstate 10 and 710, surrounded by a chain-link fence topped with five strands of back-slanted barbed wire. It's loud out here, and it smells like metal and paint and rubber. City Terrace isn't a city at all — it's L.A. Sheriff's turf. That's good because the Sheriffs are usually spread a little thinner. Usually. And I know a couple of them. On one side of Miracle Auto Body is a tire shop, and on the other is a former junkyard surrounded by a fence with shiny circles of razor ribbon on top.

I lower a window and listen to the steady roar of the freeway traffic. There are twenty or so busted-up cars out front of the body shop, like they just fell down from the one of the interstates and got in line for their miracle. Some look bad and some you can't see what's wrong. Behind them there's a big concrete-block building with a glass-roofed high bay where the pounding and painting are done.

When I cased it three nights ago, the lights inside were off and outside security floods were blazingly on.

But now the inside lights are on and the yard lights are off.

I get an odd feeling.

I know what I should do: put my foot on the brake, put the 'Vette back into gear and leave. Absolutely. No question about it. I have no reason to be here in the first place, other than my curiosity about Barry and the diamonds.

My diamonds.

Woman, put your cute little car in gear and drive away. You've got 505 horsepower under that shiny yellow hood. Use it.

I throw the car into drive and go. I feel cagey and proud of my self-control. I take a deep breath, but the steering wheel turns wide right, then sharp left, and I finish the U-turn and stop again outside Miracle. When I roll down the window, the roar of the interstates comes at me from behind the shop. The roar says, Check it out, Allison, we'll cover you.

It's a nice offer.

I try to figure the risk. If I get caught here by the Sheriffs, they'll detain me and a warrants check on my license will come back clean because I've never been arrested. The 'Vette plates will come up clean because the car is hot but the plates are not. I'll tell them I was looking for a guy who said he owns this place, we had a late date, you know, my business and not yours.

But why would the Sheriffs roll up now? It's late. It's quiet.

If there was noise or a complaint, they'd have checked it out hours ago.

Maybe nothing happened. Maybe the Miracle workers quit work early because it's a Saturday, forgot the lights, and headed home for the night. Maybe I'm imagining trouble where there isn't any. Maybe that's why I'm not in prison.

Opportunity knocks softly or not at all. It's my job to listen.

Just a look in the window.

I ease the car down the service road shared by Miracle and the tire shop. The darkness closes in a notch. The road is pitted and the Z06 bumps hard. I see the big concrete stanchions of the interstates looming ahead, and the rivers of light made by thousands of headlamps.

In the parking lot there are six cars: a pimped black Escalade, a black 500 SL, two Accords with fat tires and stingers, Barry's red Acura — thanks again to Melissa — and an older white panel van. The first four are Asian Boyz rides, but the panel van sticks out like a leg in a cast and I can't figure it.

I swing around and park away from the other cars, facing the exit. I turn off the engine, pull on my leather gloves. I think about putting on the mask and wig but don't — I'm just satisfying my curiosity now, not pulling a job. I'm innocent. I nudge the door closed with my thigh, palm Cañonita and walk toward the building like I own the place, which is how I walk everywhere.

I pass through a sliding chain-link gate to get in. The gate is open. That odd feeling comes back.

Well, I've been warned.

But I think about what's inside. My diamonds.

I start up the steps to the landing and the front door. Light spills from inside. I take long, quiet steps, quiet as I can be. At the door I look through the dirty glass to the lobby and see brown carpet, a long counter, the back end of a computer monitor, a wall with a girlie calendar and a hallway leading to the bay in back. The counter has a lift door which is open and up. Behind the counter there's an open office door, and I can see the desk and chair inside, a steel file cabinet thrown open, another chair tipped over and lying in the doorway. I check for surveillance cameras but don't see any.

I look back at the cars waiting for bodywork. There's an elevated steel catwalk around the building, and I follow it one quiet step at a time. I use the safety railing to steady myself. The sound of the freeways presses in close.

The windows are low and cranked open in the summer heat. Up on my toes I can see into the bay. It's one big room, divided into side-by-side workstations by disposable paper drapes affixed to railings with sliding hooks, an industrial version of hospital privacy curtains. Some of the workstations have cars in them, in various stages of repainting. The color of each car is the color on the curtain around it, bright reds and blacks and silvers. Big industrial fans sway the sheets. No cameras that I can see.

A dead guy lies by a red Honda. He's still got a painter's breathing apparatus over his face.

Twenty feet away in the direction of the lobby are two more bodies, apparently men and apparently dead. One has a pistol in his hand. The other's gun is a few feet away.

Another fifteen feet toward the lobby lie two other guys.

I stare at each one of the men again for a few seconds, looking for movement but seeing none. Just the lilting of the paper curtains.

I walk down to the next window. My heart is in my throat and the interstates are roaring in my ears. Other than that I feel a clarity that overrules fear.

From here I can see back farther toward the lobby, and I find exactly what I expect to. Two more men down near a yellow Thunderbird, their M243 SAW machine guns strapped around their necks.

Then, just inside the door leading to the lobby there are two more bodies. They've fallen over each other. A Mossberg military combat shotgun rests a few inches from one of the outstretched hands. The same guy has a red canvas backpack still clutched in the other.

One more man is sprawled faceup and arms out a few feet away. He's wearing a suit and tie. It's Barry.

Ten people.

Ten and out.

That's a lot of dead men.

I lean against the building and look up at the towering overpasses and their halos of headlights. I breathe deeply and try to see things for what they are. I look through the window again for security cameras: nothing. I look to the rear of the bay, to the metal roll-up door where they bring the vehicles in and out. It's closed. I see the control panel for that door, the big red button and the big black one.

Then I go back to the front door and try it. Locked.

I get a feeling that isn't quite a thought. Something to do with the guns inside and the locked front door.

Back under the second window I squat in the darkness and wonder how loud the firefight must have been. It looks to have been brief by the way the bodies fell. Nobody got very far. I try to gauge the roar of the interstates and imagine the blasting and popping of the pneumatic wrenches of the tire shop nearby, and I figure, sure, it's possible, you could have a neat little ten-man shoot-out here in this industrial wasteland under the freeways, and unless you had a customer waiting in the lobby or a bum in the Dumpster out back or a Sheriff's patrol just happen by, nobody would even hear it. The whole thing could have been over in a minute.

I can see that.

But I can't see the victors walking out the front door and locking it behind them.

And I can't see them scrambling to get out ahead of the back roll-up door as it rattled down.

And I can't see them climbing out the window right above me, either.

I can't see the victors leaving all that hardware behind. Gangsters don't leave good weapons lying around. It just doesn't happen.

The bottom line is I can't see any victors at all. I don't think anyone got away. Which makes me think of Barry's diamonds.

My diamonds.

I climb through the window.

4

Inside the fans whir and the paper curtains sway and rattle.

I move quickly to the red backpack, unzip the main compartment and look inside. For being worth four hundred and fifty thousand dollars at your local Zales, the parcels are small and trim. The gemstone papers are the size of business cards, white and crisp and held together with rubber bands. Each is lined with lint-free blue gem paper. The contents of every paper is handwritten by the grader. The diamonds are loose and brilliant. Most are half-carat, a few smaller and several bigger. One is a mondo two-carat beauty that takes away what is left of my breath. Most are round-cut, but flipping through, I see some marquises and pears and squares. In this light I can't judge quality. I'm looking down at scores of marriage proposals, engagements, anniversaries, Valentine's Days, apologies and seductions

— and thousands of hours of sex, guaranteed by these stones. I'm looking down at treasures found in dark, filthy Transvaal mines, plucked by slaves whose only rewards will be poverty and early death. No wonder they're so valuable.

Great job, Allison. You figured it right.

I stash the parcels and zip up the backpack, sling it over my shoulder and stand. Everywhere I look there's either paint or blood, and I can smell them both. I palm Cañonita and quickly tour the battlefield, walking fast and not stopping.

The two dead gunmen beside me are Asian Boyz. God knows how many holes in them.

The next two are Mara Salvatrucha — MS-13 — an L.A. Central American gang so ridiculously violent the FBI has an entire task force dedicated just to them. These are the guys with the machine guns. MS-13 always has good weapons because the U.S. supplied the Salvadoran contras for almost a decade and most of the hardware is still down there. So they bring it back up here. These dead Salvadorans are small-bodied men, young, their arms covered with MS-13 tats.

The two dead gunmen fifteen feet away are Asian Boyz.

Farther in are two more MS-13.

Now I'm to the dead guy I saw first, the

one who never had time to get his painter's mask off. He's Asian. The mask has slid to one side. He looks about sixteen years old. I have a special affection for sixteen-year-old boys. He's been shot up badly, which means the Salvadorans probably got themselves killed by using all their ammo on a car painter.

I stop for just a second and look back on the trail of bodies and blood.

You don't have to be a cop to read this mess. First, the Boyz changed the meeting time from one A.M. to earlier, sometime during regular business hours. Why? Just basic security, to keep desperate Barry from trying something stupid. Barry tries something stupid anyhow — he brings his payment as agreed, but he's cut in some Salvadorans to cancel his debt the permanent way, and probably save himself a few diamonds. Barry comes to the Boyz alone and they retire to the office and close the door. A minute later MS-13 arrives in the big white van. The Salvadorans don't know anything about an office, so two of them just go straight to the heart of the matter and start shooting up the painter. Two of the Boyz take them out, but two more Salvadorans — the smart ones with the firepower — come up from behind and the Boyz go down. Then the last two

Asian guns try to come in quietly from the office. They even take a second to lock the front door, figuring they'll trap the invaders. They make their appearance with Barry in tow, and between two machine guns, the combat 12-gauge and a machine pistol, everybody's dead in four seconds.

I think about taking their cash but realize that if the cops see this event like I do, it's case closed and nobody knows anything about diamonds.

This is one crime scene where I'm not leaving my card.

I cross myself as my great-uncle Jack taught me to do and begin a quick prayer for the dead men. A place where ten men have just been killed has a chopped-off kind of feeling. Like frayed rope, a whole bunch of ends. I believe that God hears prayers but generally doesn't answer.

I'm almost to Amen when I see light slowly advancing through the lobby hallway, then through the side windows.

Very faintly, over the whirring of the fans and the incessant rush of cars on the freeways, I hear a vehicle stop in the parking lot.

My heart is pounding hard as it falls, an acknowledgment of disaster.

But my plan is simple.

If it's the Sheriffs, I'll have a lot of explaining to do.

If it's Asian Boyz, they'll use a key and come through the front door and I'll go out the side window the way I got in.

Anybody else will likely head for the nearest window for a look inside, just like I did. Which means I'll get the door keys from one of the dead men closest to the lobby and sneak out the front door if they climb in.

I run to the lobby and crawl to the counter. There's a side window facing the parking lot, and I see an old black Lincoln Continental parked midway between the Escalade and my Corvette. Big old thing, opera windows and fender louvers, armored with chrome, seventy-eight or nine. Mint condition. Its lights are off and there's nothing moving inside. I can just make out the shape of someone in the driver's seat.

Asian Boyz, I figure — the Boyz do love their rides.

I scuttle back down the hallway on my hands and knees. When I hit the high bay, I stand and run straight for the window. I'm through the opening and crouched outside on the walkway in less than ten heartbeats.

I climb over the safety railing and drop six feet down to the dark ground.

I'm away from the light now. I'm underneath the world.

And a good thing because I hear the catwalk above me vibrate then stop. Vibrate then stop.

Someone's coming my way. Slowly.

I curl up in the darkness next to the building. Looking up through the perforated steel of the catwalk floor, I can see the dark outline of someone approaching. He moves smoothly. He stops at the first window, but he's not tall enough to see in.

A kid?

But when he jumps and locks his hands on the window frame and pulls himself up to the level of the opening, I get a better look. He's a very short, compact man. Dark hair, flat-top, straight up. He's not Asian. He effortlessly holds himself up. I can see his head moving left and right, then back again. He's got on jeans, cowboy boots and a red-and-tan plaid shirt. There's about eighteen inches of scabbard fixed to his belt and tied to his leg like a gunfighter's holster — a small machete with a handle double the size of a regular one. For swinging two-handed, I figure.

He drops lightly to the catwalk and comes my way, stops right above me, and seems to look off in the direction of the freeways. Then he pulls himself up to the second window. I watch his right shoe find a hold against the wall, then flex, then follow the rest of him as he vanishes through the window.

I give him a full minute, then unfurl and run for the parking area.

I remote the door lock from thirty feet away, then the trunk. Without probable cause cops can't inspect what isn't in plain sight, and that's why you need a car with a trunk.

I swing up the lid, fling in the backpack and slam it shut.

A few seconds later the engine roars and I'm burning rubber away from Miracle Auto Body with my middle finger in the air, which is a childish thing to do, but I haven't felt so relieved in a long time, oh man, you just can't know what it feels like to pull off something like this and see ten dead people in a place that would be happy to make you the eleventh, and I've never felt more alive than right now, just so thankful and grateful that I'm not lying back there full of bullet holes but right here with a backpack full of diamonds and almost a full tank of gas.

I hit the brakes when I see the Sheriff's patrol unit pulled over to the side of the dark road, but it's too late.

In the rearview I watch him pull out and

hit the lights, and I'm cursing really fucking bad as I drive onto the dirt shoulder and slam the tranny into park. I put my gun under my seat. I unplug and slide the police band radio under the passenger seat, too. Then I turn on the interior light as a courtesy, roll down my window, dig my CDL and registration from the center console and watch him approach in the sideview mirror.

Tall guy, slender like a boxer, light hair, alert. His summer-weight uniform looks tailored because they don't design them for guys that skinny.

He's got a Maglite in his left hand, but his right hand is free, and I see him look at my plate and reg sticker on his way by. He stops away from the door and looks at me.

"Evening, ma'am."

"Evening, Deputy."

"In a hurry?"

"No. Just a fast car."

"This the Z06?"

"Five hundred and five bhp at sixty-three hundred rpm. Just about scalp you in second."

"Where are you going?"

"Home if you don't mind."

"Drinking tonight?"

"I don't drink."

He nods and stares at me. "I need your

license and registration for the vehicle."

He steps up and I hand them over. His badge says C. Hood. C. Hood steps back and turns the flashlight on them. The registration will pass a visual from a deputy every time. It won't fool a document examiner with the right tools. The driver's license is genuine, and its bearer — Suzanne Elizabeth Jones, SEX: F, DOB 12/26/1976, 5–9, 135, BRN and BRN — has never had a ticket or been arrested. She's a good girl.

He stares at me again and I look out the windshield and sigh. He's got wheels turning behind those eyes. Someday someone is going to look at me and in their mind they'll put a black wig over my brown hair and a black mask with a crystal on it over my face and I'll be history, like Great-Great-Great-Great-Great-Great-Grandfather Joaquin.

"I support Sheriff Whatshisname," I say.

"Warm night for gloves, isn't it, Ms. Jones?" he asks.

"They're for driving."

"Remain in the vehicle."

Great.

A red Porsche 911 turbo goes by eastbound. Beautiful animal. The engine sound alone is enough to get me blushing and bothered. I can lay it off for fifty grand to the right people. Would end up in Mexico

City or Caracas or Cartagena, altered and practically untraceable. Then a Mitsubishi Lancer rolls by the other way. It's the second most often boosted car in America, right behind the Caddy Escalade. It's worth only three grand, but they're twice as easy to steal and ten times easier to sell. Bread-and-butter stuff.

The deputy is back five minutes later, handing me the CDL and registration slip.

"What are you doing out here this time of night, Ms. Jones?"

"I was visiting relatives. Now I'd like to get home."

"Valley Center. That's way down in San Diego County, isn't it?"

"It's an hour and forty minutes this time of night, without traffic."

He nods. Hood. Handsome Hood. Thirty years old, maybe not even that.

"Drive safely. You were doing sixty in a forty-five when I pulled you over."

"I promise I'll drive more slowly."

"Good night."

Hood turns for his car but stops when the old black Lincoln comes past. I flip off the Corvette's interior light, cursing silently for leaving myself momentarily illuminated.

As the black Continental drifts by, the driver studies me. Young or old — I can't tell. His hair shoots straight up from his head, then is planed into a flat-top as black as the extra-long handle of the machete on his belt. Thick neck and a big sharp nose, like a Central American Indian. The red-and-tan shirt is buttoned up all the way, like a schoolboy's. I don't know why I notice things like this, other than it reminds me of my sons. My scalp crawls.

Hood is back in his unit by now.

I start up the 'Vette and guide it back onto the street. The Sheriff's cruiser stays put for a beat, then U-turns toward Miracle Auto Body. C. Hood is going to see what I saw. I go easy westbound, come to the signal at Eastern.

The black Lincoln is pulled over to the right and the guy stares at me as I drive by. Big down-turned lips, head shaved on the sides and tapering up to the flat-top. A Mayan warrior, no doubt.

He tries to fall in behind me, but I goose the seven liters and lose him in a roar of beautiful white tire smoke and rich gray exhaust.

I hit Interstate 10 east. Things are too hot for me and Allison Murrieta in L.A. right now so I'm going home for a few days.

Not to a hotel, to my real home.

I stop in San Berdoo, park on a side street,

take off the 'Vette plates and slide them into my satchel. I remove both plates from a very sweet black Ford F-150 and drop them down a storm drain. I replace them with a set of cold truck plates then quietly load my stuff from the Corvette — toolbox, suitcase, police radio, backpack with diamonds, etc. — into the bed of the truck.

I can pull a lock and hotwire a stock car in just over a minute. Most don't have alarms, but the few that do will stop when the engine starts up. That can be a long thirty seconds while the horn wails with you inside, and that's where your nerves get tested. You beat LoJack by staging a hot car and waiting for the cops to show. If they don't show in two days, it's your car now, baby. People think the Club is insurmountable, but I just cut slots in the steering wheel with my carbide saw and pull the damned Club off. You have to replace the steering wheel at some point, but they're relatively cheap.

The truck purrs like a kitten and I hit the road for Interstate 15 south. The 'Vette had over twice the power, but I'd been driving it for five days and I get bored after five days of just about any car. And hot cars — even cold-plated ones — get risky.

I'm looking forward to seeing my main man and my kids. It's been a while. Or I

41

could stop off and see a friend of mine, give him a cute little diamond to put in his ear.

Right now, though, I just want to get the hell out of L.A.

I love this city, but there are too many dangerous people up here.

5

Charlie Hood looked at the brightly lit office lobby that was never lit at three A.M. Then he climbed the steps to the front door and looked in at the stillness. He saw the overturned chair at the threshold of the office then looked down the hallway leading to the bay.

He tried the door and felt the bolt knock against the lock plate and the housing. He looked out to where the 710 crossed over Interstate 10 and listened to the steady toneless roar of the cars.

Hood took the catwalk around one side of the building and looked through the first window he came to, at the cars and the whirring fans and the lilting curtains sprayed in various colors and the dead people strewn across the floor. It looked like an Anbar alleyway in '04.

From the next window down he saw five more dead. He waited a long time for something to move other than the curtains and fan blades, but nothing did.

He went back to the unit and called in backup and ten bodies' worth of coroners, paramedics, the homicide and gang units.

He sat on the metal office steps with his arms on his knees looking at the parked cars and wondering what kind of hell the Wilton Street Asian Boyz had stirred up.

After a minute he lit three ground flares at the entrance of the parking area to keep the county vehicles from driving in and wrecking evidence.

Within an hour there were thirteen men and women on scene and an entry/exit log taped to a front window next to the door that a deputy had forced open with a four-foot pry bar.

The homicide sergeant was Bill Marlon. He was pale-complected and black-haired and not young. When the door fell open he motioned Hood in ahead of him, a courtesy to the first responder that surprised and pleased Hood.

"Sign in, everybody," said Marlon. "The usual — look, don't touch."

Hood scribbled his name on the log and stepped in. He glanced at the office and the overturned chair. With his hand on the butt of his service weapon and his ears and eyes on alert, Hood moved through the open counter door then slowly down the hall toward the bay.

Hood recognized three of the dead as Wilton Street Crazy Boyz. Another, no more than a boy, the one with the painter's mask still half-on, looked familiar, but Hood couldn't place him. The other Asian was new to him. Maybe another Boyz click, he thought. The four Latins were Mara Salvatrucha by the tattoos, but hard to say where they came from because MS-13 wasn't about turf but about money and violence.

Hood scrolled back through his almost four years with the Sheriffs trying to remember Mara Salvatrucha and the Crazy Boyz mixing it up, but couldn't think of one incident.

"Haven't seen much of this," he said to Marlon. "Different gangs fighting it out."

"I wonder if anyone walked away," said Marlon.

"Funny they'd leave the guns."

Marlon nodded. "If there was a winner, I'd put my money on the Salvadorans. I wish this guy could talk."

They were standing next to a dead man dressed in a black suit and a white open-collared shirt and a pair of dull black dress shoes splayed out at the end of his thick legs. To Hood, shoes had come to seem irrelevant on dead men, of whom he had seen more than several in his twenty-eight years. The Racks in al Anbar wore sandals or nothing, so to him death was a shoeless thing.

He looked at the four holes in a diagonal line across the front of the white shirt, automatic fire from the Salvadorans almost for sure. The guy had no gun, apparently. He looked wrong here, like he'd wandered in from another place or time.

Without turning him over, Marlon worried out the man's wallet and stood. "Barry Cohen," he said. "Hollywood. Cohen and Cohen Gemstones in the diamond district, says this business card. What's a nice Jewish boy doing at this party?"

Hood had been thinking the same thing. "Maybe it *was* his party," he said. "Him and the Asians. This is their turf. Maybe the Salvadorans crashed it."

Marlon nodded but didn't look away from the bodies. "Him and the Asians doing what?"

"Diamonds come to mind."

"I wonder. The Asian Boyz wouldn't pay him a tenth of what they're worth retail. Barry's got a fat markup for engagements and anniversaries."

Hood considered. "How much cash did he have?"

"Eighty . . . three bucks."

"Maybe Barry was paying for something with gems instead of money. To a broker, gems are cheaper than cash."

"Maybe he was. And if tonight was the night he brought payment to the Boyz, then the diamonds are either here in this mess or went out with the winners. Good you sealed off the parking lot, Charlie. There might be some blood out there if one of these guys got away."

"If he was shot, that would explain leaving the guns."

Marlon put his hands on his hips and looked down at the bloody heap of dead men. "Looks like Cu Chi."

"Or Hamdaniya."

"Ten men. Jesus."

Marlon had invited Hood one evening after work to a bar where they drank and agreed that war is worse than hell, because hell punishes sinners but war punishes everyone.

Marlon led the walk-through, and Hood gave way to photographers and videographers, crime scene specialists, coroner's investigators, more detectives, an assistant district attorney and an LASD commander.

Hood followed Marlon at an increasing distance but listened and watched carefully. He knew that the proper deployment of personnel at a crime scene was something he'd need to learn. Here it was orderly and systematic, and people knew their jobs. But in Anbar province there had been sullen crowds and sudden lethal chaos, and Hood was hated not only by the people but by the soldiers whose actions he was sometimes called on to investigate. Sometimes it seemed like everybody wanted to kill him.

Two tours was enough. He had left a good job with the Sheriffs to go over there because his father was navy and his grandfather was navy. They put him in NCIS — Navy Criminal Investigative Service — because of his law enforcement background, though most of his time as a deputy he'd worked the jail. His last tour had ended almost three years ago, when he was twenty-five years old, but Hood still woke up in the dark sometimes with the echoes of IEDs and gunfire in his ears and the taste of Iraqi dust in his mouth.

He shadowed the Miracle Auto Body crime scene investigation for two more hours. Nobody found any evidence that the diamond broker had brought any of his wares. There might be dozens of other explanations for Barry Cohen getting together with the Asian Boyz, but Hood couldn't think of one. It looked to him like MS-13 had ambushed the Asians and Cohen, like they knew something valuable was in the mix. But they'd been a little short on manpower.

He went outside to watch the physical evidence team search the parking area in the bright white of the searchlights. A generator hummed against the distant roar of the freeways. The coroner's team wheeled the bodies out one at a time, the dead wrapped and strapped and jiggling as the gurneys came down the steps.

Half an hour later a faint pink haze appeared in the east, and the power towers stood in diminishing perspective against the growing sunlight, arms stretched and the wires drooping. Marlon and the commander came from the building. The commander was on a cell phone, and he stepped among the damaged cars for privacy.

Marlon waved Hood over.

"I'm bringing you on with us," Marlon said.

"Great, sir. I didn't know if it would happen."

"Admin's been slow but I'll push it the rest of the way through. Wyte will okay it if I ask him to. We'll have you out of patrol by the end of the week, so for now, you've got two jobs — patrol and homicide."

"Thanks again."

"You asked for it. The dogs will be glad to have you."

Hood nodded. LASD homicide called themselves the Bulldogs because they never gave up. Even in law enforcement circles they were known to be indefatigable.

Marlon ran a comb back over his head, the black hair parting into neat, close rows, an old man's ritual, thought Hood. Marlon blew through the comb teeth and slipped it into a back pocket.

"I stopped a woman tonight just before I came here," Hood said. "She drove right by, kind of middle of nowhere. Came up clean but she could have seen something. I wasn't sure what to make of her. A little eager to be on her way."

"Local?"

"No, San Diego County."

"Talk to her. You know these dead Asians?"

"I've seen three of them around. Wilton Street click."

"Notify their families and find out what

they know. The coroner will help with addresses. That part of it is lousy work, but welcome to the dogs."

6

Lupercio stood before the Bull with his hands folded in front of him, looking down at the crease in his trousers left by the tie of the machete scabbard. He repeated the license number of the yellow Corvette and watched the Bull poke at his PDA with the stylus. Lupercio wondered at the tools of men: a machete, a computer, a stylus. He didn't know the man's name.

Above him the Bull sat behind a very large brushed aluminum desk on a raised dais. The wall behind him was mirrored all the way to the ceiling, where recessed low-voltage bulbs blared down a bright white light. In the glass Lupercio saw the reflection of the Port of Long Beach behind him, the great cranes rising against the first rosy light of the morning, sunrise on steel. Even early Sunday the place was moving. Lupercio had heard that the longshoremen who ran the cranes got a thousand dollars an hour on Sundays and holidays.

"What model year was the Corvette?" asked the Bull. His voice was clear and forceful.

"This year," said Lupercio. "The license plate holder said Gooden Chevrolet." You'll get a good'un at Gooden, he thought.

Now the Bull tapped at a keyboard. There were four flat-screen monitors on the desk, two on each side of him, and four keyboards. Four printers. Under the desk were four computer towers. All of the computers were housed in handsome brushed aluminum cases, finished in such a way to catch light and reflect it in soft colors, like a muted rainbow. They were nothing like you saw in the computer stores or on the TV, noted Lupercio. They made urgent humming noises. There were very few cable connections between them.

The Bull glided to his right on a wheeled office chair that rolled on the raised platform with the sound of distant thunder. He tapped at the keys again. Then he rolled and looked down through the opening between the monitors, and Lupercio felt the weight of his attention.

"Did you see her in actual possession of the material?"

"No."

"Describe what you saw."

Lupercio described it for the third time. It was plain to him that some kind of experience with law enforcement had taught the Bull the power of repeated questioning. Lupercio had been questioned by every American law enforcement agency from the FBI on down to the local police and sheriffs, and he had never been asked a question just once. Never. He wondered again if the Bull's experience had been as the questioner or the questioned.

"Yellow?"

"Yes."

"Model year?"

Lupercio told him again. As far as he was concerned the Bull could ask him a thousand more times, if that's what it would take to convince him that a young brown-haired woman in a yellow Corvette had almost certainly driven off with the diamonds, not Lupercio. The Bull had told him before that Lupercio had "final responsibility" for his work. That was why Lupercio was paid such high commissions. Responsibility was what the Bull looked for in a partner. It was more valuable than any metal or any stone from the earth, he said. Responsibility was the son of faith, whatever that meant.

Lupercio turned and looked out the big

windows. The morning light was full now, and the container ships and tugs and port cranes continued their eternal transportation of the world's goods. One of the Bull's men passed by the window wearing a suit and sunglasses and a tiny wireless headset fixed between one ear and his shaven chocolate-colored head.

"And the year and make of the Sheriff's patrol car?"

Lupercio turned and told the Bull the information for the second time in ten minutes.

"Did you get the unit number off the side of the cruiser?"

Lupercio gave it again.

The Bull tapped rapidly on the far right keyboard, then rolled to his left and looked down on Lupercio. Lupercio heard a whirring sound.

"Describe the inside of Miracle Auto Body," said the Bull. "Focus on the location of the men and your interpretation of what happened there."

Lupercio took a deep breath and tried to clear his mind of everything but that memory.

When he had gotten to Miracle Auto Body at two-ten that morning, he assumed the outdoor lights would be on and the indoor lights off, but the opposite was true. He knew that a diamond merchant was supposed to have arrived over an hour ago with four hundred and fifty thousand dollars' worth of high-quality cut diamonds to pay off an outstanding loan to the two ranking Wilton Street Asian Boyz. The Bull had told him all of this. And he told Lupercio that four heavily armed and proven MS-13 gunmen would take control of the body shop and the diamonds by whatever means necessary. Their leader was supposed to have delivered the diamonds to a knowledgeable and neutral courier who would divide them in half by value and bring one half directly to the Bull. When the leader never showed, the courier had called the Bull and the Bull had called in his lone wolf — Lupercio. He'd told Lupercio that half of what he recovered would be his to keep.

By the time Lupercio had counted ten bodies, he knew that everyone who was supposed to be there was dead and three men who weren't supposed to be there were dead, too, which meant that the diamonds could also still be there.

"I knew something was wrong," he said. "Because of the lights."

"And this yellow Corvette, what did you think when you saw it parked away from the others, facing out?"

"That it was part of what had gone wrong."

"Why?"

"Because it's not a gangster's car. There's not enough room for men and guns and products."

The Bull looked down at Lupercio. Lit from above, the Bull's face was cleaved by shadows, so his expressions were unreadable. His face was tanned and his nose was wide and formidable. His hair was light and thin and combed straight back and the scalp beneath it was tanned, too. He was barrel-chested — built like a bull, thought Lupercio. A bull who spends time outdoors in the sun.

"Was one of the Asians very young?"

This was the second time that the Bull had asked this same question. He hadn't asked the ages of any of the other nine men, so Lupercio believed the young car painter had been the Bull's snitch within the Wilton Street Boyz. Lupercio wondered again if the Bull's other life — whatever it was and whenever he had lived it — had been that of the interrogator or the interrogated.

"One was a teenager. A car painter. I walked quickly. Then I heard the Corvette start up outside."

"Continue."

Lupercio told of his momentary indecision when he heard the car start up. He knew it was the Corvette by the sound of it. It would be faster for him to use the front door of the office, but only if that door was open. If it was locked, he'd need to locate a key and that could take seconds, minutes. So he jumped back through the window and ran down the steel catwalk to the parking area. The yellow Corvette was halfway down the access road by the time he got his car keys out.

But he got a good look at her when the Sheriff's deputy stopped her — because her interior light was on — and another good look at her at the signal at Eastern.

"Describe her."

"Light brown hair, dark eyes. *Bonita.* Unafraid. She looked directly at me both times."

"Age?"

"Middle twenties, thirty maybe."

"How far were you able to follow her?"

"I never even caught up with her tire smoke."

The Bull rolled to the left side of his desk, appeared to be using a computer mouse. The casters rumbled on the hardwood dais. Then he rolled back to the right and pulled up a sheet of paper.

Lupercio watched him study the sheet, set it facedown on the desk, then pull up a handful more. The Bull took a long time flipping through these. Lupercio heard the air-conditioning click on, then felt a faint gust of cool air on his face.

"Here," said the Bull, holding the sheets out to Lupercio.

Lupercio stepped forward and took them. Up this close he guessed the Bull to be fifty years old and strong. His neck was thick and his eyes were blue. There was something unusual about his legs.

The top sheet showed a blown-up California driver's license in color.

"Suzanne Elizabeth Jones," read Lupercio. "This is her."

"Of course it's her."

The second sheet was a photograph, apparently from a high school yearbook, in which Suzanne Jones looked years younger, naive, and pointedly bored. Sheets three through thirteen were dense paragraphs of information: DOB; Social Security number; credit rating — very good; driving history — no accidents, no traffic citations; arrests — none; interviews with law enforcement — none. There was a ten-year residence history listing addresses in Bakersfield, Los Angeles, Torrance, Norwalk, Santa Ana and Valley

Center. Also, school files from elementary through high school, abbreviated college transcripts and medical records. There was an employment history — Kentucky Fried Chicken (ages fifteen and sixteen), Taco Bell and Subway (ages sixteen and seventeen), Dominguez Hills State University (cafeteria food server while a student, ages eighteen through twenty-two), then the Los Angeles Unified School District as a teacher from age twenty-two through "current." She taught history. There was an immediate family tree that was thorough enough to list Suzanne Jones's two brothers and two sisters and their young children. Apparently she had not married.

"What grade education did you complete?" asked the Bull.

Lupercio looked up at the heavy face faceted by the recessed low-voltage lamps.

"High school."

The Bull glanced at the pages. "Is it difficult for you to read and retain information?"

"No. I read slowly and I remember everything."

"How did it feel to you, looking down at the dead Mara Salvatrucha?"

"I knew them."

"But that doesn't answer my question."

60

"I am no longer a part of them. My business and my heart are not there."

"Do you miss the structure, the friendship, the power of being a leader in the most feared street gang on Earth? Do you miss the respect?"

"Those were a child's comforts."

"And now you are grown."

"Childhood ends."

The Bull was nodding, the black shadows in his eye sockets elongating with each downward tilt of his head.

"If there was ever a time for you to be honest, this is it. I can work with honesty. Did you steal my diamonds, Lupercio?"

"I did not."

"And why should I believe you?"

"Because I don't lie."

The Bull smiled, his open lips and the lines of his face catching the downward light at new angles. "Find the woman. Find the diamonds. One-half of what you recover is yours. I remind you that several men have stolen from me. But each only once."

"This is simple and clear."

"I wish you good luck, my lone wolf."

"I would rather have information on the diamond broker."

The Bull crossed his arms. "It will take five minutes. Go outside. Sit in the cool shade and face the great Port of Long Beach. Watch the sunlight on the cranes and the towers of containers. Say a prayer of thanks for your life this fine Sunday morning."

Five minutes later Lupercio was back and the Bull was handing down to him another sheaf of papers.

7

Home.

Eight acres of scrub and savannah, a pasture and paddock, a pond, a stream, avocado, lemon and orange trees loaded with fruit.

The main house is for me and my three sons, and — at least for now — Ernest, father of the third. There is also a barn and four small cottages spread across the property for my friends. I'm never sure exactly who's here and who's not, but I've got good friends and watchful neighbors so it doesn't really matter.

I bought this place six months ago, a year after I committed my first armed robbery — a Starbucks. It's way off the beaten path. The whole compound was a filthy "fixer" with plywood for windows, insane derelicts cooking meth in the barn and rats nesting in the old mattresses. You could smell it before you got out of your car.

Across the stream is one Indian reservation and across the road is another, so when you drive in here you see how poor those people are, you see the junked appliances and broken-down cars and the trash and the burn piles and the grubby kids. You just want to keep driving, which is what most people do. Those big casinos you see out here now, they don't aim much of that slot machine cash down at the poor. No, they sponsor this group and contribute to this cause, and they give lots of money to politicians who can help them; they have swank ads on TV, but how come the rez looks so bad once you leave the casino? Ask them that.

I like the natives. There's a couple of big bad braves — they're brothers, actually — who live across the stream. Gerald and Harold Little Chief, I kid you not. Eighteen and nineteen. They're bikers. They keep an eye on my place when I'm gone, and I keep an eye on theirs. Once I saw some kids breaking into their garage so I called the rez cops. A week later the brothers brought over a minibike for my boys. They'd made it. It was a beautiful little thing, with a two-and-a-half-hp Briggs & Stratton and chrome shocks and a flame-red-and-yellow paint job. Gerald and Harold looked funny standing there at my back door, these two huge guys with a minibike between them, and Harold takes the bandana off his head and bends down and wipes a smudge off the handlebar then puts the bandana back on and picks up the minibike, must weigh a hundred pounds, and holds it out to me with two steady hands like it's a puppy or a box of long-stemmed roses.

So anyway, my place came cheap and we've been working our asses off to clean it up ever since.

Some of the down payment came from my L.A. Unified School District Credit Union, where most of us teachers bank our small paychecks, maintain our checking accounts and, if we can hack our jobs long enough, take out loans for the overpriced and often crummy L.A. homes we can afford. Some of my down payment came from my early stickups: McDonald's, Carl's Jr., Block-buster, Sav-on, Payless Shoes — anybody whose signs I got sick of looking at. But most of it came from the cars I learned to boost and sell: grand theft auto beats armed robbery any day. You can pick up a gun and risk your life for a thousand bucks, or you can steal a good car and make thirty grand without encountering another human being. And the high-end stuff, man, it's just beautiful material to work with.

Valley Center is just an hour and forty minutes from L.A., if you know when to make the drive. I get to school early and stay late, and when I'm home here I'm happy to be an hour and forty minutes away. When I retire, it's going to be to an even bigger compound, with serious acreage, horse trails everywhere, a giant wall around it and a drawbridge — I'm serious about this bridge — so I can say exactly who gets in and out. And when.

Like right now. The dogs are already barking because here comes C. Hood up the long dirt road. It's the only road in. I watch him through the Zeiss binoculars I shoplifted from a Big 5 Sporting Goods store. It's Sunday, I've been home for exactly six hours, I've had four hours of sleep, two showers, one orgasm, and now dressed in a nightshirt I've got to deal with the long arm of the law.

He's not in uniform, but his face is unmistakable behind the aviator shades. I thought he'd show, but I didn't think it would be this soon. I've got the hot pickup stashed out in the barn and the gems locked up somewhere that nobody knows about but me.

I watch him get out, glance at the "No Trespassing — Violators Will Be Prosecuted" sign. He looks at the gate, then in my direction, and I know what he sees is mostly trees.

"Who is it?" asks Ernest. He's sitting at the redwood picnic table in my big dining room wearing red swim trunks, bouncing baby Kenny on his knee. Ernest's big padded Hawaiian hands look like a life preserver around the baby's middle.

"The deputy."

"You were right."

Hood pushes the gate open and starts back to his car. The noon heat comes off it in waves. I wonder why he's driving this sweet black '86 IROC Camaro, and I figure they won't give him a county slickback because he's too junior. But they're letting him play plainclothes.

I walk outside and tell the dogs to shut up. They're big Dobermans and trained well. I stand on the porch. Hood pulls his car into a parking area marked by sections of some old cottonwoods Ernest felled down by the stream. The nose of the Camaro stops just short of the tree trunk. I can hear Merle Haggard singing behind the windows.

Hood gets out and shuts the door and comes toward the house, all elbows and angles. He's got a little notepad in one hand but I don't laugh.

"Little bit out of jurisdiction, aren't you?"

"More than a little, ma'am. I want to talk about last night."

"Last night, well. Come on up. These dogs bite but only when they're told."

"Can you tell them to roll over and wag their stumps?"

"They don't do tricks."

Hood makes the porch, looks at me, the dogs, the food bowls lined up in the shade. Hood's a one-thing-at-a-time guy, thinks he is anyway.

I let him in, introduce him to Ernest and Kenny. Hood and Ernest do the man-stare, but after a long second Hood unwraps his sunglasses and averts his gaze respectfully, then turns his attention to the infant on Ernest's knee. Kenny burps something and his eyes wobble like loose buttons.

"This will just take a few minutes," says Hood.

"You guys can have the table," says Ernest. "I'll get Kenny ready. See ya, Suze."

Ernest swings Kenny up into one of his big arms and I watch him walk out. The bottoms and rims of his feet are pale and the rest of him is a splendid island bronze. He's from Oahu. He's got a ready smile and a skein of island tattoos across the back of his shoulders. I met him at a luau, where he danced with a spear. You could get your

68

picture taken with the dancers after the show and we got to talking. A spear chucker. Months later, he showed me how he could throw that thing — with unbelievable power and accuracy, for a spear anyway. Then came Kenny.

Hood and I sit across from each other at the long picnic table and he lays it on me: the Asian Boyz, Mara Salvatrucha and diamond broker Barry Cohen. Hood is relaxed, calm and intense. He seems like an old guy in a thirty-year-old body, a pretty damned nice combination if you ask me. He wants to know everything I saw in the area of Miracle Auto Body last night, even the smallest little detail can be a help. I stare past his shoulder to a wall, where I've tacked some of my middle son's drawings and paintings. Jordan. He's ten and a very good artist.

Hood's got the cover of his notepad open and his pen in his hand. "Did you see anything unusual, out of place? Put yourself back there. Sometimes things will —"

I nod. "I saw an old Lincoln Continental, once before you stopped me and once after. First time, it was pulled off the road. That count as unusual?"

"Did you see the driver?"

"Just a guy."

"Where did you see him pulled over?"

"I don't know. In the dark. Beside the road. Sorry, I'm a history teacher, not a cop."

"What year was the car?"

"Late seventies. Just before the redesign."

Hood looks at me with surprise and doubt. He wants all the stats so I give them to him: the Continental was black, and shiny like it was just washed, and the chrome really popped because that was the last of the great Detroit chrome years, and I tell Hood I couldn't guess the age of the guy inside, just that he had this totally geodynamic planed-off flat-top haircut, and of course I know Hood is all over this, he's thinking bad guy, another one of the Asian Boyz or Mara Salvatrucha, an answer to the mystery of the dead diamond broker but no diamonds. To build intrigue I give the Lincoln driver a cell phone, glad to be of assistance to law enforcement.

"I saw that car go past when I was talking to you," says Hood. "Slowly."

I say nothing for a moment. I know Hood's hot for the Lincoln.

"What was a diamond broker doing with all these bad people?" I ask.

"We don't know."

Hood writes slowly and smoothly. I like the way he holds his pen. Then he looks at me for a moment, same look as when I said the car was a late seventies Continental.

"What."

"Last night I was surprised you knew what the yellow Corvette had in it," he says. "Most people, they don't know which engine they've got."

"You mean most women don't know."

"No, women almost never know." He's smiling now. "I didn't see it parked out front."

"I won't park it outside. If I have to explain that, you're simple enough to hide your own Easter eggs."

Hood laughs quietly. It's an old man's chuckle behind a young man's smile.

"And you surprised me just now about the Continental, before the redesign. You know your cars."

"Just the ones I like."

"Tell me about the Lincoln again. How far away was it from where I pulled you over?"

I tell him a maybe a few hundred yards, but it was dark and late and I was turned around, thinking I'd made a wrong turn but not sure. Hood writes something more in his handy little pad.

"You never told me your first name," I say.

"It's Charlie. Sorry."

"You know I'm thirty-two from my CDL.

How old are you?"

"I'm twenty-eight."

"Bakersfield High, I'll bet."

Hood clears his throat and nods. "How do you know that?"

"It's something about you. Your ears, maybe."

"Explain what."

"I can't. But I love Merle Haggard. I graduated from high school in Bakersfield, too. It was Vista West Continuation, where the pregnant girls go. We were the Gators."

I smile at him. This makes him uneasy.

"I think we got off track."

"What else do you want to know?"

"Exactly what happened at Miracle."

"Can't help you there, Charlie. Is it Charles?"

"Charles Robert."

Just then my eldest son slams through the door. He's sixteen but looks nineteen, a beautiful boy. Bradley's dad was beautiful but worthless. My middle son, Jordan, has a different father than Bradley, and of course baby Kenny's father is Ernest. It's all pretty simple. I've never married and I've named my children after *me*. Jones. I digress.

"Mom," he says. He's wearing a trucker's cap pulled down low over his long black hair.

"There's nothing I can do with the throttle cable."

He looks at Hood a beat longer than he looks at most people, including me.

"So, now what?" he grunts.

"So do what you can with it, Bradley. A Ford is a Ford. This is Charlie Hood. He's a cop."

"Hi," Bradley says.

"Hi," says Hood. "A Sheriff's deputy, actually — L.A. County."

"I'm thinking LAPD. When I'm old enough."

"They need good people."

"The pedal sucks, Mom," Bradley says to me. "Can I just go boarding?"

"Sure," I say. "Thanks for looking at it. You put the new wheels and tires on the Cyclone?"

"Before you even got out of bed."

"How do they look?"

"The shoes are too small but the meats are sick."

"Awesome. Thanks, son."

"Sheriff's pay good?" Bradley asks Hood.

"Fair."

"Good as the cops?"

"About the same," says Hood. "But we get better cars and a little more open road to drive them on."

"I'm good with large caliber handguns."

Hood raises his eyebrows.

"Nice IROC," says my son.

"Thanks. I bored and stroked it, goosed out another thirty horse."

"Glasspaks?"

"Yeah, first thing I added."

"I could tell by the sound."

Bradley hesitates then leaves, letting the screen door slam behind him. A front of hot air floats in from outside. In the sudden silence Hood closes his notepad. I see him looking past me now into the living room, a mess of a place, kind of a Polynesian party room in honor of Ernest. It's got a very nice tiki bar.

"You're climbing the ladder pretty quickly," I tell Hood. "Last night you were a patrolman and now you're a detective."

"They moved me up for the Auto Body thing. This week I'm both."

"Bet they won't pay you twice."

Hood smiles and shakes his head.

For about two seconds I wonder if I should say what I want to say. If it takes longer than two seconds to give yourself permission to speak, then your rule book is getting overlong. I hate rules.

"I like the way you look, C. Hood. I like your voice and your attitude. I teach eighth-grade history but I'm nothing like the eighth-grade teachers you had. So I think you ought to hit the road, keep yourself out of trouble. That's the last time I'll make the slightest effort to protect you."

"I'll do that."

"You'll do what?"

"Hit the road."

"I caught you checking out my legs and just about everything else."

He looks away.

"I run eight miles a week and do hap-kido."

"It shows. I apologize, Ms. Jones. My first day as a detective I was hoping not to make a complete ass of myself."

I have to smile at C. Hood. "Be honest with me right now, Charles Robert — that uniform shirt you wore last night, did you have it tailored?"

He nods and his ears actually turn red. I want to lock the doors and jump him but I won't do it here. My social guidelines are somewhat relaxed but I'd never drag Ernest's pride through the dirt like that for no good reason. Then Ernest would break Hood in half and that would become another problem I don't want to have.

"I'd like the name and a telephone number or address for the relative you were visiting last night," says Hood.

"Nice try at reestablishing your law enforcement control. But it's none of your business who I was visiting."

I watch him weigh the options, which are two: arrest me or back down. It's a mismatch.

I get up and walk over to him and lean in. I touch my nose to the bottom of his trimmed sideburn, about halfway down his ear. And breathe in.

Supermarket soap, drugstore shave cream and Charlie Hood.

Then I turn and walk back into the house, waving good-bye over my shoulder.

8

Hood sat in the activities room with his mother and father. He was still rattled by Suzanne Jones and he couldn't put her out of his mind. He kept seeing her nightshirt against her back as she walked away, the soft material creasing left then right with each step. She made him feel skinned. Now he was back in uniform and on his way to swing shift patrol that evening and he figured maybe patrol was where he belonged.

His father, Douglas, introduced Hood to his latest girlfriend, whom Douglas believed to be Hood's mother, Iris, his wife of forty-eight years. Iris herself sat beside Hood, and together they faced Douglas and his "wife" as they held hands. Douglas was young to be in such an advanced state of dementia, and it had come over him with surprising speed after he retired from the city of Bakersfield. He'd been a landscape supervisor. Hood wondered if the herbicides and insecticides and fertilizers had contributed. The doctors talked on and on about genetic predisposition, sedentary retirement and myeloid plaque. Douglas was seventy-five years old and no longer recognized his wife. He had hit her. Now he fussed over the potted plants and the frail indoor ficus trees of the assisted living center, and held hands with the girlfriend. Charlie could watch himself ebb and flow on his father's memory like a small ship on a fast tide. Iris had tried to detach herself from her husband except to appear for these weekly visits.

"Go with threaded pipe, never cement," he said to Charlie. "Make sure you've got enough silicon tape to do the job right. Never put the cement on threaded pipe. I had a guy with the city doing that out at the park and I fired him. Probably should have killed him while I was at it."

"Seen any good shows, Dad?"

"Same old."

"They've got *Bewitched* on tape," said the girlfriend. Charlie and Iris had gathered that her name was Brenda.

"Fanfuckingtastic," muttered Iris.

"We always had plenty of shovels around," said Douglas.

Later Hood took his mother out for an early

dinner, and she caught him up with his brothers and sisters, two each, all older than him by quite a bit. His memories of childhood in Bakersfield were usually of him looking up at his towering siblings or later watching them drive away in cars. He learned early to hate good-byes. He developed into a decent student, a good friend, a fair tennis player. The girls usually skipped over him in favor of the louder and more clever boys. His ears were slightly large and blushed before the rest of his face did. He dated during his years at JC and Cal State Northridge but found it disappointing and expensive. He got B's and a political science degree. The Sheriff's Department had given him a start on life, then the first Iraq tour that led him to the Navy Criminal Investigative Service, then the second tour. By the time he came home from Anbar in '05 he was twenty-five and he wanted to get his deputy's job back, find a good woman and maybe have a little fun.

Hood followed his mother's gaze out the window to the planter flowers wilting in the San Bernardino heat. The bank thermometer across the street said "102 degrees . . . 4:35 P.M. . . . TWELVE MONTH CDs TO 4.25% . . ."

When she looked back at Hood, there were

tears in her eyes though her expression was steady and unpitying.

"Mom."

"It's okay. I'm okay, Charlie."

"There's going to be more."

"More what?"

"Good things."

"The kind you have to be dead to get?"

"Not those kind."

"Tell me when you spot one coming."

"You did all you could."

"I loved him."

Hood reached out and took her hand. Her skin was cool and soft, and he could feel the hardness of the bones beneath it. The waitress brought their dinners then came back and topped off their iced tea.

"A soldier called," she said. "Lenny Overbrook. He said he knew you over there and wanted your number. I said no and he gave me his."

"I'm sorry."

"It's perfectly okay."

She dug into her purse and finally handed Hood a torn-off corner of notebook paper with a number on it.

"I'll handle it, Mom. Thanks."

"He sounds polite. He said you understood him."

"Lenny was always polite."

Hood cruised Miracle Auto Body at eleven. He saw that the Escalade was in the lot but the other cars were gone. A new Suburban with dealer plates was parked beside the Cadillac. The lights were on both outside the shop and inside, and Hood could see three young men standing on the catwalk smoking.

They looked at him with stoic alertness as he came up the steps toward them. The night was hot and still, and in the near distance the two illuminated freeways rose against the darkness like monuments.

Hood caught the leader's eye and nodded. He remembered the guy's name from the department gang book: Kyle Ko. Hood had seen him several times in a popular Garvey Avenue Internet cafe, always with a different pretty girl.

"Sorry your friends got killed," said Hood. "I was the one who found them. I'm Hood."

"Too bad you didn't find them when they were still alive, Hood."

The two others were younger. Kyle looked at them, and they moved down the catwalk out of the light, toward the window where Hood had first looked down on the massacre.

Kyle was mid-twenties. He was tall and slender with a short brush cut and a loose silk shirt for the heat. Hood now saw that Kyle looked like the dead car painter, the guy who was very young.

Hood asked him for a smoke and leaned in when the lighter clicked and flamed. The smoke went to his brain in a once familiar way.

"What happened in there?" he asked.

"You tell me."

"That would get us exactly nowhere."

"We talked all day to people like you." Kyle flicked his cigarette butt off the catwalk, and Hood watched it pop and sparkle on the asphalt below. "And it got us nowhere, all right."

Hood told him he'd never seen the Wilton Street Boyz with Mara Salvatrucha, wondered if they'd gotten together for some business.

Kyle shrugged and looked out at the freeways.

Hood played his only real card. "Sorry about your brother. I've got two. Older."

Kyle looked at him.

"Talk to me," said Hood. "I can't put ten dead men out of my mind. I bet you can't either."

"He was fifteen years old."

Hood watched Kyle and listened to the drone of the cars elevated in the night beyond them.

"And he followed you into the gang life even though you told him not to."

Kyle locked eyes with Hood. "Cohen owed us seventy-five grand. Gambling. He brought us diamonds instead. MS-13 found out about the transaction. Either they took the diamonds or you people did. So Mark died for nothing."

"There weren't any diamonds when we got here."

"There were plenty of diamonds before you got here. Tony called me from the office. Cohen brought them in a red backpack at ten-fifty P.M."

"We turned this place over more than once. No gems."

"That's interesting, then, isn't it?"

"Where were you?"

"Business or pleasure, you know — what's the fucking difference?"

One of his Internet cafe beauties, thought Hood. Add some more guilt over his little brother's death. Of course it was very possible that Kyle was lying and he'd carried off the loot himself.

"Maybe you came by an hour after the call," said Hood. "You were wondering why

Tony hadn't bothered to update you. You sized it up quick, took the red backpack and split."

"I wouldn't be here now."

"This is exactly where you'd be."

"Maybe that's what happened, Deputy. If so, then good for me. I'll drop twenty thousand on Mark's funeral, give the rest to the Girl Scouts."

Then the idea hit Hood that MS-13 was tipped to the payoff either by Barry — who could promise them, say, half the diamonds he owed the Asian Boyz — or by one of the Boyz who knew the score and had a grievance. Gangs had internal problems just like any other organization. Kyle obviously knew the score and was conveniently out with one of his girlfriends.

Kyle was still staring at Hood, mad-dogging him, which was not something a Sheriff's deputy got very often. Hood wondered if Kyle was hearing his thoughts. But Hood couldn't see Kyle leading his little brother into a thing like that.

"Don't stare at me like a damned mule," said Hood. "I'm trying to help you."

Kyle looked away and lit another cigarette.

"Cohen was greedy and afraid," he said. "This is a bad combination. He gambled away most of his money, then came to us. We helped him and he gambled away more. When he had no more cash, he said diamonds came cheaper to him than dollars. He made us the offer. But he invited MS-13 to take half and make sure not a Wilton Street Boy was left alive. That was his idea of friendship and honest business. Salvadorans? They'll do shit like this. But they didn't know how tough and smart the Boyz are. Even the fifteen-year-old. It got out of control. But one of them must have survived. He figured the cops were on their way, so he got away with the rocks and his life."

Hood dropped the cigarette butt and ground it through the metal ramp with the toe of his duty shoe. He looked out at the young gangsters down the catwalk. Kyle had just said out loud what Hood had been thinking since he saw the bloody mess, but it still wasn't sitting right. The abandoned weapons and the dead men's full wallets and the five-thousand-dollar watch left on Barry Cohen's wrist still had him wondering.

"A witness saw an old Lincoln Continental parked off Emberly last night. Black, good condition, driver talking on a cell phone. Sound familiar?"

"Not me. I got that Suburban."

Hood looked back at the parking area.

"Maybe Barry had trouble keeping a secret."

Kyle shook his head in disgust, blew smoke. "One night at Caesars Palace he tried to tell his girlfriend everything but I stopped him. If you got half an ounce of bourbon inside Barry, you couldn't shut the guy up. He loved bourbon. Worry out loud. That was his favorite thing to do — worry out loud. No telling what he said to people. Dangerous asshole. Cost me a brother and seventy-five grand and I'll piss on his grave the first chance I get."

"I need the girlfriend's name and number."

"Melissa something."

In the office Kyle dug a business card out of the desk and flew it across to Hood.

9

Lupercio walked along the stream that ran behind Suzanne Jones's property. He had a fishing rod in one hand and a container of worms in the other. A straw cowboy hat shielded him from the sun. The small bass in the stream were easy to catch and toss back, and he did this while he picked his way upstream watching the Jones compound.

Across a small tan meadow there was a main house, a detached garage, a barn and four small casitas. They were all painted soft pink, except for the red barn. There was a grassy swale between the buildings and an enormous oak tree in its center with two rope swings hanging side by side from a low branch and three wooden picnic tables in the shade. The paint on the buildings was fresh, and there were flowers in beds alongside the house and garage.

A teenaged boy in a trucker's cap roared up a half pipe on his skateboard, caught air on the free fall and extended his legs at the last minute to crunch down, keep his balance and zoom up the opposite side. The skate run had two half pipes and a couple of vertical walls and a slalom course. It looked homemade. It was painted putty gray, and it crawled with a snake's nest of spray-painted graffiti that Lupercio, once fluent in all the languages of the L.A. taggers, couldn't make much sense of. Over the years, the skateboarders had stolen the old gangland swirls, then the advertisers had stolen them from the boarders. At first it had surprised Lupercio that the style of a full-on, leave-or-die turf tag you might find in Compton could show up a year later on a TV commercial for teenagers' skateboard shoes. Now the boy flew up the half pipe for the third time and wiped out. Lupercio watched him hit then roll down the last few feet and sit for a second panting in the ferocious heat. The boy looked at him because he knew he was being watched, then sprung up, fetched his board and started in again.

From the shore of the pond another boy, half the size and age of the first, was fishing. His movements were relaxed but practiced, and when he flung the lure out and up, it sailed through the air and plopped halfway across. Then he stood still for a moment and let the lure sink before reeling it in a few feet at a time. Then he'd wait again. Over and over. Lupercio recognized the patience of the fisherman because he had it, too.

When Lupercio hooked another fish, the little boy looked at him. Lupercio waved and the boy waved back. Lupercio let the fish go, set down his rod and stood for a moment pretending to enjoy the summer day, his back to the Jones property and a hand resting on the long handle of his machete.

A while later he saw the Hawaiian come outside with a baby in his arms. Dad used a hose to put water in a plastic wading pool on a patch of grass, then he turned off the hose and got into the pool with the baby, who screamed with happiness. Lupercio smiled at the big man in the little pool because he looked like an infant.

Lupercio hooked another small bass and played it for a minute, then flipped the rod up and toward him, and the fish sailed through the air and into his hand. He pulled out the hook and dropped the fish back in the water.

Finally the woman came out. She wore a brief brown swimsuit with an open white blouse over it, sandals and a floppy red hat. Lupercio wondered why anyone with such beauty would choose to be a criminal.

Suzanne came down the back deck steps and strode across to the pond. Her face was hard to see at this distance and shielded by the hat. She stopped beside the dock and watched the larger boy ride his board. The boy upped his speed and his bravery to impress and frighten his mother.

She watched, apparently not frightened. Then she walked over to the other boy, knelt down beside him and watched him fish. Suzanne said something to him and the boy said something back, but Lupercio couldn't hear the words. He could see the similarities in the shapes and shadings of their bodies — the straight shoulders and long limbs and light brown hair. The older boy was black-haired and thickly built. Three sons by three men, thought Lupercio. *Araña.* Spider.

A minute later she walked back to the plastic pool, took off everything but her swimsuit and climbed in with the Hawaiian and the baby. She took the infant and sat down cross-legged with her back to the man, who ladled up the water in his hands and spilled it onto her shoulders. He kissed her neck.

The heat was too heavy and soon everyone had gone back inside except the young boy, who continued to fish the pond. He hadn't had a strike in over an hour but he still seemed keenly interested in what he was doing. The boy changed his lure for the fifth time. Lupercio saw that he could either kill them all and then search for his diamonds, or he could come back another time when they were gone. The trouble was that Suzanne Jones would likely fence his jewels soon, and this opportunity would be lost forever.

Then the young boy reeled up his lure to the rod tip, turned and started across the meadow toward Lupercio.

Lupercio watched the boy approach and the distance between them shorten, and he rapidly weighed cause and effect and made up his mind what he would do.

The boy was slender and dark-skinned and his eyes were gray. "How do you catch the fish?"

"With patience."

"I mean bait or a lure?"

"Worms."

Lupercio picked up his Styrofoam cup of worms and handed it to the boy, who lifted the lid and pried through the earth with a finger.

"These look good," said the boy.

"They are good."

"You don't have a bobber. How do you see the strike?"

"By feel. The small fish are brave and confident. You can feel them take the worm if it's hooked right."

"Teach me how to catch them," said the boy.

"They've stopped biting in the heat," said Lupercio. He lifted his hat and wiped his forehead as if to prove this, then set the hat back in place slightly higher up, enjoying the new strip of cool. "And I have to go home now to my family."

"Maybe later today when it's not so hot?"

"Maybe."

"No, never mind. We're going to the movies today. Sunday afternoons. I just remembered."

Lupercio smiled inside. "Then some other time. Keep the worms. Put them in the refrigerator and they'll stay alive for days."

The boy looked at him. "I'll pay you for them."

"Okay."

The boy pulled a wallet from his back pocket. It was smooth leather, and new, and Lupercio read the name embossed across the back: Jordan.

Jordan tucked the worm cup under one elbow, took out a dollar and handed it to Lupercio.

"Thank you," said Lupercio. "When you feel the hook move, set it. Even at the slightest movement, set it. If you're not sure, set it. You'll be surprised."

Jordan nodded, then turned and walked back across the meadow.

Lupercio watched him go, understanding that he had just determined his own fate. He had revealed himself for the diamonds. He'd always believed that he would die in the pursuit of something beautiful but never imagined his death would begin with a boy trying to catch a fish.

When the family drove away at four in a red Yukon, Lupercio rose from the shade of the greasewood trees alongside the stream.

He had a good feeling about the barn and decided to search it first. Two hours was plenty for the barn, the house and the garage, so long as you had a feel for where to hide things. Lupercio had that feel from years of hiding his own earnings — the cash and dope and jewelry and stolen everything that he'd spent a lifetime amassing and protecting.

He picked open the padlock, slid the heavy rolling door aside just a little and slipped in. He found the lights. He saw the pickup truck and had an even stronger feeling that this was where she'd put the gems.

He had just put his hand on the green latex

painter's gloves in his pants pocket when the door thundered open to a bright sky and two men appeared in the doorway silhouetted by the orange sun.

They walked toward him. They were young and even bigger than the Hawaiian, with long black hair and faces that looked chipped from stone. Indians from the reservation, thought Lupercio.

Their hands were empty and then they weren't. Shiny blades appeared. They moved apart, putting some space between them as they advanced. The sun was behind them and Lupercio still could not see them clearly.

"Suzanne hired me to do landscape maintenance," he said.

"So you sneak into the barn?" said the big one.

They came out of the sunlight and Lupercio truly saw them for the first time.

"Put up your hands," said the big one. Lupercio guessed him at six feet four, two-ninety, maybe three hundred pounds. The other was bigger. They were both very young and Lupercio felt relief.

"She told me to use these tools," said Lupercio, nodding to the far wall, on which dozens of yard tools hung on hooks in pegboard. He raised his hands and looked down at his boots, humbly.

"You know her number?" Big asked Bigger. "We could call her."

"I don't know her number."

"Then let's just chain him up and wait," said Bigger. "If Suzie hired him, fine. If she didn't, we'll tie him to the truck and drag him through Indian country. You ever had your ass dragged through prickly pear?"

"No," said Lupercio.

"It's the worst thing there is."

"I'm a gardener," said Lupercio. "Why do you need knives for a gardener? I ask you to be reasonable. I would like to do my job because I need the money. I have identification in my pocket. You can hold it until Suzanne comes back. And I can work."

Bigger stepped closer to Lupercio, and Big went behind him. With one huge hand Bigger flipped his knife closed and slipped it back into the scabbard on his belt. Out came his wallet on a chain, then the wallet went back into his pocket but without the chain. Bigger stepped toward Lupercio to bind him.

"My identification," said Lupercio. He stared into Bigger's eyes now and lowered his right hand toward his pocket deliberately but not quickly.

"Leave it where it is," said Bigger.

In a flash of steel in sunlight Lupercio popped the machete out of its breakaway scabbard and cut off Bigger's right hand at the wrist. Then he pivoted left and swung the weapon in both hands across Big's belly, high and deep enough to feel the tip scrape vertebrae as it passed through. Following the blade Lupercio completed the circle and augured down on his short strong legs then jumped and brought the machete straight down through the top of Bigger's head with the sound of an axe splitting a log. Bigger collapsed, but Lupercio held tight to the long handle and braced his foot on the man's face to pull the weapon free; then he spun again and brought the blade down with all of his considerable strength onto the fallen brother's neck. The steel cleanly split the big column before bouncing sharply off the concrete floor in a rooster tail of blood.

For a moment there was no sound but his breathing and the weakening splashes of blood on cement then Lupercio searched the barn and the house and the garage and found no diamonds.

From the house he took jewelry so that this whole mess would look like a burglary gone wrong, but he knew that Suzanne Jones would instantly see it for what it was. He took a battered leather address book from a desk in a room full of books.

Lupercio was an optimist, though as he made his covert way back to his car he admitted his problems: the police would soon be crawling all over this place, Suzanne Jones would clear out and try to sell the diamonds very quickly, the Bull would be angry.

All that, and the boy could identify him.

But throughout his eventful life Lupercio had found that chaos is opportunity. He made his plan as he drove the dirt road toward town.

10

"We'll call her Allison Murrieta because we don't know who the hell she really is," said the captain.

His name was Patmore, and he was leading an interagency task force briefing on the armed robber Allison Murrieta. He stood in a Sheriff's headquarters conference room beside a television screen on a stand, with a remote control in one hand and a laser pointer in the other. There were cops and deputies from all over Southern California, FBI, even a popular Channel 4 reporter. It was Monday morning and already ninety degrees.

Hood sat in the back of the room holding a cup of coffee on his knee. Marlon had put him on the task force because they needed bodies and Hood could take the hours out of his patrol schedule. Overtime was always good. Marlon seemed fascinated by the masked robber.

Patmore cued up a series of stills of Allison's face, taken from a video of her robbing a Taco Bell up in Van Nuys.

The first thing Hood thought was that Allison seemed to be hamming it up for the camera, then when Patmore rolled the whole video clip Hood realized she really *was* hamming it up. She was enjoying herself, pointing a big-barreled derringer at the video shooter, who backed up squealing like a teenager on a thrill ride. Then Allison whipped the gun back at the clerk, who smiled big-eyed as he stuffed the bills into a plastic Taco Bell bag. The other clerk looked uncertain how she should react to all this, then she grinned. Christ, thought Hood, is this what it takes to entertain people anymore?

The second thing Hood thought was that Allison Murrieta looked like Suzanne Jones.

He lifted his coffee and sat back. He studied the shape of her body and her face, comparing it to what he'd seen the day before down in Valley Center. *I caught you checking out my legs and just about everything else.* True enough, Hood thought, which gave him some pretty clear images to work with. He wondered if Allison's hair might be a wig. He tried to imagine her with Suzanne's brown waves and no mask. Look at the jawline, he thought, and the forehead and the tip of her chin — what do you see?

Well, he wasn't sure what he saw.

He remembered that Suzanne Jones had pretty hands, but Allison Murrieta wore gloves.

Patmore was saying that she was suspected of thirty-four armed robberies of various southland retail businesses in the last eighteen months, good for over twenty-five thousand dollars. In addition she was suspected of four *Auto Trader* scams where she set up marks dumb enough to bring cash to buy used high-end cars, such as the one up on Laurel Canyon over the weekend. These jobs had gotten her another ninety-six thousand dollars. Patmore said that Allison Murrieta had also stolen at least twenty-two high-end vehicles for the so-called export market, which meant the cars were sold whole — usually out of country — instead of chopped for parts.

"We know this because she's left her card in place of twenty-two very fine automobiles," Patmore said. "And God knows how many more of her cards blew away, or maybe she just ran out and had to get more printed up. In our estimation those vehicles have gotten her something in the ballpark of one million dollars. So she's doing okay for herself. We've got reason to believe she's lifting plenty of Toyotas and Fords, too, but she only brags about the high-end stuff. Oh, here's the card she leaves."

He clicked the remote, and the screen almost filled with an enlargement of Allison Murrieta's card. It looked like a standard rectangular business card, but the paper was pale pink and the writing was a graceful black cursive:

YOU'VE BEEN ROBBED BY
ALLISON MURRIETA
HAVE A NICE DAY

"Ten years ago, we'd have been all over the print shops, but now anybody can make these with a PC and a printer," said Patmore. "The card stock you can get at the big office stores."

Next he ran another cell-phone video, of Allison Murrieta holding up a Huntington Beach Blockbuster. This time the clerk — a big boy with a bad complexion and his hands in the air — froze and backed away from the cash register. Allison Murrieta jumped the counter and bagged the money herself. The boy was backed against the far side of the employee pen, and when Allison turned her attention and gun to him, he slumped unconscious in a dead faint. She said "Shit" quietly, then straddled the kid and tried to slap him awake. The video shooter actually stepped forward to the counter to get the shot, and Allison wheeled and aimed the cavernous barrel of the derringer straight at the camera.

For just a second Hood clearly saw the imminent death and destruction that nobody in these videos except the big boy seemed to be aware of. Even Allison Murrieta looked like she was acting out a part. The clerks were supporting cast.

But Hood knew how quickly things could happen. That was the first lesson you learned in Anbar province. So you had to change the way you drew conclusions. You had to see every moment of silence as an explosion or a burst of gunfire, every quiet alley as an ambush, every piece of roadside clutter as an improvised explosive device, every helpful citizen as a suicide bomber. Allison Murrieta didn't know any of that. The clerks didn't either, except maybe the boy who fainted. Which was why, Hood thought, somebody was due to get killed at one of her stickups. It was a wonder it hadn't happened yet. Then, Allison Murrieta would turn from a popular televised news bite into a murderer, and some outraged citizen or off-duty cop would take her down in the middle of one of these performances. Or try to. Hood figured the derringer was at least .40-caliber by the diameter of the twin barrels.

Patmore explained that she'd driven a different vehicle for almost every stickup — all stolen and quickly dumped. Of course they'd dusted them for prints and gone through them for hair and fiber, but no prints because of the gloves, and plenty of random hair and fiber that might or might not relate to her.

"I'm going to just let some video run here," said Patmore. "It's all pretty much the same. Some is taken off security cameras, some from cell phone cameras. I think what it mainly shows is that this dingbat is going to end up shooting somebody if we don't get to her first, and the whole deal is going to turn sour."

Amen to that, thought Hood.

Allison robbed a Pizza Hut. Allison robbed a Starbucks. Allison robbed a Burger King, another Taco Bell, a Subway, a Payless Shoes, a Circuit City and a Radio Shack. She hardly said a word, Hood noted. All you needed was a gun and a mask and people instinctively knew what to do.

Then Patmore cued up a map of greater

Los Angeles. It went as far north as Fillmore and as far south as Temecula, and all the way from San Bernardino to the Pacific Ocean. There were red triangles marking the armed robberies and black squares marking the boosted cars.

Hood heard the low murmur rise up from the audience — they were impressed by Allison's success, by the sheer numbers she had run up. Hood noticed that Marlon was shaking his head in wonder.

"That's a lot of activity," said Marlon.

"Maybe you can see a pattern," said the captain. "Shelly, you do these radius plots for bank jobs, don't you?"

Hood watched the FBI woman nod. "There's nothing directional in this one," she said. "Nothing that looks like a pattern of entry or exit. It's more round, which usually makes us look at the center. That would be, what, Pomona, Fullerton?"

"Yeah, about that," said Patmore.

"Did you plot time of day?"

"Right here," said Patmore. "You're dealing with the big boys, Shelly."

Chuckles, scattered applause, one "eee-haw."

The time-of-day map was just like the first one, but above each red triangle or black square was a date and time.

The roomful of law enforcers went quiet for a moment.

Hood saw patterns, general as they were. The jobs were pulled close to freeways — not hard in greater L.A. Almost nothing at rush hour. Heavy on Saturdays and Sundays, light on Mondays, hardly a Friday at all.

"She knows the traffic," said Shelly. "She avoids rush hour and likes the weekends."

"Easier getaways," said Patmore.

"Look at all the three o'clocks and eight o'clocks she's pulled," said Shelly. "Just before, then right after the crush. That's good timing. Just enough traffic to get lost in."

Hood remembered what Suzanne Jones said: *It's an hour and forty minutes this time of night, without traffic.*

He looked at the time-of-day map. It was a big area, but there were roads all over most of it. Thousands of miles of roads, hundreds of miles of freeways. That was the thing about L.A. — in just two hours, at the right time, you could be way up Highway 395 or Interstate 5 to the deserts north, or just about make the Arizona border to the east, or be sitting in a cantina in Rosarito, Baja California, Mexico.

Or be back to your family in Valley Center.

"I'm going to change gears here," said Patmore. "I brought in Dave Boyer from NBC because he's . . . Well, Dave, maybe you should just tell it."

Hood had watched Dave Boyer on and off for the last five years. Boyer was an affable, wide-faced ex-quarterback for USC. He did mostly local color, human interest and an occasional exotic adventure. Boyer had talked to Hood once about a "young deputies back from the war" story that never aired. Hood always thought he was a good reporter: fair and curious, reluctant to incite fear.

Boyer came up and introduced himself, then pushed a disc into the player below the monitor. Patmore gave him the laser pointer and remote.

"I got this FedEx last Friday," said Boyer. "From our friend Allison. Let me know if you can't hear it in the back."

Boyer pushed something on the remote, then crossed his arms and stared down at the floor.

Allison appeared on-screen, black hair loosened from the usual ponytail, crystal-studded mask in place. She was sitting at what might have been a hotel room desk, visible from the waist up. The window or mirror behind her was draped with what looked like a wine-colored blanket or bedspread. She wore a tailored Western-cut blouse, black satin and long-sleeved, with red piping along the pocket slits and mother-of-pearl buttons. Her earrings were gold hoops. The pendant around her neck looked to be diamonds and rubies. Her gloves were black and shiny enough to look wet. An ivory-handled derringer lay on the desk in front of her.

"Hi, Dave, I'm Allison Murrieta, as I'm sure you noticed. Love your reporting. I especially liked it when you went to Indonesia and got attacked by the Komodo dragon, but I'm glad you weren't hurt. I thought the big-wave surfing story from Baja was good, too, how the surfers risk their lives for not much money. I did not care for the La Brea Tar Pits story because I find the pits boring and smelly."

Her voice was electronically scrambled but understandable. The effect was eerie and B movie at the same time. It was an octave lower than it should be, thought Hood.

"But we're not here to talk about you, are we? I've been watching your network's coverage of me, as well as the other networks, too, and I want to set the record straight. I am the great-great-great-great-great-great-granddaughter of Joaquin Murrieta. Our family tree has been accurately recorded. Joaquin was born in 1830 in Mexico and I was born in 1976 in Los Angeles. I am a physical and a spiritual descendant. He was hunted down and shot dead in 1853. They cut off his head, put it in a jar and displayed it for money in Northern California cities. Two other men were shot and beheaded along with him, because the posse wasn't sure which one was Joaquin. The posse was led by the so-called last of the Texas Rangers, a guy named Harry Love, of all things. The beheadings were not done purely for profit and cruelty, though there was certainly some profit and cruelty in it. Back then, before widespread photography and refrigeration and fingerprinting, it was common to cut off a dead man's head so they could ID him later. The man who actually cut off Joaquin's head was named Billy Henderson, and he was self-admittedly haunted by Joaquin's headless ghost until the day he died. In every appearance as a ghost, Joaquin told Billy that he would not rest until he got his head back."

With this, Allison ran a gloved index finger across her throat.

"Think about that," she said. "What they actually did to him."

Then she cleared her just-cut throat and shook back her hair.

Hood wondered if it was a wig, and if so, where did you go to in L.A. to get a good one? Or in Valley Center.

"They say that Joaquin's head was lost in the great San Francisco earthquake of 1906, but this is not true," said Allison. "It was actually stolen by his great-grandson, Ramón — or Raymond, if you must — and passed down the generations to me. I have it now and keep it in a cool place where I live. His face is still very handsome, just as the books say he was. Frankly, his color isn't good. But the main trouble is his long black hair fell out decades ago and now it's just like black grass at the bottom of a lake. Historians have disagreed on the preservative medium — some claimed it was brandy, others said whiskey, others said medicinal alcohol. I don't know what it was at first, but I can tell everyone this: Joaquin came to me in a brown liquid that smelled slightly of alcohol and meat, so I switched it out for a premium brand of rubbing alcohol and now he looks a lot better. I was extra careful with his hair."

History, thought Hood.

A history teacher.

The room was quiet. From Hood's point of view in the back, he saw dozens of capable and dedicated law enforcers all looking at a TV screen from which a masked outlaw held them to a fascinated silence. It was reality television — a real person with a real gun.

Allison signed off:

"Okay, Dave, I've got plenty to say about the way they treated Joaquin all those hundred and fifty years ago, but I've also got some cars to boost and some chain stores and fast-food outlets to rob, so I'm going to say good-bye for now.

"Oh, as you know, I've been donating a generous percentage of my earnings to various southland nonprofit organizations. The following organizations will vouch for receiving cash donations from Allison Murrieta, unless of course they've pocketed the money: the Los Angeles Boys & Girls Club, the Olivewood Home for Children in Orange, the Assistance League of La Cañada/Flintridge, the Laguna Club, Children's Hospital Los Angeles, Project Concern in San Diego, the Make-A-Wish Foundation, Amnesty International, the Heart Association and — I love this one — the Los Angeles Police Foundation!

"Now, obviously, you can put this video of me on TV if you want. I might even do a Channel Four interview with you sometime. The public is ready for me. Your ratings will spike. Just let me tell them and you and everybody else out there not to mess with me while I'm working. I get a little nervous sometimes when I'm onstage and that little derringer is loaded and the trigger is light and I don't want anyone to get hurt. Don't any of you try to be a hero. Stay out of my way.

"And one last little thing: it's M-U-R-R-I-E-T-A. *Two R's and one T.* I've left enough cards behind, so tell your print media friends to get it right. Oh, and my favorite color is chrome. Thanks, Dave."

She raised the little gun and aimed it at the camera.

Dave Boyer paused the video. Allison aimed at the law enforcement community, her expression hidden behind the ivory-handled derringer and the jeweled mask.

There were murmurs and a few chuckles then someone finally spoke up. "She won't last another month."

"She's lasted a year and a half," said Patmore.

"Hey, Dave, you gonna run this on Channel Four?"

Boyer turned up his palms in a show of innocence. "Actually, that's one of the reasons I came here. I, ah . . . thought you all should see this. I want to keep the lines of communication open between the law and Channel Four. And to answer your question, well, yes, we are going to show it. This is news."

"You're just pumping up a delusionary

babe with a death wish," said a burly cop from Whittier.

The woman sitting next to him said, "Yeah, and you don't know if one word of what she says is true. You really think she's got a head up in her closet?"

"Yeah, really, Dave," said an L.A. Sheriff's detective, "if you get people on Allison's side and they start thinking she's cool and cute or something, well, that's going to make our jobs a lot more difficult. That's already starting to happen. My kids think she's cool. You might want to think this one through."

"We already had it out with the network attorneys," said Patmore. "Our lawyers said there's no way to stop them from running it."

"Show the damned thing," said a strong, clear voice near the front. Hood recognized it as Captain Wyte's. "You show it, and I guarantee you that somebody will strip off that mask during one of her jobs and it'll be over. The citizen hero will get shot, Murrieta will get made, and the LAPD Foundation will need to find new sources of development."

This got a chuckle.

"We're going to give you in law enforcement plenty of airtime in response," said Boyer. "I'm on your side. That's why I'm here. But this is a good story and people need to hear it. We're checking facts as fast as we can. We know you've got genuine concerns. We do, too. We'll let the public know that this isn't cute or funny. My goal? Bring Allison Murrieta to justice without anybody getting shot. That would be a good story for all of us."

"And bring up your ratings," someone called out.

"Ratings up, crime down," said Boyer with a smile.

When the briefing was over, Hood loitered up near the podium to overhear Patmore and the others. Boyer was assuring them that Channel 4 wasn't about to spin Allison Murrieta as Robin Hood or Bonnie Parker. He had burned a stack of Allison's CDs to help the cops, and Hood took one.

"Congratulations on making homicide," said Wyte.

"Thank you," said Hood. He knew Wyte only by reputation. He was considered bright and cursed. Years ago his wife had died of a rare cancer. She was thirty. Not long after that, Wyte was seriously injured in an onduty helicopter crash. He came back to work full-time, though limping and deskbound. He rose to gang unit coordinator, and now oversaw crimes against persons, which made him Hood's distant boss. He seemed fit and strong in spite of his injuries, Hood thought, and looked like he spent plenty of time outside.

"I heard the auto body shop was pretty bad," said Wyte.

"Ten men."

Wyte nodded. "What do you have?"

"A diamond broker tried to pay off a loan from the Wilton Street Asian Boyz, and MS-13 found out. Shot each other dead."

"Did MS get the diamonds?"

"We think so. Somebody did. We just can't quite nail that part down."

"Let me know if I can help," said Wyte. "I've still got some decent sources for MS-13 from my gang days."

"I appreciate it, sir."

"The members of Mara Salvatrucha have no fear of us."

"That's what I hear. It looks like they underestimated the Asian Boyz."

"Kyle Ko might help you."

"I talked to him. Some help, yes."

"Keep me in the loop," said Wyte.

In the new detective pen cubicle of which Hood was proud, he called Barry's girlfriend, Melissa Levery. He offered his condolences and was quiet for a moment while she cried. He explained that he was a junior detective assigned to the case then made an appointment to meet with her.

"Melissa, right now I'd like to clarify one bit of information that will help us very much," he said.

"What?"

"The night that Barry died, did he have diamonds with him to pay back gambling debts?"

"Of course he did. That's why they killed him, isn't it?"

"What was their approximate value?"

"Four hundred fifty grand if sold retail. Forty grand plus change on the black market."

"Did you actually see him with them in his possession?"

"Yes."

"That night?"

"Afternoon. He showed them to me. He said that they would buy us back the way we used to be."

She sobbed again. Hood waited and she hung up.

He thought a minute, then dug Lenny Overbrook's number out of his wallet.

He dialed the number then punched the off button on his cell phone and set it on the desk. Hood couldn't think of a single good thing that could come of talking with Lenny, but he felt duty bound to call. He picked up the phone and hit redial.

"Lenny."

"Charlie Hood."

"Thanks for calling."

Hood let the silence stretch out a little. "You're a long way from West Virginia."

"I came to L.A. to see you, sir."

"There's nothing you can say that will change anything for the better, Lenny."

"It will make it better for me."

"It's too late."

"Are you God, sir?"

Hood felt his ears grow hot and the heavy beating of his heart. "Okay."

He let Lenny set a time and place.

11

The interagency e-bulletin about the slaughter in Valley Center hit LASD late that morning. Hood made it to Suzanne Jones's property in an hour forty minutes just like she said he could.

There were two Sheriff's cruisers on the property, a coroner's van, Escondido Police and a Tribal Police unit. Reporters and news crews had stationed themselves in the meadow under the huge oak tree for shade. Hood parked his Camaro where he'd parked the day before and drew the unhappy attention of the sergeant manning the sign-in log outside the barn.

Hood identified himself and signed in, then defaulted to the neutral stare and brevity that they all had adopted in the otherworldy heat of Anbar.

"You're completely out of jurisdiction, Hood."

"We've got a case open and she's our best

witness," he said.

"Who?"

"Jones," said Hood. "She lives here."

"I know who lives here."

"I appreciate this, sir."

And then he walked past the sergeant. There were no bodies by now but Hood saw the blood pooled on the concrete and splashed against the rough-hewn stalls and thrown across the floor almost to the door. He had learned from a Shia executioner that a decapitated adult will send twin jets of blood about ten feet, sometimes more, depending on how afraid he is at the time of his death. A trail of bloody boot prints faded toward the barn door. They seemed hardly larger than a child's.

He convinced a San Diego Sheriff's photographer to scroll back through his digitals, and he saw how the big men had fallen, and the terrible work of the blade or blades that had butchered them. He saw practice and efficiency and something that was harder to put into words. Hood asked if they'd found a weapon, and the photog said just a Buck knife still gripped in the fist that was chopped off — actually chopped completely off — one of the Indians. He had several close-ups of this. He said the other one's head was still on but barely; it must have been one helluva

118

sharp sword or axe or whatever.

Hood looked up into the eaves and saw the pigeons unmoving in the heat. Dust climbed a column of sunlight. He thought of riding horses with his father once when he was a boy, on a clear October morning in the desert when the world was clean and beautiful.

He found a Sheriff's homicide detective, Felton, who told him that one of the boys who lived here had found the bodies about eight o'clock last night. The dead men were brothers — Harold and Gerald Little Chief — and they lived right across the stream. Almost kids themselves, he said, just eighteen and nineteen years old. Rincon Indians.

"One perp?" asked Hood.

"One set of prints leading out. That's all we've got so far."

"The Jones family still here?" asked Hood.

"They left last night."

"I'd appreciate a number."

"Who the hell are you again?"

"Los Angeles Sheriff's homicide," said Hood. He showed his badge. "Suzanne Jones is a witness. The ten gangsters."

"I heard about that one."

"We don't have much either."

Felton looked at him doubtfully then flipped open his notepad, wrote something and tore off a sheet for Hood.

"So what?" he said. "This Jones babe happens to see ten bangers get shot dead in L.A., then she comes home and this happens in her barn? She the angel of death or something?"

"She's a schoolteacher." Hood didn't try to explain Suzanne Jones and Miracle Auto Body, wasn't sure he could.

"Give me a call when you got it all figured out, son."

"I'd be glad to."

Hood walked across the barnyard, felt the sun heating his neck and shirt. He stayed away from the reporters under the enormous oak tree. As he passed them he looked up at a knocking noise and saw two acorn woodpeckers working an upper branch near a tree house. The house was way up there, not quite hidden by the twisted black branches of the tree. Hood saw no ladder or rope, no way to get up to it.

The front door of the house stood ajar, and there was a crime scene notice in a clear plastic sheath thumbtacked to the wall. Hood saw that the dog bowls were gone. He opened the door and called loudly then walked in. It was hot. Things looked the same as they had the day before, but the house felt abandoned. There was no burglar alarm console in the entryway.

He walked into the dining room with the picnic table where they had talked, then he went into a large living room with a big-screen TV and two unmatched couches pushed side by side, with plenty of pillows misshapen from use. There was a tiki bar at one end of the room, complete with a thatched roof and woven bamboo bar stools. There was a set of island drums in the corner near the bar, and decorative wooden clubs and spears and ukuleles hung on the woven-grass-covered wall.

In the kitchen there were dishes in the sink, but the refrigerator was empty of perishables. No alarm console here either. In the corner of the pantry floor was an open space with nothing but two dog kibbles on it. He walked through the teenager's room and a boy's bedroom and a nursery.

Another room had books on shelves, a couch with reading lamps at each end and a small desk with a computer, a printer/copier and a telephone on it. He looked for a personal address book but found none. In a file cabinet in the corner he found the household bills for electricity, propane, water and phone. He took the most recent phone bill, ran a copy and put back the original.

He folded the copy and studied the shelves, mostly books on history and some best sellers. There were stacks of magazines on cars and skateboarding, fishing and cooking.

In another bedroom that appeared unused Hood glanced at the pictures on the shelves and walls: mostly Suzanne Jones with three boys who looked several years apart and not a lot alike, and a few shots involving Ernest, the islander, and other men Hood didn't recognize. There were commendations from the Los Angeles Unified School District, including a framed Primary Teacher of the Year Award. Hood saw Suzanne's diplomas from Dominguez Hills State University and Vista West High School. She'd graduated from high school four years before him. He wondered if he might have seen her at a football game or a rodeo or a store.

The master bedroom was spacious and shaded by a big coral tree outside the French doors that framed a view of the wooded valley and the stream. Bright orange orioles hopped in the thorny branches. Against one wall was a dresser with the drawers hanging open. There were mounds of clothing on the floor in front of it. A wooden jewelry box had been rifled and tossed on top of the clothes. The closet shelves were bare because everything had been pulled down to the carpet.

A plainclothes investigator glanced over his shoulder at Hood, a video recorder in his hand.

"Someone went through here pretty good," said the man. "Watch the stuff on the floor."

"Did you talk to her? Jones?"

"No. I'm crime scene, part of the second wave. She'd gotten her kids out before I arrived."

The bedroom smelled lightly of human beings and laundry soap and perfume. The bed was unmade. Hood looked at Suzanne Jones's pillow.

He wondered how much four hundred and fifty thousand dollars' worth of diamonds weighed, and how much volume it would occupy in space. Not much.

In the hallway he checked the thermostat, which was turned to off. Back in the family room he played the recorded message — Ernest saying to leave a number and they'd call back. There were three incoming messages. Hood took down the names and numbers and locked the door behind him on the way out.

He stood for a moment in the big three-car garage, half expecting to see the yellow Corvette, but the only vehicles were a nice little minibike caked with red dust and a small tractor fitted with a mower.

Hood crossed the stream rock-to-rock and climbed the embankment toward the home at the top of the rise. It was beige stucco, peeling and rain-stained, and the shingles on the roof were warped. There were three huge satellite dishes and some old appliances in the dirt patch beside it. A window-mounted air conditioner was held up by two-by-fours placed at splaying angles.

Betty Little Chief was a large, big-faced woman with black hair and a soft, singsong voice. Her cheekbones were high and pronounced and the whites of her eyes were bloodshot. She wore reading glasses on a lanyard around her neck. Hood could see that Betty's blouse and her glasses had been recently cried on, and the lenses were not yet wiped.

After he identified himself and gave her his commiserations and told her his purpose, she looked straight through him and nodded. For a moment Hood felt that he had vanished.

"I saw a car parked down by the stream on my way to the store," she said. "And I saw it on my way back home, too. There was a man fishing the stream. The fish in that stream are about four inches long. That's the only thing unusual about that day, except my sons being murdered."

"What did the man look like?"

"A hat. A pole. A fisherman."

"What time?"

"Afternoon. Three-thirty and four-thirty, about. No one fishes down there."

"What kind of car?"

"Lincoln Continental. Black. My old man bought one like that once. Used and he was proud of it."

"When? When did he buy that car?"

"Late seventies. He died in eighty." Now Betty Little Chief focused her gaze on his face instead of through it. Her eyes shone like black suns beyond the peaks of her cheekbones. "Evil was here. I've had that feeling twice before in my life and both times I was right. It's still strong."

"I have it, too."

"You don't look like you could."

"You can't know what other people have seen."

"No. That's why secrets are good to keep."

"Did Suzanne Jones ask you about a car parked down by the stream?"

She hesitated as her eyes scanned his face.

"She did. And all of you police, too. I told everyone."

"Thank you. I'm sorry what happened to your boys. I truly am."

She closed the door on him not impolitely. Hood touched the wood with his fingers before he walked away.

In the streambed he found the small boot prints and followed them down the stream on one side then back up the stream on the other. Where there was a view of the Joneses' meadow and pond, the toes faced another set of prints in the soft earth and these were certainly a child's athletic shoe of some kind. The child had walked from the direction of the Joneses' property. Hood wondered what they had talked about. Fishing, maybe. A child and a man. He retraced the child's steps toward the pond, then lost them in the dead summer stubble of the meadow.

On the way to his car he dialed the number he'd gotten from Felton and listened to the computerized voice telling him to leave a message.

He asked Suzanne Jones to call him and left his numbers. He said it was important.

Five minutes later Ernest called back to say that Suzanne was out of town and not available.

"I want to talk to your child," said Hood. "The middle one."

"I'll bet you do."

12

So I'm up in the Hotel Laguna and Ernest and the boys are safely stashed in Oceanside. I still can't believe that flat-topped Lincoln-driving machete-wielding son of a bitch tracked me to my home in less than one day and killed two of my neighbors. Fishing. Yeah, Jordan's an observant boy. I've got the diamonds, and in my satchel plenty of cash and a very nice .45-caliber Colt Gold Cup that shoots like a dream.

I've already called the people who might know about this man, this violent collector, and I've gotten not one single call back. I think he's MS-13, maybe the boss, and he knew about the diamonds and came sniffing around Miracle Auto Body when none of his boys returned. Now he wants my rocks and I've seen what he'll do to get them. But I'm betting on me.

My son Bradley found the bodies late last night and he was still clammy and near silent when I kissed him good-bye in Ocean-side a few hours ago. This from a kid who skateboarded two miles home with a compound fracture of his arm when he was ten. I will not forgive that man for making Bradley see what he saw. It was indescribable. Something in Bradley was changed by it. The look on his face. They were Gerald and Harold and then they were hacked meat. Buckets of blood. The cop said it happened with tremendous speed.

I'm still betting on me.

It's evening now and the sun is still up over the water, but I turn on every light anyway. My heart is beating quickly and not deeply. I upend the red backpack and shake the parcels to the bed.

I study them. There are only six. According to the wholesaler's writing on the paper, one parcel contains sixteen one-and-a-half-carat diamonds, near colorless, SI1 and SI2. They are a mix of round and princess cuts. Another parcel contains a like amount of one-carat stones, same color, clarity and cut. Three others contain the same stones, but in diminishing sizes, from three-quarters down to one-third carats. The sixth parcel contains one round-cut two-carat diamond, near colorless, SI1 in clarity. It's beautiful and it's worth twenty grand if you want to buy it in a store.

I set one of my black leather gloves on the bed pillow, swing out the reading light, then unfold the gemstone paper and place this rock on the glove. There's an explosion of light and color. The red of the sun and the blue of the sky and the deep green of the Pacific and the electric lights of the hotel all find their way through this stone. The diamond doesn't just reflect light, it radiates the light. I see this with my own eyes, though I know it can't be true. The facets shift up and down the color spectrum as I slowly pivot the glove atop the pillow — fresh detonations of blues and reds and yellows. Does a diamond shine if there is no one there to see it? Dear Joaquin in heaven — it must. I can't take my eyes off it, and I think it's watching me, too. Besides a very few men and maybe three cars, it's the most beautiful thing I've ever seen. Millions of years in the making. Harder than steel. Sharper than the blade that killed the Little Chiefs. Extremely difficult to find. Unseen by the masses and untouched but by the few. Stunning. Brilliant. Hypnotic. Seductive. Pure. Eternal. Worth a potload.

Mine.

I put it in the palm of my hand and walk around the hotel room, watching the plays of light. I drop it and catch it in my other waiting hand. I toss it back up to the first. I foxtrot as my great-uncle Jack taught me, with the diamond in my right hand, then I flick it to my left hand as I *one-two-three-four* into the corner near the entertainment center then *one-two-three-four* back out of the corner then balance the heavy jewel — yes, two carats have heft — in both cupped hands as I do an unhurried spin like Jordan's daddy Joe used to do to me and I'll tell you I miss that man, reminds me of Charlie Hood, not so much the way they look but they both have that good man thing inside them that you can't move no matter how much woman thing you push against it, then I glide between the window and the couch and watch myself as I pass the mirror, nice-looking woman there, then I'm into the alcove with the closet and the bathroom, and the diamond rolls from hand to hand, *one-two-three-four,* I, Allison Murrieta.

An hour later the papers are laid out open on the bedspread, each gem gleaming in the light. There's a total of eighty-one stones. The two-carat whopper sits in the middle of the bed, shining like a beacon on all the little twinkling ships around it.

The buyer is named Cavore but he has no

idea I know this. I saw his car once when I arrived early for a meeting, and later gave the plate numbers to my DMV acquaintance. The registered owner was Carl Cavore. I've dealt with him before and he is just barely tolerable. He calls himself Jason.

I make the Jack in the Box in Redondo Beach in an hour twenty minutes in the light traffic. He pulls up in his conversion van, a hulking black GM with cobalt blue pinstriping along each flank. No windows except the ones up front. I step up and put one knee on the captain's chair and swivel around for a look in. He says hi and I ignore him. The van smells like a man's bed, not recently laundered. I've been here before: up front is the cockpit, then a small built-in table with two folding chairs facing each other, a very small bathroom, and at the rear, poorly lit and unmade, the bed. We're alone, so far as I can tell. I swivel forward and drop the satchel between my legs.

Cavore pulls out of the lot. I still haven't said a word to him. He takes us up Pacific Coast Highway half a mile, to the Beachside Center parking lot. He parks up close to the stores with the other cars tight around us. As soon as the engine and lights go off, he motions me to the back.

"No. You know I sit closest to the exits,

Jason. Claustrophobia."

He chuckles and moves past me. The van shifts with his great weight. I don't take my eyes off him. He steps down into the pit of the vehicle, lifts the table in order to get around it, then lowers it behind him.

When he's settled in at the far end, I lug my satchel back to one of the folding chairs and I sit.

I clap my hands and the lights come on. Cavore snaps his fingers and they go out.

I clap again.

"You're cute," he says. He smiles.

"Thanks, but I'm really not."

"I know cute when I see it."

Cavore is big, fat and wears his hair in a pompadour. The pompadour is orange on top and brown down at the roots. The rest of him is pale and moist. Large gums and small teeth. His yellow Hawaiian shirt is tight to his enormous arms and the tail rides up over the revolver he carries in a holster approximately at his waist. I don't know how he could find that gun under all his blubber. But I've seen the benches and weights and the heavy bag in the warehouse he used to rent, and by the stacks of fifty-pounders I think Cavore has something capable under all that fat.

He sets a magnifying glass on the table

and smiles without opening his lips. "Maxine, I'll pay any reasonable amount to take you to my bed."

"The answer's still no. You'd crush me."

"I've been told I can be overwhelming in a good way. Huge is huge."

My LASD staff acquaintance ran a records check on Cavore. Among other things, he has raped. Got her in the backseat of a car and let his body weight almost suffocate her while he did his thing. Suspected in two others, but never charged. This was a while back, for what little that matters. The first time he propositioned me was at his warehouse, and I put Cañonita against his gut and cocked her. At that moment, standing pretty much face-to-face with him, feeling like I was in the backseat of a car about to get smothered in fat and raped — I would have shot him. I *wanted* to shoot him. Cavore had understood.

"I'll just have to believe it, Jason. Let's get down to business, okay? I've got things to do."

If I knew a fence who paid better than Carl, I'd go to him. In this business it takes decades to build up the right associates. I've had about eighteen months at it. Carl pays good dollar, such as the 10 percent he offered for all this lovely ice, because he moves a lot of product. The other L.A. diamond guys, they'll give you 5 percent, maybe 8 or 9 for the big stones. Greedy. Diamonds are easy to sell again because only a very few out of millions can be identified.

I bring my satchel to my lap so I can get what I need without taking my attention away from Cavore for more than half a second.

I lay the Colt .45 on the table, stare straight into Carl's small, quick eyes, then fan out the papers facing up and away from me, so he can read the labels. I set the satchel on the floor. He reaches out and presses down lightly on the two-carat masterpiece, his finger circling the paper. His knuckles have dimples and they are hairless.

"You going to palm my best rock?"

"Just feeling the nipple through the blouse."

"Eighty-one stones," I say. "Mostly round, but some nice princess cuts. Uniformly fine clarity, colorless, excellent cuts. The smallest are one-third of a carat and the biggest is that poor thing you're crushing under that hand of yours. Jason, take your goddamned hand off my diamond right now."

He flinches just a little. Then pulls away his hand and reaches into his shirt pocket and lays the calculator on the table beside the papers. Gives me what he thinks is an injured look.

"Good man," I say. I pick up the envelope to make sure he hasn't pulled some kind of magic trick on me. I can feel the big rock inside. I look at it just to make sure. My heart slows down a little.

"Maxine," he says in mock disappointment.

"It's out of respect for your cleverness," I say.

"I've never even tried to cheat you. And when you leave, I drive this lonely city, thinking about you."

Shifting my gaze quickly between Carl and the papers, I unfold them slowly, one at a time, to reveal the treasure. Carl's eyes move as he watches my hands, but the rest of his mass is pale and damp and still.

When I'm done, Carl sits up straighter and leans forward with the magnifying glass. I look at him and he smiles and brings the glass up to enlarge his big gums and little teeth. He wiggles his fat tongue and laughs and the glass steams up then clears.

"You probably scared the girls with lizards," I say.

"Toads. I'd throw them as high as I could into the air, and when they hit —"

"Yeah, yeah."

"Graphic. And the sound was unexpectedly loud, because they fill up with air when they're scared. The smaller ones lasted longer — five, six throws."

"Never learned the difference between scary and disgusting, did you?"

"I was not popular."

Cavore looks through the magnifying glass in his left hand and with his right hand slides a gemstone paper directly under the lens. He studies the rocks, using the tip of his right little — actually big — finger to reposition certain diamonds, then others. Then without looking he reaches out with his right hand and taps at the little calculator resting on the table by his elbow. He pushes the buttons by feel. I can hardly see the calculator beneath his big mitt of a hand. He deftly moves the packet to his right. Outside I hear the voices of a family trying to get into their vehicle, not six feet away from where I'm sitting: "Wait until I unlock the doors, Cody. Cody, wait!"

Cavore examines and taps, examines and taps.

He lingers over the two-carat trophy. "You wonder where they come up with the ratings."

"They're quantifiable."

"This isn't SI2 clarity. It's less."

"Smarter people than you say it's SI2, Jason. They're professionals, not thieves."

I expected him to criticize the product, but I'm not in the mood to indulge him.

"This is four hundred and fifty thousand dollars' worth," I say. "If you want to come up with my forty-five grand, I'll be on my way."

"Ten percent for this quality?"

"Jason, that was the agreement."

"Contingent."

I lean back in the little folding chair and look straight at him. "A gemologist rated those stones."

"But *I'm* buying them. I've been doing this since you were ten years old. This is not four hundred and fifty thousand dollars' worth of stones, Maxine. It's four hundred, even. Quantifiable. The quality varies from good to only fair. The slight inclusions? I see them at only five-times power, when you know that ten-times is the GIA standard. Don't try to fool me. I'll give you eight percent — thirty-two thousand. They'll be hard for me to sell because of the quality, and I am not eager to have them. But a deal is a deal. This is my best and final, pretty woman."

This is a new obstinance from Carl. He always starts low and comes up.

"I'll take forty-two thousand."

138

He shakes his head. No smile. Just the little eyes sucking at me like he's draining a pond to see what's at the bottom.

"Talk to me, Jason."

"How did you manage this? Why? Everybody is talking. MS-13 is very unhappy about those stones. And the Asian Boyz *hate* to lose anything. They're asking questions everywhere. They're looking. They're listening. Someone always knows something. Someone always sees. Someone always talks. Maybe tomorrow or maybe already. They'll discover your sources and stomp your luck flat. The diamond market people won't buy the stones together as they are. Not at five percent, not at any percent — I've talked to them — try them if you don't believe me. They're afraid of the same things you should be afraid of. They'll turn you over to the MS or the Boyz. I can't imagine what they would do. There are rumors of Lupercio."

"Explain Lupercio."

He gave me half a chuckle.

"Mara Salvatrucha, OG, original gangster, *Maxine*. Then he left them, dramatically. A lot of blood was spilled but Lupercio endured. Mara Salvatrucha offered the truce. They say he can see in the dark. They say he's the devil himself."

"He's a little guy with a machete."

"It's more than a machete."

"More how?"

Cavore shrugs and yawns. "I wasn't told. Magical powers, no doubt. Did you hear about the Indian brothers in Valley Center?"

"No. Why?"

"Nothing," he says. "It was nothing." Cavore keeps his small-eyed stare on me. I know he can't link me to Valley Center so I stare back. But I wonder at his thinking, the way he put things together so quickly.

"So, Maxine, what are you going to do? Take it or leave it. I can deliver you to the money in under ten minutes. Thirty-two thousand dollars for something you found like litter in the souls of ten dead men."

"Your spirituality moves me."

"I'll add five hundred for you-know-what, right now, back there."

I watch Carl as I fold and collect each gemstone paper. I square and riffle them like a deck of cards before the shuffle, then slide them down into my satchel without taking my eyes off him. I pick up the gun and stand.

"I'd rather you tried to rape me," I said. "Then I'd have an excuse to shoot you."

"I'm not sure you could do it."

"There's a way to find out."

"Have you ever killed a person?"

"You're not a person."

"Maybe you just would."

"I promise you I would."

"You won't survive where you're going. You believe in yourself because you've had good luck. Good luck always changes. You won't survive."

"I'm glad I didn't sell these diamonds to you, Jason. If you offered me the full forty-five right now, said this was all just a prank, I'd still walk out of here with them."

"That's why you won't survive, Maxine. Because you become emotional about the wrong things. You are emotional about inert stones. You should be emotional about saving your life."

"It would break my heart to put such beauty into dimpled, hairless hands."

"It doesn't matter what you do with the rocks," Jason says. "They already belong to someone else."

"No. You're the only one who's seen them. You're the only one who knows what I have."

"Don't forget Lupercio. What if he's been pointed in your direction? They say he never gives up. If he brought MS-13 to its knees for a truce, he'll find and crush you, easily."

"There's no evidence of Lupercio," I lie.

"No evidence that anyone knows except for you. The last few days have been peaceful. If I see evidence, I'll attribute it to you."

"You don't have the weight to hurt me."

"Believe in that."

Carl opens his hands palms up. "The only two things I know about you aren't even true. A first name that isn't yours. And a phone number that will be useless before the sun comes up. I'd betray you, if I had enough of you to betray."

"How about you just get me back to Jack in the Box?"

I'm put out and hungry so I hit the drive-through. A few minutes later I pull into a driveway in Hollywood, roll down the window and drop a paper grocery bag to the ground.

In my rearview I can see Melissa grabbing her ten grand in cash as I head back toward the freeway.

A deal's a deal.

I'm still pissed off.

I want to shoot Cavore so badly I have to stop by the indoor range, where I fire fifty rounds of .45-cal wadcutters at twenty, thirty, forty and fifty feet. Nice groups except for my occasional stray. I love that Colt.

Then I fire Cañonita at ten and twenty feet. I'm in the black of the silhouette at ten, but at twenty it's tough to keep them on the paper.

When the range master isn't looking, I fire both the Colt and the derringer at the same time, left and right hands, a brief Armageddon featuring Cavore's blubbery greed-bag rapist's body at the receiving end.

I breathe deeply and listen to the ringing in my ears, in spite of the foam plugs.

Then I reload Cañonita and slip her into my waistband and close my eyes. The target is at twenty feet. I breathe deeply, then see Cavore at twenty feet, coming at me. I open my eyes and draw the derringer. The first shot flies over his left shoulder, but the second one hits the middle of his black little heart.

I smile at the range master on my way out.

13

Hood found Ernest and the boys at the beach down by the Oceanside pier. A summer swell pushed the waves high along the pilings, and Hood watched the surfers carve the green walls with their short, quick boards. The sign outside the lifeguard headquarters said the waves were six to eight feet and the water temperature was sixty-six degrees.

Ernest sat in the cool of a portable sunscreen. There were blankets and backpacks strewn in the sand and a cooler with its lid ajar. Kenny lay on his back in his portable crib, head to one side, his eyes locked onto towering Hood.

Hood squatted for a moment, trailing his fingers through the fine gray Oceanside sand.

"That's Bradley, with the black wet suit and the red-and-white twin-fin," said Ernest. He nodded to the surfers.

"Big waves today."

"He's fearless."

"Children can afford that."

Ernest's face was unyielding and his eyes calm.

"Where did your wife go?"

Ernest shook his head. "She's not my wife and she didn't tell me."

"She just took off?"

"There are times when she needs to be out of sight. She doesn't tell me where she is and I don't ask."

"Kind of an odd arrangement."

"There's nothing odd about trust. Why do you care where she went?"

"I think she's in trouble. I think the man who killed the brothers was looking for her."

"Why does he want her?"

"Maybe she knows."

"Who is he? Tell me where he lives. I'll settle it."

"I don't know either of those things."

"But you say he's looking for Suzanne? You're not making sense."

"Why did she run away?"

"Staying out of sight is not running away."

"Why is she staying out of sight?"

Kenny rolled over to his stomach and strained his head up from the floor of the crib. Ernest looked at him then at Hood, then out at the waves. "I respect her fears and her worries."

"Ernest, if I could talk to her I might be able to put some things together. The other night she saw this man near a crime scene in L.A. He saw her, too. I think he's the one who killed Harold and Gerald. But he didn't go all the way down to Valley Center to do that. He went for Suzanne. He was on her property. He thinks she saw something in L.A., or has something. That's why I need to talk to her."

"I don't know where she is."

Hood watched Bradley ride a wave. It didn't matter if Ernest was lying if Ernest wasn't going to tell where she'd gone. "Tell her to call me."

"She got your message."

"Tell her again. Is she going back to school? It starts in a few weeks. She can't teach history and stay out of sight."

"We haven't planned that far ahead."

"Plan ahead if you want to stay alive," said Hood.

Ernest stood and reached down into the crib, touching the baby's head. "Watch the baby. You wanted to talk to Jordan."

Hood watched the Hawaiian amble down to the surf line. A dark-skinned boy ran past him, slid his skimboard into the receding backwash and jumped on. He raced along, threw a rooster tail and shot into the incoming white water, landing on the back side of it still balanced on the board. The boy said something to Ernest, who shrugged and took the board and waited for the next backwash. Ernest was big-chested and short-legged, but he rode the board with an easy power, managing most of a three-sixty just before he got air then wiped out. He was smiling and shaking his head as he pointed up to Hood.

Jordan wrapped a towel around his slender shoulders. His teeth chattered while he said that the fisherman was short, dark-skinned and dark-haired. No mustache or beard. His hair was cut flat on top. He was "not an old man and not a young man, either." He wore jeans and cowboy boots and a short-sleeved plaid shirt and a straw cowboy hat. He was small but powerful. It was really hot that day. His fishing rod and reel looked new and he caught several fish, which he threw back. When they talked, the man said the worms worked best, but you had to hook them so you could feel the tug when the fish bit them.

"Show him what you did," said Ernest.

Still hunched in the towel Jordan hustled

bent-legged over to a backpack and came back with two folded sheets of paper. Hood remembered the child's paintings and drawings he'd seen on the wall of the room where he'd embarrassed himself in front of this boy's mother.

Jordan gave him the papers and Hood unfolded them. They were better than any IdentiKit or police artist's drawing that he'd ever seen. They looked like a well-observed man — not a composite, not an interpretive sketch of someone else's memory. A man. There were two versions: one with a straw cowboy hat and one without. With a pencil Jordan had shaded in a little behind the portraits. He had signed them. Hood rubbed his fingertip across one penciled corner and it came back without a smudge.

"Mom said you would come," he said.

Hood eyed Ernest silently.

"May I have these?"

"She told me to give them to you. She told me to tell you it was the guy from Miracle Auto Body."

Hood looked at the drawings again. This run of good luck was making him uneasy. "Why did he take off his hat?"

"To wipe his forehead, but only for a second. His hair was exactly like that — short and straight up and cut flat. Like the deck of a skateboard."

Hood looked down at the drawings. Jordan's skill was a gift, he thought. When Hood looked at the boy, his teeth had quit chattering but his lips were pale.

"Will you please tell me everything again? Every single thing you remember. I'm going to ask you all those questions again. Maybe something new will come out. Something you overlooked."

Hood thought that Jordan Jones, or whatever his last name was, overlooked very little.

"I gotta stand in the sun."

"Ernest," said Hood. "Can we go up to the snack bar for a drink?"

"Up to you, Jordan."

Jordan kept the towel around him and led the way. "That guy caught like eight fish. He put them back. Did he kill Harold and Gerald?"

"I believe he did. Did your mom keep the originals of your drawings?"

"Yeah. She saves a lot of my stuff. We have a whole wall of it at home."

"Is Ernest your father?"

"My father was Joe Iverson. He died when I was two. There's me and Bradley and baby Kenny and we all have different dads. Bradley's cool. Kenny cries a lot."

"Bradley's dad come around much?"

"Not a lot. He's afraid of Mom."

By the time they went to the snack bar and back Jordan had told Hood his mysterious fisherman story three more times. He remembered nothing new and did not change a single detail from his original version, right down to the number of different lures he used to try to catch a bass that day: thirteen. Hood found it significant that Jordan told Lupercio that the family was going to the movies that day. Apparently, Lupercio had waited down by the stream for them to go, and was interrupted in the barn by Harold and Gerald.

Ernest held his right hand out to Hood, who thought it was to shake, then saw the business card in it. The card was for Ernest Kaleana Electric and featured a graphic red lightning bolt. On the back was a handwritten phone number.

"Try that," said Ernest.

On the way to his car Hood dialed the number and got a computerized voice telling him to leave a message, which he did.

14

Captain Wyte handed the drawings back across the desk to Hood.

"A ten-year-old did those?"

"Yes."

"We should hire him."

"Do you recognize the man?" asked Hood.

"Lupercio Maygar," said Wyte. "One of the original MacArthur Park MS-13 gangsters. Our most recent photograph of him is ten years old. He broke ranks with Mara Salvatrucha and vanished. They say — well, they say a lot of things. Have you heard any of them?"

"No, sir."

"People need heroes and enemies. So they make them. Look at Allison Murrieta."

Wyte went to one of the three black file cabinets along one wall. Hood saw that he moved slowly and unevenly. He pulled open the top drawer of the left-hand cabinet, reached in and removed two thick files.

He set the files on his desk and sat. "Here's the last known photograph of your man."

Hood looked at the picture. Lupercio Maygar was thirty-eight years old at the time of the picture, about to be discharged from San Quentin State Prison in September of 1998. Lupercio looked like many of the Salvadoran gangsters: compact, fearless, ageless. Even at thirty-eight he looked like he could have been eighteen, or forty-eight, or anything in between. Hood set Jordan's drawings on either side of the photograph. The flat-top was new. But if you put that haircut on the ten-year-old photo of Lupercio Maygar, you had the same guy.

"When he got out, his own people turned on him," said Wyte. "When they couldn't catch up with him, they killed his wife and his family, sent their heads to him UPS. He vanished, then MS gangsters started dying even faster than usual — seventeen of them in 1999 alone. These weren't youngsters. They were high-ranking OGs, captains and pistoleros. Lupercio looked good for twelve of them, possibly more, but we never got to warrant because everyone was afraid to talk. They're still open, all twelve of those murders."

"Twelve," said Hood. He studied the

photograph some more. He'd lost faith in numbers in Anbar — the numbers of people killed by soldiers, IEDs and suicide bombers. The numbers of Shiites murdered by Sunnis, and vice versa. There was never agreement. There were U.S. Command numbers, Coalition numbers, UN numbers, Iraqi army and police numbers, American media numbers, BBC numbers, Al Jazeera numbers and of course the numbers muttered in the mosques and marketplaces and alleyways.

"Mostly with a machete," said Wyte. "That's the village method from Salvador — because a machete is personal and quiet and makes a dramatic statement. There was a truce in late 2000 between Lupercio and Mara Salvatrucha. There was some fond hope he'd gone to Salvador for good. Maybe run into a death squad and tasted a little of his own medicine."

"Do we have anything working on him at all?"

"Just this ancient history. After prison came the murders and the truce, then — he disappeared. Next thing we know, he's down in Valley Center murdering Native Americans."

"It's tied to Miracle Auto Body," said Hood. "But I don't know how. Lupercio was both places — the body shop, then Valley Center."

"Lupercio at Miracle? Can you put him there for sure?"

"Close to for sure. We've got a good witness."

"The woman from Valley Center," said Wyte. "This kid's mother."

Lupercio in two bad places, thought Hood. And Suzanne in two bad places, too.

Wyte leaned back and frowned. "Why would she be at an auto body shop a hundred miles from home?"

"She was driving by. Heading home after seeing a relative who lives up there. She saw Lupercio pulled over, in his black Lincoln, talking on a cell phone."

"The Lincoln," said Wyte. "I remember it well — always polished and perfect. He drove something else for a few years because he knew we were onto the Lincoln. Now it's apparently back in action."

Hood told Wyte about pulling her over for speeding and hearing her description of Lupercio. He silently cursed himself for failing to get the name and number of Suzanne's alleged relative that night, then failing to get them again the very next day. Wyte listened, tapping his keyboard. Hood noticed that Wyte's computer wasn't a department-issue plastic one like everybody else's but a brushed aluminum laptop that looked like it could withstand an IED. He remembered hearing that Wyte built his own computers, had built one for the sheriff himself.

"Then Lupercio must have seen the woman, just like she saw him," said Wyte. He shook his head slowly, as if only grand stupidity on Suzanne Jones's part could have allowed this. "And he's after her because she's a witness, or he thinks she is. Where is she now?"

"Her boyfriend isn't telling."

"Forty-eight hours in a holding cell would help."

"I don't think he knows."

"Where's the boyfriend?"

"Oceanside."

Hood wondered again if Suzanne had seen Lupercio doing more than just sitting in his car in the vicinity of Miracle Auto Body. For instance, seen him making off with four hundred and fifty thousand dollars' worth of diamonds that several people knew were about to change hands. That was another pretty good motive for Lupercio to track her down, he thought. But if she'd seen something suspicious that night, why didn't she tell him? Because she didn't know what she was looking at? Maybe. Or maybe she knew something about the deal. Or maybe she, too, had been after the diamonds. Hood hadn't even considered these possibilities until he'd seen Patmore's video of Allison robbing the Taco Bell in Van Nuys. If Suzanne Jones was Allison Murrieta, things got possible. Strange things. And if she wasn't Allison, well, then she was just a schoolteacher on her way home from seeing a relative.

"How did Lupercio find her so fast?" Hood asked.

"Maybe he followed her home."

"No. She lives out in the country. Just a narrow dirt road the last mile to the house. She would have seen him. And he didn't show up until the next afternoon, dressed as a fisherman and casing her property. If he'd followed her all the way to her house without being seen that night, they'd have found her body instead of the brothers."

"I give up."

"I don't."

"You shouldn't. I was young once, too. And hungry."

Hood didn't like that things were fraying: Lupercio seemed to know things he shouldn't know. Suzanne Jones didn't look super clean anymore, but she did look like Allison Murrieta. And Allison Murrieta was just brazen enough to think she could lift diamonds from gangsters and live to tell about it, as if the underworld was just another fast-food joint and all she needed to conquer it was an attitude and a gun.

Hood thought of the way Suzanne Jones allowed him to see her in a nightshirt, and what she'd said about liking him and protecting him, and of the way she'd touched her face to his cheek and drawn breath. She had rattled and skinned him.

He began to feel the same clench in his stomach that he had lived with day and night on each of his Iraq tours. He could almost taste the antacid he'd swilled for those months — slippery and separated, crusted on the bottle neck and hot to his throat.

"Where do I find Lupercio?" he asked.

Wyte nodded toward his office window. "After the murders we looked under every rock in L.A. We never laid eyes on him. I suspect he found a woman to take him in and hide him. I suspect he's no longer living in this city."

"He finds Suzanne Jones easy enough," said Hood. "Maybe we can use that."

"Can you get her to cooperate?"

"I'm not sure I can get her at all."

Hood silently reviewed his clues: a cell phone number she might or might not answer, an empty home, a boyfriend unable or unwilling to give up her whereabouts, a job she wouldn't need to report to for another few weeks, three callers who had left her messages on the home phone after she'd taken off with her family early that morning.

"She'll have to be damned well behaved if we're going to try that," said Wyte.

Hood tried to think it through. He stared across the desk at Wyte and saw some locomotion behind his blue eyes. Wyte was large and well built but somehow unstable at the same time. The helicopter crash had killed the pilot. Wyte's expression now went optimistic and eager, and Hood wondered if Wyte missed the action.

"Listen," said Wyte. "You might have some luck with this. Bait and wait — we did it in gangs all the time. You keep it small. You stay patient. It could work, Hood. Dangle Jones, then wait and watch."

"Like a goat on a stake," said Hood.

"But you'd have spotters, listeners, SWAT if you can get them, and someone close to her. You, Hood — you can hold her hand, calm her down."

Hood didn't imagine that.

"I can help," said Wyte. "I'll show you what I know."

Hood nodded.

"But you'll have to find her first," said Wyte. "Keep her alive until we can set up. It can take a little time."

"I'll find her."

"Let me know when you do. When she's onboard I'll talk to Marlon."

"Yes, sir."

Wyte sat back. "Hood, if Lupercio saw her at or near Miracle, he'll kill her. You should be very aware of that. He's never let people interfere with him. It's why he's alive and a dozen men he used to work with aren't."

Hood went out to the lunch truck and got an orange soda and stood in the shade of the headquarters building. His undershirt was stuck to his back and he felt a trickle of sweat behind each ear.

He called the number Ernest had given him and Suzanne Jones answered on the first ring.

"It's Deputy Hood."

"Who is that son of a bitch?"

"Lupercio Maygar. Former Mara Salvatrucha. You're in danger."

Suzanne Jones said nothing for a moment.

"Where are you?" asked Hood.

"Laguna."

"A public place?"

"A hotel room."

"Can you get to that lifeguard station by the boardwalk without having to drive your car?"

"I can walk to it."

"Meet me there at three. Stay with the beach crowds."

"This place is one big crowd."

15

Hood spotted her sitting on a bench near the lifeguard station. She wore a Raiders cap and big reflective sunglasses, and had a pink mesh tote at her feet.

He was sweltering inside his Target sport coat but it hid his gun. His chinos were a thick winter-weight cotton and his work boots were suede, steel-toed and heavy.

"You look comfortable," she said with pleasant sarcasm.

"It's the best I do on an average day," he said.

They headed north up the boardwalk. The air here in Laguna was cooler than L.A. by twenty degrees and he liked the smell of saltwater and sunscreen. The gulls keened and the boom boxes throbbed away down on the beach. The ocean quivered silver and green, and the children screamed and splashed in the small, firm waves.

"He wants what you have, Ms. Jones." He

watched for her reaction to his suggestive words but saw none.

"He wants me dead. Because I saw him."

"Maybe he's after something more than your life."

"What's worth more than my life if I'm dead?"

"Did you see him again that night? Apart from the three times you told me about?"

She looked at him briefly. "No, I did not."

"Did you see him take anything from Miracle Auto Body?"

"Take? I was never in that place, Hood."

"Because if you were and if you saw something you're not telling me —"

Suzanne Jones stopped walking and took his arm, turning him to face her. The river of tourists parted around them, and Hood heard Japanese and French and Tagalog trailing past him.

"I've never even *seen* this body shop," she said. "And I don't take things that don't belong to me. I'm a schoolteacher who saw a man. I didn't even know about your crime scene until you came to my home on Sunday. Now my neighbors are being murdered and my son is finding butchered *bodies* in my barn."

A kid with a skimboard stared at her big-eyed as he walked past.

"Let's find a better place to talk," said Hood. "Maybe along the water."

They stepped off the boardwalk and trudged across the sand toward the ocean. Hood watched the sand flies scatter as he crunched through a patch of seaweed drying in the sun.

"Give me the name and number of the relative you were visiting when I pulled you over Saturday night. Don't say it's none of my business."

He punched in the number as they walked. Mary Jones picked up on the third ring and confirmed that her sister-in-law Suzanne had visited her last Saturday night, left around one-thirty in the morning and had not been drinking. Hood thanked her.

"Alibi confirmed?"

"Did you coach her?"

She shook her head and said nothing.

"You're telling me the truth, right, Ms. Jones?"

"You're the most distrustful man I've ever met."

He thought of Anbar and the price of trust. "It's part of the job, Ms. Jones."

"I've told you nothing but the truth, Charles Robert."

"How much of it?"

"Everything. Christ, you're difficult."

Hood stared down at her as she said this, and he weighed her words and the tone of her words against everything he knew, and he believed them. Unrelated to the fact that she rattled and skinned him, he believed them.

"Tell Ernest to keep moving," he said. "One place — one night. No ground-floor rooms. Use public places. The more people around the better."

"Okay."

"The same goes for you."

"Yes."

"I can offer you protective custody."

"You'd have to kill me first."

"What I figured. When you left your Valley Center home, did you take your personal phone and address book?"

"I left it in the computer room."

"It's gone."

They looked at each other, mid-step. Near the shoreline they continued north. The sand was hard-packed here, and Hood watched the white water chase a sandpiper up the berm. Ahead the tide pools shimmered in the sun and a tall outcropping of black rock stood out against the sky.

"Lupercio must think you have the diamonds."

"I have no diamonds."

"Why are you running?"

"To protect my family. When Jordan drew the picture, I knew that man was after me. Because of the night before. He wasn't after Harold and Gerald."

"He was looking for something in your barn."

"Believe me, I know what's in my barn. I'm sorry my word isn't good enough for you, Charlie."

"Help us set him up," said Hood.

She looked up at him. He couldn't see behind the reflective glasses but her mouth was set firm.

"Be the bait?" she asked.

"Yes. Listen."

Hood stopped but Jones kept walking, swinging the tote in a carefree arc, then looking back at him. She turned and climbed the rocks then crossed a spit of sand and ducked into an archway and disappeared.

Hood trotted after her, scrambling up the rocks and across the sand then ducking through the same arch and finding himself in a small enclosure with rock walls and a wet sand floor.

The white water flooded in and soaked them to their ankles.

"What would I have to do?" she asked.

"We'll want you up our way, for jurisdictional reasons. We'll pick the place, but you'll register yourself and pay the charges, just like you did here. We'll set up outside, in the lobby, in the room next door. We'll use cameras, mikes, whatever we need. We'd be fluid and lean. The moment he shows, we swarm him."

"Who picks up the room charges?"

"We're trying to save your life for cryin' out loud, but we'll pay for the room, too."

"Good. How's he going to find me?"

"I don't know, but I think he will. He's got help — a network, old gangster friends, maybe a DMV connection. If he found you in Valley Center, we figure he'll find you again in L.A."

She studied him from behind the glasses then sloshed forward through the receding suds and took his face in her hands and kissed him. Hood stared point-blank at her forehead and the light brown hair curling out from under the cap, and he felt the bill of it touching his own head up near the hairline. He heard the rush of the water up the sand and against his ankles. Hood had never been kissed with such generosity.

"I need your help checking out of the hotel, Hood. Due to heightened security."

"I understand."

In room 302 he took off his coat and hung it on a chair and sat. She showered and came out in a black slip and stood in front of him, and Hood lost most of what reason he had left. He carried her to the bed. It was like two tornadoes competing for the same trailer park. When they were done he lay on his back with his head over the edge of the bed breathing hard and looking out the curtained window to the upside-down Pacific. He wondered at the path that had led him here but he couldn't see any path at all. Then he was up and herding her back into the bed and truly believing that at this moment he ruled the known world.

"Oh, Hood. *Charles Robert.* Let's hear it for Bakersfield."

16

Lupercio stood on his back patio and watched the tumbleweeds shiver against the chain-link fence. Beyond the fence a dirt devil augured across the desert floor then spun itself out. The sun hung red and wavering and his outdoor thermometer read 104 degrees. It was good to be home.

Adelanto lay around him, a struggling city in the desert north of L.A. It was poor and dirty but had just enough Latin Americans to make Lupercio more or less invisible. There was hardly a window in the city that wasn't protected by iron, and although some of it was decoratively wrought, the rest was the straight vertical bars of jail cells around the world. Up until a few years ago the police were running a casino and a brothel, the streets flowed with drugs, and the civic leaders were pocketing public money as fast as they could grab it. In this it was like the El Salvador of Lupercio's youth.

But Lupercio knew the true difference between the *norte* and the *centro,* because nowhere in Adelanto or anywhere else in the Estado Unidos did freshly murdered bodies appear each morning as they did at Puerta del Diablo — unexplained and uninvestigated. Piles of them, thrown from the verdant heights above — decapitated, dismembered, hacked, beaten, burned. News would spread through the village each morning, how many new bodies were found "on top." When his brother disappeared, Lupercio had climbed over the piled bodies at the Devil's Door many mornings, turning over the fresh ones on top in search of him. When his father disappeared, Lupercio had done it again.

And he had found them.

Thousands of times Lupercio had driven by the sign welcoming drivers on Highway 395. It said: "Welcome to Adelanto: City of Unlimited Possibilities."

He understood what the sign meant but he saw another side to the words. When you came from San Salvador and your youth was death squads and the disappeared and mysterious piles of bodies at Puerta del Diablo, or El Playón, or bodies in the jungle or on the roadside or in the *barrancas* — you didn't want to live in a city of unlimited possibilities.

Lupercio turned and went inside to the small living room. An air conditioner labored from one window and a large oscillating fan sent intermittent gales throughout the room. The TV was turned down low to an L.A. news broadcast. He'd learned English from American TV and newspapers and he liked the news.

The twins — Lucia and Serena — sat side by side on the sofa, identical faces with identical expressions locked onto the television screen. They were strong girls and pretty, and Lupercio had long seen a forcefulness in them that made him respect them. He had used them for increasingly important, work-related errands and found them capable. They understood that his work was serious. They never asked questions and they never complained. They were seventeen years old now and they both had B averages at the high school. Lucia played soccer and Serena was in the theater club.

Lupercio had taken up with their mother, Consuelo Encarnación, while being on the run from his onetime partners in MS-13. Ten years ago. Practically a stranger to him, she had cursed two assassins out of her kitchen one night while Lupercio hid in a cabinet with the pots and pans, and in a corner of Lupercio's heart this had made him hers forever.

He came back to that kitchen in Los Angeles one year later — one year after the murder of his wife and family — and asked Consuelo to marry him. She had lost her husband to gastrointestinal infection in San Salvador. Nearly destitute, she had brought her young children through Mexico then up the Devil's Highway into Arizona, where two of the older men in their group had died of sun and madness and where her shoes had decomposed in the heat and her feet had been lanced with cholla spines that ten years later still occasionally emerged from her flesh during the cool baths she loved to take in her Adelanto bathroom. Connie had become plump with American prosperity but had not lost the beauty of her face. She cleaned motel rooms and understood that when their little family needed money, her small, quiet husband would deliver it. He had given her everything but his name, because that would be a great risk for her. She trusted him in everything and asked him nothing.

"Serena, I need to have my hair cut," he said. They spoke only English in the household because Lupercio thought that good English would give them all an advantage in this gringo world. Lupercio had made sure that his wife and daughters became legal residents, a blessing made possible by Hurricane Mitch, which ravaged El Salvador in 1998 and temporarily changed U.S. immigration policy. Later, they became citizens. Lupercio had remained a fugitive felon.

Serena got the electric clippers, comb and a bath towel, and Lucia brought a dinette chair into the living room.

Lupercio sat and Serena wrapped the towel around his neck. "It looks good, Dad. High and flat like you like it."

"I want it very short now. So my head is almost round. Nothing flat. The world is not flat after all, Serena."

The girl laughed and the clippers buzzed on. "Your mustache is sure coming in fast."

"Fast, yes."

When his haircut was done, Lupercio looked into the mirror that Serena held before him.

"Round as a football," he said.

"You look more gentle," she said. She laughed again and unwrapped the towel from his neck.

When Serena came back from putting away the cutting tools, Lupercio sat between them, a small man between strong, pretty girls. On the coffee table in front of him he moved aside a vase of the cut flowers Consuelo bought at outrageous prices from a curio shop along Highway 395. Then he put up his boots on the table and watched the news while enjoying the safe warmth of the girls on either side.

He could smell the *bistec* cooking in the kitchen.

Late that night Lupercio was still in front of the TV but his wife and stepdaughters had gone off to bed. He watched the late night host interview his guests, then a segment called stupid pet tricks. When a housecat had jumped onto his master's shoulder then stood on its hind legs and eaten a portion of anchovy stuck behind his master's ear, Lupercio muted the television and wandered the house.

It was a familiar routine. First he went to the garage and sharpened his machete using a bench vise and a series of increasingly fine files. The metal was soft enough to take an edge beautifully. It took time to get all eighteen inches of blade but when Lupercio was finished the edge gleamed in the overhead fluorescents. He broke down and inspected the springs and levers inside the big handle to make sure they were working correctly.

He hung the reassembled weapon on the pegboard wall along with the other yard tools.

Then he went into a spare room, where he lifted a section of the carpet in one corner and spun the combination lock open. First he brought out the revolver and set it aside. Then Lupercio braced himself on his knees, bent over and with two hands hefted the tangled mass from the safe below the floor. There were thirty watches — Rolex and Patek Philippe and Baume & Mercier and others — all studded with jewels and made of solid gold or platinum. There were fifty-two gold wedding rings, most engraved, some with diamonds, too. There were twenty-two engagement rings with diamonds ranging from slivers to one that weighed 1.55 carats and was worth close to thirteen thousand dollars if sold in a store. If sold to a black market buyer, it was worth maybe thirteen hundred. There were ruby earrings, sapphire necklaces, diamond bracelets, strings of pearls, even an envelope containing eight gold-filled molars that had been offered to him as payment by a desperate Salvadoran refugee.

Lupercio set this mass of treasure on the brown-and-cream swirled shag carpet. Although he knew exactly what was here, he separated the tangle and itemized it all again in the half light of the spare room. He loved the bold brightness of the diamonds and the rich blue glow of the sapphires and the happy red rubies. The pearls were his favorite because they were unrefined and simple. He thought the elaborate watches were funny. They had stopped running because they were either self-winding or battery operated. The stopped watches were worth over four hundred thousand dollars to a retailer, and about fifty thousand to a thief. The entire pile was worth just over seven hundred thousand dollars on the legal market and about one hundred thousand to Lupercio.

But he had no interest in selling any of it. It was for his wife and daughters when he died, though they had never seen so much as a glimmer of it. They knew about the safes, of course, but such was their respect for him that they had never touched them, just as he had ordered. The treasure would be theirs when the time was right. Consuelo would see to it.

He ran his fingers over the pieces then swept them gently together into a pile and pushed them back into the hole. He ran his fingers through the shag again to make sure he hadn't left behind an earring backing or even a truant jewel, but there was nothing. He popped open the cylinder of the .38 and checked the loads, then set the gun on top of his booty. He locked the safe, set the carpet back in place and rose upright on his short, strong legs.

In the closet he knelt again and spun open the big safe. The smell hit him as it always did — slightly damp, slightly chemical, slightly sweet. The safe was almost full of United States hundred-dollar bills in stacks of one hundred each. The bills were nonsequential and not new. There were 156 bundles in here, totaling 1.56 million dollars. In the small space that had no cash lay a nine-millimeter Taurus. He didn't touch a thing. He just nodded, closed the door and spun the dial. He had no interest in spending this money, either. More for his family.

Later, in the driveway, he washed and waxed the black '79 Lincoln Continental he'd owned for twenty years. He used two new sponges to spread the automotive cleanser across the body, working in slow circular motions, feeling the contours of the body panels registering in his hands and arms. Then the chamois to dry, then the wheels and tires, the insides of the doors and trunk lid and the frame, the windows and the interior.

When he was finished waxing it he walked around it with a critical eye, brushing with his finger the small imperfections that an older car will develop.

Lupercio remembered that evening in December of 1979 when he was nineteen years old and finishing up his shift on the construction site of a new American hotel on the Salvadoran coast. He was stowing tools in the boss's truck when a car came up the winding road toward them. It was new, black and shiny. He recognized it as a Lincoln Continental Town Car. The shimmering ocean reflected on the flank of the car, and the blaze of the setting sun crept along the hood. It stopped and out stepped a man in a tan suit and a woman wearing a white dress. They were *norteamericanos.* The man was heavy and poorly shaped and the woman was tiny and nervous. It had been six months since Lupercio had found his brother dead in the pile of bodies at Puerta del Diablo, and two weeks since he'd found his father in almost exactly the same place. And the hope that had fled from him now suddenly rushed back as he looked at that car. Not at the people, not at the ocean, not at the sunset — but the car.

At first he didn't understand why. How could hope come from an automobile? But he couldn't take his eyes off it. It was large and he sensed that it was very heavy. The sides were great black slabs of steel and the fenders were blade-like chrome. There were triple vertical vents behind the front wheel wells that looked to him like shark gills, and the chrome trim twinkled.

Then Lupercio realized that this car was not only beautiful and useful, but unkillable. He would never find it chopped into parts and dumped into a mountain of other parts. It would never bleed.

He walked over and humbly acknowledged the man and woman, then placed his hands behind his back in a gesture of subordination and walked around the car. Twice. He drank in the overall posture of this machine, its firm stance and its powerful body lines and the fit of the quarterpanels and brilliance of the black paint even in the falling light. He saw the little things, too — the simple elegance of the spoked wheels, the depth of the wells, and again, the splendid chrome. His heart fluttered when he saw the indentation down by the edge of the driver's side door, a deep rounded pit that he first mistook for a bullet hole. But he saw that the body steel hadn't been penetrated.

The paint had not broken away. A rock, he thought, thrown by a peon or maybe just dislodged by a bus.

Eleven years later he found the car for sale on a lot in Azusa for fourteen hundred dollars. It had one hundred and ninety thousand miles on it. The orange painting on the windshield read: "EXTRA CLEAN." Lupercio had placed his finger in the pit in the door, which looked exactly as he remembered it. He tried to reason how this car had gone from Salvador to the United States. He couldn't. Just like the car's effect on him all those years ago, its appearance here went beyond reason. It was a miracle.

Late that night he came back and stole it. The first thing he did was have the dent fixed. There was no way to tell that the door had ever been anything but perfect.

Two years later when he was becoming more prosperous Lupercio had actually purchased another such Lincoln — same year and model. It was a dark forest green. He had hoped to double his pride and his luck. But the second car carried no history and no magic at all, though it ran well and looked good. He gave it to Consuelo.

Lupercio had just pulled the Lincoln back

into the garage when his cell phone rang. He saw from the call number that it was the call he'd been waiting for. El Toro.

The Bull.

17

I finally get Hood to leave Laguna ahead of me. My legs buzz as I hustle him out the door, and by his expression I can see that I've shaved fifty points off his IQ. Don't worry — it's temporary.

I confirmed something about Hood today that I suspected: he has a secret. I don't know what it is. But I know from the way his heart beat against my ribs after the second time — or maybe it was the third, what a blur — that he's got a secret. It's big and unhappy and it hurts him to carry it. I love men with secrets. I'm going to figure his out.

Hood is also adorable but I can't let him see my truck because he'll wonder how a yellow Z06 Corvette turned into a black F-150 pickup truck pretty much overnight.

So, far back in the long-term parking lot for John Wayne Airport, I find a shiny, almost new Mustang GT for my drive up to

L.A. I park beside it, glove up, remove my cold plates from the pickup truck and slide them into my satchel. I strip off the 'Stang plates, and put them in the pickup bed, then fill out one of my photocopied dealer registration slips. I shim my way into the Mustang — no alarm, nice, and I'm figuring no LoJack either, because Mustang buyers are often bargain hunters and LoJack is expensive. Even if the car has LoJack, it won't start transmitting until the Mustang is reported stolen. And based on the long-term parking and the car's lack of dust, I'm willing to gamble that I'm good for a few hours. Which gives me plenty of time to get this thing to a LoJack-proof metal building with no windows. I know exactly where to find one.

I tape the registration to the inside of the windshield. There: pretty woman, new car, no plates yet from DMV. The Mustang has black leather, a five-speed manual, three hundred mighty horses under the hood, premium sound. It'll do 143 miles per hour. The leather smells like heaven, and when I match the ignition leads to the screwdriver, the engine growls to life with a vibration that goes straight through my feet and up my legs to where Hood just was. Mmm. The horses idle as I load in my bags and the backpack, then touch the flank of the black pickup with the back of my hand and say thanks.

Halfway to L.A. Hood calls and tells me to check into the Residence Inn in Torrance. It's not where they're going to set up for Lupercio — that will happen tomorrow — it's just a safe place for tonight. Twenty minutes later I let myself into the room, eat the pillow mint, put out the "Do Not Disturb" sign, then drive the Mustang across town and check into the airport Marriott. The place is so busy nobody will notice me. I can self-park. I don't have to worry about Hood showing up, wagging his tail. I put the diamonds in the room safe. I'm ready in thirty minutes.

I've got work to do.

When I was a girl, my first job was for Kentucky Fried Chicken in Bakersfield. I told them I was sixteen and looked it, but I was barely fourteen. Back then girls were front store — filling orders and taking money — and boys worked back store doing the prep and cooking. I fell seriously in love for the third time in my life then, with a cook named Don. He was an older man, actually — nineteen — and he had a great smile and a nice touch with the chicken and coleslaw. When it was slow, I'd hang out in the back with him and the guys, watch them slide across the slippery floor from the stoves to the cooling racks with the huge pots filled with boiling grease and chicken parts. You wouldn't believe how slippery a floor can get when it's layered with grease and flour and eleven secret herbs and spices. One big slip backward and a pot would end up dumping on someone's face, but Don and his buds just careened around the kitchen like ice skaters, hefting the pots onto and off of the burners right on time, slamming and locking down the lids. Then when the chicken was cooked, they'd reach over the pot and release the pressure valves, which would explode in a deafening hiss as the steam shot all the way to the ceiling, and of course there was the story of the valve that broke off and went through the cook's head, killing him right on the spot, and Don said it was true, but you know, he might have just been trying to impress me.

Ruby was the manager, and she was usually in a good mood even though her sons were in Tehachapi Prison and her husband had a bad heart. She'd go out and get us Taco Bell for our dinner because we all ate so much KFC we got tired of it, though I still think their original recipe chicken and coleslaw are particularly good. Anyway, Ruby rocked, and knew I was fourteen, but then corporate KFC sent us Victor and Ruby trained him and we tolerated his little yellow smile. He set his hand on my fanny once and I let it go, then he did it again a few days later and I turned and slapped him once hard, but none of it mattered because corporate fired Ruby like we knew they would and Victor became the new manager. When they announced it, the whole crew quit and took Ruby out for steaks and too many drinks at the TGIF, and it really was a Friday and we really were thanking God we didn't have to work for that prick Victor.

So I rob KFCs pretty much every chance I get.

This one is down in Long Beach. I've cased it three different times. I like the parking lot out back and the fact that the entrance is on the side, not facing the main street. No drive-through, which means at least one less set of eyes on you, and no pain-in-the-ass Joe Heroes already saddled up for a chase. I like the quick access to the boulevard and an on-ramp for the 405 a quarter mile east. Two signals, no U-turns necessary. The nearest police substation is two miles away. Fast-food outlets aren't wired into the cop houses like banks are, and the FBI sure doesn't come after you, so if you time it right you're good for eight hundred, maybe a thousand, maybe two thousand bucks. I can use two thousand bucks but I'm doing KFC a favor, too — I truly hope the shortfall will cause corporate to be just a little more careful about who they accept into the management program instead of blowing money on guys like Victor.

It's dusk now. Most of the dinner business has been done because this is a working-class neighborhood and these people eat on time and get to bed early. They're more likely to pay cash than to use a card. In the parking lot I check my wig and put on my gloves, then slide Cañonita into one side pocket of my black leather vest and my crystal studded mask into the other. I breathe deeply, check my look in the mirror one more time. I can feel Allison Murrieta being born inside me. I can understand her thoughts and hear her voice and I ignore the last little whispers from departing Suzanne. I'll come back to her. I see Allison now. I see as Allison now.

I move as Allison, head up and eyes level as I count my steps from the car to the door. A family comes through it and I turn away from them and put Cañonita to my ear and start blabbing loud like anyone else on a cell phone. When the family passes I get a look inside: a girl and a middle-aged woman working the front, a young Paki and his girlfriend ordering and behind them a couple of brawny dudes who look like long-shoremen off shift from the Port of Long Beach.

I put on my mask, throw open the door and aim my gun straight into the face of the biggest longshoreman.

"Hi, cutie," I say.

"Oh, shit."

"Come on, smile for me."

He does, so I swivel Cañonita to his smaller buddy.

"You too, Hot Rod. Give me a smile."

His buddy just stares at me.

"Behave yourself," I say to him.

The Paki man is already backing away with his hands up and his girl is hiding be-hind him, so I step right to the front of the line.

I point Cañonita at the young clerk, then at the woman, then at the security camera behind them up by the ceiling, then safely down at the ground.

"No bullshit, ladies. I'm in kind of a hurry."

The woman has that indignant look that only a good and honest person can get. She's disgusted that I would take what belongs to someone else. She's offended. From the right-side periphery of my vision I can see Hot Rod hitching up his shirttail. It's exactly what an off-duty cop would do to pull his sidearm — an off-duty cop being my worst nightmare except for *two* off-duty cops — and all I can do is draw down on him.

"What are you going for, Hot Rod?"

His hands freeze and he looks at me. "Phone. Picture?"

My heart is beating so hard in my ears I can barely hear what he says. And I can barely hear what I say next:

"Just don't mess with my stickup."

"No. Not me."

By then the middle-aged manager and the young girl are chattering away in Spanish and the Pakis are wide-eyed and silent, but the register is open and the girl is downloading the cash into a white KFC bag with the Colonel's face on it. The woman won't look at me and she's muttering mainly to herself, but the girl loads the bag in a quick, helpful manner. I tell her not to forget the rolls of quarters. I see over eight hundred dollars go into that sack. I set one of my cards on the counter.

Less than a minute and I turn to go. Hot Rod has his cell phone camera aimed at me and I brandish the weapon and the bag of money. Cutie steps in front of me then kneels facing the camera. I can't resist this kind of publicity. So I set a friendly hand on his shoulder — the money hand, not the gun hand — while Hot Rod clicks another two pictures.

I flick a card to each of them.

YOU HAVE BEEN ROBBED BY
ALLISON MURRIETA
HAVE A NICE DAY

"For the next ten minutes the first person through that door gets shot," I say.

By then I'm heading back to the airport Marriott, the northbound traffic light and the Mustang burning through the fuel which is a feeling I love. But I'm strictly speed limit now. Suzie Jones, citizen, teacher of history. My feet have gone cold and my hands are shaking because all the concentration and calm I force upon myself during a holdup dissolve when I've gotten away, body and mind suddenly able to admit what a scary dumbass business this is, pointing guns at people you don't want to shoot while you take someone else's money. Pulling a job is the best — well, *second* best feeling in the world. But the comedown — these jittery minutes when your heart pounds in your eardrums and you can hardly draw a full breath — man, that I can live without. So I do the speed limit and watch the rear-view and turn on the news and think about Joaquin because Joaquin makes me calm and proud.

Lots of legends sprouted up around him. One was that he became an outlaw because a group of Anglos raped his wife and made him watch. Another was that he became an outlaw because his brother was hung for stealing a horse he didn't steal at all. Another was that Joaquin became an outlaw because he was whipped. I have his leather-bound journal so I know what's true and what isn't. The journal itself is only eighty-one pages long because he died when he was twenty-three. The pages are small, yellow and brittle. The handwriting is neat but fading. The journal won't last forever, just as Joaquin's head will not. They rest next to each other in a secret room in my barn in Valley Center.

Interestingly, all three of those legends are true, and they all took place on the same day outside of Coloma, California, in 1849. Gold had been found at Sutter's Mill. In the Sierra foothills you could pick it right off the ground, pan it right out of the rivers and streams. Talk about a rush.

Joaquin had a claim and a camp with his wife, Rosa, and his brother, Jesús. Joaquin was nineteen years old. My great-great-great-great-great-great-grandmother was a beautiful woman — a girl, really, just seventeen — and like Joaquin she was educated at a Jesuit school down in Alamos, Mexico. She was three months pregnant on that day outside Coloma.

They were panning the creek, doing well. Their claim was legitimate, too, because the foreign miner's tax — which pretty much made it legal to shoot non-Anglos mining for gold — wasn't enacted until 1850.

It was July and I know it was hot because I spent a July up near Coloma camping with Bradley a few years ago, just to pay my respects to Joaquin, and to get the feel of the place where his life was shaped. I told Bradley a little about Joaquin, but not too much. The sky was a beautiful turquoise blue and most afternoons we saw wispy cirrus clouds blowing toward the mountains.

This is how it went down: six young Anglos rode into Joaquin's camp with their guns drawn, yelling that Jesús's horse belonged to them. They were drunk. Joaquin writes in simple, clear Spanish about being held at rifle point and tied to a tree, then watching Jesús "struggle and strangle" (my translation) at the end of a rope slung over an oak branch and pulled taut by all six of the men. They lowered his boot toes to the ground then yanked him up, lowered him to the ground again then yanked him up again. They laughed. Finally they hoisted him up and watched him die. Joaquin wrote about the horsewhip that "drove fire" into his back — six powerful lashes that would bleed and fester for weeks — and how the men "obliterated" the camp and found their tiny bags of gold flakes taken from the stream. And he wrote finally of the sounds of Rosa's screams against the bandana she was gagged with, the grunting of the men, and the bucking and whinnying of his tethered horse, Jorge, "as if he could understand."

I've stood on that ground. I've slept there. It's a quiet place, mostly pine trees. But the oak tree where they hung Jesús is easy to find — it's the only oak tree by that stretch of the stream — and it's got plenty of good stout horizontal branches. You don't hear much but jays during the day and crickets at night. You might see a squirrel or a lizard, maybe a deer flitting between the trees. It's like nothing ever happened. Nature forgets history just like we do — something I often tell my students. Bradley and I panned the stream and got some trace, but that was all.

By the time I get to the Hapkido Federation studio in L.A. my nerves have settled and I feel focused. I'm in time for sparring with Quinn and some other black belts. Quinn was the one who taught me this method way back in Bakersfield before he moved south to the city.

In case you don't know, hapkido is a deeply vicious martial art — you break bones and dislocate joints and gouge eyes and crush windpipes and smash testicles in about the time it takes to unlock a car with a key fob.

Of course for sparring at the black belt level you have to control yourself, and your whole body is padded to the max — head protector, mouthpiece, cups for the guys, even pads for your feet and hands.

You can't believe the adrenaline-driven clarity that settles over you as a six-foot, 190-pound hapkido warrior bows to you, then flows into his fighting position and waits for you to attack. You see every shift in his balance, every tiny feint, every flicker in his eye. You know when his breathing changes. Then all hell breaks loose. A two-minute round never seems to end. And the second you get tired is the second that some-one lands a fist to your solar plexus or a foot to your head.

I go six rounds. At the end of the session I'm bent over and breathing hard and I can hardly hold myself upright to bow to Quinn before I head for the locker room.

18

An hour later I'm standing in Angel's shop up in Phelan. Phelan is in the desert north of L.A., not far from Interstate 15. Angel is the man who taught me how to steal cars and what to do with them once they're mine.

Here in Phelan they've got black sky and nice stars but not much else. The shop is made of metal and has no windows, which defeats the popular LoJack device. I can hear the wind knocking against the panels. Angel is doing a walk-around on the Mustang, nodding, clicking and sending pictures and text messages with his phone. Demand is high. Angel is always selling. He might have sold the thing already for all I know.

"Thirteen," he says.

"Fifteen."

"Thirteen seven fifty, and no higher, Suzie."

"Fourteen."

"Fine, fine, fine."

"Where will you send her?" I ask.

"Mexico. I have a buyer waiting. Someone who prefers American. You've always had good instincts for the right car."

A loaded Mustang GT is a thirty-two-thousand-dollar car new — drops to twenty-five if you sell it low-mileage to a private party. Angel will take it from here: pay me, replace the VIN with a clean one, forge counterfeit title and registration, remove LoJack or any other antitheft devices and transport it by truck to a Tijuana leather shop for custom upgrades, where it will change trucks and be taken south to Mexico City, maybe Sinaloa, maybe Puerto Vallarta or Cartagena or Bogotá. Angel will be paid in dollars. Since the airlines got tough after 9/11, roughly one million American drug dollars a day journey by car through Tijuana to points south. *A day.*

So the *narcotraficantes* have plenty of cash on hand. For the Mustang Angel will get about twenty-two grand. The cartel guys who buy them aren't getting a steal, but they're getting something they can't buy legally in the United States. One reason that Angel's stolen cars are so popular in Mexico is that suspected drug heavies are banned from spending money here in the States, a law originally passed to keep them from financing "dream teams" of lawyers for their defense in U.S. courts. What *narcotraficantes* get now is a court-appointed defender. But they can always get a VIN-switched Beemer, Benz, Porsche, Jag, Ford, Chevy or Chrysler from Angel. In most corners of the world, money talks.

Angel pours us each a shot of reposado tequila, offers it to me on a varnished wooden tray. It's a ritual of ours.

We sip and I stare at the Ford. It's a bitchin' ride — honestly aggressive, capable, fun just to look at.

"Angel, I might want to move some diamonds."

"Oh." He frowns. He studies the car, then me. "There's Jason."

"I won't deal with him."

Angel nods. One of the many things I like about Latin men is that they understand that many things in life are fated and final and beyond discussion.

"They're beautiful, Angel. Gem quality — the best. One is two carats and close to perfect. They're unbelievable. Retail is four hundred and fifty. I'll take forty and there's five in it for you."

"Ten percent is top dollar. But let me see."

I thank Angel but I don't like the look

on his face. He's a strong man with broad shoulders and chest, a lion's gut and a high, back-sloping head blessed with thick silver hair. He dresses beautifully. His face is all crags and he's got a smile like a sunrise. We were us for a while, but we both knew that wouldn't last long. Mostly we were business. Angel charged me five hundred dollars to show me how to steal my first car. Later, when I'd learned the craft, he had a custom slide-hammer made just for me, a little shorter than the usual ones and the handle a little thinner for hands my size. I rarely sell a car to anyone else.

But I see no sunrise in Angel's face right now.

"Does this relate to the diamond broker in the body shop?"

"Directly."

"A terrible thing."

"I wasn't involved. I was lucky."

"I've never had good luck with diamonds," he says. "They seem to have minds of their own. But an automobile, it always goes where you steer it. Speaking of this, come with me."

We walk past some very choice American cars — two loaded Escalades with twenty-inch shoes and big meat, two Suburbans with more of the same, a Mustang GT, a black-on-black GM Yukon and a genuinely beautiful custom cobalt blue Denali XL that actually makes certain parts of me tingle. The paint and chrome gleam in the fluorescent lights and each one seems smug with its own secret behind the heavily tinted glass. Customers love heavily tinted glass.

This is the domestic part of Angel's operation, which is different from the high-end German stuff that Angel processes in a warehouse down in San Ysidro.

See, the German cars are more valuable per unit but they're also a lot harder to steal. If you physically move a Beamer or a Porsche more than a few feet, the systems all lock down — the antilock brakes take hold, the steering fails, the ignition and injectors and electric all go spastic and all you've got is a three-thousand-pound paperweight. The only practical way to steal the German cars is with a key or a tow truck. Both work. But keys are difficult to get — although some people leave the valet keys in their glove boxes, which is the first place a thief looks. And a tow truck usually means a broad-daylight lift, which takes time and a partner.

So, for business I steal American. They've got lousy security systems that are easy to override and there are more of them to choose from. Angel sometimes has a customer interested only in a specific color or option package, and that's almost never a problem because when Detroit does something they do it in a big way. Great selection!

But the best part of stealing American is the huge market in Europe and in the Middle East. Those guys know a deal when they see one. Especially in the Middle East. They hate us, but they love paying oil cartel cash for our SUVs and trucks. The Mexicans have the drug cartels and the Arabs have the oil cartels. I have a friend who did a tour in Iraq and another in Kuwait, and he saw American cars with California plates still on them being driven all over the place. The American cars hold up well over there and they're functional. You try driving a Mercedes SL or a BMW M5 on dirt roads across the Yemeni desert and tell me how far you get. You know how much German *air filters* cost? But get yourself a Ford Explorer, man, and you'll make it on time with a decent sound system, the air conditioner still blowing ice, and you'll get decent mileage, maybe seventeen miles per gallon with the six cylinder. Then you just hose it off and vacuum it out and head to Dubai for a round of golf or some indoor skiing or some gambling at the casinos. Plus, if you show up in an Escalade or a trick Denali XL with the big chrome shoes and the subwoofer pounding like the bass drum in a marching band, it says you kick ass.

So all these American cars will go overseas, and to get them there Angel will load them into containers and truck the containers to the Port of Long Beach. Angel has his system and his people in place. I've seen the operation. The port is one gigantic buzzing hive of cargo containers, cranes, trucks and thousands of workers and drivers and longshoremen and hundreds of *millions* of tons of cargo coming and going every hour. It's a full-blast throbbing city out there, everything timed out to the minute. In the apparent confusion, which is actually not confusion at all, Angel's containers get handled by the right longshoremen and they get on the right vessels inspected by the right people. They're not on the ground for more than a few hours. This is the meat and potatoes of his business because Angel sells twenty American workhorses for every one high-end German stallion.

"I love that blue Denali, Angel."

He smiles with pride. "It's better not to look."

Outside the wind whips and the stars

glimmer. And we come to something that's included in the price for the Mustang. It's something to get me home, in this case a nondescript white Nissan Sentra. Angel has done a strip-and-run on this car. Here's how it works: one of Angel's guys stole it six months ago, stripped it for parts, then ditched what was left of it. The cops recovered the frame, canceled the theft record, and sold it at an auction. Of course the guy who originally stole it is the one who buys it. Back here at Angel's they put the parts back on the "clean" frame and now they have a car no longer listed as stolen. That's low-end, pay-the-rent car theft, but everybody needs a simple clean ride that won't draw attention and won't come up hot on the DMV check.

"Think about those diamonds," I say.

"I am thinking about them already."

"I love you, Angel."

"As I love you, Suzanne."

I kiss him on the cheek, and Angel gives me the keys and sends me home safe and secure in my little Sentra, which has a full tank of gas, gets twenty-six miles per gallon and has a paper grocery bag containing fourteen thousand dollars in hundreds and fifties in the trunk.

The eight hundred in the KFC bag is right

next to it, weighted down with two rolls of quarters.

It's payday, man, and I'm still on summer vacation.

I leave my booty and work tools in the room safe at the Marriott, except for Cañonita, of course, which I put in my satchel. I shower and trade the loose work clothes for tight jeans and a blue silk tank, and the boots for heels, just in case handsome Hood has ditched his night patrol shift and is waiting around to make sure I'm okay.

At twelve-thirty I pull into the crowded Residence Inn self-park, find a space and park.

An old black Lincoln pulls up behind me at an angle, headlights on high beam. The thought races through my mind that I'm about to die.

I slam the Sentra into reverse and floor it. The car jumps backward about a foot before crashing into the Lincoln's formidable front end. While my front tires scream and smoke, I know that the Sentra doesn't have the strength to budge the Lincoln.

There are cars on either side of me and a hedge of oleander in front. In front of the oleander is a concrete tire block and behind it is a chain-link fence. I throw the car into drive and floor it straight ahead over the block. I aim the Sentra between the shrubs and into the fence. I hear the rip of metal on metal, and I see the right headlight burst in a bright shower of safety glass shards, and I feel the awful stretch of the chain-link fence as it slows the Sentra almost to a stop. It's like getting stuck in a spider's web. Then I feel the fence weaken and see it collapse over the front of the Sentra, and suddenly I'm accelerating and the uprooted metal fence posts are shooting sparks as I drag them along each side of my car. Then I'm under the fence and past it and in the rearview I see the fence posts skidding and the chain link bouncing to a stop, and I am thinking, This is a miracle, but the big black Lincoln suddenly barrels through the mess toward me. Willpower is no match for horsepower.

I gun it out of the parking lot and onto Hawthorne Boulevard before I realize I'm running on a blown front tire. At fifty miles an hour the Sentra is shimmying so hard I can barely hold the wheel, then it zigs hard right and all I can do is follow onto the first side street, which leads to another side street, then another, and it's all tract homes and driveways and streetlights and Father in Heaven I never thought Allison Murrieta would die in the suburbs.

I pull up curbside, get Cañonita and sling the satchel over my neck and one shoulder as I walk across a neat front yard. It's dark and still. I throw my CFM heels in a rose bed. Then I jump a side fence and pray there's no Dobermans or rotters or pit bulls waiting.

I'm across the dogless backyard in seconds. I can hear the Lincoln idling on the street near my Sentra. Then I'm over the back fence and across the adjacent backyard to another side fence and fast over that one, too, and dogs are barking now and some of them sound real close but I'm on the sidewalk, one street over from where Lupercio is maybe still parked and scratching his flattop and figuring what to do. Hustling across the front yard, I can see that Lupercio's got a fair way to go to bring that Lincoln around to me. It's a long street, families sleeping, alarm clocks set. And as soon as I hear or see an approaching car, I'll cut back through more yards the same way I got here. Then I'll make it back to the boulevard, where the people are. My heart is pounding painfully hard as I ease into my runner's pace, get the satchel balanced evenly and tell myself that I might have to run until the sun comes up in order to make it through this night alive.

I look behind me and see no one.

God bless this long Torrance street. And

the next one, which takes me back toward Hawthorne, which is where I need to be. I finally hit my rhythm — my heartbeat and my breathing mesh — and I stretch out my stride a little more and remember what a pleasure it is to run barefoot down a sidewalk on a summer night.

I look behind me and see Lupercio.

Not in his Lincoln, but running after me. His short legs work like pistons and his plaid shirt is tucked in and the machete in his right hand flashes in the streetlights.

He's gaining.

I cut across a front yard, over a fence, through a backyard, over a fence into another backyard, then leap another side fence and find myself one full street closer to where I started.

When I turn I see Lupercio advancing through the shadows, as if he's matched my every footstep with two of his own.

The new street is older and not as generously lit as the first two. The trees are larger and the sidewalk is narrower and I can hear the tap of Lupercio's boots behind me. I stretch out my stride again, get my knees up higher, eating up longer and longer bites of ground, but I can tell without looking back that he's closing in. I pass a living room lit behind the blinds, a "Security Solutions" sign poked in the middle of a lawn, a trike on a walkway leading to a front door.

I run harder.

And harder.

I don't need to look back. The boots are hitting faster than my bare feet and this is the time to live or die.

I stop and turn. I point Cañonita.

Lupercio stops, too. He's under a street-light, fifteen feet away. He angles quickly for the light pole and I fire.

There's an ear-splitting boom and a loud twang and sparks jump off the streetlight stanchion. I've missed him by five feet. All I can think to do is turn and run again. I've got one shot left.

So I'm across another front yard and over a side fence but my tank top catches on the top as I go over. The blouse is half ripped off and half hung up. I can hear Lupercio charging as I get the material in one fist and yank it free, but by then he's half over the fence himself, above me, and I point Cañonita at him, but there's this terrible blur coming at me from above his head and instead of pull-ing the trigger I pull the gun away just as the top of the fence splits and the machete blade lodges deep and true in the wood.

I'm gone.

I hear him cursing, and the sharp squeak

of steel caught in lumber. I take the next two fences vault style, with Cañonita in my mouth and both hands braced on the fence tops and my arms burning as they push me up and over.

I tumble onto the wet grass of a front yard and I can see the boulevard just a hundred yards away now and I roll and stand and run, digging down for everything I've got. I'm drenched in sweat. Running to stay in shape is different than running to stay alive.

When I look behind me I see no one.

I make Hawthorne Boulevard, press Cañonita into my pocket and put out my thumb.

The third car pulls over and the passenger window goes down. Two boys in the front, white shirts, ties, young Republican haircuts.

"Do you need help?"

"I need to get in your car. Then I need to make one call, and I need you two guys to wait with me while Triple A comes."

They look at each other, then the nearest one nods.

Yep, Jehovah's Witnesses in a five-year-old Malibu. A gift from heaven. I open the door and push aside a bound bundle of *The Watchtower* and sit.

"Where's your car, ma'am?"

"Let's give it a few minutes. There's a bad person involved. He ripped my blouse. How about donuts? You guys like donuts?"

"Yes, we do. There's a Winchell's up here."

And plenty of cops.

"Perfect," I say, digging my phone out of the satchel.

Back at the airport Marriott, door locked and chain in place, and reloaded Cañonita on the bathroom counter, I sit on the edge of the tub in the dark with my feet in the warm soapy water. There are cuts and splinters all over them and my heels are badly bruised. It hurts.

But my brain hurts worse because I'm trying to figure out how Lupercio always seems to know where I am and I really don't like the answer I'm getting.

How did he know about Miracle Auto Body? How did he know about Valley Center and Torrance?

Be logical here.

Okay, maybe Amanda, the clerk who checked me into the Residence Inn, was a friend of Lupercio's. She was a plump redhead who looked about twenty and was reading a Harlequin romance when I walked up to the front desk. You tell me.

Or, maybe someone else at the Residence Inn was a friend of Lupercio's — a higher-up who could scan the computer for the names of the guests checking in and out. Sure, maybe. But Lupercio is freelance. He works alone. He murdered half of his own gang. So how many friends does he have in how many hotels in a city with hundreds and hundreds of them? You tell me that, too.

I didn't tell anyone where I was staying. Not Ernest, *no one*.

Now consider this: Handsome Hood and Lupercio are related by time and space. Hood shows up at Miracle Auto Body; Lupercio is there, too. Hood shows up at my home in Valley Center; Lupercio is right on his heels. Hood suggests the Residence Inn for a good night's sleep and who should be there waiting for me?

They connect. So, maybe Hood was covering Lupercio at Miracle Auto Body that night. That's why he rousted me — just in case I'd seen something. Man, *did* I — and I was dumb enough to tell him all about it. He knew I lived in Valley Center and he knew I'd come back to the Residence Inn. On the beach in Laguna he pretty much accused me of taking the diamonds, so maybe he knew about them all along.

Hood buttered my toast in the Hotel Laguna but maybe the heavy secret inside his heart was that I was about to be killed — no witness to Lupercio that night, no witness to himself. And there's this, too: if Hood is tight with Lupercio and if he reasons like I've reasoned, he knows that I've got the diamonds, and he knows I'll keep them close, in the very possible case that I need to buy my life with them. Thus, close enough for them to find. Then they've got no witness *and* my forty-five thousand dollars' worth of rocks in their pockets.

I lift my feet from the water and towel them off. They hurt like hell. I hope there's nothing stuck in them. I see Lupercio's machete flashing like lightning above me and then hear the dry bark of the metal splitting wood. Probably would have sounded about the same splitting my arm. I turn on the light and the bathtub water is pink. I hobble into the bedroom and lie down and look at the clock radio. My feet hurt and I want my mother, even though she probably wouldn't be too happy with me.

If I'm right about Hood and Lupercio then I'm wrong about Hood. It would disappoint me to think that my judgment could be so poor. But I'd rather be disappointed than dismembered. I thought I'd outgrown my attraction for cute losers sixteen years ago when I threw out Bradley's father for taking his niece to our bed. Before I threw him out I shot his bare ass with a .22 pistol. The bullet went right through both cheeks, left big ugly wounds. Made me feel better. He's still afraid of me, which should be the natural order of things with guys like him.

But Hood? I hope I'm figuring wrong. I want to be wrong.

It's late. I can see the gray ellipse of morning coming through the slit in the drawn blinds. I can hear the murmur of L.A. around me and the roar of the jets and the thumping of closing doors and the distant ding of the elevator.

I get Hood on his cell.

"Hi, Hood."

"Where are you?"

"Not telling, don't ask."

"I've been calling all night."

"My good night's sleep in Torrance just about got me killed. Lupercio came a few inches from cutting my arm off with that machete. Where were you when I needed you?"

"On patrol. I drove the Residence lot at six o'clock and once again every hour until midnight. I knocked on the door of your room each time. Where were *you*?"

"Never saw the old black Lincoln?"

Silence then and I wonder what Hood is thinking.

"I got there at twelve-thirty," I say. "Lupercio pulled in right behind me. I ran through a fence to get away. He didn't follow me in. He was there, waiting."

"Goddamn, Suzanne."

"Goddamn is right. I ran a mile barefoot on streets and sidewalks. I jumped a million fences. Everything hurts."

"Have you checked your car for a location transponder? That's a —"

"I know what it is, Hood."

I can't tell him how many cars I've stolen and driven since Miracle Auto Body, that you'd need a team of confederates just to keep those cars in transponders. This thought brings me a very brief smile. And I also can't tell him that I checked Barry Cohen's backpack for a transponder, too — just before I boosted the F-150 in San Berdoo after I'd lost Lupercio and his lame-ass Lincoln at the signal at Eastern in City Terrace.

"Yes," I say. "I checked."

"How?"

"Got on my back, crawled under and looked."

"Are you driving the Corvette?"

"You can't crawl under that car. No. My old Sentra."

"What about your purse, or a briefcase, or something you carry with you?"

"No transponders that I know of. When could he have put one in place, Hood? I saw him for a total of four seconds that night and we were never less than twenty feet apart."

"You have to look again. Look everywhere again. They're small now."

I take a deep breath and let it out. Can't believe how tired I am. "Hell's bells."

"Did you tell Ernest where you were?"

"No."

"I'll come get you."

"I don't know about you, Hood. Every time I see you, Lupercio shows up. Every time I see Lupercio, you're in the picture, too. That really bothers me."

"You're being ridiculous."

"Then how did he know about the Residence Inn?"

"Hell, Suzanne."

"Maybe someone you work with — your boss or something."

"No."

"Easy for you to say. But I was the one looking up at that machete. By the way, Lupercio's got a new hairstyle. It's a buzz."

I hang up and call in for my messages. Ernest has called twice with full reports on how the boys are doing. Bradley caught a six-foot barrel at Oceanside, got tubed and came out. Jordan caught four fish off the pier. The dogs are fine. The Sequoia is leaking oil. Ernest misses me.

Hood has called ten times in the last twelve hours. I hear his voice go from gently polite to annoyed to worried to fearful.

Maybe he really is who I thought he was. Maybe I have him figured wrong.

Same way he's figured me.

19

Hood stood in the Residence Inn parking lot and looked where the chain-link fence had been. The flattened mesh lay a hundred feet into the adjacent lot along with three ripped-up stanchions.

Torrance PD had taped off the area sometime during the night, but they were gone now, a little after sunrise. They'd made no arrests, had not identified the vehicle involved. They wrote it up as vandalism.

On the sun-faded asphalt Hood saw the tire marks in front of the cement parking bumper, and the broken headlight glass behind it. There was another set of tire marks — the kind left by heavy acceleration or heavy braking — and these were set more widely apart and the tires were fatter than the first set. Hood pictured the big black Lincoln bearing down on Suzanne Jones, whose little Sentra had already lost a headlight. Too bad she wasn't in the yellow

Corvette. He had the thought that Suzanne Jones had used up a lifetime of good luck in the few days he'd known her. He called her again but she didn't answer.

Hood spent an hour in his temporary homicide cubicle, writing an affidavit for an arrest warrant for Lupercio Maygar. It was his first warrant request and he knew the wording had to be right. He was a slow but accurate writer and when he was done with the statutory page he read it to himself and was convinced that the judge would issue.

He sat in the empty courtroom as the judge read the request in chambers. He called Suzanne again but she wouldn't pick up. He was starting to think that he couldn't help her if she wouldn't let him. He regretted what they had done in Laguna but wanted to do it again. A few minutes later a bailiff walked the signed and stamped warrant to Hood and said good luck, I hope you stick this guy.

Hood sat across from Melissa Levery in a coffee bar on Gower. It was noon by now, but they got a corner table in the crowded little room. Melissa was a fair-skinned and dark-haired young woman with a pretty face. She was heavily made up in spite of what appeared to be a nearly flawless complexion. Her eyes were green and remarkably beautiful. She had wiped away a tear when Hood sat down, but now, several minutes into the story of her poor treatment by Barry, something hard and eager had come into her eyes.

She told him that Barry had owed money to the Wilton Street Asian Boyz, and that he wanted to pay them in diamonds, which of course were insured. The Boyz were happy because Barry totally misrepresented the value of stolen diamonds. Barry got the idea of cutting in another gang for less payment and he knew some Salvadorans — a rob-Peter-to-pay-Paul thing and that was pure Barry because he was smart but not real smart. Story of his life.

Melissa told Hood about the money she'd lent him and he'd promptly lost at the Caesar's Sports Book — ten thousand dollars of a Roth IRA she'd earned as a Lancôme rep — and the way Barry thought he could run her off and cancel his debt to her by taking up with other girls and he'd done just that, taken up with them. This was where Hood had seen the hardness in her eyes. She began describing the girls. One had been a friend. Hood liked the way she talked on without a comma because it bode well for his main purpose here. He wanted to get her back to the bigger picture, but it was a hard thing to be subtle about.

"How much did he owe the Asian Boyz?"

"Seventy-five grand." She took another sip of the elaborate coffee drink that she had ordered a few minutes ago. She had been drinking one when Hood got there, so this was at least her second.

"You told me the rocks were worth forty-five grand on the street. So Barry was underpaying them, dramatically."

"The Boyz didn't know that. And they sure didn't know they were going to get ripped off by MS-13. I read the papers. There were more people there than Barry thought would be there. It was a bigger thing than he was ready for."

She looked down now at the cheap wooden table, scratched at the surface with a manicured nail, exhaled. "Barry didn't deserve that. He was basically a good guy. He was Barry. He didn't deserve what happened."

"He stole from you and betrayed his partners and brought this upon himself," said Hood. And he thought that Barry had set up five Wilton Street Asian Boyz to be murdered by Mara Salvatrucha. Maybe Barry wasn't sure about numbers, but he was sure about outcome.

"But he didn't deserve to die for that."

Hood wanted to explain that according to the rules of the Asian Boyz and Mara Salvatrucha, Barry certainly did deserve to die. And he'd walked into that world, full of bluster and bad ideas. To Hood the definition of a fool is he who can't see consequences. But none of this would help Melissa.

She looked at him. "I talked to your boss, the guy with the fish's name."

"Marlon."

"Yeah. He asked me straight-out if I knew about the meeting and I said I did. So next he wants to know if I came in and scooped up those diamonds. Then Barry's insurance company investigators, they pretty much *told* me I'd ended up with the diamonds. They've been following me not very cleverly. They want to sweat me. Is that why you're here? You going to bust me?"

"Should I?"

"Should you?"

Hood shook his head. "I don't think you have the diamonds."

"Why not?"

"You don't seem the type to come waltzing into a place with dead men all over, steal something, then step over your boyfriend's body to make your getaway. I apologize for the images."

"A cop who believes in innocence here in twenty-first-century Los Angeles?"

"I believe in non-guilt." Hood smiled and Melissa did, too. "But someone did take the diamonds."

"Really?"

"Really. Not a diamond was found at Miracle Auto Body."

Melissa sat back. "Who?"

"It was someone who knew."

"Barry talked a lot."

"So did other people, Melissa. It's the natural thing to talk. I need the name of every person you told. Every one. This is very important, maybe the most important thing you can do for me, and for Barry."

Even through the makeup Hood saw her blush. She admitted telling some of the people she worked with, some of the women in her book group, some of the people in her AA group, some friends, her hairstylist, mother, father and an aunt, and a guy she happened to be sitting next to in a restaurant bar one night.

"You told them *all?*"

"Well, yes. I did. But not everything to everybody."

"Who knew the most?"

Melissa thought, green eyes roving up. "Octavia, from work."

"Did she know the time and place of the payoff?"

"Yeah, eventually. She asked me about things almost every day. You have to know Octavia to know what a sweet and absolutely harmless person she is."

"Melissa, this is very important — who else knew the time and place of the payoff?"

Melissa thought, and Hood slipped a short stack of coffee napkins across to her, along with his extra pen.

"Oh, come on," she said.

"Please, Melissa."

She shook her head and squared the napkins on her left, then picked up the pen with her left hand. "In order of who knew most?"

Hood found Octavia Dumont at Macy's in the Sherman Oaks Galleria. She had even more beautiful skin than Melissa's. She struck him as good-hearted but dim, and she freely admitted to telling the "Barry and His Diamonds" story to several people. The main ones were her boyfriend Derek and his roommate Frank. Octavia said Frank was in the market for an engagement ring, and when he heard about Barry's situation with the gangsters he thought he smelled a deal. Frank managed the two Heavy Petal flower shops in L.A., but they weren't making him exactly rich. So Frank was curious. He always wanted to know how it was going with the diamond broker. He asked lots of questions. Octavia figured he was looking for a way to buy a good rock on the cheap for his future wife.

Hood found Frank Short at the Heavy Petal on Wilshire. The shop was sunny and cool and smelled of blossoms. Frank was early twenties, tall and pale, with straight brown hair in a ponytail and a gold stud in his left ear.

Hood had him get an employee to work the front, then followed Frank to his office.

It was cramped and humid and smelled not of blossoms but of bleach. Frank spoke softly and without apparent emotion. He said he would have loved a distress sale on a good piece of ice, but mainly he was curious about Barry because it was such a cool story. Barry getting killed in the shoot-out seemed appropriate, Frank said.

"I never met him, though, you know?"

Hood nodded and watched the young man. Diffident people disturbed him.

Then there was a knock on the door and a young blond woman pushed through. She wore jeans and hiking boots and a sleeveless blue plaid blouse. Her arms were wiry and tanned.

"What," she said, looking at Hood then Frank.

"Not a problem, Ronette," said Frank. "You're early today."

"I've got some killer protea."

"Uh, Ronette, meet Deputy Something-or-other. He's interested in Barry."

She was blue-eyed and freckled and didn't smile.

"Ronette's one of my suppliers. I should let her show me what she's got. That's all I know about the diamond guy."

On his way to the Camaro, Hood noted the faded and slouching Growers West van parked at the deliveries curb outside the store.

He interviewed three more people on Melissa's tell-list that day. One was a very talkative hairstylist, one was a girlfriend named DeVry, one was Melissa's Aunt Shirl. He made notes as they talked, but nothing popped or contradicted what he knew or pointed in the direction of who might have used Melissa's generous gossip to interrupt the diamond payoff from Barry to the Asian Boyz.

The next day he tracked down the other

six, putting close to two hundred and fifty miles on his old IROC. In a traffic jam on the Hollywood Freeway the car began to overheat, so Hood pulled off and found a place to park and wait awhile for the radiator to cool before he put in some fresh fluid from the trunk.

He got more names, but each new possibility was further removed from Barry than even Frank, who had never met him. Hood sensed the degrees of separation widening with every interview, wondered if he was sniffing the wrong trail. Then he worried that he might have overlooked something obvious, or maybe seen something rough and ordinary on the outside but missed the gleaming diamond within.

20

That Friday evening Hood was off patrol duty and he met Lenny Overbrook down in Muscle Beach. They joined the skaters and boarders and joggers and walkers northbound on the sidewalk. The ocean flashed silver and black and an old red biplane lugged a banner that said "Lose 20 lbs. in One Month — No Drugs" across the powder blue sky. The outdoor stalls offered everything from falafel to Mexican sandals to pendants with the wearer's name hand-painted on a grain of rice. Hood smelled incense and tobacco.

Lenny Overbrook was slight and short, with a ramrod posture and a luckless face. He still had a military haircut but Hood knew he'd been discharged nine months ago, just before his own tour had ended. Lenny wore jeans and sneakers and a light jacket against the breeze.

Hood had first encountered Lenny in a

Hamdaniya living room in which an Iraqi father and his three sons had been shot to death. Hood had blundered into the crime scene during the tail end of a late evening firefight, drawn by a ferocious outburst of automatic fire. In the hot, smoke-filled twilight Hood saw soldiers running from the house — six of them — and he'd yelled for their attention, but they ignored him as they vanished into the labyrinthine Hamdaniya alleys.

Hood rounded a doorway inside the house and saw a young corporal wiping down an AK-47 with his shirttail. When he was done, he placed it in the hands of a bullet-riddled Iraqi man slumped against a blood-splattered wall.

At that moment Hood knew that for the rest of his life he would be tied to this bloody young marine corporal who positioned the machine gun in the dead man's lap then turned with a look of blue-eyed innocence. That look would come back to Hood in dream after dream after dream.

I wish I hadn't seen that, soldier.
You see what I did.
I saw the others.
There weren't no others.

And that was how Hood's investigation went. That was what it all boiled down to.

Lenny Overbrook from a holler in West Virginia refused to admit that there had been other soldiers with him in the Hamdaniya living room when the Iraqis were slaughtered. Nothing Hood could do had an effect on Overbrook. When Hood said that he'd seen Overbrook wipe down the AK, the man shook his head and denied that he'd ever touched the gun at all. When Hood said he'd seen six men leaving the home where the dead family lay, Overbrook said he was alone in the house. When Hood turned Overbrook over to senior investigators, nothing changed. The little corporal told the same story, day after day. In spite of the evidence and Hood's testimony, the senior NCIS field people wanted to believe it.

Hood interviewed the soldiers in some of the door-to-door platoons but he couldn't identify anyone with certainty — the massacre had taken place in late evening and the soldiers were running, laden with battle-rattle, their faces hidden under their helmets. During these interviews Hood learned the full meaning of contempt. The soldiers thought he was there to betray them. He sensed that there was a bullet out there looking for his back.

Hood quickly learned that the Iraqi father ran a small produce stall in a nearby marketplace. The two youngest boys helped him, and the oldest son was a journeyman auto mechanic employed by an uncle. They were nonviolent, moderate Shiites, used to being subordinate under the old regime.

Hood also learned that Lenny Overbrook had an IQ of seventy-two, had not yet completed his junior year requirements for high school when he joined the marines on his eighteenth birthday. He'd never had a grade above a C-minus. He'd been working full-time at a filling station when he enlisted.

Even with the crude investigative tools at Hood's disposal, it was apparent that the Iraqis — the father was forty-two years old, the sons were eighteen, fifteen and thirteen — had been shot sixty-one times with six different weapons. But Overbrook said no, that wasn't possible because he'd done it himself in self-defense against an insurgent with an AK. He had acted alone. He had done what he thought was right. It all happened "so dang fast."

When Hood did the toolmarks comparison on Overbrook's dust-choked M-16, he found that only one of the sixty-seven casings recovered from the Hamdaniya home had been fired through it.

When Hood explained to him that this was a capital case, that the Navy could execute him for murder if he insisted on confessing to it, Overbrook had just turned his clear blue eyes on Hood and nodded.

So Hood released him. He figured if he couldn't even identify the six men who'd done most of the shooting, he wouldn't allow a man who had fired one shot to take the rap for killing four people. Overbrook was willing to lay down his life for six men who ran out on him, but Hood wasn't willing to let him.

Now, nine months later, Overbrook looked at Hood with the same calm conviction with which he had falsely confessed to the slaughter of four people.

"I want to tell the truth," said Overbrook.

"It's too damned late, Lenny. It's over."

"Nothing is over when it's still in your heart."

"I'm sorry it's in your heart but you had your chance."

"There shouldn't be a time limit you have to tell the truth by."

"You're going to name the six?"

"Yes, myself first. I fired once, just like your test said I did. I shot the father. I hit him square, too."

Hood stopped and Lenny stopped and Hood looked into the corporal's placid eyes.

"I gave you a chance to tell the truth,"

said Hood. "And I gave you a chance to let it go."

"I don't want to let it go. I murdered, sir. My heart needs to tell it."

"Tell it to who, Lenny?"

"You, Mr. Hood."

I wish I hadn't seen that, soldier.

"I'm nobody, Lenny. I'm just a guy who saw something once. But go ahead. We'll walk and you can tell me what happened."

Hood leaned into the breeze coming off the ocean. Overbrook was hunched in his jacket and looked like he weighed maybe a hundred and ten pounds. Hood saw that since the discharge Overbrook hadn't put on weight, hadn't grown out his hair, hadn't changed really one bit since Hood had first laid eyes on him in the bloody Hamdaniya living room.

"We followed some bombers off the street but they got away. There were voices inside. Loud voices. I was the first one in. One of them moved his hands and I shot him. After that there was no sense. It got mighty loud. We were furious at the bombers that got away. We had a lot of hate inside us."

They cut across the sand toward the beach. A flock of seagulls standing in the sand regarded them but didn't move.

"It was Cowder what had the AK. Called

it his throw-down gun. Cowder told me what to do with it and said if anybody told, they'd get personally killed by him and that went for me, too."

Hood recalled Cowder, a PFC with a cool look in his eyes who told Hood later that maybe the Racks had it coming.

"See, Mr. Hood, the thing is I was raised by churchgoing folks and I believed what I was taught back then and I believe it now. I don't know how to get this blood off my hands except by suffering the consequences of what I did."

"You did as good as you could do, Lenny. You never asked to go to there."

"Yes, I did ask. I wasn't old enough after 9/11 but I made up my mind when the buildings came down I was going to do something."

"I can't reopen the investigation, Lenny. I wouldn't even if I could. I did the closest thing to right that I could come up with."

"Letting four men get murdered and nobody pays is right?"

"You're paying, Lenny. We all are."

"I don't think it's enough."

"You're not the judge of that."

"It's about consequences and terrible dreams. I have the most awful dreams you can imagine and they never stop."

Lenny turned around and looked down at the gun in his hand.

Hood dove for it.

Never took his eyes off it. He hit the sand gut-first with his arms extended and the pistol locked between them, and when he rolled over and aimed up, Overbrook was looking down at him with an expression of crushing hopelessness on his face. Hood popped to his feet and Overbrook charged him, screaming. Hood threw the gun to the sand behind him and got Overbrook in a bear hug and took him down. Hood used his weight and held tight, and Overbrook's screams slowly devolved into moans, and his struggling ceased, and Hood loosened his grip enough so the man could cry but not break away for the gun.

A while later Hood untangled himself from the still-blubbering Overbrook and retrieved the pistol. It was a Smith & Wesson .22-caliber rimfire revolver, each of its eight cylinders containing a live load.

Hood blew the sand off the gun. A family dragging towels and bodyboards and swim fins stared unabashedly at him and the gun, then at the man lying faceup in the sand breathing hard and sobbing quietly. Hood slipped the gun into the right front pocket of his chinos.

Then he walked back over to Overbrook and squatted in the sand. "So what am I going to do with you, Lenny?"

"I thought I'd be dead by now."

"I'm glad you were wrong."

"I hope you don't think I was going to shoot you, Mr. Hood."

"I don't. But it worries me that you were going to shoot you."

Lenny struggled to his knees, then sat back on them. He wiped the sand off his sleeves, then his thighs. The fine beach silica had stuck to the tears on his face to form a dark sludge that framed his bright blue eyes.

For a long time Lenny stared out at the heavy orange sun beginning its melt into the Pacific. "Okay."

"Yes, it's okay."

More time passed.

"Something's different, Mr. Hood."

"What's different?"

"It's hard to describe. Like something got lifted off."

"Yeah," said Hood. He wondered if grappling with Lenny had left him light-headed, or if maybe the charge of adrenaline had made him giddy. But what he really thought was the truth had lightened their burdens, at least for a moment.

Lenny pulled a folded piece of paper from

the pocket of his jacket then stood and walked it over. "These are them. The six. They should say what really happened, too. They were my friends. I did my part."

Hood took the paper and put it in his shirt pocket without opening it.

"Lenny?"

"Yes, sir."

"You hang in there. I'm keeping the gun."

"Yes, sir."

"Go home. Take care of yourself. I like you."

Hood backpedaled away from Lenny Overbrook then turned and jogged back to the boardwalk.

21

That night in his small Silver Lake apartment Hood watched and recorded a TV news special on Allison Murrieta. He ate his dinner and drank beer. The windows were open for the cool air, which in August smelled like nightshade and frying tortillas.

The show was hosted by Dave Boyer. It had jolting edits and a soundtrack of very loud and sudden noises, like bullet trains passing or maybe cell doors slamming. The images were of Allison robbing businesses, intercut with the self-promotional video that Boyer had played at the interagency task force briefing.

There was a still shot of an old drawing of Joaquin Murrieta. He was long-haired and appeared crazed. Then the screen split and a still image of masked Allison appeared beside that of her alleged great-great-great-great-great-great-grandfather. If there was a resemblance, it was faint at best to Hood.

But again he thought he saw Suzanne Jones behind Allison Murrieta's jeweled mask. When they showed a clip of Allison leaving a McDonald's after robbing it, Hood watched the way the back of her blouse creased in alternate directions with each step, and he remembered comparable creases in the nightshirt Suzanne wore that Sunday after she'd smelled his face up close then walked away, waving over her shoulder.

As evidence I now present comparable creases, he thought. He burped and shook his head. What were the hundreds of people who knew Suzanne Jones thinking when they saw Allison Murrieta on TV? Good question. Apparently not what he was thinking.

He got out the copy of Suzanne Jones's phone bill and flattened it against his knee so he could read it.

He chose a Los Angeles number and a woman answered. Hood identified himself as a Los Angeles County deputy and said that he was trying to locate Suzanne Jones. She had suddenly gone out of contact and he was concerned. Hood offered his badge number and a number to call at LASD if she wanted to verify that he was a deputy on official business.

"Did you talk to Ernest?" she asked.

"He's out of contact, too."

"And she's not at home?"

"The family moved out suddenly on Sunday night," said Hood. "There was an incident in the neighborhood."

"Incident?"

"She was fine. Her children and Ernest were fine. Then — she stopped returning our calls."

Then, thought Hood — I almost got her murdered at a motel up in Torrance and I can't figure out why she hit the wind.

"I'm sorry," said the woman. "I just don't know where she would go. We work together at L.A. Unified. But she lives way down in San Diego and I rarely talk to her during the summer. I wish I could help."

Hood got an idea but he was afraid it was a bad one. At least that's how it struck him at first but he decided to air it anyway. Maybe it was the beer, but Hood figured if Lenny Overbrook could tell a difficult truth then he, Hood, could ask a difficult question. Something in this woman's voice made him believe he should try.

"Are you close to a TV set?" he asked.

"Why?"

"I'm asking for your help. Turn on Channel Four."

"Are you serious?"

"Yes."

There was a pause. Hood could hear the phone hit something solid like a table or counter. A moment later she was back.

"Allison Murrieta," she said. "She robbed a place over in Long Beach last night. I kind of like her but I'm afraid she'll kill somebody someday. What's this got to do with Suzanne?"

"Do they look alike?" asked Hood.

"You're kidding, right?"

"I'm not."

"Well, no. They don't look much alike. Suzanne is tall and athletically proportioned. This robber is thicker. Look at her. She's not tall, and she's full. Allison has black hair but Suzanne's is light brown. Of course the mask hides the important features, so there's no resemblance to be seen."

On-screen Allison was finishing up her KFC heist of Tuesday night, hamming it up with a burly workman who was down on his knees in front of her.

To Hood the guy looked big, even on his knees — thick thighs and heavy arms and a head the size of a Dutch oven — which could make someone standing beside him look shorter. And Allison Murrieta's loose-fitting black leather vest and roomy, run-for-it trousers — they widened her, suggested a few pounds that might not really be there.

"What if that's a wig?" Hood asked.

"Possible, but I doubt it. You can almost always tell."

"What about the face?"

"Same basic face type, maybe, but it's not her. Suzanne doesn't carry herself that way. I know how she walks and moves."

She gave Hood her name, Julie Ensley, and Hood gave her his cell number and asked her to call if she learned anything. Hood said that he would have Suzanne call her when he found her.

"You're right," he lied. "Suzanne and Allison don't look that much alike to me. It was a false hunch."

"Women notice women more than men do sometimes."

He got another beer and dialed another Los Angeles number.

Sid Welch, Suzanne's principal, had not spoken with her since the last day of school back in June. He had no idea where his teachers went for summer break. Suzanne had a way of showing up at pretty much the last minute. Welch's words were slightly slurred and his attitude was jocular, but Hood didn't ask him to turn on a TV.

He dialed a Temecula number and got the recording for Oscar's Septic Service. And another recording for Quality Motors in Alpine.

Then he tried an Anza Valley number.

"Growers West," said the voice.

And Hood pictured the dour blonde and thought: There it is — a connection between Barry Cohen and Suzanne Jones.

The message was interrupted by a female voice.

"Ronette West."

Hood reintroduced himself, told Ronette the Suzanne Jones story, offered his shield number.

"Sorry, Deputy. I don't know any Suzanne Jones. Where'd you get my number, anyhow?"

"From Suzanne's phone bill."

"Then you have a problem, dude."

"What do you grow?"

"The most beautiful flowers on Earth. Nice talking with you. Good-bye."

Hood stood up and went outside to his deck. From Barry to Melissa to Octavia to Derek to Fred to Ronette to ... Suzanne Jones?

He felt flush with luck. Back inside he cracked another beer and called information and wrote down the address of Growers

West down in Anza Valley, Riverside County. Meth country, thought Hood, Tweak City.

He blew into his hand as if it held dice then dialed a Bakersfield number and got a woman with a dusky voice but few words.

She listened to his intro, and he could hear her writing down his badge number and the HQ number that would confirm his identity, rank and assignment.

She asked him to call back in ten minutes, which Hood did. Her name was Madeline Jones and she was Suzanne's mother. She agreed to talk to him in her home at eight the next morning. She gave him her address and hoped that he would be on time.

22

Hood came up the driveway five minutes early. The desert air was cool and the sky was tinged orange with sunlight and dust. The highways north from L.A. had been a trance of darkness and headlights followed by an ordinary desert sunrise of inordinate beauty. He'd seen an LASD recruiting billboard: "Every Community Needs a Hero. Will It Be You?" In the new light he'd watched the yuccas passing outside the windows of his Camaro, put on some Merle and let the music and the flat, dry land take him back to his days as a boy.

Madeline's home was a walled adobe alone on a crest of hill northwest of the city. It looked secure, but in Anbar province Hood had learned that all appearances are just appearances, and he was alive now because of that. So as he came up the drive, he thought again of Lupercio and the address book missing from Suzanne's computer room and slid his .38 Colt from the glove box into his coat pocket. Hood had cleared this visit with Bakersfield PD through Marlon and Wyte, and Bakersfield had agreed to let the LASD investigation proceed so long as Hood behaved himself. He had a number to call if things got hot.

He parked at the adobe wall, between two large clay planters with saguaro cactus reaching up. The weathered wooden gate was open and he stood there looking at the courtyard inside. The floor was decomposed granite sand, clean and raked. The roof was a crosshatch of heavy lumber that filtered the early morning sunlight into a slanting forest of beam and shadow. The fountain was large but made only a soft trickling sound. The rock fireplace was blackened from use. A large black kettle sat in the pit, but Hood saw that it contained not food but an explosion of red canna lilies. There were four heavy wooden chairs held together by black iron studs and upholstered in red horsehair, from one of which a large black cat fixed its yellow eyes on Hood.

"I am Madeline Jones."

She had materialized without Hood's knowing.

"A pleasure to meet you," he said.

She looked mid-fifties, on the tall side, built with a strength and femininity in which Hood saw her daughter. Her face was an older version of her daughter's, too — dark eyes and high cheekbones and a general expression of capability and doubt. Her hair was honey-colored and worn loose almost to her shoulders.

"Come in."

Hood followed her through the courtyard and into the house. It was dim inside, with few windows and the lamps turned low. They passed through a living room and a kitchen. Adjacent to the kitchen was a breakfast alcove with windows looking out on the courtyard. There at a small table sat an older and smaller replica of Madeline — her mother or an aunt, Hood thought. She was reading what looked like a Bible, making notes directly on the pages with a pen. Same distinctive face, same skeptical calm as she looked up from her reading, quietly closed the book and watched him walk by.

Then they passed an entertainment room with east-facing windows and better light. Hood noted the couches tossed with colorful blankets, a big TV and framed posters from a Mexican soap opera featuring a very beautiful woman who looked like Madeline might have looked thirty years ago, or like Suzanne looked now.

Madeline sat him at the end of a long dining room table and took the head for herself. On the walls were framed paintings of old California — Spanish missions, vaqueros, bullbaiting, horses. Hood watched the oddly muted play of the paint lit by the electric candles of a chandelier.

The long table was dark oak and appeared old, and Madeline folded her hands on the wood and looked down it at him.

"Are you a policeman or her friend?" she asked. Her voice was slow and mannered. Like an actor, thought Hood, or a person used to being listened to.

"I'm both. What does she say?"

"She trusts but doubts you."

"I grew up here, too. Bakersfield High, class of '98."

"Tennis."

"Well, I made the team."

"Then law enforcement."

"College at Northridge — political science — then Sheriff's Academy, then the navy, now L.A. Did you grow up here, Ms. Jones?"

"Mexico City. A Spanish family — my mother was an actor and my father was her writer. My father died years ago, and as you saw, my mother lives here with me. I fell in love and moved to Hollywood when I was very young. I married an unlucky writer, Jones."

"I met Ernest."

"Like Suzanne I've left a collection of interesting men behind me. We're drawn to good lovers and good fathers. A very rare combination. It makes for a life of ecstatic disappointment."

"Where is she?"

"Why should I tell you? The last time she accepted your protection she was nearly murdered by a man with a machete."

"Because without my protection he'll find her again."

"Who is this man? Why does he want Suzanne?"

Hood told her about Miracle Auto Body, Barry Cohen and the missing diamonds, Lupercio Maygar.

Madeline nodded. "I find it hard to believe that such a small coincidence — seeing a man from your car, in the course of your travels to visit a sister-in-law — can lead to a sentence of death."

"In some worlds it's common," said Hood. "Suzanne entered that world without knowing it."

"What has this civilization come to? Why

can't you guardians guard the innocent?"

"We try, but we need help. That's why you should tell me how to contact her. She has a new cell number by now. That would be a good place to start."

She looked down the table at him. "As a girl she was rebellious, like her mother and her mother's mother. I tried to instill two things in her: courage and independence. As a young mother I wanted Suzanne to make history. As an adult, she wanted to *teach* it. Neither one of us ever saw the value of compromising our desires, if there is any value in compromise at all. So, I became her captain and she became my mutineer. This is the story of every mother and daughter."

"She's a bright and beautiful woman."

"Do you believe that beauty is a curse?"

"It can open doors that should be left shut."

"Are you one of them?"

Hood shifted his weight in the heavy old chair. Down at the other end of the table Madeline stared at him, her eyes reflecting the light of the chandelier.

"I don't know if I'm better left shut. I'm pretty much what I seem."

"She says you have secrets."

"I think she does, too. I'm not sure that

Suzanne is what she seems."

Hood sensed the stillness at the other end of the table.

"Explain," she said.

"I can't explain one thing about your daughter. I don't even have a number to call."

"You need to know who you're looking for."

"I need to find her."

"I can show you what she was," said Madeline. "Here, come with me, Mr. Hood."

He stood and took a better look at the painting on the wall as he pushed in his chair. He saw that it was not a painting at all but a print.

He followed her to the entertainment room, now awash in full morning sun. She pointed him to a leather couch and handed him two big, heavy scrapbooks from one of the bookshelves then sat down not far from him. Hood looked through the pages of the first volume — a birth certificate, baby and toddler pictures, birthday and holiday pictures, soccer and swimming certificates, a record of baptism, report cards and class pictures from kindergarten, first and second grades. From what Hood could see Suzanne had been a skinny, big-toothed tomboy: Suzanne holding a snake, Suzanne with a fishing pole, Suzanne in a white martial arts uniform breaking a board with her hand and a grimace and a Bakersfield Hapkido Federation emblem on the wall behind her.

The next page contained a report titled: *A Day in the Life of the Outlaw Joaquin Murrieta. By Suzanne Jones.* The cover was orange construction paper, and the title was printed in a large old-fashioned typeface, like a wanted poster from the Old West. Below the title was the same image that Dave Boyer had used in his TV special the night before — Joaquin Murrieta with his long hair and his wild eyes.

Hood looked up at Madeline. She had leaned closer, and her closeness startled him. He thought that her eyes looked like Joaquin's with less wildness, and that Suzanne's eyes did, too.

"Fourth grade," she said. "California history."

Hood lifted the plastic protector and turned the orange cover.

Joaquin woke up with the sun that day as he always did. He could hear his beloved mount, Jorge, neighing in the barn. His young wife, Rosa, slept with her head on a pillow and her mind in dreams. It was a glorious morning outside the small town of Coloma, California.

"She liked this outlaw," Hood said.

"She talked about him a lot back then. But you will learn someday that children talk about a lot of things. Her best friend wrote about Father Serra and mission life. This bored Suzanne. Suzanne always chose the underdog, the outlaw, the doomed. Later, she became interested in Frank James — Jesse's brother — who lived out his life in Los Angeles and died in 1915. She visited his home there. Then there was Tiburcio Vasquez, the outlaw who hid in the rocks north of L.A. Of course we visited the rocks, spent a night there to communicate with his ghost. When they tried O.J., she was eighteen. I couldn't get her to turn off the TV. Hours, days, weeks watching that trial. I don't know how she kept her grades up."

"What did she think of O.J.?" Hood asked.

"He fascinated her. She thought he did it."

Hood turned pages.

Then Joaquin watched as they hung his brother. His black eyes burned with an anger that would never leave them until the day he died. In spite of Joaquin's great strength he was helpless against the Anglo ropes that held him.

"She tried to put herself into his mind," said Hood.

"Like a writer or an actor."

Hood closed the report, lowered the protective plastic cover and turned the next pages of the scrapbook.

He saw Suzanne's rush of adolescent growth in junior high school. When she graduated from eighth grade, she looked more like a high school junior.

Hood set aside the book and looked through the next one. Suzanne was still swimming and playing soccer her first year of high school at East Bakersfield. She still worked out at hapkido, but the yellow belt of her youth had turned black. She wrote sports reports and movie reviews for the school paper. She attended several dances, never with the same date. She looked lovely and bored. She went to the junior prom with a boy who looked very much like her son Bradley. Most of her sophomore year was missing. Because of the birth of Bradley, thought Hood. But there were no pictures of the young mother and her son. There were snapshots of her at work: Kentucky

Fried Chicken, Taco Bell, Subway.

Allison Murrieta's favorite haunts, thought Hood.

Her junior and senior years of high school were scarcely represented at all — school photographs, a graduation announcement and her diploma from Vista West Continuation. Busy with the baby and work, thought Hood. Amazing she'd gotten her diploma.

But suddenly there were junior college and state university report cards, newspaper clippings of her triumphs at hapkido tournaments in Los Angeles, Las Vegas and Dallas. She was knocked unconscious in the Dallas finals. There were several pictures of Suzanne with various boyfriends. Several with small Bradley, already about two years old by the look of him. He simply appeared in her life, unexplained, but increasingly present. He was cute. There were local newspaper clippings about Suzanne graduating summa cum laude from Dominguez Hills, a columnist's note about her being hired by the Los Angeles Unified School District, articles about awards and commendations she'd earned in her early teaching career. The last page had just one small item on it, a Chinese cookie fortune taped diagonally beneath the plastic cover sheet: "History is not made by the timid."

Hood set the book on top of the other. "Thank you."

"The past is now. A sigh. A generation. A grave and a birthplace. It's all one instant. Look at me and you see my mother. Look at her and you see Suzanne."

Hood thought there was truth in that. "When I look at my father, he's losing his mind."

"And you see yourself someday," said Madeline.

"Yes."

"The old become infants."

"I like your daughter very much."

"You've captivated her."

"Why did you bring me here?"

"To see if you're the one," said Madeline.

"The one who what?"

"Who sees my daughter as she really is."

"Am I?"

"I have no evidence of that."

Hood said nothing for a moment, just looked out at the flat land and the power lines drooping north. A high school buddy had crashed his new motorcycle into a power pole at over a hundred miles an hour. He was a heck of a bull rider and a wrestler, too.

"I have something to show you," said Hood.

He pulled the DVD from the pocket of his

sport coat and held it up to her.

"Unfortunately, this television needs repair," she said. "I have a small one in my bedroom. I'll bring it out."

Madeline left the room. Hood stood and went to the window and looked out at the desert. There was a breeze now, and he could feel a hint of its heat coming through the glass. He looked at the book titles. At eye level there were hardcover histories and commentaries on world cinema and television, entertainment biographies and nonfiction, most in excellent condition, all neatly arranged and alphabetized by title. The bottom shelves were stuffed with paperback bodice rippers, westerns and thrillers bloated by use and haphazardly arranged.

He studied a poster for the Mexican soap opera starring Madeline Mercedes. The show was called *Nosotros,* and the poster was dated 1971. There were similar posters for '72, '73 and '74. Hood touched the dusty poster glass.

He wandered into the breakfast alcove, but the grandmother was gone. Her book and pen were still at her place, and when Hood stood near her chair and looked down, he saw the book was a Bible with a crossword puzzle pamphlet inserted between its pages.

Back in the entertainment room Madeline

set down a small TV with a DVD player built in.

Hood plugged it in, slipped his copy of Dave Boyer's special into the play slot and sat at the opposite end of the couch from Madeline.

They watched the first ten minutes in silence. Allison robbed and hammed it up and talked about Joaquin from behind her gem-studded mask.

"Did you see this last night?" asked Hood.

"Yes."

"Is that Suzanne?"

"Of course it is."

He crossed the room and hit the pause button. His heart was going fast. "Are you going to help me find her or not?"

"That depends on you."

"Maybe you should tell me what's on your mind, Ms. Jones, because I sure can't read it."

"Sit. Please."

Hood hit the play and mute buttons on the little TV set then sat down again.

"How long did it take you to recognize her?" asked Madeline.

"A few seconds. But I wasn't sure."

"It took me longer than a few seconds. She carries herself differently when she plays this role. The second time I saw video of Allison Murrieta, I knew. My daughter. There she was, with a mask and a wig and a gun."

"Do you know where she is?"

"I have a cell number for you. It's all I know."

Hood handed her a pen and his notebook, and she wrote down a number from memory then set the notebook and the pen on the couch between them.

"What's the deal with Joaquin Murrieta?" he asked.

"There is no consensus that such a man ever existed, outside of the stories about him. Some historians say he was only legend, a product of Anglo fear. Some say he was a real man. Of those, some claim he was born in Chile, others in Mexico. For every story about him, such as the ones that Suzanne tells on TV, there is a contradictory story about him, too."

"She doesn't have his head in a jar?"

"No, she does not." Madeline looked down.

Hood wondered if the positive identification of a person wearing a mask — even by the suspect's mother — would be enough to get a warrant for arrest.

"Why is she doing this?" he asked.

"Because it's profitable and exciting. Because it stimulates and arouses. Because it makes the routine of work and family responsibility tolerable. Because she becomes famous and infamous."

Hood doubted that Suzanne Jones had sat down in her kitchen one day and asked herself how to make teaching and being a mother more fun, and come up with the idea of armed robbery and grand theft auto.

"Because she wants to please you?" he asked.

"How does this please me?"

"She makes history instead of just teaching it."

Madeline looked at one of the soap opera posters, then back at Hood. "Perhaps. Perhaps it's competition, too. I was a bright star in a small universe. Briefly. I gambled with my ambitions and failed. I saw myself in Suzanne until I saw Allison. Then I knew she'd moved beyond me. Far beyond me. She possesses the courage that I never had and always wanted. I'll confess to you, Mr. Hood — I'm very proud of her and very sad for her."

"You do understand how this is going to end," said Hood.

"She'll almost assuredly be killed."

"Someone will."

"I doubt that she could pull the trigger of

that silly little gun."

"There's nothing silly about a forty-caliber bullet."

"Find her, Mr. Hood. Stop her."

Hood pocketed his notebook and pen, stood and went to the window. Outside, the breeze was now a wind, and he watched a swirl of dust scratch against the window with the sound of a snake passing over a sheet of paper.

"I don't understand," said Hood. "Of all the people who know Suzanne, and all the people who've seen Allison on TV, why hasn't anyone stepped forward and identified her? She started making the news months ago. Just a little at first, then more and more. Now she's telling the world about herself. But we haven't gotten a single call, a single suggestion that we consider Suzanne. Her students, the parents of her students, her coworkers, her friends and acquaintances — what are they seeing? Why did I recognize her in two seconds but they still haven't?"

She looked at him with mild surprise. "People are busy and inattentive and absorbed, Mr. Hood. Truly seeing is an inconvenience the mind will avoid. It's possible you saw her because you're a good detective. It's also possible that you saw her because your hearts have touched."

After the Hotel Laguna Hood had the same irrational idea, this touching-of-hearts thing, because he wanted Suzanne Jones like he'd never wanted anything or anyone. He barely knew her but was famished to know more. She fired his imagination. He wanted to be great for her. He started slotting her into his future like the last gleaming plank of a ship he'd been building all his life.

"She denies being Allison," said Madeline.

Hood figured she would.

"When I told her I knew, she laughed at me. She said Allison Murrieta was an attention-starved child and obviously three inches shorter and ten pounds heavier than her. I reminded her that television adds ten pounds to any actor and she reminded me that I was getting old. She said that she'd have me committed if I continued to degenerate at such a rapid pace. She laughed. She finished eating the ice cream from my freezer straight from the tub like she did when she was a girl, then kissed me on the forehead as if I were a child. Like I used to kiss her. Her lips were still cold. Then she sped down the driveway like the bandit she is, the tires of her car smoking."

Madeline smiled. It was the first smile he'd seen on her, and he saw Suzanne in it in a way that gave him desire and dread. "As a concession, and because something inside told me to, I admitted to Suzanne that I could be wrong."

"But you're not?"

"I am not wrong."

"Does Ernest know?"

"I would find it frightening if he didn't, but possible. She doesn't let him be the man in her life because of his high intelligence."

Again Hood thought of Lupercio. It wasn't hard to imagine that Suzanne's address book could lead him to this place, just as the telephone bill had led Hood to it. It wasn't hard to imagine what Lupercio would do when he got here. If Marlon petitioned nicely, Bakersfield PD might step up patrol of this area, but that would almost certainly not be enough to deter Lupercio. Hood had a bad feeling about this day and he believed he should act on it.

"Have you had any calls recently about Suzanne?" he asked.

"Just yours."

"Any vague or unusual calls from a man with a Hispanic accent?"

"No."

"Any unusual visitors or solicitors?"

"I would have told you immediately."

"Can you leave this house? Go stay with

someone who doesn't know Suzanne? You'd need to take your mother. Say five days. Maybe less. Hopefully less."

"When?"

"Right now."

"Mary, Mother of Jesus."

Madeline left the room and Hood heard voices from the alcove. They spoke in Spanish and Hood caught only some of it. It went from a discussion to an argument back to a discussion. A moment later Madeline was back.

"I'll pack."

"There's one more thing." Hood took out his notebook and pen again. "Every place she might go. Every place she likes. Hotels or resorts she's mentioned. Vacation spots. Favorite restaurants, bars, clubs. Friends. Relatives."

Madeline talked and Hood wrote. It took some time. Later, while she packed, Hood called the first five places on Madeline's list. No one had seen Suzanne; she was not a recent guest. When Madeline was packed, he put her bags and her mother's bags into a dark blue Durango.

Outside the vehicle Madeline took his hands in hers. They were warm and strong. Her eyes were wet and Hood saw the tremble in her chin.

"Don't let them kill her, Mr. Hood. That's really what everyone wants, because that's how outlaws are supposed to end. And it's such good entertainment — a real person dying a real death. Maybe she'll listen to you. Maybe she'll stop. Maybe she won't."

"I'll do all I can."

"I'm not expecting a promise. I don't require theater. I used to but now I do not."

"Don't tell her that you told me. Tell her you sent me the wrong way. It might leave us something to work with."

"Of course." She climbed into the SUV and started it up. "Are you going to wait for him here? For this collector?"

"For a while, yes."

Madeline hoisted her purse from the console and produced a house key, which she handed to Hood.

"Eat the food and drink the coffee."

"Thank you. Call here when you get where you're going. Don't leave your location on the machine. If you find out where she is —"

"I know."

Hood watched the Durango lumber down the drive then turn toward Bakersfield. In the dusty windblown distance he saw it join a line of traffic. Standing in the heat he dialed Suzanne on the new number and no one answered so he left a message. He said he was just leaving her mother's house and she was a nice woman but she wouldn't tell him where Suzanne had gone or much of anything about her. All she'd conceded was this number. He tried Ernest again but Ernest didn't answer. He got his .25-caliber autoloader, ankle holster and big flashlight from the trunk of his Camaro.

For a long while he stood leaning against his car, letting the dry, hot wind press against him. It was nice to feel it again. He had loved the Bakersfield wind when he was a kid, sending plastic kites up into it and feeling the string unspool in a steady rush while the kite urgently vanished into the blue brown sky. And he'd loved the Bakersfield wind when he went out riding a borrowed horse with friends along the roads between the cotton farms and the oil fields, the way the wind shivered the white fluffy balls and whistled through the derricks. It was the same wind that blew through Anbar province, but he had few pleasant memories of Iraq with which to associate it. He wondered if Lupercio had ever felt that wind down in El Salvador.

Hood slung the holster and gun over his shoulder and stepped back into the courtyard. He stopped in front of the fireplace. He touched the big black kettle and confirmed that it was made of plastic. The canna lilies were paper.

23

That evening Hood went into the city. He bought food, underwear and shampoo at a Kmart. Then he turned the Bill Woods music down low in the Camaro and drove slowly past the Blackboard and the Corral, where Woods and Owens and Haggard had created the Bakersfield Sound — electric twang, raw and rough, "too country for country" according to the Nashville smoothies.

This had all happened decades before he was even born. But as a boy Hood had loved the sound of their recordings, and their straightforward tales of prison, drinking, working the rigs, truck driving. To teenaged Charlie Hood the music had seemed truthful and moving — dispatches from a pained world of which he caught glimpses in the Bakersfield all around him. And this is what he heard in it still.

He swung by his old high school, home

of the Drillers, then the house where he'd grown up. The house hadn't changed much in ten years. The paint was new and the trees were taller and the campaign signs on the bumper of the pickup in the driveway were for Hillary Clinton instead of Bill.

He was back in Madeline Jones's home before sunset. He checked the answering machine: Madeline had checked in and that was all.

At dusk he sat for a while in Suzanne's room. It appeared to have been abandoned about 1994, Suzanne's senior year of high school, when Suzanne wasn't really a graduating girl of eighteen but a mother with a small child and a job in a fast-food place and plans for college so she could teach history. There was a small plastic infant's bed in one corner. There were teenagers' clothes and infant clothes still hanging in the closet. How had she managed all that?

Hood ate his dinner in the darkness of the courtyard, with the fountain turned off and his .38 next to the cat on the chair beside him, waiting for Lupercio.

An hour later the cat had taken up position on Hood's lap and he was petting it when he heard a light concussive thud from the desert beyond the driveway.

Hood froze and listened. It might have been a car door opening, or a gate tapping against its post, or an errant foam food container slapping up against a fence, or some other faint event within the play of wind and silence and the purring of the cat. He knew how far sound could travel in clear, dry desert air.

Hood picked up his gun, and when the wind died for a moment, he turned his ear toward the desert and listened.

Opened car doors usually get shut, he thought.

Silence.

The cat slipped away when Hood reached over and picked up his flashlight off the floor.

He stood just inside the entrance to the courtyard, saw the moon low in the west and the glint of the moonlight on the fender of his Camaro and the stars flickering in the canopy of the night like diamonds caught in black mesh, and he thought of Suzanne then dropped her from his mind.

He followed his flashlight beam across the driveway, boots crunching on the gravel, gun in his right hand. At the fence he stopped and aimed the light into the desert, which easily consumed it but revealed little of itself. Within the limited beam the branches of the sage and creosote shivered white.

In the middle distance Hood made out the shapes of sand hills. He had chased lizards through such sand hills when he was a boy. On the dunes their tails left long, straight lines and their feet left pointillist claw dots on either side of the lines. Sometimes Hood would follow a track for hundreds of yards, over hill and dune, until it ended at a hole.

Now in the moonlight the sand hills were pale and dotted with sagebrush, and he remembered that they could be steep-sided and softly packed and treacherous to climb.

He turned off the flashlight and walked toward the hills. Gradually the sand under his boots hardened into a dirt road. He didn't like the crunch of the road so he moved off to one side of it, and as he got closer to the sand hills, he saw that they were higher than he had thought. The faint dirt road wound into them and vanished.

The road comes out of the sand hills, Hood thought, so it probably comes in on the other side of them. But he also remembered the odd incompletion of man-made things in this desert: a section of fence connected to nothing, a foundation slab poured but never framed, a mine abandoned after eight feet of progress, and everywhere fragments of dirt roads connecting nothing to nothing.

He walked the road between two of the lower sand hills. The moonlight diminished while the shadows deepened, and Hood had trouble clearly seeing the hills ahead. He stumbled in a rut and caught himself but the sound was sudden and loud. He stood for a moment feeling his heart race.

At the foot of the next hill Hood jumped onto the slope, leaned forward and wide-stepped his way up, sand giving way, gun and flashlight out for balance. Thirteen steps. On top the moonlight was stronger, and he clearly saw the old black Lincoln Continental parked on the road between the hills.

He swung around as fast as he could, gun first.

A bad taste rushed into his throat — of hot spoiled antacid pooled on top of fear — the taste of Hamdaniya and Miracle Auto Body and the Valley Center barn.

But all he saw was darkness and the way he had come and in the near distance the lights of Madeline Jones's driveway.

Hood turned back and looked again at the car. Then he crouched and scuttled across the hilltop. From the far side he could look almost straight down on the Lincoln. The windows were darkly smoked and revealed nothing, but through the windshield he could see the glint of moonlight on the dashboard and on the upper circumference of the steering wheel.

He knelt with the unlit flashlight braced in the sand for balance and let his eyes wander the desert around the car. He thought of the carnage that Lupercio had left behind in the barn, and of the dozen men he'd killed before the most violent gang in L.A. had sued him for peace, and how Lupercio seemed to be prescient and ubiquitous.

Hood used his flashlight hand to slip the phone off his belt, punch it on and dial the Bakersfield PD number they'd given Marlon.

He gave the sergeant Madeline's address and his location, said he had reason to believe a violent felon was in the vicinity. He asked for the car to run with no color, no sirens. The sergeant sounded skeptical and he took Hood's cell number.

Five minutes went by.

Protect me, Hood thought.

He rose and hopped off the top onto the slope, leaning back and stepping big down the flank of the hill, his heels sliding through the loose sand and sending the gravel down with a hissing sound that he could not prevent.

He jumped onto the dirt road and used his

momentum to jog toward the car.

His flashlight was in his left hand, his .38 Mustang in his right, wrist on wrist for control. Hood sighted down the barrel of the pistol. Up close to the car the flashlight beam passed through the windshield and diffused. Through it Hood could see inside the car — rearview mirror and empty front seats and the dome light and the glistening buckles of the shoulder restraints that were folded neatly as bat wings beside the rear seats.

Crouching, he shuffled counterclockwise around the car. Empty, no alarm lights flashing on the dash, door locks down, the driver's seat positioned up close to the wheel for a short man. When he came back to where he'd started, Hood lowered the gun and swung the flashlight beam up to the top of the nearest dune. Then the dune on the other side of the road. Nothing moved except what was moved by the wind.

Hood sensed something behind him. He spun around and aimed the beam into the empty desert, his gun steady and his chest knocking against his shirt. Then he swung hard right where the pale flash at the edge of his vision was only the darkness pulling an owl back in.

Be still, he thought: still.

He turned off the light and lowered both it and the gun and stood in the road in the bare moonlight. He turned slowly in a circle, moving his head to keep the wind from blowing straight into his ears.

Owls have wings and men have feet.

With the beam pointed down to the road, the tracks were easy to see and distinguish from his own. They were boot prints, small — like the ones Hood had seen by the stream in Valley Center, where Lupercio had talked with Jordan Jones and surrendered his precious identity.

The prints led away from the car then down the road toward Madeline's house then disappeared where Lupercio had given up road for desert.

It took Hood a while to find the trail again but when he did the footprints were easy to follow.

He was halfway back to the house when he saw the cruiser coming up the road from the signal. A moment later it bounced onto the driveway and started up the hill toward the house.

He turned on his cell phone and it rang almost immediately.

"Hood? This is Officer Jackson, Bakersfield PD, here at the Jones residence. Talk to me."

"He's there. He's close."

"Whoa, podner — what are you talking about?"

"Lupercio Maygar. Ex–Mara Salvatrucha. We like him for two murders down in San Diego four days ago."

"What's your ten-twenty?"

"The middle of the desert about two hundred yards north of the driveway you're coming up. His car is out here but he isn't. His footprints are aimed straight at the house. He's armed and extremely dangerous."

"What's he doing here?"

"He's after the Jones daughter. She's a possible witness. The house off to your right belongs to the mother."

"We'll have a look. Maybe you should get back here."

"If he gets around you, he'll head back to his car."

"I've got a good partner and a twelve-gauge. He's not getting around us."

"Get backup."

Hood saw the cruiser stop outside the Jones house. A spotlight blasted on, bleaching the adobe wall white. He turned and looked back in the direction of the Lincoln. He couldn't see it, but he could see the two sand hills that it was parked between.

"It's Friday night in Bakersfield, Hood

— we're thin. We've got a spot on the place right now. We'll look around. If we see anything interesting, we'll get backup. If you want to stand out in that desert and watch a car go nowhere, be my guest."

Hood punched off as he watched the spotlight roam the wall, and the garage outside the wall, then the courtyard entryway.

The cruiser headlights went out and the doors opened. In the interior lights Hood watched the two officers climb out, flashlights on, one patrolman carrying a combat shotgun, the other with his sidearm drawn. Their beams searched the wall and together they disappeared around one side of it. A minute later they had come full circle. No Lupercio scattering into the night. The shotgun cop turned and looked into the desert in Hood's direction.

The one with the pistol swung open the wooden gate to the courtyard, backing up and using it for cover. The cop with the shotgun stood with his back to the adobe, and when the opening was wide, he crouched low and followed his light inside. It looked like the pistol cop was trying to secure the gate open, but he gave up and followed his partner in.

The gate slammed shut in the wind.

Hood saw the dull explosion of light behind the courtyard wall, then another. A second later came the muffled reports of the shotgun.

He ran for the house, gun still drawn, flashlight still in his left hand.

They got him, he thought. Two shots from the riot gun at close range.

He heaved across the desert and the driveway and swung open the gate. The shotgun cop lay on his back just inside the entrance. His head was intact but his face and everything behind it was gone, and through this crude tunnel Hood saw the gravel of the courtyard floor wet and red. The dead man's finger was still inside the Remington's trigger guard.

His partner was sprawled faceup over the chair that Hood had been sitting on with the cat half an hour earlier. He was breathing fast, his upper chest and neck in ribbons, eyes staring out at Hood from behind a mask of blood. He reminded Hood of someone but Hood had no presence of mind now for memory. The cop breathed faster and tried to stand but the chair began to topple. Hood caught him and eased him to the floor but by the time he did this the cop had stopped breathing and Hood could hardly get a pulse.

He pulled back the man's head and closed

his nose and breathed for him twice, then straddled him and continued the CPR with twenty stiff-armed, flat-palmed compressions against the sternum. He ventilated again, the compressed. And again. Hood lost count. His mouth filled with liquid copper and his throat clenched to keep the bile down. His face and hands and thighs were sticky and warm, and he thought, Jesus, this guy isn't going to make it but he talked to him anyway, saying stay alive, stay alive, man, open those eyes and come back here right now, man, you come back here.

Hood fumbled out his cell phone, punched 911 and speaker and set the phone beside the cop as he did the cardio thrusts. Through the wind and his own grunting breaths he heard the operator come on, and he gave her the address and said officers down, *two officers down* but that was all he managed before it was time to breathe again for the cop. Hood got himself off the man and pinched his nose and breathed into him again while the operator assured him in a distant voice that police and medical were on their way.

Immeasurably later the medics pulled Hood away mid-thrust and took over with the oxygen machine.

Hood sat panting in a corner of the courtyard. He wiped the blood from his mouth with the back of his sleeve and stared wide-eyed and straight ahead. He saw Lupercio's small boot prints in the gravel and the gore on the gate above the shotgun cop as the paramedics swung it open and took the gurney out.

A while later Hood and two BPD officers were standing atop the sand hill above Lupercio's car, but the car was gone. He saw the flashlights of two more cops on the dune across the road and two more lights down where the car had been. A helicopter crossed overhead and a spotlight raked the ground below it.

Hood didn't remember trudging through the desert to get here.

He turned and took a knee and looked out at the chaos of vehicles and flashing lights backed up for what seemed like miles down the driveway of Madeline Jones's house.

24

Hood's first and only crime spree, and his first thoughts of becoming a cop someday, both occurred when he was sixteen.

He'd gotten his driver's license and the world was open to him through the ancient Chevrolet that he had bought from a neighbor with saved money.

His father had shown him how to pull the block and pistons to be ground at an auto shop, had helped him rebuild the carburetor and put in the new oil pump, radiator, solenoid assembly and brakes.

As they worked, his father asked Hood what he wanted to do with his life, and Hood said be a cop, maybe, because he liked the TV shows about them and the idea that you joined a department of people who became your friends. His father, as a municipal employee himself, praised the medical benefits and retirement packages offered to Bakersfield policemen and agreed that there was plenty of "camaraderie" in law enforcement.

When the car was finished, Hood had not one penny left for paint, but the engine and tranny were sound and the retreads still had some miles on them. It had a radio that pulled local FM stations and the AM news stations out of L.A., and a cassette deck.

He was free.

It was a summer night, a Friday. Hood had a full tank of gas and some metal on, and his parents had given him permission to over-night with a friend.

He drove through downtown with the window open and his elbow on the door and a cigarette in his lips and wondered what he really *would* do with his life, given that he was sixteen and there was lots of life ahead. He cruised the East Hills Mall parking lot and watched the pretty girls and knew that whatever he did with his life, it was going to include one of them. Girls liked cops, right? He smiled and waved at some, tried to say hello, but his voice stuck high in his throat like something he'd forgotten to chew.

Back on the boulevard Hood realized that the trouble with law enforcement was that he'd always liked outlaws.

He'd always wondered what it would be like to be one, to walk alertly through space and time following his own code and no other. He'd always silently pulled for the bad guys.

When he saw *Butch Cassidy and the Sundance Kid* as an eight-year-old, he'd thought it was the most powerful movie he'd ever seen, though his mother said, "The chuckleheads got what they deserved."

In seventh grade, when the genuinely tough kids began getting expelled from school, he'd secretly admired them.

When a local man had been arrested for stealing horses from a Bakersfield rancher, Hood had recognized him immediately on the news — he was the cool guy who worked at the bike store, the young guy with the old voice who'd talk chicks and liquor while he adjusted the brake cables and chain on Hood's Schwinn for free. Hood wrote him an anonymous letter, care of the Kern County Jail, telling the bike shop dude to hang tough.

When his father groused about the state of California halting executions, Hood had been secretly glad because the idea of waiting in a cell to be killed terrified him.

A world beyond the law, he thought. Give me freedom to find a code of my own.

So that Friday night Hood walked into the Bakersfield Warehouse, picked out a hundred and twenty dollars' worth of head-banger tapes because he already owned everything related to the Bakersfield Sound, and ran out of the store.

He was burning rubber out of the parking lot, mud slopped over the Chevy plates to obscure the numbers, before anyone even bothered to follow him out.

He dined and dashed at Coco's, shoplifted a bottle of vodka and a handful of Slim Jims from a supermarket.

High on fear and heart pounding hard, he strode into a Wal-Mart, then strode back out with a one-hundred-and-fifty-dollar boom box and plenty of D batteries to run it. The pleasant old man who greeted customers at the entrance croaked drily at him as Hood ran out the door.

That night he took all his loot out to a desert campground he'd used over the years. There was a ring of fire-blackened rocks and a plywood lean-to and empty food cans brown with rust. He collected some wood and got a fire going, then set up the boom box, put in a tape, cracked the vodka and opened a meat snack. Two hours later he was very drunk, so he got the sleeping bag from the trunk of the car and curled up in the backseat with nothing but his shoulder for a pillow.

In the morning his head was killing him but he put more wood in the fire ring and got the flames going strong. Then he dropped what was left of what he'd stolen into the fire and watched the plastic soften and writhe and the audiotape curl and vanish. He was ashamed of himself for reasons he could hear in his aching head, specifically enumerated by the voices of his father and mother.

He was hung over the rest of the day and went to bed early that night, complaining to his parents about the weird-tasting chicken he'd gotten for lunch at the Target snack bar.

"Watch the alcohol, son," said his father as he turned off the light.

Before falling asleep, Hood decided on law enforcement.

Now Hood sat in the trailer in Anza Valley that served as the Growers West office. It was late morning. Through the windows he could see a tan meadow and rocky hills and the greenhouses battered by the desert wind, their white skins hanging in shreds.

Hood looked out at the ruined greenhouses. They were difficult to comprehend because he was still back in Madeline's courtyard. It was two days later and he still hadn't really come away from it yet. He felt like he had left something important there but he didn't know if there was a word for it, let alone a way to get it back.

Ronette West lit a cigarette and looked at him with annoyance. "I already told you I've never heard of Suzanne Jones. So you just drove all the way down here to hear it again."

"I ran a records and warrants check on you before I made the drive," Hood said.

"I'm clean."

"You're on work furlough for felony possession of cocaine with intent to distribute. You've got a pager on your ankle."

She exhaled a mouthful of smoke at him. "I'm not using anymore. Are you threatening me?"

Hood shook his head and pictured Lupercio's tiny boot prints in the blood on Madeline Jones's courtyard.

"You sure are dreary for someone who grows flowers," said Hood. "Aren't they supposed to make you happy?"

"I am happy. I don't like cops. You guys badgered me into selling that coke to you. Week after week after week. You literally pressured me into it. To a fucking narc."

"You'd have sold it to someone else."

"I needed capital to keep my business

afloat. But I kicked, I'm clean, and I don't know Suzanne Jones."

"But you knew about Barry Cohen's problem."

She nodded. "Yeah. Frank's a talker and I'm a listener. It was like a soap opera. Melissa blabbed to him and anybody else in earshot. She wanted her ten grand back."

Hood had the idea that Suzanne wouldn't talk to Ronette West about gambling debts and diamonds. But someone else might.

He took a DMV picture of Suzanne Jones from his wallet and set it on the desk in front of Ronette. She stubbed out her cigarette in a Raiders ashtray.

"Allison somebody," said Ronette.

"Tell me about Allison," said Hood.

"She showed up in a new red Kompressor. Said she lived in Valley Center, wanted to grow some tropicals."

"Greenhouse flowers?"

"That's what I said. She wanted to see how you do it. Which, believe it or not when you look outside, I actually know a lot about. I was in county lockup for a week last winter, worst storm of the year. Worst week of my life. My entire business got blown away and I was sitting in a cell, thanks to you . . . people."

Ronette sat back and crossed her arms.

She looked out the windows, and Hood followed her gaze to the ruined screens of the greenhouses, the PVC frames splintered by the storm, the irrigation lines dangling. There were stacks of empty black planting trays everywhere, like tossed poker chips. Only one greenhouse appeared whole and perhaps functional, and Hood figured it was where Frank's protea had come from.

"Did you talk to Allison about Barry Cohen?"

"I mentioned him. She was easy to talk to, you know? We kind of hit it off. She felt bad about how fucked up my greenhouses got and I told her right off how they got that way. I mean, she could see the damned pager on my leg. Then she said something about money solving legal problems and I said unless money *is* the problem. And she said only lack of money is a problem and I thought about Frank's story and I made a crack about running out of money and using diamonds instead. It went from there. Barry, the gambling, the Asian gangsters, the pissed-off girlfriend and her ten grand. Allison wanted to know more. So."

"So?"

"So. I put her in touch with Melissa," said Ronette. "Then I shut my mouth and washed my hands of that whole thing. I was trying to rebuild this business, you know? Next thing I hear Barry's gunned down up in L.A. somewhere — I read it in the papers."

"Give me Allison's numbers."

Ronette came up with a phone number and that was all.

"Good luck," said Hood.

"It'll start when you get off my property."

Melissa met him in the Nordstrom cafe in Beverly Hills. She had come from a manufacturer's show. Her dark hair was weaved through with faint lavender streaks that matched her nails.

Hood asked about the woman who Ronette West put in touch with her.

"Oh," she said, sipping her coffee drink and blushing beneath her makeup.

"Start with her name," said Hood.

"Allison. I never asked her last name."

"Did you meet her?"

"Never. We only talked on the phone."

"How much did you tell her?"

"Hardly anything."

"Melissa, if you lie to me again I'll arrest you right here. This is a promise."

"I told her everything."

"Did you meet her?"

"No. That's the truth."

"She knew the time, the place?"

"Yeah. Everything."

"How long did it take Allison to get your ten grand back?"

"A few days."

"Cash?"

"In a market bag. She called and left it on my driveway."

25

Hood volunteered to check credentials at the press conference Monday evening because he was no longer working two assignments.

He'd never seen so many reporters for a law enforcement news conference. Not only were the national networks and local affiliates here, but PBS, all of the big cable news outfits, several of the small ones, ten or so radio networks and stations, student newspapers and radio from half a dozen Southland universities, and maybe twenty print writers and photographers. They came from as far south as Tijuana and as far north as Portland, Oregon. Many of them were from towns and cities that Hood had never been to.

He stood at the entrance to the big room and checked the names off a master list. Well over half of the media participants weren't on the list because they hadn't come to a LASD press conference until now.

But no one was going to miss the story of Lupercio Maygar and the trail of blood he was leaving across the Southland, and of the vanished L.A. schoolteacher wanted for questioning as a possible witness.

So he logged in the reporters and gave them temporary passes. There was an oddly festive atmosphere. Hood gathered that the Monday conference was good timing for what must be a slow local news week. He signed in a lovely blonde from a Bakersfield radio station, but when he said he'd grown up there, she looked at him pityingly and said she was from Boulder.

When the media had all been admitted and the room was nearly full, Hood found a seat near the back. His legs were still stiff from dune climbing and running in the Bakersfield desert. He could still taste human blood, though he reasoned that this was his imagination and memory playing a trick on him. But his body was the least of it. His soul felt filthy, and the faces of Officers Jackson and Ruiz — which Hood hadn't seen clearly until the Sunday papers — waited at the center of it. Ruiz was DOA at a Bakersfield hospital. His HIV test had come back negative.

Beside all this Hood was inordinately focused on the fact that Jackson's riot gun had never been fired. Two shotgun blasts had killed the men, but Lupercio had not taken their weapon and used it against them. Hood had seen it in Jackson's hands. Since that moment he'd fastened onto this anomaly like a life raft. He had used part of his bleary Sunday to read every page of Wyte's jacket on Lupercio. There was not one mention of the man ever using a shotgun. When Hood tried to picture Lupercio trotting across the desert and into Madeline's home with a shotgun, he couldn't quite see it. A shotgun wasn't an assassin's tool. It was efficient but loud, difficult to conceal, effective only at close range. Reviewing the Bakersfield PD crime scene report, Hood saw that the shot pattern had expanded rapidly — more rapidly than even a sawed-off barrel and an open choke would suggest. It was as if the shells weren't fired through a gun barrel at all, but from some truncated handheld contraption. A zip shotgun? Possibly. How about through his fingertips, like lightning bolts — one more example of Lupercio's black magic? But two shotgun blasts had killed the officers, this was a fact. Each charge contained number six shot, which Hood knew was typically used for large birds such as pheasant and was fabulously destructive of a human up close. It was also a fact that no empty shot shells had been recovered.

Twenty minutes later Captain Patmore had finished his synopsis of the facts surrounding the murders of two Indian brothers in San Diego County and the murders of Bakersfield Officers Burt Jackson and Steve Ruiz.

Then the monitor beside him filled with the ten-year-old California Department of Corrections release photos of the suspect, Lupercio Maygar — left profile, right profile, front.

Hood listened to the murmur that rose in the room, though he wasn't certain what it was for. The man in the photograph looked fearless and unhappy, but far from unusual. L.A. was full of fearless and unhappy men. His short black hair was parted on the side and partially covered his forehead. Then Hood heard Lupercio's name being spoken by some of the reporters, and he realized that they remembered him — his break with the gang he had helped establish, and his bloody war and peace.

Next came the sketch done by Jordan Jones. Hood was relieved to see that Jordan's proud signature had been removed. And he was relieved that Jordan's sketch of Lupercio with his straw cowboy hat on was not shown. Hood had explained to Patmore and the other media relations people that if Lupercio saw the drawing with the hat he would know who had described him. And that Lupercio might wish to silence this person. The new Lupercio looked out at his audience with a different haircut but the same steady eyes and compact, ageless face.

Patmore described Lupercio's criminal career, from his early days around MacArthur Park, where he helped form the deadly Mara Salvatrucha, to his break from the gang ten years later.

"We've issued a warrant," said Patmore. "We're hoping that somebody will recognize this man and call us. There is currently a reward of one hundred thousand dollars, pledged from some of the fine individuals and businesses served by our department. If every one of you watches and listens, we can stop this man. There's a number at the bottom of your screen, and for those of you listening on radio . . ."

Next up on the monitor was a synopsis of Lupercio's criminal record, followed by a physical fact sheet. He stood five feet three inches tall and weighed 120 pounds. Brown eyes, black hair. Knife scars on his belly and forearms, bullet scars on his right front thigh and right stomach.

Patmore pointed to the next image on the

monitor, which showed Lupercio shirtless from behind.

"Mayans in gangland," said Patmore.

Hood stared at the hypnotic tangle of serpents and eagles and big-toothed jaguars all wound together in a tattoo that covered Lupercio's whole broad little back. Hood remembered that in school textbooks he'd found these motifs mysterious, but stamped into a man's skin they were ominous.

"Now, we've got a possible witness to some of this," said Patmore. "Her name is Suzanne Jones. She's thirty-two years old, and a teacher here in Los Angeles Unified. An award-winning teacher, no less. She's a Dominguez Hills graduate, a single mom. She got herself into the wrong place at the wrong time. She was working with investigators but suddenly dropped contact with us five days ago. That was right after Lupercio Maygar attempted to murder her in a Torrance hotel parking lot."

What came from the crowd now was more than a murmur.

Suzanne Jones's face filled the monitor. It was apparently a school district employee photo from the year prior — poorly lit, not well focused, unrevealing.

"We have no reason to believe she's come

to any harm," said Patmore. "We need to talk to her. We need to find her. I can't tell you how important this is. Again, please call the number at the bottom of the screen if you know anything about the whereabouts of Suzanne Jones. Ms. Jones, if you're out there, please contact us."

Patmore filled in the Jones biography. Another photographic image swept over the monitor, a shot of Suzanne at a podium. She wasn't smiling and she suffered red-eye from the flash, but she had a plaque in her hands and she looked serious and proud.

Hood's reaction surprised him: he was proud of her, too, and wanted her to be safely alive to mother her children, teach her students, drive her Corvette fast and maybe spend some quality time with Los Angeles County's most recently minted homicide detective. Nice guy, bright future. For a moment he was able to see her like everyone else saw her and it was good.

He told himself it was possible that both he and Madeline were wrong about Allison Murrieta, even though he knew they weren't. It didn't matter that no one else on Earth could see what they had seen. What they saw was true. He had told Marlon but Marlon was skeptical because the two women didn't look enough alike, in his opinion. Wyte had agreed. Hood felt like an unwanted witness — alone, unheard, doomed. Which is exactly how he figured Suzanne felt, running for her life.

"I think my kid had her in eighth grade," said a reporter near Hood. "U.S. history."

"Good teacher?"

"Beats me," said the reporter.

"They say she is. The awards and all."

"What's the tattooed pygmy want with her?"

"I think she just stumbled across a crime scene," said Hood.

"And now he's after her? That's a story."

"Write it up. Run the pictures real big. It could help."

When Patmore opened up for questions, they came fast and loud.

Hood drifted out with his cell phone throbbing against his hip.

"Why?" she asked.

"We had to."

"I will not be hunted. And don't tell me some story about a good night's sleep in the hotel of your choice. Everybody in Southern California is going to be looking for me and it's your fault."

"There's nothing else we can do, Suzanne. We can't help you if we can't find you."

Hood suddenly felt a sharp and unexpected sorrow for Suzanne Jones. Had she invented the Murrieta guise as a joke, or out of boredom, or because of competition with her mother, then been seduced by the action and the notoriety? Was she simply insane? He came close to telling her what he knew — that she was Allison Murrieta — and what he almost knew — that she had taken the diamonds from Miracle Auto Body after picking Melissa's vengeful brain. But he didn't, because that way he'd never see her again except in a hospital or in a morgue.

And because it was his duty to arrest her.

"Okay, say you've found me. Say I'm sitting right across from you. What the hell are you gonna do with me?"

"We've got safe houses."

"Where?"

"Desert, mountains, beach. Take your pick. We'd have two deputies there, twenty-four seven."

"Hood, I can't believe you did this to me."

"I'm trying to help you."

"He would have hacked Mom and Grandma to pieces."

Hood couldn't get Jackson and Ruiz out of his mind, his mouth, his nose, his eyes,

297

his dreams. "Yes."

"He killed two cops."

"Suzanne. Come in. I want you safe. The best thing you can do for them is stay with us for a while."

"What's a while, Hood? Two days? A year? What if Lupercio decides to wait me out, just lets me go back to work and bides his time?"

"He'll kill you for sure is what."

"I'm not going to be run off my job. I'm walking into my classroom in September. I'm going to teach those thick-headed kids whether they want to be taught or not."

Earlier Wyte had suggested that if Suzanne would come in they could stage a video "statement" in a good location, subtly reveal her whereabouts, televise it and wait for Lupercio.

"Help us set a trap," said Hood. "You come in. We help you video a statement where you refuse to come in for questioning out of fear. But you want your family and friends to know you're okay, safe right where you are. You send it to the newspeople and they run with it. We'll make sure it gives Lupercio an idea of where you are. Just a touch, just enough to get him to come around. Then you're free to go. Or you can take a safe house. Up to you."

"You do remember my last *safe* house?

"Do you have a better idea?"

"You're unimaginative, Hood."

"I'm trying to save your ass."

"Why bother?"

"So I can enjoy it."

Suzanne was silent for a long moment. Hood slipped outside the headquarters building into the heat of the evening. Again he almost told her what he knew, but he could not.

"You have to help me help you. Come in."

"Okay," she said. "You work out the details. You get the location set up and figure the clues and get the video camera ready. Then I'll do it. But no safe houses. No protective custody. No cages of any kind. None of that. I'll tape a statement then I'm splitting. Deal?"

"Deal. There will be at least two more of us, a sergeant and a captain. They've done this before."

"Comforting."

"I want you to be okay, Suzanne."

"You busy tonight, Charlie?"

He hesitated. If she was with him she was safer. Suzanne and Allison were safer. He would protect them and bring them to justice.

He couldn't think of any meaning of the word *idiot* that didn't apply to himself. "I hope so."

26

Which leaves me three hours to boost a better ride because I can't entertain Hood in a Sentra. And I need to hit the Burger King on Reseda Boulevard, which I cased last week and looks very good.

I take a taxi to a long-term parking lot by LAX where I've got an arrangement with one of the shuttle drivers who has a nice black GTO in a private corner. I pull out the door lock with the slide-hammer, grab the ignition assembly and go to work on the wires. My heart is not steady but my fingers are.

When I'm done I check my time on the Rolex I bought from Carl Cavore for a grand. It's got ten diamonds on the dial and a rare mother-of-pearl face that tells me I'm gone in seventy-five seconds, not bad for a history teacher who steals cars only as a hobby.

Ten minutes later I'm at the Pep Boys in San Fernando, where another associate of mine replaces the GTO door lock with an off-the-shelf universal that looks fine. And he pulls what's left of the old ignition and installs an aftermarket imitation that operates on a regular key. Which means I don't need a key with a microchip to start my new beauty, just a freshly cut key that costs me next to nothing. The work and parts run me six bills but I'm out in less than fifty minutes because this guy doesn't fool around.

Then to work. I park on a quiet residential street not far from the BK and I get suited up for the job: wig, gloves, pepper spray on my belt, Cañonita in the satchel, mask in my pocket. I'm already wearing the loose trousers and blouse and vest that allow for unrestricted movement in the event I need to run for miles and climb fences to get away from a homicidal maniac. The clothes help disguise me, too. I think a very quick prayer of thanks that the only person in the world who has recognized Allison as me is my own mother. I think I put some doubt in her, however, by questioning the agility of her mind. A little doubt goes a long way.

One of the things that Joaquin liked to do was to work fast, hit three or four remote ranches in one night, steal the good horses and run them up north into the mother lode because that's where the miners and the money were. Three-Fingered Jack, who rode with Joaquin, used to complain about the thirty-six-hour runs to steal and sell the horses — no sleep, no time to drink or whore or gamble until they'd sold off the horseflesh. In his journal Joaquin admitted to drinking "many gallons of powerful coffee" on his three-day crime binges. He brewed the coffee and carried it in cloth-covered canteens wrapped in serapes to keep it hot and protect the horses.

Jack's real name was Manuel Garcia. His hand got mangled in a roping accident when he was a boy, thus the finger loss. He was killed alongside Joaquin by Harry Love and his "California Rangers," and they cut Jack's three-fingered hand off for ID. The hand was purportedly displayed in the same jar as Joaquin's severed head, and I've seen posters advertising the exhibition of the "HEAD OF JOAQUIN! And the HAND OF THREE-FINGERED JACK!" but there was no hand in the jar I was given by my great-uncle Jack and now keep in the barn down in Valley Center. I miss Valley Center.

Joaquin was credited with stealing roughly fifty thousand dollars' worth of gold and over a hundred horses. According to his journal it was more like twenty thousand in gold and a hundred and forty horses. Historians said he and his gang killed nineteen men, mostly unarmed Chinese mine workers. But according to Joaquin they killed four, and there is nothing dishonest, boastful or evasive in his own account.

All of which runs through my mind as I park in the lot beside the Burger King lot. The two lots are separated by a hedge of lantana and there's a nice body-sized opening to let me through.

I stride toward the Burger King, all those nice yellows and reds brightly shining within.

I must have timed out the dinner rush pretty well because the dining room has only a few customers and there's nobody at the counter as I step up and point Cañonita at the young Latina girl whose smile freezes on her pretty face.

"The money."

"Yes."

A boy with pimples and a French fry basket in one hand stares at me. The girl working the drive-through stops mid-sentence. A stout older woman with short red hair barrels out of the kitchen wiping her hands on a dirty white towel and glares at me.

I swing the gun on her. "Sit and stay."

"Where?"

"Right where you are."

She crosses herself and kneels on the tile while the pretty girl empties the cash register into a plastic take-out bag.

"Double-bag it, please," I say. "And don't forget the quarter rolls."

"Okay, yes."

"Any dye packs, locators, I'd appreciate it if you'd leave them out."

"We don't have those."

"Somebody's going to get hurt," says the manager.

"You volunteering, Red?"

Right then the door opens and in wobbles an old couple, the kind you look at and think, Wow, that's what I've got to look forward to if I'm *lucky.* Mr. Geezer stops, balanced on a cane. He's nodding. He's wearing a blue shirt with a green cardigan over it even though it's a hundred degrees out. Mrs. Geezer has monumental hair, a scowl and heavy-duty therapeutic nylon support hose. She looks at me.

"We will not eat here, Frank," she says.

The old man regards me with beautiful gray eyes and he smiles, then pivots and places his cane for the turn.

He's still nodding as he drops to the floor.

The old woman just stares at him.

The pretty cashier gives me the heavy

double bags with one hand and the other goes to her mouth. The kid with the French fry basket says, "Whoa," and the manager suddenly jumps up and looks over the counter. Two customers rush in from the dining room. The front door opens and three teenaged boys shuffle in then stop, bumping into each other.

I aim Cañonita at the teenagers while I walk across the room and stand over Mr. Geezer. I kneel down and find his carotid pulse with my left hand, my right still holding Cañonita firm on the boys. There isn't much pulse and his mouth is hanging open some so I figure he's not breathing right.

"Get down here and CPR this guy," I say to the wife.

"I don't know how."

"Boys, you know how to do CPR, right?"

They mumble and shy away.

"Fuck, what's wrong with you people? Pretty face, you know CPR?"

"I forgot, I used to know, but . . ."

"Shut up! *Red!* Get over here, sister. Your lucky day. And make it quick."

The manager bursts into the lobby through a windowed kitchen door.

"Do you know CPR?"

"I do not."

"Watch me. I'm going to show you *once.*

306

I'm going to explain what I'm doing. Then you're going to take over. If you make a move on me while I'm breathing for this guy — like if you try to get this mask off or the gun? I'll come off him and shoot you. Got it?"

"Yes, ma'am."

"Watch and learn, Red."

I put Cañonita in my left hand, hook my right thumb deep over the old man's tongue and lift his head back to open the trachea. I explain this to Red, who is nodding quickly. Then I get Cañonita in a funny grip so I can use my left hand to pinch Mr. Geezer's nose shut. With my mouth I cover my thumb and his mouth and give him a nice, slow, even exhale. I taste my breath going into a small cavern that smells mildly of meat. I feel my breath come to the end of the cavern, like blowing up a balloon. I look up sideways to see Red nodding even faster. I count to four and breathe for him again. Red practically elbows me away so she can get in and try it. So I swing around and straddle the guy and join my hands over his firm but oddly thin and light chest. It feels like he's made of aluminum, like an office blind or a soda can. Down-up. Down-up. Down-up.

"Count seconds, Red. Every other second you press in. *One,* two, *three,* four — all the way to twenty. Got it? It'll keep his heart going or maybe even start it back up."

"Push on every other count."

"Then ventilate him, like I just did. Some of the new protocols say to skip this part, but I wouldn't. Look at this guy. *It's four breaths, twenty pushes. Four breaths, twenty pushes.* The damned experts change the ratio every year or so just to confuse people like us. But this can work. Good luck."

"Yes," she says, then grabs Mr. Geezer's nose and swoops down to get him in a mouth lock.

I jump up, swing Cañonita in a semicircle and make sure the parking lot isn't crawling with innocent bystanders or cops.

And if it were, what choice would I have but to run out through them? I feel as if I've been breathing for that old guy for hours, like the whole world has had time to get here and get their cameras ready and their guns drawn and wait for me to walk into the shitstorm. I feel like I'm never going to make it to those swinging doors. I step in that direction. The teenagers part.

I'm too rattled to even hand out my business cards.

But miracle is in the air tonight. The GTO beckons from the other side of the hedge like a burning bush.

Four hundred horses.

And the lot is empty of pedestrians, just a minivan looking for a place to park.

I'm almost to the door when Mr. Geezer coughs and sputters. Red looks at me with pugnacious wonder. Mrs. Geezer throws tears as she silently kneels over her husband with her hands folded under her chin like for a prayer.

Too bad nobody has a camera to show me saving the old man's life on TV — fame to go with my infamy.

I walk out, palm the gun and shorten my stride. I take a deep breath. Mask off. Head high, back straight, eyes alert.

I know I look right.

I'm a just a hungry consumer with a hard-earned bag of burgers and fries. Maybe even a family to feed. Nobody can stop me.

I can't even stop myself.

I have just enough time to secure my tools in the adjoining room, shower and change before Hood arrives. Short dress. Of course I brush my teeth.

When he comes through the door I swarm him.

A thick bunch of roses and a bagged bottle of something drop to the floor and I pull him through them toward the bed. I hear the crunch of the stems on carpet and the rattle of the paper bag. Hey, I can drink wine or smell a flower anytime but right now I got Charlie Hood where I want him and no conventional weapon can keep me off him.

It doesn't last long but after it I'm starved so I take him to dinner in the GTO.

"Nice car."

"I have nice friends," I say. "I choose them on the basis of the cars they can lend me."

"This have the three-fifty horse?"

"It's the six-liter, Charles — a full four hundred. Sick torque, and I love that it looks like something my grandmother would drive. No wonder they quit making it."

"Where's the Corvette?"

"In for service."

He's looking at me with an expression I've never seen on him before. Like he's discovered something and locked it up for safekeeping. Up until now I made Hood nervous or least uncertain but now I wonder if my mother might have got him thinking about my unorthodox girlhood and or that I shot Bradley's father or that I've had more boyfriends than Hood has had dates.

Or maybe he changed his mind about me and the diamonds.

Or . . . Allison?

I pick a Persian restaurant on Sunset with

private rooms where we can sit on beautiful pillows and eat spicy food and I can touch him. Hood seems gently befuddled by his surroundings and I wonder if it has to do with his time in Iraq. Or, again, if it has to do with me.

"You're quiet," I say. "Remind you of the war?"

"Just the way the people look."

"I want you to tell me about it someday."

"I will."

"Tonight?"

"Not tonight," says Hood. "Have a glass of wine."

"I told you I don't drink, Deputy."

"Maybe you should."

"Like having a cigarette before they shoot you?"

He looks at me then with genuine amusement. I like a guy who can enjoy your joke without having to make a better one. I like a guy whose ears turn red once in a while. Most of all I like a guy who's got the kind of Man Thing that you can't fight or ruin or dissolve or avoid — this big blocky clunky Man Thing right in the middle of him. The Man Thing is a nuisance, I'll admit, and early on I learned every trick in the book for eliminating it. Mom taught me some of them. Grandma some. Girls just learn most of them on their own. The deal is, some men will let you take the Man Thing and dispose of it. They actually think that's what women want. I've got no time for men like that anymore. Because the Man Thing is half of what makes the time shared by a man and a woman interesting. It's like this dirt track we had out in the Bakersfield desert when I was a kid. It was a little oval and we'd race our bikes around it as fast as we could. It was flat and smooth and level and you could haul ass. But there was one hairy thing about it — a big sharp rock lodged right in the middle of the far turn. It stuck up, pointing back, like a big dull fishhook looking to stab you. We had some bad wipeouts trying to miss that rock. We didn't always miss. There were stitches and broken bones. Terry Lilley knocked out his front teeth on it. I picked them out of the dirt but they couldn't fasten them back on. So one day we got together like intelligent human beings and dug the thing out and rolled it off the course. We filled the hole and packed the dirt down hard and rode around that track for a few hours. We made some good time. Very fast. Very smooth. And very boring. So we dug the hole and rolled the rock back into place and buried it just like it was. That's what the Man Thing does — it makes the race dangerous and difficult and worth running.

And Hood's got it loud and clear, even in his smile.

"You don't have to get shot to enjoy a cigarette once in a while," he says. "The wine makes you peaceful and the smoke makes you calm."

"But I don't want peace or calm."

"What do you want?"

"I can explain by conducting a Socratic dialogue, as I sometimes do with my brighter students."

"I'll try."

"Rather drive a Rolls Silver Shadow or turbocharged Porsche nine-eleven Carrera?"

"Carrera, for sure."

"El Do or GTO?"

"I'd go Goat."

"Escalade or Mustang GT?"

"Well, the 'Stang, no contest."

"Me too. See, Hood, it's just human nature to want to go fast. And feel it. *Feel it.* That's what I want."

I get up real close to his ear with my mouth, just like that first Sunday he came to my house. I like it here. Now I just have to whisper: "I mean, Charlie, what if a doctor could give you a pill that would give you ten back-to-back o's but you couldn't feel each one of them separate and distinct?"

Hood actually thinks about this one. Just the trace of a frown passes over his brow. Even if he's just acting dumb I still love it.

"What's an orgasm if you don't feel it?" he finally says.

"That's what I'm trying to explain, you Bakersfield hick."

"You value your hot spots, Suzanne."

"I know I do. And I know this, too, Hood — I won't be young very long. I'll use 'em while they're usable."

Mr. and Mrs. Geezer come to mind right then. I see Hood and me fifty years from now as Mr. and Mrs. Geezer and I know that's supposed to warm my heart but it just plain doesn't.

"You're pretty much everything my mom told me to stay away from," says Hood.

"That's nice to hear. The old bag ever let you have any fun?"

Hood smiles again, nodding, eyes bright and not quite reckless. I kiss him with feeling and when the waiter comes through the ornate curtain into our little nest I tell him to beat it. He smiles and bows and pulls the curtain tight.

Then it's just a small underwear adjustment and a pull of zipper and I'm riding Hood right there in the pillows. He looks straight into my face. Soon comes a point when my heart is pounding so loud I can't hear much else and Hood's usually sharp brown eyes glaze over, and I'm welded to this guy.

When he finally manages to stand and put himself back together, he turns away so I won't see. Imagine. His hair sticks up on one side. He excuses himself to the men's room. His wallet has fallen out and is half-hidden under a lush satin pillow so I look it over, finger the bills — eighty-two bucks. I take out two of the twenties, rub them together, then stuff them back. I don't know what's wrong with me. I set the wallet at his place on the low table.

A few minutes later Charlie is back with his hair wetted down like Jordan does his before school. Charlie looks proud of himself, like he just got away with something, which he did.

"My wallet," he says.

"Better count the cash."

He sits down and a while later we have a dessert made of dates and cream. Most excellent.

Hood has another glass of wine and we don't say much.

I look at him and he sees I'd like to do it again but he shakes his head *no* with a toothy smile and raises his fingers in a cross like I'm a vampire or something.

I drive him up Sunset fast in the GTO and blast up into the Hollywood Hills to this turnout I know.

We park and sit in the car just like real lovers, looking down on the city lights with the windows down and the breeze bringing us the smells of the arid hills but not so strong that they interfere with the new car smell, the finest fragrance on earth in my opinion.

I hold Hood's hand and rest my head on his shoulder.

27

Hood sat on the safe house couch and loaded a new disc into the recorder. He made sure the time and date were right. Wyte's aluminum-cased laptop sat on the coffee table before him. Out on the deck Marlon was setting up the tripod. Suzanne stood with her back to Marlon, taking in the afternoon view of Marina del Rey through the shaggy-headed palms.

Hood could hear their voices through the screen door:

So this is what a safe house looks like.

Safe apartment is all.

What makes a safe house safe?

Only the good guys get in.

Bora Bora Way. Fifth floor. Sunset views. Nice.

We try. You bring the sunglasses?

All I own. Three pair.

Turn around.

Hood watched Suzanne stand at attention

before Marlon as he adjusted the glasses like she was a star and he was a director who wanted everything just right. They stood face-to-face, and the breeze blew brown strands of her hair into his face, and they both smiled. Then Marlon positioned her facing the Pacific again and stood back beside the tripod and studied her for a moment.

Try another pair.

I've got my Jackie O's.

Hood watched her trade out the first pair of sunglasses for her Jackie O's. They were big and curvaceous and dark and Hood figured they'd be perfect for Lupercio.

I don't get why all the sunglasses. Something tells me it's not about the way I look.

It's about the message you send.

She cocked her head and looked at Marlon. Then she turned just enough to see the palms and the beach and the whitecapped ocean beyond them. She turned further and looked through the sliding glass door to Hood.

The reflection. He'll see all this in my glasses.

But we want you to look good, too. The Jackie O's are perfect.

Hood took the camera out onto the deck.

Ten takes later they had it right. Suzanne

reassured her friends and family and colleagues that she was fine, she was safe, and this would all be over soon. She told everybody not to worry.

Hood and Marlon listened from the curtained kitchen so as not to be caught on the video. Later, watching the various takes on disc, Hood could see the apartment complex and the palms and the beach and the ocean reflected in the dark lenses.

"It's Marina del Rey, all right," said Suzanne. "It's these apartments. It can't be anyplace else."

"Not if you know L.A. like Lupercio does," said Marlon.

"And Valley Center, Torrance and Bakersfield," said Suzanne.

She looked at Hood, then at Wyte's computer, then back at Hood with an odd expression. Hood wondered if the laptop looked as orphaned to her as it now did to him. If so, it might be dawning on her where its owner was, which was downstairs working on her car.

"We appreciate this," said Marlon. He ran his comb through his shiny black hair. It was a rockabilly do and Hood knew that Marlon was proud of it and wanted Suzanne to notice.

"I appreciate it, too. Thank you. Well, gotta go."

They shook hands, and Hood walked Suzanne to the elevator then out to her Sentra.

"Where's the Goat?"

"Resting."

"Give it back to your friend?"

"Don't try to figure where I've been, Charlie."

Which is exactly what Hood was doing, going back to the night before. He figured she'd boosted the Goat for the BK job but as yet it hadn't made the hot list. Sometimes, if the car's owner was out of town, a stolen car went unreported for days or weeks. Long-term airport parking lots were popular places to make a grab that wouldn't immediately hit the hot list. But he'd looked hard at the ignition when Suzanne wasn't aware and it looked new to Hood, factory. And if she pulled the door lock with a slide-hammer, then she'd either gotten lucky and been able to work the assembly back in or she'd replaced it.

"Guess I don't have to tell you to keep moving," said Hood.

"No. *Vaya con Dios,* Hood."

"You, too."

"Always."

Back upstairs Wyte was on the couch tapping the keypad of his laptop. A man that Hood had never met sat at the dinette table, two more laptop computers open before him and a box of discs off to one side. He was slender, silver-haired and tanned. Hood recognized him from headquarters — a surveillance specialist. Marlon sat across from the specialist, watching playbacks of Suzanne on the camera viewfinder.

Wyte introduced Hood to Bruce Lister from tech services. "Bruce and I got the tracker on the Sentra while Jones did her video."

"Take eight's the best," said Marlon.

"Check this out, gentlemen," said Wyte.

He set his laptop on the coffee table. Hood and Marlon sat on either side of him and leaned toward the screen, which displayed a map section of Marina del Rey. A blinking red indicator light moved northbound on Via Marina. The light advanced and the map quadrant slowly scrolled down in accordance with the speed of Suzanne Jones's Sentra.

"Solid," said Marlon.

Lister nodded but didn't look up from the discs and laptops before him.

They watched the Sentra head toward the 405 Freeway. Hood found something mesmerizing in this, something covert and omnipotent.

Lister brought over the two laptops and set them up on the coffee table, one for Hood and one for Marlon. The same map of Marina del Rey scrolled slowly south as the Sentra moved north on the freeway.

"Just follow the IBEX icon on the desktop, it'll take you to the real-time feed. Wherever the car is, you'll know. The GPU can get you an exact location and you can turn the location into a nearest address with the FIND tab under options. You won't even lose the map if you minimize. It's simple enough for a five-year-old."

The men continued to watch.

Wyte gathered up his custom machine, hit the keypad and waited, then tapped again.

"More goodies," he said.

He set the laptop on the coffee table and swiveled it out for all to view. On the screen were split images of Allison Murrieta talking about Joaquin, and Suzanne Jones talking to friends and acquaintances.

"Naw, Charlie," said Marlon. "No matter what you and her mom says, different women."

"Funny," said Wyte. "In the flesh Jones doesn't look a lot like Murrieta, but you get her on video, squeeze them both onto a screen and you can see the resemblance."

"Exactly the problem," said Marlon. "With a small screen you're creating parallels that aren't there."

"It's her," said Hood. "The sunglasses help. They hide part of what the mask hides."

"I thought that, too," said Wyte. "The less you see of Jones's face the more it looks like the *bandita.* There's enough resemblance to bring her in, put some questions to her."

Marlon shrugged. "Sure, bring in the man in the moon, too."

"Lister, what do you think?" asked Wyte.

Lister wrapped a USB cable around his hand as he looked at the screen. "Your call. But either way, thanks to that locator you can find Jones whenever you want."

Hood remembered how many cars Allison Murrieta had allegedly stolen — Patmore had it at twenty-two — and doubted if she'd transfer the locator with each newly stolen car so they could keep up with her. No, it was sayonara to the transponder the next time Allison jacked a ride.

Lister set the cable in his briefcase, clicked it shut and with a curt wave walked out of the apartment.

Wyte sat back and watched the screen. "If we bring her in and can't crack her, she'll walk. We don't have prints, we don't have

DNA, we don't have a witness except her own mother and Hood here."

"Not exactly," said Hood. He told them about Suzanne calling herself Allison in talking to Ronette West about Barry Cohen's diamonds. And about the faceless phone-only Allison who had followed Ronette's lead back to Melissa and learned everything she could about Barry's payoff. Then delivered ten grand in cash to Melissa a few days after Miracle Auto Body. He felt that he was betraying Suzanne but he couldn't let her break the law and get herself killed.

"You think Jones is Allison *and* she has the diamonds?" asked Marlon.

"Yes."

Marlon laughed. "Some history teacher, Charlie."

Hood nodded.

"Look, you did some pretty good detective work, Hood, but what you got is a rope made out of smoke."

Hood said nothing, looked at Wyte.

"Really?" asked Wyte quietly. "I think Charlie has come up with more than smoke."

"Can't you just unscramble the voice on Boyer's video?" asked Marlon. "Or maybe scramble Jones's voice the same way as Allison's, and see if they match? Then we'll know for sure. No more moms and coke-heads and pissed-off girlfriends and maybe it is, maybe it isn't. If you can't convince me — the homicide sergeant — how are you going to convince a DA or a jury?"

"I'm working on the voices," said Wyte. "There's dozens of scramblers she could have used. Some of them you can buy for six bucks in toy stores. Some of them render a human voice one hundred percent unrecognizable, by any means."

"Well, if Jones is Murrieta then we got the transponder on her car," said Marlon. "We can catch her right in the middle of one of her stickups."

"A good way to get someone shot," said Wyte.

"Then let her pull the job," said Marlon. "We'll have helicopters in the air and we'll spike-strip her car."

Wyte seemed to ignore Marlon. But he gave Hood a long look. "You sleeping with her?"

"No, sir."

Now Marlon stared at Hood. "What? You're not, are you, Charlie?"

"I just said I wasn't, sir. I can say it again."

Marlon looked hard at Wyte. "Where'd that come from?"

Wyte shrugged and very small smile lines ringed his mouth. "Sorry, Charlie. Things get into the air. Must have been just me."

"*You're* fucking her?" asked Marlon.

Hood didn't laugh with the other two men, and he stayed seated though he knew he was giving off bad heat. Lying about Suzanne Jones felt something like not filing charges against Lenny Overbrook but in Hamdaniya he had been covering a fellow soldier's ass and now he was just covering his own.

"None of us is fucking her but Lupercio's trying to kill her," Hood said quietly.

"After we've got him in custody we can figure Suzanne and Allison Murrieta," said Wyte. "We'll have a little time to get it right. Some wiggle room — I like that."

"I do too," said Marlon. "Just a laugh, Charlie. Lighten up. We'll stop this guy."

28

Lupercio watched the scenery in the lenses of Suzanne Jones's sunglasses. She was part of the evening news that was now playing on a large screen behind the Bull. The picture was vibrant and clear and Suzanne Jones's face was almost as tall as Lupercio's entire body.

"Marina del Rey," said Lupercio. "One place I know not to look."

"Exactly," said the Bull. "She won't be hard to keep track of now."

"Why not?"

The Bull shrugged.

Lupercio was used to having his questions dismissed by the Bull but this gesture seemed particularly brief and disrespectful. After much thought, Lupercio had decided that the Bull had once been a law enforcer, perhaps still was. Little else could explain his arrogance and his abundant information. That the man was also a successful criminal set off no alarms in Lupercio — witness to the disappeared, finder of loved ones' bodies in the human piles of Puerta del Diablo, brother and son of El Salvador, the Savior.

The Bull sat above Lupercio as usual, surrounded by his aluminum-cased computers and peripherals, the low-voltage bulbs overhead throwing shadows down his face. He rolled his chair across the dais, casters echoing lightly upon the wood. He tapped at a keyboard.

Lupercio turned, and through the windows of the big office he could see the Port of Long Beach, its legions of trucks and trailers tending the immense walls of stacked containers. The sun was still high and the harbor was silver and the great cranes cast black reflections on the water.

"Watch," said the Bull.

Lupercio turned back and watched the big TV screen split. On the right side of the screen Suzanne Jones's face froze in all its oversized beauty. On the left side appeared another face of equal size and similar shape. This one had straight black hair and wore a jeweled mask.

"Allison Murrieta," said Lupercio. He enjoyed her exploits and liked it that she gave some of her money to the poor. She had saved the life of an old man. Lupercio's wife and daughters were much more interested in Allison stories than in the "reality" shows they watched. Lupercio hoped that the cameras would be there when she died in a hail of bullets.

"What do you see?" asked the Bull.

"What can anyone see behind a mask?"

"Are they the same woman?"

"I don't know. That is why she wears it."

"Are they the same woman?"

Now Lupercio shrugged. There was too much in the world that went unseen to speculate on what was not even visible.

"A mask can hide many faces."

"This only hides one."

"Jones has the diamonds unless she sold them," said Lupercio. "If Allison Murrieta also has them, it is not my concern."

The Bull stared down at him. "I admire your economy of thought."

"Yes."

The Bull still stared down at him. "Are you feeling pressure, Lupercio? Because of the attention in the news, your pictures being shown on television, the various law enforcement agencies all focused directly on you, the reward money?"

"I do what I must do to remain unseen."

The Bull smiled. "You cut your hair."

Lupercio nodded.

"I find it very entertaining," said the Bull, "that here in the twenty-first century, some of our deadliest enemies hide from us in caves. And that here, in this huge city, with all of our manpower and technology, all of our vast and fast lines of communication, our most wanted man simply cuts his hair to remain invisible. And our most wanted woman wears a simple mask. And for a time, it works."

"Few see."

"True. But then where did they get the drawing of you they showed on TV? Someone not only saw you, but observed you closely. Right down to the hair you had to cut."

"Her son. The shirt in the drawing I have worn only one time."

"Why did you let the boy see you?"

"He was my opportunity to search for the diamonds."

Lupercio wondered if the Bull had been a federal enforcer or a Sheriff's deputy or a municipal policeman, or perhaps an insurance investigator.

"Will he live?" asked the Bull.

"He chose his path the moment he talked to me."

"You are an unforgiving thing, Lupercio."

"I'm simple and true."

"He's a boy."

The Bull turned and looked at the big screen behind him, which still contained the split-screen images of the women.

"Where is she?" asked Lupercio. "I want to finish this work."

"I want you to finish it, too."

The Bull rolled over to one of his computers and guided the mouse. He consulted his laptop. The light from the monitors shifted on his face. A moment later he leaned back and crossed his thick arms over his thick chest.

"She's in Lake Arrowhead, at the Gray Fox Cabins. She's driving a white Sentra."

The Bull gave Lupercio the address and the license plate numbers.

"How many police are with her?"

"The police are in Marina del Rey."

"If you know where she is, then they must know where she is."

The Bull smiled and entered something on a keypad. "No. I've got a little helper. I control it. If I want, it talks only to me and gives static to everyone else."

A little helper, thought Lupercio. The Bull has many little helpers. A criminal policeman with many helpers, such as myself.

"She might have a friend with her," said the Bull.

A sheet of paper emerged from a printer and he plucked it out and looked at it. He set it on the edge of the big desk, and Lupercio stood on his toes in order to reach it.

"The deputy from Miracle Auto Body," said Lupercio.

"His name is Hood."

"Was that him in Bakersfield? Someone came across the desert when he heard the shots."

"Yes."

"He's young."

"I want my diamonds, Lupercio. I want them tonight."

Lupercio was coming up the mountain at nine P.M., his Lincoln Continental swaying comfortably through the winding curves. Once in a while a switchback would carry him out into the night and he could look down at the vast ocean of lights south of L.A. The lights were dimmed by the dirty air of the basin below but up here above the cities the air was cool and clean. His car was still scratched and dented from plowing through the chain-link fence after Suzanne Jones, but Lupercio had had time to wash the desert sand of Bakersfield off it.

He wondered if he should make Suzanne Jones tell him if she was Allison Murrieta or not before he took the diamonds and killed her. He failed to see the importance of who Allison Murrieta really was, even though it seemed unlikely that she could be the great-great-great-great-great-great-granddaughter of an outlaw from long ago who might not have ever existed. In fact he'd wondered at first if Allison wasn't just a made-up character, part of a new kind of show made to entertain Americans, in which a character is introduced to audiences on the news as if she were real, then gets her own time slot if she's popular enough. He wondered what it would be like to have his own show, *The Lupercio Maygar Show,* or just *Lupercio.*

He parked a quarter mile away from the Gray Fox Cabins and got out. He hooked the curve of the pry bar over his left shoulder then pulled on his oversized brown sport coat, arranged the machete scabbard to be almost invisible beneath it and buttoned it. He set the black felt cowboy hat on his head, hooked his thumbs into his belt and headed down the dark road toward the cabins.

An SUV swept past him, headed for town. Then a minivan, then a pickup truck. Their side mirrors sent breezes against Lupercio's face, and he noted how close most drivers were willing to get to him, how little reality a small brown man possessed in the world of *norteamericanos*. It was like being disappeared but you were still here.

The Gray Fox Cabins came into view as he walked over a gentle rise in the road. The office was a large log structure, two stories, and atop the peaked tin roof sat a large sign cut out in the shape of a fox, outlined in a string of blinking red, white and blue lights. The fox wore a blue officer's jacket and red fez and was up on his hind legs, dancing. The paint was faded. Beyond the office lay the cabins.

Lupercio walked past. There were two rows of five cabins facing one another across a small patch of trees. The forest grew up behind them. Each unit had a car parked in front. The lights around the fox reflected weakly on the Sentra and advanced slowly across it as Lupercio walked by. He saw the light on in the cabin with the Sentra parked in front, though the shades were drawn. It was the end unit of the uphill row.

Lupercio walked two hundred feet down the road then crouched and trotted into the forest. The trees were fragrant and widely spaced, and he had no trouble navigating his way back to the Gray Fox. The red, white and blue lights winked silently. Lupercio lowered his boots evenly and slowly, and when he came up behind Jones's cabin, he stood still and stared at the faint orange glow of the drawn shade. The units all had back doors. He heard voices and music and laughter coming from the cabins.

An hour later, still within the trees, he had not moved except to breathe and not once had anyone passed behind the drawn shade of the back window. The music and laughter had ended.

Lupercio shrugged the pry bar off his shoulder and into his hand then crept lightly to the door. He stepped onto the small concrete landing. A thin line of interior light issued around the door, and Lupercio could see where the line was interrupted by the lock. He hefted the pry bar up and gently worked the tip into the space where the lock was. Then he pushed on it with all of his strength, and the steel lock ripped through the soft old pine of the frame and the door wobbled open.

Lupercio was inside in an instant, his machete held up over his right shoulder in a two-handed grip.

The little dining area where he had entered was clear. He was aware of the empty bathroom as he passed it. On his right was a bedroom with its door open and no one in it.

But ahead of him up the hallway the front bedroom door was closed and the light inside was off, and he knew this was where she would be, so he flung open the door and jumped inside. In the dim light from the hallway Lupercio saw the woman sleeping in the bed, covers turned up against the mountain chill. Then he saw the blade of his machete disappear into the pillow and the severed head jump into the air and land on the floor.

After the flash of white that should have been bone Lupercio saw the foam head rocking to a stop on the cabin floor and the wig caught by his blade in the deep gash in the pillow. He buried the machete in the head, the two halves skittering across the knotty pine floor.

Voices now rose from the unit next door, and he thought he saw movement through the window facing the office.

He saw the index card propped against the lamp on the nightstand.

"I trusted you" was written in a graceful feminine cursive script across it.

Beside it lay some kind of electronic emitter or transponder, likely a vehicle locator.

Lupercio ran back into the forest.

29

Hood knelt beside the bed in Suzanne's cabin and photographed the transponder with his cell phone.

He was bewildered by Lupercio's supernatural ability to find Suzanne Jones, but he knew the explanation would be simpler than ESP. There was an odd-looking line of solder on the transponder housing, just below the manufacturer's etched logo — Assured Surveillance.

A San Bernardino County Sheriff's detective worked beside him, videotaping the note on the bed stand, the transponder, the wig, the two neatly cleaved halves of the Styrofoam wig stand and the deep, fresh cut in the old wood floor. His name was Pettigrew. Outside a team of investigators waited for the sun to rise.

Pettigrew turned off the recorder and let it hang at his side.

"So this woman is the witness against the

badass Salvadoran everybody's looking for."

"Lupercio Maygar."

"Animal."

"He's more than that."

"She's a schoolteacher, right?"

"Yes, eighth grade."

"Was that locator on the car out front?"

Hood nodded but said nothing.

"Even with that TV press conference, I still don't understand how she got mixed up with him," said Pettigrew. "A schoolteacher and a killer. They have a history?"

"Not that we know."

Pettigrew shook his head doubtfully. "I don't see how you do it, day in and day out. I hate going down the hill now. You hit that brown stuff they call air, you just know nothing good can happen."

Hood said nothing. Lupercio's black art had left no room in his mind for Pettigrew's fearful opinions.

"I was L.A. Sheriff's for eight years," said Pettigrew. "Mostly East Los Angeles Station. So I know what I'm talking about."

A few minutes later Hood went down the hallway and looked at the splintered door. Lupercio had used a pry bar. Hood could see where the blade had forced the steel lock assembly through the door frame. By the punky look of the wood, it seemed it wouldn't have taken great force.

For a moment he stood behind the cabin and watched the sunlit morning vapor drift through the branches of the pine trees. He called Suzanne's cell number again, but she was, as usual, unavailable.

Then he called Assured Surveillance in Worcester, Massachusetts, and talked to an engineer named Schlinger. Schlinger couldn't explain the solder line on the AS-210, but he was happy to look at the pictures and gave Hood an e-mail address. Schlinger would call back.

Hood stood outside the cabin in the cool dawn as the pictures raced across the continent. Blue jays flitted in the upper branches of a jack pine and Hood could see Pettigrew's flash unit popping light against the cabin windows.

Five minutes later Schlinger was back.

"It's been modified," he said. "We don't ship them that way."

"Modified to do what?"

"Open it. Send more pictures. You'll need a small cross-tip."

Hood got Pettigrew to dust the transponder but not a single latent came through. Using a screwdriver from the trunk of the Camaro, he opened the housing. The short screws unseated quickly and he set aside the lid.

Hood looked down at the tightly packed microelectronics, which meant little to him. He shot them with his phone camera and sent them through to Massachusetts.

Another five minutes and Schlinger called again.

"It's been reworked," he said. "Cleverly. It's got a signal splitter with a digital arm switch. That switch can be thrown on and off by remote by an operator who knows the frequency."

"By whoever added the splitter."

"Correct."

"So, two signals," said Hood. "I can turn yours off and leave mine on. You get nothing and I get signal."

"Right. You should report this to your superiors."

Hood thanked him and rang off.

My superiors.

He thought of how Lupercio had shown up at Suzanne's home in Valley Center, at the Residence Inn in Torrance, at Madeline's home in Bakersfield. How could he do that? Because he's clairvoyant or because he was tipped? Who knew that these were the places where Suzanne would likely be?

Hood did. Marlon. Wyte almost certainly.

Marlon or Wyte, running Lupercio? Delivering Suzanne to the killing floor for a handful of diamonds?

But no one had known that she'd drive up to the Gray Fox Cabins in Lake Arrowhead.

So someone tracked her electronically. Someone who could kill one signal coming from her car and pick up another frequency.

And guide Lupercio here.

My superiors, Hood thought, who approved and arranged for the transponder on Suzanne's car.

Hood began to feel the same sense of unreality that he had felt in Anbar, the sense of entering a world that only outwardly resembled the one he knew. After the murders of Jackson and Ruiz his soul had felt like an open wound that he wanted to hide, but now the wound had grown large enough to be seen on his face and heard in his voice. He could feel the new sunshine on it.

He thought about last night, ordering the flow of events, trying to see if there was a flaw in his logic, something that could blow away his suspicions with cold, bright truth: at six o'clock the evening before, the Sentra had been in Oceanside, not moving, apparently content. He'd kept thinking about Suzanne. He thought about her resuscitating the old man at the Burger King. The news media had really run with it. *Armed robber Allison Murrieta turns lifesaver.* His Silver Lake apartment windows were open and his music was down low, and the darkness outside seemed lazy and open so he sat awhile on his deck with the laptop balanced on his thigh. Hood liked the simple things about his tiny portion of L.A. — the soft nights, the sounds of car engines on the boulevards, the sweetness of the roses in the beds by his complex swimming pool, the inviting smell that slowed him as he walked by the laundry room.

Then, at eight o'clock, in the middle of his takeout Mexican dinner, the Sentra had begun moving north on PCH in Oceanside. Hood had watched it as he ate his rice. A few minutes later the locator light on the GPU map went dead. Marlon called him immediately to see if Hood's was still working. Wyte called a minute later to say his was down, too, and that he'd already talked to Lister. Lister called a few minutes after that to say that vehicle transponders were prone to interruption by magnets, heat, cold, moisture and vibration, but Hood thought it was odd that this one had worked so well then failed so completely. Lister said he was doing what he could, and that there was a chance that Suzanne had found the transponder and destroyed it. Hood noted that when the signal went dead the Sentra had been eastbound on Highway 76 from Oceanside, where Suzanne had no doubt been with her children, dogs and boyfriend.

All they could do was wait. Wyte said he'd stay on Lister. Marlon, who sounded pleasantly drunk, said he'd deal with it in the morning.

Hood had finished his dinner and sat on the couch with the laptop beside him and his head bobbing back against the wall every few minutes, which would wake him up for a look at the GPU map screen. But the locator never reappeared.

Suzanne called just before midnight and cursed Hood violently. She told him she'd found the transponder, driven to Arrowhead to arrange a little surprise for clever Hood and the assholes he worked for but it was Lupercio who'd tracked her to the cabin. Lupercio! From a motel room across the street she'd watched through binoculars as he drove by, then a few minutes later walked by, passed the cabin and slunk into the trees. Hours later there was some commotion and she saw the manager hustle across to her cabin. Hood got the name of the cabins from Suzanne before she cursed him again and hung up.

Fuck you, Charlie. What kind of an idiot do you think I am?

Hood went back inside the cabin, thinking: Marlon or Wyte?

Marlon was uncomplicated and Wyte was smart.

Marlon liked Suzanne and Wyte had never met her.

Marlon was strong and Wyte was injured.

Marlon was a family man and Wyte was a widower.

Marlon had others to provide for and Wyte was alone.

Lister? Hood didn't know the first goddamned thing about Lister. There was little likelihood that Lister had even heard of Suzanne Jones before the Valley Center massacre, or had known that Hood was going to conduct an interview in Bakersfield. So Hood took him off the list.

He tried to decide which man was more likely to jettison the law, abandon his morals and deliver a woman to be murdered for diamonds and silence. Maybe Marlon and Wyte were in it together.

But Suzanne Jones could blame no one but him.

Fuck you, Charlie.

The uniform with the camera came inside and started shooting interiors. Through the window Hood saw a deputy squatting and running a finger through the pine needles.

Detective Pettigrew set the video camera on the bed. "The schoolteacher is a brave lady. Maybe foolish. That could have been her head instead of a wig stand."

Hood nodded. He wondered again if Suzanne and Lupercio had pulled the Miracle Auto Body job together and gotten crosswise after. He didn't think so, but until a few minutes ago there were other things he hadn't thought either, and now they wouldn't leave him alone.

"Shit like this is why I don't come down the mountain. You can have your animals, your whackos. When you've seen enough of them down there, you'll find a way out of L.A."

"I like L.A."

"You're young. You'll either figure it out or you won't."

30

"I apologize, Suzie," says Angel.

"I'm a big girl."

"It's necessary."

He hands me the black sack and I put it over my head. Immediately I feel myself becoming Allison. A blind Allison. Of course the hood makes me think of Hood.

"It's okay, Angel," I tell him. My breath is hot under the heavy fabric. Solid black. I can't even see a twinkle of oncoming headlights. "I know how these VIPs can be."

"It's necessary for both of you."

"I said it was okay."

"Please tie the strings behind your head."

Last I saw we were in Angel's Tundra pickup truck, the loaded one with the big V-8, headed south on Interstate 5. Now blinded, I can still feel him pulling over to the right lane, which puts us in place to pick up the 710 south toward Long Beach. But for the life of me I can't tell if we've merged south or not. I hate this blindness.

So here's the deal: Angel talked to the smartest, toughest-to-get fence in L.A. and told him about his friend Laura and my parcel of beautifully cut gem-quality diamonds. Angel has worked with him twice before and he says this man is dependable and professional. He is interested. He is not known for paying high but he understands quality. His name is Guy. Angel says he's a man who will "buy and sell anything," but I can't tell if Angel is speaking with respect or denigration.

Guy's five conditions for meeting me were: I am to arrive in the company of Angel and only Angel; I will be hooded for the last half hour of the journey to the meeting place and for the first half hour of my journey from it; I can bring no cameras of any kind, especially a cell phone camera; I will be checked for recording equipment; and I will not be allowed to be out of sight of Guy or one of his associates, including trips to the bathroom.

I asked Angel if I could arrive with a .40-caliber derringer in my purse and he said that Guy would have no problem with that, though I might want to declare it before the pat-down.

It's almost midnight now, Friday, two nights after Lupercio used a LASD transponder signal to track me to the Gray Fox Cabins in Arrowhead. I can't begin to explain how Hood's betrayal and/or stupidity broke my heart. My mother used to describe my heart as "that little wooden thing in your chest," but wooden or not it broke when I saw that device stuck to the chassis of my Sentra.

The first thing I did when I got away from my video session in Marina del Rey was pull over and check for homers. I was surprised to be treated as if I were stupid. I guess Hood had one of his buddies attach it while I was upstairs in the safe house trying on sunglasses. Safe. Right. Safe for whom?

I haven't talked to Hood since except to cuss him out from Arrowhead. I'm afraid to call him because I'm afraid he'll act dumb. It infuriates me when people act dumb. The best explanation Hood can give me is that he is not in league with murderers, but his bosses are. And all that really says is that Hood is incompetent and his superiors are without souls. So piss on all the brutes. You bet I know *Heart of Darkness.* I read it when I was fifteen at continuation school, working nights at Taco Bell and pregnant with Bradley. I was rereading it a few months later because I didn't quite get what he was saying about race and power the first time.

It was on my bed stand the night I shot Bradley's father through the butt cheeks with the twenty-two. Some blood mist got on the cover and by the time I got around to wiping it off it had dried and stuck. I don't think any of that was symbolic but I've never forgotten it.

So I slide down low and lay my head back against the seat and bump along in Angel's Tundra — nice truck, Toyota does a good job on the suspension, which is firm but nimble, and the lumbar support is just right though I can't enjoy it slumped down like this — wondering if we've gotten onto the 710. But the hood is truly blinding so I finally just give up and try to breathe slow and shallow because it's hot in here, even though I sense Angel, always the gentleman, adjusting the AC vents to blow directly at me. Slowly, going by feel, I move my GPU from the right-side waistband of my jeans — hidden by my loose blouse — to the seat.

"You could have made me happy, Angel."

"I was too old and saggy and temperamental."

"True."

"But I would love to be young again, with you," he said.

"That's what you say to all your hotties."

"It won't be too much longer, Suzie. Be

comfortable. You didn't bring something unnecessary like a cell phone with a camera?"

"Of course not."

"And the derringer in the purse?"

"It's in there. You *said* —"

"It's okay. It's okay. I'll make sure Guy knows."

"I hate people who think they're important."

"His privacy is our privacy. It benefits all of us."

"I really don't like this hood, Angel. I'm claustrophobic. It makes me feel trapped and I hate that even more than people who think they're important."

"It won't be long."

"I'm going to recline the seat and meditate," I say. What I do is recline the seat and dangle my GPU down between the door and the seat, then drop it. "Put on the news, would you?"

"Of course."

"What do you think of that Murrieta chick?" I ask.

"She saved an old man's life, so I admire her. The police will kill her, though. It's unavoidable."

I'm sitting on a leather sofa. It's soft and

smells good. When Angel lifts the hood from my head I look up at a beefy middle-aged man sitting on a dais above me. He looks like a cop even though I know he's Guy, the fence, the man who will "buy and sell anything." There's a very long desk in front of him and the desk is littered with computers, monitors, printers, faxes, scanners, the works. The computer cases are made of a brushed aluminum and engraved with an abstract pattern that shimmers like the play side of a CD. The lights behind and above Guy cast long shadows down his face, and though his hair and forehead and cheeks are visible in bright relief, his eyes are hidden.

"Hello, Laura," he says. His voice is clear and powerful. "I apologize for all the security. Thanks for making it easy. I'm Guy."

He stands and leans over the desk and extends a hand. I stand and step forward and stretch out my own and we touch fingertips. He doesn't bend very well and I wonder if he's injured or just likes making me work hard to touch him.

A black man with a shiny head and a nice suit appears at my side.

"Relax," says Guy. "This is Rorke."

"There's a gun in my bag," I say. Rorke the dork.

"Yes, the scanner told us that."

Rorke pats me down, gets close to overly personal but not quite. He wands me. He smells like those men's magazines that Bradley's worthless father used to bring home.

"Turn around please, Laura," he says.

When I turn my back to Guy I can see that this room is elevated — part of a tower, maybe, or built on a hill — and through the high windows the port unfolds all the way to the ocean. Port of Long Beach, or of Los Angeles? In the cold blast of light from the incandescent light banks, the cranes are pivoting and the immense stacks of containers are either growing or shrinking as the megatonnage of goods flood into America or wash back out. My Mustang GT is probably out there in one of those containers, packaged up with more of Angel's vehicles for sale in the Middle East. I look down on what appear to be miniature trucks but I know they're actually full-sized tractor trailers filled with all things imaginable. Perfect setting for Guy, I think, the man who will buy and sell anything.

"Thank you, Anthony," says Guy. "Rorke will take you down for coffee or breakfast while I talk to Laura. Will that be okay with everyone?"

"See you in a while, Anthony," I say to Angel. "Save me a donut."

In the darkness to my right a door opens to a neat rectangle of light into which Angel and Rorke pass.

"He has nothing but the highest praise for you," says Guy.

"He speaks very highly of you, too," I say.

"The port is fascinating, isn't it?"

"It makes me feel small and slow," I say.

"Me too. It's pure capitalism — controlled chaos. Just barely controlled. I'm sure you know that very few of the containers are inspected, coming or going. Which of course is good and bad. It helps me in my business. It saves me money when I purchase foreign goods. But it may someday allow in a dirty bomb that will blow me and my little world here into eternity. Or an anthrax dispenser. Or ten thousand rabid vampire bats all hungry for blood, bursting out into the night when the container is opened."

"The cost of freedom," I say.

"May I see the diamonds?"

I tap my jacket pocket. "We sort of do things together."

"I understand. Join me up here. There are steps if you go to your left."

A moment later we're standing across from each other, on either side of a worktable built off his long curving desk. The desk and table are a dark wood with red tones in it — mahogany, or maybe Hawaiian koa. Ernest has a decorative Hawaiian spear with a koa shaft.

I see an aluminum-cased laptop on the desk, turned away from me to face Guy. It's got the same finish as the desktops, shiny and brushed. It's very unusual looking. It's also identical to the one I saw in the safe house in Marina del Ray. Is Guy a cop? A flush of suspicion breaks over me and for a moment I can't look at him. I turn and watch the port. I calm myself as the skyscrapers of cargo containers grow and shrink under the powerful lights.

Guy is a large man and he's tan — an outdoorsman? He's got a thick upper body but when he brings a chair for me I see that his legs are slightly wrong and he moves slowly. Being from Bakersfield I think of a bull rider who mashed up some discs over the years, or maybe a guy who crashed his BMX bike one too many times.

I sit and remove the parcels of diamonds from the jacket pocket and set them on the black velvet jeweler's pad that Guy has thoughtfully supplied. There's a jeweler's loupe, too. I smile at him.

Starting with the smallest stones I tap them out into discrete groupings. With a fingertip I swirl each group. You can imagine how dazzling they are in the fierce incandescent light beaming down from above. They've never looked this good, not even when I danced with the two-carat monster in my Hotel Laguna room. By the time I set this mondo rock on the black pad I can sense Guy trying to keep his breathing deep and even.

"This is the gemologist's writing on the papers?"

"It is."

"I'd love to hear the story of how you got them."

"You won't hear it from me."

"I know. I know. I wish our business could be lighter and less formal, don't you? I'd love to hear the stories behind things. All the tales of how we work and how we steal and how we get what we want."

"Tales can be testimony."

"You're right, of course."

Guy is staring at the rocks. He reaches out with a blunt fingertip and rearranges them slightly. The newly revealed facets throw back the light in new ways. He uses the loupe, taking his time, finally setting it down to look at me.

"Twenty-five thousand dollars," he says.

"My heart just broke."

I stare at him and he stares back. Guy has

cool blue eyes and they don't let on much. I'm not really sure what I look like to him. I'm mad enough to pull my gun and shoot him and I don't care if it shows.

"Guy, say something better to me. The situation demands it."

"Laura," he says, leaning forward confidentially. "These jewels are from the Miracle Auto Body massacre. They are hotly pursued. Everyone knows it. You must."

"I know they're worth four hundred and fifty grand at the mall, and forty-five grand to you. Twenty-five? All I can say to twenty-five is the obvious — it's two in the morning and you are wasting my time."

"Then in deference to Anthony, and to your valuable time and your skill in acquiring these stones, I offer you twenty-seven thousand, five hundred dollars. I will not pay more."

I shake my head and look out at the busy port. I think of plenty of things to say, but I don't.

Guy finally breaks the long silence.

"Laura, you're new to this. Listen. Let's say that we do business but you don't get your price this time. If you sell to me now, I'll be here for you again. We can build respect. Respect leads to responsibility. We would become responsible for each other. Back and forth. Left and right. Containers going and containers coming. I buy and sell almost everything. You can continue your relationship with Anthony, whatever that might be. I can be an ally and a source for you. There would be times when I hear things that can help you. There would be times when you need something I can supply. I am a man you want to be in business with. I can help your friends. You can put your ear to any door in this city and you'll never hear an uncertain word about me. Why? Because I make money for everyone around me. If you say no to me now, Laura, you're closing the door on a secure and profitable future."

I stare at Guy through this whole proclamation. He's unflinching. Slowly, he sets a card on the table before me. It's blank except for a phone number, handwritten in blue ink.

I look down at the diamonds. Even the minor, involuntary movement of my head makes them shine with unpredictable brilliance.

"You can take the diamonds and go. You're free to do that, of course. If you change your mind, you can leave a message at that number."

"I can find another buyer."

"Yes. But really, it doesn't matter what you

do with them now."

"How can it not matter?"

"Because they don't belong to you. Do what you want. But the diamonds will come back to me."

"I fail to see how," I say.

"No matter what you do, they'll be revealed. Blood diamonds are always revealed. That's what makes them blood diamonds, correct? And when they're found they'll be brought to me or someone like me. And my offer will be taken because it's fair."

"It's not fair. You didn't do the work."

"I'm management and you're labor."

I take my time sweeping the diamonds back into their papers. My heart is beating hard and I have this terrible sense of doom and defeat inside me. I hate this man and everything he says because in my heart I know he's right.

"Fourteen men have died for these diamonds," I say.

"Yes."

"Not counting the ones who died in the mines, searching them out."

"Yes again."

"How can I take less than what they paid for them?"

"That sounds noble but really it's just sentimental. The stones are only worth what they are worth."

"I like them," I say. "I've become attached to them. Maybe I'll have some set for people I love. Maybe have some set for me. Maybe just enjoy them for what they are rather than selling them. Some things are more precious unsold."

The look on Guy's face is authentic disappointment. He exhales softly but keeps his cool blue eyes on mine.

"We all know that Lupercio is going to find you, *Ms. Jones.*"

Of course Guy saw Lupercio and me on TV. Half of L.A. saw Lupercio and me on TV. I didn't think someone would use that story to rip me off. Honor among thieves? What a pitiful notion.

"Maybe he'll pay me a better price," I say.

"He's going to kill you and take them. But the diamonds aren't why he's going to kill you. You can hand all of those over to him, and a hundred thousand dollars in cash, and give him your beautiful young body, then move to another state, and change your name and your appearance, and he'll still kill you."

"Why?"

"Because you *saw* him. Maybe you described him to the police artist. Or, maybe someone else saw him and described him to a police artist. Maybe. But Lupercio is free now because he doesn't allow people to see him. I'm not trying to frighten you for yourself or your family. I'm not trying to negotiate with you. I'm not trying for a better price. I can get a better price just by waiting."

"Can you stop him?"

"He can be influenced."

"If you get your price."

"Which is a fair price."

"In exchange for allowing you to steal my diamonds you *influence* Lupercio?"

"Correct."

So, Guy is basically what KFC and Burger King and Taco Bell and all those other businesses were when I was a kid — a low-wage employer with a feeble benefits package and the proud ability to save me from terrors that he himself will bring upon me. They're all poverty vendors with protection rackets on the side. I swear for just a second that Guy looks like that damned Victor they brought in from the East to take Ruby's job at KFC.

I'm also pretty sure that Guy's swank laptop is the one I saw on the coffee table in the Marina del Rey safe house. I've never seen one like that — not in a store, not in an ad, not in a movie, never. So I think Guy is not only a cop but one of Hood's bosses. A thought: in Marina del Rey he was downstairs outfitting my Sentra with a locator for Lupercio to follow, while I was upstairs making a video to lure Lupercio into a trap. A fucking cop, helping Lupercio kill the only witness who can put him near Miracle Auto Body that bloody night. And now trying to steal her diamonds for a song. A bad song.

Cute.

Too bad I can't tell Hood about it.

It would all be kind of funny, if I didn't have my life to consider. And the lives of my boys. Ernest, too. Even my students. I teach a mean hour of history to eighth graders for nine months a year, and believe me, they need some tiny sense of the past. They need to know that there was life before cell phones. They need to be relieved of their overstimulated, overscheduled, overamplified, overcommercialized, overrated, overpandered-to present. But a classroom hour a day isn't enough to accomplish that, and teaching is not a way for me to get ahead in life. I took this extra job partly for my family, though I'll admit it was mostly for me. I took it because I was tired of following the orders of corporate drones and compromising with district fools. And I took it because the blood of Joaquin runs through me. It pulls at me like a hand from the grave. I did *not* become an outlaw to get more laws to live by.

"I'm keeping the diamonds, Guy. Get Anthony back in here. I'm gone."

"Let me be the first to say good-bye."

"Say good-bye to yourself. You don't impress me."

"I'm not trying to."

"You don't have enough balls to impress me. You just rent them from Lupercio."

He offers me a dull smile.

I stand as Angel and his ward come back through the invisible door. Wise Angel senses disaster.

"May I have a few private words with Guy?" Angel asks.

"Give me the truck keys," I say.

"Why, Laura? I'll just be a minute."

I look at Guy. "I can't *take* another minute of this."

"Of course, Laura. Of course." Angel hands me the hood.

"Is there a navigation unit in the truck?" asks Guy.

"There is none, Guy," says Angel. "I can still read a map."

"Escort Laura to the truck," says Guy to Rorke. "Confirm Anthony's statement."

I give Rorke a hateful stare as I put the

hood back on. He cinches up the ties behind my head and I feel the knot go tight. He walks me out with firm pressure on my arm and beeps me into the truck. He guides me into the passenger's seat. I'm sure he's looking at the dashboard to confirm that there's no screen, and I hope he doesn't bother to look under the seat for my portable. Thank God it's small and black. I hear the driver's door open and the clink of keys as he slips one into the ignition, then closes the door. I hit the door locks and give Rorke a blind wave, then turn on the radio and crank the volume. I give Rorke a moment to get inside and lose interest. A minute later I've got my hand around the GPU and I push the current location save button. I've practiced this in the dark and I can do it with either hand.

Then I lean my head back against the rest and try to figure out what to do about Guy.

31

On his first tour Hood spent time at the "Baghdad Tennis Club," a Green Zone facility with a single court made from Tigris River clay and patrolled by men with machine guns. The Chinese-made tennis balls were pressureless and heavy as rocks. But the Iraqis love tennis almost as much as soccer. The play usually took place during the evenings, under the soft hiss of the Green Zone palms.

Hood was a steady player, having been number two on his Bakersfield High School team. He enjoyed having a racket in his hand again. He had a big forehand that was somewhat mitigated by the yellow Tigris clay, though sometimes the gravel composition gave his shots some horrendously advantageous bounces. He didn't mind hitting with the Iraqi youngsters just learning to play.

The club was often visited by Nasir al-Hatam, Iraq's number one player. Amid the rubble and chaos of Baghdad Nasir was trying to get an Iraqi Davis Cup team together. Hood could rally with him, but in games the Iraqi's serve and his deep, steady ground strokes easily did Hood in. Al-Hatam was good-natured and generous with his time, and he became the club pro, giving lessons to American soldiers, who played in combat boots and fatigues.

Hood remembered all of this as he drove away from Officer Steve Ruiz's funeral that Saturday afternoon in Bakersfield, one week after the shootings in Madeline Jones's courtyard. The palms lining the cemetery road looked like the Baghdad palms, and the cooling evening had the same rosy desert light. And Steve Ruiz and Nasir al-Hatam had looked very much alike — tall and dark-haired and slender, with a warm smile and kind eyes. At least that was how Ruiz looked in the portraits on easels beside his coffin. Hood had seen the similarity when he'd first laid eyes on Ruiz, terrified and dying in Madeline's courtyard, but his mind had been too frantic to make the connection.

Hood drove to his old high school and parked and walked out to the tennis courts. There were players on one of them. He sat on a bench and watched. He tried to concentrate on the ball going back and forth but all he could think of was Ruiz.

Ruiz was his age — twenty-eight. At the funeral Hood had seen his widow and his children, his brothers and sister, his mom and dad. There was no point in approaching any of them, in telling them that his own carelessness had contributed to Steve's death. He believed that anyone who looked closely at him would see this. It surprised him that no one at the funeral truly saw him, but no one truly saw Suzanne Jones either, and millions of people had watched her commit armed robbery on TV. Maybe seeing was a lost art.

So he loitered far back in the standing crowd, black as a crow in his weddings-and-funerals suit, wondering if better CPR would have saved Ruiz. And wondering if it was Marlon or Wyte or both who had guided Lupercio to Bakersfield that night. Marlon or Wyte? The names had been endlessly ratcheting through Hood's mind since Arrowhead. *Marlon, Wyte.* Hood had told Marlon that he was going to Jones's mother's house in Bakersfield. Marlon had likely informed Wyte. Where was the leak? Either way you cut it, Lupercio knew where Hood would be and that Hood was looking for Suzanne Jones. Hood had set the stage on which the force of Lupercio's character collided with the luck of two young, strong, unsuspecting deputies — a mismatch.

Hood watched the ball go back and forth over the net. He remembered winning a big match against his crosstown rival, Suzanne Jones's alma mater, in fact, right there on that court. Now the players were middle-aged and rounded, mixed doubles teams grunting and shrieking and playing hard.

Hood thought of Nasir al-Hatam again, his smoothness on the court and his humility off of it. The story that Hood later put together went like this: Nasir was approached by his old homies to drive a bomb into the Hunting Club, a ritzy tennis club where Nasir had learned the game during Saddam's reign. Nasir said he wasn't sure that he wanted to do that. His family was relocated, and Nasir kept teaching and training for the Davis Cup, stayed low, varied his schedule. His old friends caught up with him and two teammates in the Baghdad neighborhood of Sedeya one day and gunned them all down. Nasir and his buddies were wearing the green-and-white warm-ups of the Iraqi tennis team and the Adidas knockoffs that were all you could get in Baghdad. Bullets and fake tennis shoes, thought Hood, all that Iraq could offer its number one player.

Hood watched the ball go back and forth

but he didn't see it. He was back in the Baghdad, hitting with Nasir. Then he was in Madeline Jones's courtyard. Then all he could see was the names Marlon and Wyte scrolling through the window of his mind's eye, like symbols in a slot machine.

He watched the tennis for another few minutes then drove south to L.A.

Hood sat in the activities room with his mother, Iris, beside him. His father was across from them as usual, but without the girlfriend he had mistaken for his wife. Earlier in the week Douglas had punched the woman, and now his activities were restricted. He had lost his swagger and sat with his hands folded in his lap and a hangdog expression on his face.

Hood had brought a picture album he'd assembled from the shoeboxes of photographs he'd gotten from his mother. The doctors had said that visible tokens from Douglas's past might help to slow the deterioration of his mind, or at least please him. So Hood went and sat next to his dad and flipped through the pages.

"Look, that pool you got me when I was four or five," said Hood. He sat in the small blue pool with the bright shapes of seahorses and shells on the walls all around him. He was startlingly skinny but smiling big.

"You look like a POW," said his father. "They should have fed you more."

"I always got enough, Dad."

"Where was I living then?"

"Right there at the Bakersfield house."

"That was the last year we were all together," said Iris. "Donny moved out that December, and Sharon left the next spring."

"I have no memory of them," said Douglas. "But the maintenance yard I remember very well. That's where we'd pick up the trucks and sprayers and pipe and fertilizers. I remember a stack of new Rain Bird sprinklers, brand-new, still in the boxes, that got stolen on Good Friday, 1989."

"You miss work, Dad?"

"I miss the donuts."

Hood flipped through. Douglas nodded but Hood could tell that he wasn't remembering much of what he saw. When Douglas pointed to a picture and asked a question, Hood saw that his hands were still strong and steady, and Hood wondered that a man's mind could wear out so much faster than his hands.

But Hood found himself enjoying the closeness of his dad, the touch of his bare arm along his own, his familiar smell. He remembered Douglas taking him up to Yosemite on fly-fishing trips when he was a boy, the cold water and the elusive fish and the painstaking knots that his father taught him to tie. He could remember his father standing behind him up on the Merced River, taking his hands and showing him the rhythm, how to cast the line with his wrist firm and his elbow doing most of the work and the left hand paying out line. Hood remembered getting it right once in a while, and having brave little rainbow trout crash his fly, and the silver red flash of the fish in the sun as it jumped, then the furtive darts back and forth underwater as he reeled it in. The rainbows were impossibly beautiful, the brook trout even more beautiful. His father always let them go, carefully working the hooks out while keeping the fish submerged. Hood had never loved fly-fishing like his father loved it, but he had fished hard to please him. When he was on a river with Douglas it was always a time of beauty and slowness and that absurd concentration in which anglers become lost.

Hood also remembered riding horses with his dad, especially one warm spring day when Douglas trotted past him on a black warmblood and Hood had so thoroughly admired the way he sat that horse that he tried to emulate it on his own, sitting up and squaring his shoulders but trying to look relaxed also and being thankful that this man so good with horses was his father. In Hood's memory his father trotted by, then trotted by again.

"Look, Dad, remember Taffy?"

"Not one iota."

"The collie you got us. Remember? And she dug up the yard so bad you took her to the pound and came back with a kitten. We named her Noel because it was Christmastime. And Mom put little squares of masking tape on her feet and we laughed when she tried to shake them off and she knew we were laughing at her."

"Sorry to have missed all that."

"You remember, honey," said Iris. "The Webster's boxer got ahold of Noel and you ran him down and got her back out. Christmas Day, 1986. Four stitches in your hand. Charlie and I were in the front yard and we saw the whole thing."

"Charlie being one of my sons?"

"Yes, hon, the one sitting right next to you."

"Oh."

"Look, Dad, here's my first year of Little League. The Angels. You were the coach."

Douglas set his finger under the team picture and appeared to give the photograph his complete attention. He leaned away and looked at Hood.

"Charlie. Right?"

"Right, Dad. Charlie. Perfect."

"I'm hungry."

They ate in the dining room. For Hood and his mother it was an anguished hour of nonsense piled over sense, of imagined events crowding out the memory of real ones. There were moments of pure lucidity but even in these Hood saw nothing of his father's once capacious heart. Mostly he complained.

Hood forced down the dinner and thought of what Madeline had said. *The past is now . . . a grave and a birthplace . . . it's all one instant . . .*

His father looked at him. "I hate my life."

Hood drank at a bar in Hollywood, watched the Dodgers beat the Cards, chatted up two nurses from Chicago and came back late to Silver Lake.

His cell rang as he came through his door.

"Talk to me," said Suzanne.

"Where are you?"

"Far from you and Lupercio."

Hood toured the little one-bedroom place to make sure everything looked the way he had left it, a habit and nothing more. He turned off the lights and sat in the dark in his living room.

"We shouldn't talk here, like this," he said.

"Remember Laguna, before you helped me check out?"

"Hard to forget."

"Then walk across that sand in exactly two hours. Alone."

Two hours later he walked alone across the sand north of Laguna's Main Beach. The sky was close and starless and the moon trailed a river of silver on the water. The waves were small and sharp and they crashed hard. He remembered that the rock archway had been easy to find at low tide but now the tide was high and the beach was smaller and steeper.

He hugged the cliff to stay dry and when he was close enough to make out the shape of the archway Hood heard a crunching sound behind him.

Suzanne skidded down the cliff face and her boots landed quietly in the sand. Her face was mostly hidden under a cowboy hat, and she wore a faded denim jacket against the beach chill.

"Keep going," she said. "Talk."

Hood walked, and she almost caught up

with him but not quite.

"I've got a leak," he said.

"No shit. A cop. How many lives has he helped rub out?"

"Four for sure."

"I liked my neighbors, Hood. I liked Gerald and Harold Little Chief. They were men. What were you thinking?"

"That I was working with good people. I am, mostly. I think I am."

"That's really damned comforting."

"It's a soul killer, woman."

He stopped and turned, and Suzanne stopped, too. He looked at her and felt the good thrill of having her here, caught in his eyes, unmoving for this moment.

"When I found the transponder on my car I thought it was you."

"It was not."

"Prove it."

"You know me is the only proof I've got."

"You don't strike me as a chickenshit coward."

"I care about you." Hood hadn't planned to say that, had never quite said it to himself. It was against all the rules, but that list was long by now. The odd part was that he cared about Allison Murrieta, too.

She cocked her head slightly, as if to hear something better.

"All this, because I saw a guy one night."

Hood knew that the only way to keep her close was to honor her lie. Back in Anbar he'd vowed to never honor a lie again — not after Lenny Overbrook's false confession on behalf of the men who used him. Now he was doing it again.

"It was bad luck," he said.

"What are you going to do about it? School starts in a few days and if I don't work I don't get paid."

Past the archway they came to a place where the beach widened and the pitch of the cliff face softened. Hood looked up at a gazebo outlined atop the bluff in the faint moonlight.

Halfway up the stairs to the gazebo they stopped and Hood looked back at the beach below them and the soft black Pacific.

"There's a way, Suzanne. There are two people other than me who've known where I was going, and where you might be. If I give each man a different place to find you, and Lupercio shows up at one of them — we'll know."

"Who are these assholes? How high up are they?"

"A sergeant and a captain."

"Men, women, white, black?"

"It's better you don't know."

"You don't know what's better for me. So we find the leak. Then what?"

"There's internal affairs. There's feds."

"More cops. Great."

They climbed to the top of the bluff and stood in the gazebo and looked down again. They were alone. Up here the breeze was stronger and Hood could hear the cars swooshing along behind them on Coast Highway. Suzanne brushed back her hat and the strap caught her throat. She stood in front of him. Over her shoulder he saw a restaurant long closed for the night and a lamplit patch of highway.

"I saw my boys today. It made me happy."

"I'll bet that made them happy, too."

"I'm a good mother."

Hood said nothing.

"I've raised them on independence and they know they're loved. I've exposed them to good things, a lot of them. I've taught them to think for themselves, to be curious about everything and to doubt everything. I've never missed a birthday, a holiday or an illness. Well, not many."

"They seem like good boys. Really. A good look in their eyes."

"After you arrest Lupercio I'll let you take me somewhere no one knows us. Somewhere beautiful. We'll be lazy."

"Ernest might not be too happy about that."

"Listen. Ernest is a truly good man. But he knows that things end. I told him they would. And I told him that again, until he really got it. I wouldn't take him until he understood that our time would be short. Because of that I treated him like a king."

"I'll stay out of that one."

"You're smack in the middle of it, Charlie. Here's the deal: I'm not easy and I'm not property. I'm not up to you. I'm up to me. I'll help you find your murder-loving boss and I'll help you nail Lupercio. I want them both to rot in hell. I'll trust you, Hood, but I'm still up to me. Those are my terms. Acceptable?"

"Those are fair."

"Good, because I got us our old room at the hotel."

32

So I'm down in Little Saigon, Orange County. The people here aren't likely to know Suzanne Jones and there's a nice little hotel on a side street built to look like a French one in old Saigon.

Hood needs time to set his trap and I have things to do.

First I get my hair cut short and dyed light blond. I tell the stylist to brush it back and let it fall where it falls. It's chaos. Good. Sometimes a girl needs a change.

I meet in the afternoon with Quang, a jewelry maker and acquaintance of mine. We sit in the back of his shop on Bolsa with the front doors and the security screen locked tight and the OPEN sign turned out. Quang chain-smokes and when he smiles his face creases with wrinkles and smile lines. He's been hit by armed robbers twice in the last four years and he won't open up for anybody who doesn't look right. Lots of the Vietnamese businesspeople keep their cash in floor safes right on the premises just like their parents taught them back in Vietnam, which encourages armed robbery. They'd be better off with their profits in banks but there's no convincing them of that.

I sketch out a setting for Ernest's ring, which will be an eleven-stone bolt of electricity on gold. Gold, because it looks so good against his dark Hawaiian skin.

Quang smokes and smiles and nods.

I draw a masculine silver ring setting for Bradley's half-carat diamond, which will be mounted inside a crescent of lapis cut in the shape of a wave.

I sketch out a broad, flat fish with a trail of dorsal diamonds that will hang from Jordan's neck. Both the fish and the chain will be brushed stainless steel, built to last.

Quang suggests a simple ring box for baby Kevin's third-carat diamond, which I can set on his dresser until he's old enough to wear something valuable. I think briefly of having Quang affix the stone to the grip of a teething ring but this seems gauche.

I ask Quang to set the two-carat whopper as a ring for myself, something shameless in platinum.

For Hood I draw a pendant shaped like an H, studded with smaller third- and half-carat diamonds, totally dope. And it will ride with 'tude around his neck because the chain hole is in the left vertical bar of the letter. I've got no idea how I can give him this without him questioning where I came up with the money to buy such a thing. I don't think he still suspects me of having something to do with the Miracle diamonds, but I can't be sure. Hood is honest and he blushes and I can read him like a book but he holds things back, too. He's smart.

Quang smiles and nods and smokes and pokes at a little calculator so old the figures on the keys have worn off. When he turns it around to me the charge looks right but I haggle anyway and get him down a few hundred. I think of Guy and how he tried to rip off my diamonds. I'm all but sure he's a cop and that he's running Lupercio. I'm still furious about that but I've pushed it to the back of my mind. I pay Quang half his fee in cash. The other half will be in diamonds, due on delivery.

One week, he says.

In my Rendezvous Hotel suite in Little Saigon I put on my work clothes and check that all my tools are in order. I don't put on the wig or mask.

I know I can't publicly contribute to my

favorite charities in a Sentra, so I find a very nice Escalade in a South Coast Plaza parking lot and use the slide-hammer that Angel had made for me. It fits my hands perfectly and it's got torque galore. I hate ripping out the lock assembly of a fancy newish car, but I love fancy newish cars so what am I going to do?

I'm southbound on the 405 in less than a minute, wig on and the AC blasting because it's late August and I run hot when I work. I work on the wig, saving the mask until the last minute.

The Laguna Club is just a preschool but it's got good people running it and they always need money. They helped out a friend of mine once by keeping her son an extra fifteen minutes a day. Not for just one day either, but for an entire school year. So I've given them four thousand dollars over the last year, and I've got another four thousand in a large clasp envelope beside me here in the Escalade. I should mention that this Escalade has the big V-8 in it, 345 hp, and it handles very well. It's also got twenty-two-inch chrome wheels that retail at $2,995 if you can believe that, and of course a navigation system, a rearview camera and a DVD player. It's kind of garish — bling on wheels — but it's got attitude and it hauls butt.

I've timed it right at the Laguna Club because the staff is escorting the students up from the playground and the parking lot is filling with the cars of parents who are there to pick up their kids. On goes the mask.

I gun the Escalade into the lot, stand on the brakes and yank the steering wheel hard left.

The tires scream and smoke and the moms and dads scatter. They stare at me. Some of them realize who I am but they don't know what to do — it's like seeing Jesse James walk into your bank: do you dive for cover or say what's up, Jess?

Then from the clubhouse marches a very angry young woman in a red Laguna Club T-shirt.

I hurl the envelope through the open window and it lands at her feet.

"Allison Murrieta says thanks!"

In a screech of tires and white smoke I'm back to Coast Highway. Here, I slow down and pick my way to Interstate 5 south of Dana Point. Mask off, then on again.

At the Project Concern headquarters in San Diego I just walk and in and set five envelopes on the receptionist's desk.

"I'm Allison Murrieta," I say. "And this is fifty thousand dollars for a new water truck down in Ethiopia."

"Ayisha District. It's terrible."

A few weeks ago I read the Project Concern brochure about this dilapidated old water truck that breaks down all the time. It brings water to — get this — seventy *thousand* people, and when the truck breaks down they go without water. One truck. Of course these people are in the middle of nowhere in Ethiopia or they wouldn't need a water truck to begin with.

"I was happy you saved that old man," says the receptionist.

"He was, too."

"We can't do anything with this money, Ms. Murrieta. We have to turn it over to the police."

"Deny those people a new water truck? Honey, talk to your boss. Declare a couple grand. Figure it out."

"Oooh. Tempting."

"Temptation is good. Now give me the keys to your car. Don't report it stolen. If you write your number on this card I can tell you exactly where it is. I won't hurt it."

I transfer the remaining charitable contributions and my work tools to her Kia and head for the Olivewood Home back in Orange County. Incidentally, the Kia is a very nice little car, firm and peppy for a four-banger, a value car.

One of my students lived at Olivewood before he found a foster family in my district. It's a place for children who don't have anyone to take them in when their families explode or dissolve or, in the case of my student, simply disappear and leave the child to be found. His name was Tim and he was a cool kid and the Olivewood people looked out for him.

The trouble with Olivewood is that it's right next to the Sheriff's substation and not far from Juvenile Hall, so this corner of Orange is crawling with law enforcement.

I take off the wig in plenty of time. I wait for a Sheriff's cruiser to pass before I turn into the Olivewood lot and look for a parking place. A Santa Ana Police car backs out ahead of me. I turn the A/C vent straight onto my face and hit Max.

I park and put the envelope in my satchel. I walk through the lobby to the restrooms and lock myself in a stall. The door has a coat hook and I set the handles of the plastic shopping bag over the hook. Inside the bag is ten thousand in cash and a note that says: "Olivewood Home for Children — Allison Murrieta thanks you for all of your hard work!"

On my way back out of the lobby a plainclothes cop holds open the door for me and gives me the cop eye. I smile slightly without making eye contact and I'm very happy to be a blond.

I backtrack to South Coast Plaza, where I leave the Kia and pick up my Sentra. I call the Project Concern receptionist on my way up the 405.

By the time I get up to L.A. it's sunset and the charitable organizations have closed for the day. The evening is warm and touchable and the sky is layers of blue, black and orange.

There's something nice about giving thousands of dollars to an organization you believe in. It lightens the heart almost as much as having a two-carat diamond set for yourself. I can't wait to see that thing on my hand. I stop by the admin building of the Los Angeles Boys & Girls Club, then Children's Hospital, the Make-A-Wish Foundation and the Heart Association.

I slide the envelopes into the mail slots and walk away. Each has a large sum of cash and a note from Allison Murrieta — I write them left-handed so it won't look like my own rather graceful cursive script. Of course I'm hoping that the PR departments of these organizations can find a way to thank Allison publicly for at least a portion of the money.

If they can't quite declare the full amount, I understand. Even with my new haircut I'm not insane enough to brave the LAPD Foundation, so I'll mail the money to them as usual. I only give them small amounts because I know they'll set it aside as evidence. Maybe they check it for numbers or secret watermarks or something. It tickles me that they have to deal with Allison in this way.

On my way back to Little Saigon I stop in Carson to rob a 7-Eleven. I park on the street, past the entrance. The freeway is a blessed two hundred yards away. I adjust the rearview mirror so I can check the storefront, then I get Cañonita ready and clip the pepper spray to my waistband. I get the mask on, the wig right, the gloves snug.

I have to turn to see the police car pulling up behind me.

I drop Cañonita into a box of tissues then swing the mirror back in place and the sun visor down. I strip off the wig, mask and gloves and jam them under my seat. I make sure my leather vest covers the pepper spray at my waist. My heart smacks my chest and my breath gets faster. It's a solo car, one officer getting out now, his flashlight on. He walks toward me, hugging my vehicle to discourage a shooter. I get my purse onto my lap and come up with a mascara pencil, which I now use to touch up my left eye in the vanity mirror on the top side of the visor. When the officer gets to my window I look at him and power it down. He's a big-shouldered white guy, looks like a weightlifter.

"Good evening," he says.

"Hi, Officer."

"Driver's license please."

I drop my mascara pencil back into my purse and dig out my wallet. I give him my CDL, where I have long brown hair. The officer looks at me, then again at the license.

"Suzanne Jones," he says. "The witness? The schoolteacher?"

"Yeah."

He takes my license back to his unit and I can see him on the radio. He's not sure what to do with me, and his watch commander won't be sure either. For one thing, I'm not under his jurisdiction as a witness, and for another, I'm not wanted. I'm just a schoolteacher being victimized by a killer. They can even run the Sentra plates, but thanks to Angel the vehicle title is in order and it hasn't been on the hot list since the cops recovered the stripped chassis months ago.

My lucky day.

He comes back and hands me the license.

"Do you need help, Ms. Jones?"

"I'm very well, thank you. I appreciate

your asking."

"This is just a no parking zone here tonight. Street cleaning ten to midnight. Sorry."

"Is it that late?"

"Yes, it is. Far from Valley Center, aren't you?"

"Good friends are worth a drive."

"Thank you for standing up to that guy. You did the right thing."

I start the car and put it in gear. "Thanks, Officer."

"Thank *you*. And have a nice night."

So I hold up a 7-Eleven down in Huntington Beach instead.

I'm the only customer. The clerk is Indian and quite polite as he puts the bills into a plastic bag. He's a young man but he wears glasses and he looks over the top of them at my face, then my gun, then my face again.

"You should go," he says. "The police come here almost every hour."

I turn just as the door swings open and three surfer dudes spill in — flip-flops and sweatshirts and matted hair. They laugh until they see me coming their way, then they quiet down, bumping into each other as they come to a halt. Their eyes are slits and their Adam's apples bob.

"Whoa."

"Allison."

"Gun."

"Hey, can I like take a picture?"

"Sure, but be quick."

The clerk comes around the counter. "Perhaps I can be in the picture, too?"

"Cool."

"Get close," says one of the surfers.

He steps back toward the door, a cell phone out. His buddies and the clerk join me but they're too scared to get up close so I gather them in. The smell of weed is strong.

The surfers laugh their stoned laughs and I'm in a little bit of a hurry here so I yank one of them in by the hood of his sweatshirt and Cañonita goes off.

The roar is deafening.

The surf dude screams and drops. The cameraman runs outside. The third surfer dives to the floor and scrambles down the aisle on hands and knees, flip-flops jumping off his feet. The clerk backs away from me with terror in his eyes.

I stride to my car, mask off, head up, plastic bag containing maybe a quart of beer or a box of cereal swinging in my left hand. But my right ear is ringing from the gunshot and my heart is racing and my nerves feel they've been stroked with a wire brush. Once again I've forgotten to hand out business cards. I wonder if it's a run of bad luck or if I'm losing my nerve.

An HBPD patrol car swings into one of the 7-Eleven lot entrances as I exit another and goose it for the on-ramp.

Back at the Rendezvous Hotel I shower and change and go down to the bar in the ballroom. The Vietnamese dance to an orchestra. Everyone is Vietnamese, not a round-eye in the room except for me. Most of the people here are older and established. They had the means to flee the war and ended up here, where they built a place to remind them of home. They're good dancers — cha-chas and fox-trots and waltzes. The men are in suits and the women in dresses and the air is thick with smoke. The walls are mirrored.

I'm tired all the way to my bones. I think about my boys and my mom and Hood and almost blowing the surfer's brains out. Wait until that makes the news. I must have had a tighter grip on Cañonita than I thought. I must have been more nervous than I thought. I don't know. But I do know that luck changes like everything else and I get the idea that Quang should have names and addresses to send that jewelry to in case I'm not able to deliver it personally.

Joaquin wrote in his journal about coming

across an old man and his white dog walking the road to Nevada City one day. The man wore clothing that was little better than rags and his shoes were held together with baling wire. Joaquin slowed his gang of bandits and got off his horse and walked along with the old man and they spoke Spanish and the man told him that he had once been rich and now he was poor and rich was better. He said the worst thing about being poor wasn't hunger or cold but being made to look ridiculous. Joaquin unloaded a bundle from one of the packhorses and in the grass he unrolled it. Inside was a new suit of clothes, a pure woolen suit in black, with a white cotton shirt and a black satin necktie. From another packhorse Joaquin got a new pair of leather boots, black and beautiful. Joaquin loved clothes. The bandits waited while Joaquin used a needle and thread to shorten the pant cuffs. The old man went into the trees and when he came out he was wearing the suit and boots and his chin was up and his eyes looked clear and he was smiling. Joaquin and his men then mounted up and pounded away in clouds of dust and continued on to Nevada City. They gambled and drank and bought women and things. Joaquin bought two new suits. Three days later on the road out of town they came across the old man, hung by his neck from a big sycamore tree, still dressed in his finery. The white dog lay beneath him, baying and growling. A note pinned to the coat lapel said: "This is what happens to friends of Murrieta."

Joaquin said a prayer for the old man, called the dog and rode away.

When I first read that part of the journal I could feel Joaquin's luck changing. He could feel it, too, and he said so. He said it was like a dark cloud he couldn't see but he could feel the way it blocked the sun and made the world a cold place. Thirty days later they shot him down and cut off his head and you know the rest.

I wonder what I'll do with Joaquin's head. I don't love it but it is rightfully mine and it is my personal history, love it or not. Is it a curse? Is it a blessing? Either way it will belong to my sons after I go. I wonder if it's time to have the talk with Bradley.

The talk.

I'll never forget the talk I got. My great-uncle Jack — Mom's side — took a liking to me when I was very young. He paid special attention to me. I remember him holding me on his lap, listening to my early words, just sitting and watching me. He read to me. Later I noted that none of his other great-nieces or nephews or even his own grandchildren had anything nice to say about him. But he continued to give me special gifts for my birthday and Christmas. He taught me to dance.

He was a slender, quiet man, silver-haired and dark-eyed. He had been a farrier by trade, which is a person who shoes horses. He had a vertical scar on his forehead, curved as a hoof is curved. He had a mobile farrier service that was successful in the seventies and eighties. He drove all around Southern California shoeing horses. He told me later that he was also a bookie — a "front" as they call them in that business — which is the person who takes the bets. His mobile farrier business made it easy. He drove a junkyard crane part-time because the money was good and his brother owned the wrecking yard. When I was little he'd take me there, let me work the levers and push the buttons of the big crane, let me grab some junkers with that big magnet hoist and put them in the stack. Fun, but all the dead cars made me sad.

One day when I was fifteen and he was sixty-two he took me out for a "driving lesson" in my mother's 1974 Alfa Romeo Spider. Jack loved cars. I had my learner's permit, so I could drive with an adult in the car, and we raced all around Bakersfield in the little red roadster and I can't explain what a joy it was to drive that thing. It was the last year the Spiders had the cool bumpers, and the last year before catalytic converters were required, so it put out 129 very adequate horses. And the four-speed had a short, sweet throw, with a lively clutch. That car stuck to the road like a tick. The air conditioner didn't work. The door handles kept falling off. Radio? Forget it. Nothing on it really worked, but Jack just sat back and let me blast around, the top down and the wind blowing back his long silver hair. Of course I wasn't exactly learning to drive because by then I'd been taking my mother's and several other cars for joyrides for months. I was good. Thought I was.

When we came back I pulled the Alfa into the garage and shut off the engine.

Jack turned to me and put his hand on my knee.

"You are a special child," he said.

"Thank you, Jack," I said. "You always made me feel that way."

He handed me a key with a tag attached. On the tag was an address and a number.

"This is yours," he said. "My great-great-great-great-grandfather was Joaquin Murrieta. You will come to understand."

"I wrote a report on him."

"One night while you slept I told you his story. You were very young but I think you heard me."

"I remember every part of it, Jack. The wind was blowing that night."

"It seemed like the right time for an outlaw story."

It took me a week to get out to that address, what with school and hapkido and my jobs at KFC and Taco Bell. Bradley's father-to-be drove because he was three years older than me. I was two months pregnant with Bradley. Funny how that first walk across the floor in the morning would leave me queasy back then but the eighty-mile-an-hour Alfa jolt left me wanting more.

The address was a storage facility down in the south part of Bakersfield. I made Bradley's cute fool of a father wait in the car. The key fit a well-oiled Schlage and got me into unit number 227.

There were two large cardboard boxes, big enough for a microwave or a small TV. They were taped shut. I picked the one on the left, slit the tape with my knife — a beautiful four-inch, walnut-handled Buck I'd shoplifted from Oshman's Sporting Goods when they refused to hire me one summer. I still carry it in my satchel.

The first box was filled with papers,

books, yellowed news clippings, flyers for exhibitions of the head of my great-great-great-great-great-great-grandfather, the outlaw Joaquin Murrieta. There was a leather duster with bullet holes in it, worn boots folded over and stiff with age, a lariat, an Indian arrow. His journal was at the bottom.

In the other box was his head in a jar of yellow liquid. A bit of a shock, even to a knocked-up fifteen-year-old with no discernible sense. I looked at all that hair lilting around near the bottom and the face as dead as a face can get, and I felt that I was a part of this man and he was a part of me.

I didn't go back there for thirteen years. I took over the rent payments when Jack died.

I moved it all out to Valley Center a year and a half ago. It's not hard to hide two boxes. The property is big and truly, people don't see what they don't want to see.

The Vietnamese are dancing to "The Tennessee Waltz." I turn and look at the nearest mirrored wall and I see a blonde looking back at me. She looks confident. I take the elevator up to my fourth-floor suite.

I keep thinking of the surf dude I almost blew away. I can feel the dark cloud that Joaquin wrote about and I wonder if it's going to pass by or stay right over me, freeze my bones with me still on them.

I call my boys and talk an hour with each, not counting Kenny of course. Ernest is quiet and gentle as always, willing to let me avoid all truth.

I call Hood and listen to him say hello then I hang up and turn off the phone.

33

In the darkness Hood waited for Lupercio to come into the motel parking lot. The Mariposa was on Aviation near LAX, and when the jets roared over, Hood heard the window glass buzz and the lamp stand rattle on the table.

Sitting back from the window in room 6, Hood could see each parking place and the side of the motel office. Fog had broken the heat wave and now the night was heavy and damp. The Mariposa's security and courtesy lights were yellow, casting the property in false colors.

There were twenty-six rooms. The parking places were nearly all taken. Around the perimeter was a cinder-block wall that had been heavily tagged and sandblasted and tagged again. A low concrete planter lit by a yellow ground light stood in the middle to divide the incoming and outgoing traffic, and in it grew three sagging queen palms blanched by the foggy illumination.

A pale minivan pulled in, circled around and found a place at the end of the row. So far tonight Hood had seen six new arrivals and eight departures. The Mariposa offered a park-and-ride deal at ninety-nine dollars according to the sign out front.

Suzanne had checked in at four P.M. then met him at a liquor store on Sepulveda to give him the room key and exchange cars. She had already talked to Betty Little Chief about parking Hood's Camaro out of sight in her garage. Hood hoped she could make Valley Center by six-thirty, which would still be well before dark. He left a cigar box full of tapes of the Bakersfield sound on the passenger seat for her.

Hood drank coffee straight from a thermos and had a bag of snack food under his chair to keep up his alertness. Suzanne's white Sentra — tinted a sour yellow by the motel lot lights — faced him from the parking space directly in front of his door.

The bait now sat before his superiors.

That afternoon he had told Wyte that Suzanne was checked into the Mariposa for one night. Wyte told him that he and his bride had stayed there when they first came to L.A. The planes kept them awake all night, or maybe it was each other. Then

Wyte gave him a look that Hood couldn't read and turned back to his monitor.

Later Hood told Marlon that Suzanne Jones was spending the night at her home in Valley Center. Marlon questioned her wisdom because Lupercio had already found her there once. Hood said he'd told her the same thing but Jones was stubborn. Marlon said if Lupercio showed up there tonight it would prove he was psychic and they'd have to get the psychic crimes team on the case.

Hood drank more coffee and listened to the window vibrate and the lamp stand start up again. His department-issue Glock was holstered over his left shoulder and his own eight-shot Smith AirLite .22 was strapped to his right ankle. He had brought his folding chair from home, with armrests and a low seat that was surprisingly comfortable.

He thought of Suzanne down in Valley Center, perched in the tree house in the massive oak that grew in her barnyard. He had remembered the tree house and thought that if Lupercio materialized on her property, Suzanne would be as safe in that tree as an observer of Lupercio Maygar could get.

The idea got better when she showed Hood how Ernest and Bradley had rigged the hidden line that released a rope ladder so you could climb into the tree house, then hoist the ladder up and out of sight once you were in. Hood had sat on a derelict couch on the deck of the tree house and confirmed that you could see the back of the house, the barn, the pond, the outbuildings, the drive and part of the road that led past Betty Little Chief's house. But there was small chance that anyone approaching could see you.

Hood had given her his twelve-gauge Remington automatic and a box of number sixes just in case, and that was how Hood now pictured her, sitting on the couch — how did they get that up there? — with the scattergun propped against it, listening to the coyotes yapping and the night birds singing and waiting for a glimpse of Lupercio. He liked her new do, but in his imagination her hair was still brown and wavy.

Now Hood scanned the cars parked in the motel courtyard, looking for movement. The perimeter was poorly lit, and the cinder-block wall with its bold swirls of graffiti fooled him into seeing motion. He half expected to see Lupercio emerge from one of the cryptograms.

If so, Hood would deal with him. And later, somehow, with Wyte.

If Lupercio went to Valley Center then Suzanne would see him and they would know that Marlon was their betrayer.

And if what Hood thought would happen happened — if Lupercio stayed out of sight tonight — then either Marlon or Wyte had sensed the trick and called him off.

There was also the possibility that they were in it together.

Hood drank more coffee, slapped his face and pulled a packet of donuts from the bag under the chair while he scanned the yellowed parking lot again.

At 4:14 a dark old Lincoln Continental rolled into the courtyard, hugging the wall on the far side of the planter.

Hood backed his chair farther away from the window without taking his eyes off the car.

The Lincoln moved along the wall, turned and turned again, then came back toward Hood alongside the cars parked outside the rooms.

The windows were smoked and he couldn't see the driver, or if there were passengers. It looked like the one from the sand hills outside Bakersfield. When the car had come full circle to the exit, it turned hard left into the entrance lane and began the circle again. Like someone looking for a good parking place, Hood thought, or someone looking for his room.

Or someone else's.

A jet roared over, and Hood's heart beat steady and fast as the Lincoln cruised the lot again. It slowed at Suzanne's Sentra, almost stopped. He couldn't see in. When it got to the exit, it stopped then bumped onto Aviation and went south toward the airport.

Hood hit the door running, made the Sentra in seconds. He started it up, slammed it into reverse, then punched it off the lot and onto Aviation southbound.

Ahead he could see four sets of taillights, red halos in the fog. He closed hard on them, flashing the brights and honking, hoping to cut Lupercio away from the pack.

The Lincoln jumped into the fast lane and accelerated. Hood floored the little four-cylinder and closed the distance as they approached Century. He thought he saw a backseat passenger in his high beams, a faint face looking at him.

Hood rode the Lincoln hard, flashed his lights again, backed off a little.

To his surprise the Continental signaled right and pulled over.

Hood followed it to the curb then gunned the Sentra again, shot past the Lincoln and skidded to a stop ahead of it. The Lincoln didn't move. He hit reverse hard and backed almost into the Continental, then rolled out of the Sentra and came up with his Glock out and ready as he crouched and ran toward the car. He stayed outside of the headlight beams and yelled for the driver to step out. He kept the door of the Lincoln just above his front sights, and when it opened slightly, he dropped to his knees in a shooter's stance and swung his left hand up to support the weapon.

"Get out and step away from the car!"

He watched the door open halfway, then swing all the way out.

A heavy, round-faced woman dislodged herself and took three hurried steps through the fog, away from the car toward Hood. She raised her hands. Hood saw the car keys dangling from the right.

"Don' shoot! Don' shoot! I have my daughters! We are not a gang! We are lost!"

She whirled and rattled off rapid Spanish toward the car and then Hood saw the back door open and a young woman get out, followed by another who looked exactly like her.

Away from the yellow lights of the Mariposa lot, Hood now saw that the Lincoln was not black but dark green.

The girls raised their hands and stood on either side of their mother. Hood brandished his shield and came toward them, pistol pointed up at the sky. He kept them in his vision, but what he focused on was the interior of the car.

"Los Angeles Sheriff's," he said. *"Don't move."*

The mother and the second girl out had both left the doors open, and Hood saw no one else in the car, but he knew Lupercio was small and nimble, so he trotted past the women and aimed his gun into the car as he walked completely around it to make sure it was empty.

Back at the driver's side door Hood leaned in and ran his left hand along the bottom of the dash until he found the trunk release.

He pulled it and heard the lock disengage and saw the trunk lid open an inch or two.

He walked closely alongside the car, and when he got to the trunk, Hood reached over with his left hand and lifted it up.

Then he stepped back and circled the rear of the car, aiming his gun in.

There were three large suitcases, a folding garment bag and three carry-ons.

He holstered his pistol.

"Please come over here," he called to the women.

They hustled over, and suddenly Hood smelled their perfume and hair products and makeup. Their eyes were wide and their faces looked stunned but hopeful.

"What were you doing at the Mariposa?"

"We want to go to the Hacienda."

"It's south of the airport. El Segundo."

"Please tell me how to go there. We are lost. We have very early flight to Caracas."

"Caracas."

"I am a United States citizen. My daughters are United States citizens. We will show you passports."

"Thank you."

Hood eyed the three big pieces of luggage in the Lincoln trunk.

Then looked down at the mother's passport: Consuelo Encarnación, DOB 12/26/1970.

In his dawning humiliation Hood asked to see her driver's license also.

The daughters obeyed, too, and Hood examined all three CDLs, every few seconds glancing over at the big suitcases in the trunk of the Continental.

"Thank you," he said, returning Serena Encarnación's current and valid driver's license.

"Thank you," he said, returning Lucia's. "Wait here, please."

He walked over to the Lincoln and pulled

the carry-ons and the folding bag from the trunk and set them on the ground. He unzipped the big black suitcase that was on its back, saw clothes and no Lupercio, shook his head. He wrestled the other two over and checked them next. He heard one of the girls giggle. He felt like a fool.

Back with the women he apologized and said he was looking for Lupercio Maygar.

Hood saw recognition on the mother's face.

"We saw the TV," said Consuelo. "We don' know him."

The twin girls silently looked at the ground.

Hood had seen the same look on Iraqi people, a look of anger and shame at being mistaken for criminals or killers or sectarian rabble. But it was a look that not only the innocent could produce.

He checked the Lincoln's registration and wrote down the plates, and the names, dates of birth and address for the Encarnación family of Fontana. Consuelo gave him a phone number.

Hood apologized then gave them directions to their hotel.

He trailed them three cars back, down Century to Sepulveda, then south to the Hacienda. They turned into the busy check-in area, and Hood passed them, then swung a U-turn back toward the Mariposa.

In room 6 he waited out the sunrise with donuts and lukewarm coffee. He wanted badly to do something right. He thought about the mother and twins and if he should drive out to Fontana for a look around. He doubted that Lupercio had shown at Valley Center either, but the plan was for Suzanne to call when it was light.

At six-thirty she called — no Lupercio, she said, and no sleep, not a creature stirring except an owl that floated out of the big oak tree at three-twenty and just about gave her a heart attack then flew back into the tree thirty seconds later with a pale shiny rattlesnake that buzzed until the bird ate its head. The owl was still perched there, eyes closed and the shredded carcass hanging over the oak branch. She wanted the rattle for Jordan but couldn't figure out how to get it.

"No Lupercio, Hood?"

"No. Just a mother and two daughters on their way to Venezuela."

"Tell me about that."

Hood did, as he pulled the curtains almost shut. He returned to the chair, stepping through the snack wrappers and chocolate milk cartons and the spent energy-vitamin packet.

"Now what?" she asked. "We still don't know which of your bosses is ratting me out."

"He sensed the trap."

"But we're okay if nobody saw us, right? We've got our little traitor wondering if we're as dumb as he thinks we are."

"Exactly."

"Who are your suspects, Hood?"

"You don't know them."

"What do they look like?"

"Cops."

She was quiet for a beat.

"When I get a mouse in the pantry, I put the peanut butter on the trap but I don't set it the first night. I just let him eat. Second night I put on peanut butter and set it. Kills them every time."

"He's smarter than a mouse."

"I'm not going to live like this anymore. If I wait for Lupercio to find me, he will. I have to act."

"Act how, Suzanne?"

"I don't know yet."

"You sound like you do."

She didn't answer, and Hood listened to the silence then the rumble of another jet lumbering out of the sky toward the runway.

"You must really miss me, Hood."

"Yeah."

"It's light here now and I'm still in the tree house. I've got your shotgun leaned up against the wall. The sun is coming up over the hills and colors are starting to form. The pond is dark shiny gray. It looks like the mercury that Jordan spilled out of the thermometer a couple of weeks ago. There are hills the color of lions and no houses on them. If a herd of wildebeest came down from Betty's right now it would look perfectly natural."

"That's nice."

"It's more than nice."

Hood pictured her. "I wish I could have met you some better way."

"You get what you take."

"It's the other way around."

"The other way around is bullshit."

Hood saw Allison Murrieta from the news the night before, nervously clowning around with the surfers and the 7-Eleven clerk just before her gun discharged. The clerk said he thought it was an accident. One of the surfers said he thought she was showing off. She took seven-hundred-plus dollars. The TV reporter said that in the last two days, five Southland charitable organizations had reported cash donations apparently made by

Allison Murrieta, *one as high as twelve thousand dollars.* A San Diego charity said they got five thousand. The LA Police Foundation admitted getting an envelope in the mail with an undisclosed amount of cash and a card from Allison Murrieta.

"How should we have met, Hood?"

"Maybe you would have won a big hapkido tournament and I would have won CIF at tennis, and the *Bakersfield Sun* would have run our pictures on the same page."

"What's better about that?"

"It's better than you being stalked by a killer."

"Naw. What if we were back-to-back winners on *Millionaire*? And they'd want our pictures together after the show — you and me and Meredith? And after drinks at a very posh bar our natural-born hotness for each other just took over? And we each took a year off work to do nothing but travel and learn the history of the world and have sex in totally cool hotel rooms?"

"That's a good one, Suzanne. There should be a great car in there, somewhere, for the U.S. portion of our travels."

"With a million bucks you can buy a lot of great cars."

"I like the Camaro, but if I had the money I'd get the Cayenne Turbo."

"I'd get a Saleen Mustang and a Harley fat-boy and still have more money left over than you."

"You know how to stretch a dollar."

Suzanne laughed and Hood laughed, too. He was still sitting in his canvas fold-up chair, back from the window, where he could see the flash of cars coming and going from the Mariposa and hear the slamming doors of travelers and the rising noise of traffic out on Aviation.

"You know, Hood, we could actually do all that without winning a game show. We just take a year off, put our money together and go. *Make* a perfect world."

Hood thought about that one. He had eleven grand in the bank but eight of it was an IRA.

"What about your boys?"

"They got this thing called mail. And telephones. Ernest is a very good father and stepfather. They all might like me gone for a year. I'm overcontrolling when I'm home too much. I get fussy about the littlest things. I even drive *me* crazy, but I can't help it."

Hood reached down under the chair and retrieved his last donut. He had the surprising thought that running away with Suzanne for a year would be a good way to keep Allison Murrieta from getting shot.

413

"I could do it."

"But you won't. You're chicken. You'll stay straight and narrow, try to get your sergeant's stripes before you're eighteen. Or however you deputies prove your greatness."

Hood laughed again. "You don't know what I am."

"I can tell a lot about a man just by being sexually assaulted by him."

"Assaulted?"

"Yeah," she said dreamily. He heard her yawn. "The owl just spun his head around and he's looking at me with one eye. It's yellow."

"The parking lot of the Mariposa Motel is hopping."

"There's a mockingbird down in the coral tree outside my bedroom. They make such pretty sounds."

"A bus just pulled in, big black cloud."

"Smells like damp grass and fresh water here."

"I got floor cleaner and cigarette smoke."

"If I go to the edge and look straight down, I see where the trunk goes underground and I know there's a root ball the size of the tree itself under there."

"If I look down, I see an empty pack of donuts."

"I had donuts last night, too. We're so

414

much alike — great minds, and all that."

"That's us."

"This is us," she said.

They were quiet for a long minute. Hood watched the cars jostling in and out of the lot and listened to the sound of Suzanne Jones's breath in his ear. When she spoke again, it was almost a whisper.

"Charlie, back when I was a teenager I had this policy about people moving me around, making me do what they wanted instead of what I wanted. My policy back then was don't let it happen. Ever. Don't give in and don't turn away. Fight until you bleed if you have to. I based it on Roosevelt's 'Speak softly but carry a big stick.' And that's still my policy today. I won't let someone move me around. Not your bosses and not Lupercio and not anybody. You should know that."

"Let me figure out what to do about Lupercio, Suzanne."

Another silence, another jet. "You figure it out, Hood."

"Bye, Suzanne."

"Bye, Charlie."

Just before nine A.M. Hood pulled up to the Encarnación address in Fontana: The Hosier & Reed Funeral Home.

On the off chance that Consuelo and her

daughters actually lived there — perhaps one or more of them acting in an after-hours capacity — Hood walked the building in search of an apartment or guest quarters.

The building was one story and not yet open for business. Around the side Hood walked a chain-link fence that surrounded a healthy green lawn. There was a covered patio with some plastic chairs and an ashtray on a stand. A fountain stood in the middle of the lawn and a raven dug its head into the water then straightened and gave Hood a canny stare.

The building looked too small to accommodate a business and living quarters for three. The rear half of it had few windows, and the rear door was not a residential one but an electric roll-up large enough to accommodate a hearse or a van.

He dialed Consuelo's number on his cell phone but was told that the call could not be completed as dialed. He tried it twice more with the same results.

Hood felt less foolish for having rousted the woman and girls. They'd fooled him with fake ID but he still wondered if they were somehow connected to Lupercio Maygar. If so, Lupercio would soon know that instead of Suzanne Jones, a young LASD deputy had been waiting for him at the Mariposa. And if that was true, then she had been betrayed by Wyte.

34

Hood doesn't have to figure out what to do with Lupercio because I already have.

I call Guy and tell him I changed my mind. I'm ready to sell the diamonds. I'll call back tonight at ten to arrange the meeting.

And I know what he's going to say when I call: *I'll come to you.*

Meaning Lupercio will come to me.

Then I call my friend who works for the Los Angeles Sheriff's Department, a secretary who's been there twelve years and knows things. I had her son at Franklin five years ago, nice kid, a curious mind. I tell her about my friend Guy. I describe him in some detail. I put him into the department hierarchy above Hood, but not so high up he's deskbound. She listens, says she'll think on it. What I think is, she'll be able to help.

Now I'm at the Sunset Tower Hotel because it used to be the Argyle and I loved being close to the ghosts of movie stars, I loved the stainless steel and the deco mirrors, the cast iron palms around the pool and the great view of the city. That's all gone now, except the views, but it's a five-star property. Hood's got no idea where I am. I may lure him here later tonight if everything goes right, feed him a couple of room service martinis and give him a bath in the silver tub.

I've already made my arrangements for Lupercio, and now it's time for a nighttime jog. I run up one side of the Sunset Strip and back down the other. It's nice to be blond and not look like Suzanne or Allison. I feel free. I run past the Whiskey and the Rainbow and the Jaguar dealership I'd love to hit someday, past the Viper Room and the sidewalk where River died, past Hustler Hollywood and the cigar shops and boutiques and sushi bars all lit up under huge billboards flashing tits and ass for movies and TV shows and booze and clothes — man, the models look about Bradley's age.

Around me on the sidewalks are the people the ads are trying to sell to: couples walking close, single guys and dolls tracking each other down, some working girls, young queers with their cute walks and old ones with their cute dogs. I can smell the need in the air, in the mix of perfume and cologne and the exhale from the Armani store and car exhaust and meat smoke from the grill at Kings Road. Some of it comes from me.

I get some looks and this is good.

I get more looks an hour later in my almost new black Pontiac Solstice, which puts out two hundred and sixty horses and two hundred and sixty pound-feet of torque from a turbocharged four, though the steering is vague. I got it down in La Jolla on my way back from Valley Center earlier today. It was easy. I chose a good restaurant, watched this chick park her cute little car, let her get inside, then called the restaurant to say there was a black Solstice in the lot with the headlights on. When she came out to solve the problem, keys in hand, Allison introduced her to Cañonita. She told me she'd seen me on TV up at her boyfriend's place in L.A. Later I cold plated it so there's no reason to pull me over.

Superior Wrecking & Salvage is east of L.A., way out by the riverbed, dead automobiles stacked ten high, mountains of them rising from the flats along the Orange Freeway. Around it are rock quarries and billboards. My friend Phillip owns the place and he's showed me a few things and turned the keys over to me for the night, no questions asked, just two thousand dollars cash for his generosity. If anything happens, I'm a trespasser.

The office is in a metal building that reminds me of Angel's staging place for his cars. The lights are off in the front of the building where the customers lean against an old counter and deal with Phillip's employees. Behind the counter are two large cubicles, and down a short hallway is the inner sanctum, Phillip's personal lair.

I sit at his desk. I'm Allison but without the mask. Phillip has disarmed the security alarm system, as I asked him to. For a moment I watch the bank of video monitors built into one wall. There are twelve screens in all, four rows of three across, each a live feed from the security cameras positioned around Superior's eight fenced acres. Most of the ground lights are on, per my request. The wrecking yard glows in the night, steel and paint and chrome vibrant in the floodlights. Even the rust seems bright. I never knew there were so many different shades of it. The cranes hover over the automotive bodies like undertakers. There are four of them, and their big engines are all idling against the night, another arrangement Phillip has made at my request.

I dial. Guy answers and I tell him where to meet me. I tell him not to let the activity in the yard bother him. He says he's on his way. He sounds pleasant and sincere.

I like that.

A few minutes later I'm seated high up in the cab of one of the power-operated electromagnetic cranes, a seven-thousand-pound capacity Ortlingauer that Phillip bought used two years ago. Its monstrous diesel engines idle throaty and deep and I can feel the rumble through the very thin padding of the steel cab seat. The power of these machines is intoxicating. The yard buzzes with sound and light.

Phillip has positioned the crane right inside the fence that separates the yard proper from the small parking lot in front, just like I asked him to. And right here where I sit in the crane cab, he's left the yard lights off. The parking lot lights have their backs to me, so it's dark right here, the only valley of darkness in the entire yard. Anyone looking at me from the parking lot would have the lights in his face.

I spent an hour with Phillip earlier today, relearning how to operate the big machines — the push-button controls and the joy-stick and most important the servomotors that control the electricity to the magnet at the end of the huge cable. They've haven't changed much since Great-Uncle Jack's days — the basics are the same.

Now I sit almost fifteen feet up in the cab, the Plexiglas side panels open for air. The fence is almost directly below me. I can see the empty access road. In the distance I can see the opposing rivers of freeway lights — the headlights oncoming fast and white and the taillights streaming red and away. I've hung my satchel on one of the steering levers because the cab floor is grimy with oil and dirt. Cañonita is in the bag, reloaded, although right now I don't think I'll be needing her tonight. I've got Hood's shotgun propped up beside me in case all hell breaks loose and I feel the need to contribute.

The shotgun reminds me that one night in a rainstorm a band of Cahuilla Indian raiders stole a string of ten horses from a meadow near Joaquin's camp. They would have taken beautiful Jorge and the other outlaws' mounts, too, but these lucky animals had spent the night under tarps in camp, which is where Joaquin always kept his most valued personal possessions. The stolen horses were all good strong quarter horses, well bred and healthy. Joaquin had worked hard to steal them and he was furious. In the morning he and Jack and two more of their gang easily tracked the hoofprints across the wet meadow and down a Butterfield stage road, then for miles along a game trail that led him into the rocky hills at the base of Thomas Mountain. It took them almost half a day to get there.

Looking through the thick madrone and manzanita, Joaquin could see Indians and horses in a corral. There were twenty in all, and half were his. But instead of a small band of raiders, Joaquin saw an entire village. There were women grinding acorns on the high stones and sewing skins and washing clothes in a spring. Children played in the dirt and the men made arrows and spears. He counted thirty able-bodied men. He watched for a while, then motioned for his gang to follow him away.

When they were out of earshot of the tribe, Joaquin told his three men that it would be a sin to kill thirty Indians over ten horses but a greater sin to surrender such fine animals to savages. He looked at his men. Writing in his journal, he said that Jack looked crazy, Jesús was drunk already, and Juan was "a fearful worm" (my translation). Joaquin wrote that he removed his finest wool jacket from one of the mule packs, brushed it out and slipped it on. He set his best rifle behind the pommel — not the "friendly" little Plains rifle from the saddle scabbard but a full-length Hawken Mountain rifle he'd won from a deputy marshal in a card game way up near Clovis the summer before. He took a single deep swallow of Jesús's whiskey.

Then he spurred big black Jorge off toward the Indian Village.

Joaquin wrote that he cantered straight into the village with the rifle across his lap, his head high and a scowl on his face. I know from pictures that he was a handsome man and that he wore his hair long, and I can almost picture the look — the arrogance and menace and hint of the prankster and the very fine riding coat that would make you respect him and want to agree with him. You'd want to see things his way.

When they'd surrounded him, Joaquin spoke to them in a simple version of their own language, which he'd picked up from a Cahuilla cowboy he'd worked with near what is now Palm Springs. He told them that he had come for his horses. If he did not return with them, his army would come back to the village by morning and shoot every man they could find. And, of course, claim his horses. He had come to get his animals, and to save the village.

He watched as six of the senior braves huddled and discussed. He urged his horse into a tightening circle around them, looking down impatiently, the long barrel of the

425

Hawken gleaming in the afternoon sun, and as I picture the scene I see the buttons of his coat catching the sunlight, too, and I hear the heavy clomp of the horse on the ground and I can see the warriors glancing back at him up on that big black animal, thinking, Maybe we should give this fucker his horses back.

One of the braves turned and smiled and led him to the corral. Joaquin watched as two of the men entered and began cutting away the horses in question. Looking down on the warriors in the corral, Joaquin saw that they were having trouble separating the animals, then he saw that the other four men had drifted toward the big boulders where their weapons lay.

The men in the corral looked to the other braves, clearly waiting for them to act.

Joaquin watched more of the male Indians easing toward the rocks for their weapons. It was going to be thirty on one.

He spurred his mount into the corral, which sent the horses scattering and the two braves jumping out of the way. He raised his rifle in one hand.

"No! *All* of the horses! *All* of the horses or my army will slaughter you by morning!"

He raised his Hawken and fired into the air, which sent the quarter horses running and the Cahuilla horses fleeing in fear and the tribe scurrying for cover.

An arrow pierced his saddle as Jorge pressed the horses down the trail. Of course, that was the arrow in the box that Great-Uncle Jack led me to in the storage area. The arrowhead isn't very sharp because the Cahuilla didn't have the best rock to work with, but it did penetrate a very tough saddle. I keep it hidden with Joaquin's head down in Valley Center.

The trail leading through the thick madrone was narrow and the horses had no real choice but to follow it all the way down the mountain slope to the old stage road, and from there, tired but settling, they followed Joaquin and Jorge back to the camp beside the meadow.

The Cahuilla braves never came to claim their rightful horses. Joaquin broke camp late that night and followed the moonlight north toward the dusty town of Riverside.

Just after midnight a car comes up the road and turns into the Superior parking lot. It's a big old black Lincoln Continental Town Car, the same year and model as the one that chased me out of the Residence Inn parking lot. The parking lot lights are good and strong, but all I get from the windshield is reflection. Then the driver bears right and begins to circle. When he comes at me, the lot lights blast the window straight on and I see the trim, dark face of Lupercio, up close to the steering wheel, peering over the top, scanning slowly left to right.

He looks toward the office lights and the Lincoln rolls forward and right, following his line of sight.

I glance at the shotgun.

I look at the push buttons and levers on the cab console before me and I remember Phillip's voice: *Use enough muscle . . . These things aren't delicate, they do what you tell them just like a car or a horse . . . Remember to undershoot the hoist when you go to place it . . . it always looks on target because it's so much smaller than the target . . . In daylight I use the end of the boom to line up the magnet and the car, but at night you can't see the damned thing . . . Don't push the servo with a load in the air or you'll lose it . . . The guys here do that for fun sometimes, drop a Suburban or a Hummer from full up, like an earthquake when it hits . . .*

I've bet that Lupercio will park in the darker third of the lot, which is underneath me, where Phillip has left the yard lights off. It's a nice little pocket of darkness, an easy walk to the inviting lights of the office and away from the brightly lit part of the yard where the cars are stacked high and the cranes idle like snoring dinosaurs.

The Lincoln eases into the dark patch of the parking lot but goes right through it. The car hesitates as if Lupercio is going to park, then he slowly continues to the exit and turns onto the access road. I watch his taillights grow smaller and closer together. They vanish.

Ten minutes later he's back. This time he cruises the parking lot in the opposite direction, brushing up close to my crane as he enters the dark patch. I look almost straight down on the roof of the Lincoln and I feel like a god up here in the dark sky, a patient and cunning god. But again he passes through. He stops in front of the office, and although I can't see him through the glare of the lights on the Lincoln's windows, I can imagine him squinting hard at the invitation before him, at the partially opened door and the play of light coming from the rear.

Suddenly the Lincoln reverses. I'm confused for just a second then I understand: Lupercio doesn't want to take his eyes off of the office. My lucky day. He backs into the darkness below me and swings parallel to the fence.

He stops.

The tranny clunks into park.

My moment.

. . . Use enough muscle . . .

The Lincoln idles. I can smell the exhaust up here. The headlights die. The second I hear the engine shut off I press forward hard on the control lever and the big electromagnetic hoist lowers through the sky, straight and true on its heavy cable. I hit the servomotor button and feel the massive charge as the generator comes to life, sending wave after wave of current to the magnet hoist.

The hoist crunches onto the Lincoln's roof and I see the huge circular magnet clamp on. The car shudders. I watch for a door to fly open while I pull hard but steady on the lever to bring up the hoist.

This is my moment of truth. From fifteen or twenty feet off the ground Lupercio can still jump out — if he thinks fast enough and understands what's happening. Which is a tall order in the dark, with your beautiful prized car suddenly taking flight with you inside it.

But over twenty feet it's a leg-breaker and he's trapped and he's mine.

The Lincoln rises fast into the air. It swings left to right because the magnet isn't quite centered and the sedan is heavier up front.

Fifteen feet and the door swings open.

Twenty and it's still open but Lupercio is still inside.

Thirty and I've got him.

The car pivots into the faint light of the yard and I can see him through the windshield and he can see me. We're eye to eye, forty feet apart. I expect him to look like he's being chased by a bear but he looks calm and unexcited. His window and the window behind him go down.

Then he astonishes me. He slams the door shut and climbs halfway out the open window, clenching the Lincoln's body pillar with his left arm.

He's up forty feet now, ten feet above me, and he draws his machete from the darkness inside the Lincoln. What can he possibly do with a machete from a distance like this — throw it?

He drops the blade back and flat over his right shoulder and I think he *is* going to throw it.

I'm wrong.

There's an orange flash and a loud crack above me then the close rip of something hitting my crane hard. The Plexiglas window splinters into snowy perforations, high and right of me. BB's! He's got shot shells in the big black handle of his machete, and a way to fire them.

But I'm not hit and he's sixty feet up. I can see the bottom of the Lincoln as it twists slowly skyward. The struts relax and the wheels droop.

Seventy feet, eighty feet.

It's a hundred-foot cable.

All the way up now, the Lincoln stops and sways and slowly turns.

My heart's pounding like distant artillery and I think of the last time I saw Lupercio stalking my Gray Fox cabin up in the mountains.

Then I think of those two Bakersfield cops he killed in my mom's courtyard and how it could have been Mom and Grandma or Hood.

But most of all I think of Harold and Gerald standing there on my porch with the custom minibike for my boys and how Lupercio turned them into bloody slabs of meat and left them in my barn for Bradley to find.

So I punch the push button and cut the power to the magnet and the car silently detaches from the hoist.

It falls slowly at first. I can't take my eyes off it. The Lincoln makes a soft hissing sound as it accelerates. The heavy front end tilts downward. Suddenly the car is dropping very fast.

At fifty feet I drop to the bottom of the cab

just in case Lupercio has another shotgun shell and the nerve to fire it.

But there's no blast.

Half a second later I'm up again, my face just high enough to peek over the console and see the Lincoln below me, its nose tucked down and the lighter back end coming around in an almost graceful pivot. It hits the parking lot with a tremendous shearing crunch and the windows explode and two of the doors fly open and the roof buckles. I hear the tinkling of glass and plastic on the asphalt as I jump into my seat and grab the lever to lower the hoist and pick it up again.

Which is when I look up at the hoist and see Lupercio inching along the boom toward me.

He's got his arms and legs wrapped around it like he's climbing a tree. He looks calm and unhurried. The machete is clenched in his teeth.

He's not halfway down the boom yet, maybe fifty feet from me. The only thing between us is the pellet-riddled Plexiglas window.

Yanking on the lever, I raise the boom as high as it will go, which puts Lupercio almost straight up, looking down on me. Then I reverse the lever and lower it. Then I raise it up again. I wait for Lupercio to fall off but he's tight to the steel struts of the boom and he's crawling closer six patient inches at a time.

He's got the machete in his right hand now, with the handle bottom pointed at me and the blade folded back over his shoulder.

This one's for Betty Little Chief.

And for me.

I lower the Plexiglas window and grab Hood's scattergun. I push the safety off right where he showed me and raise the heavy thing and sight down the barrel.

I try to hold the bead right under Lupercio's chin. Then I pull the trigger. There's a clanging noise and a bright spray of sparks on the boom ten feet behind him. In a flush of panic I yank the trigger again and miss everything — no sparks, no sound of contact.

I duck down just as his shot blasts through the crane cab. A red-hot needle punches through the top of my scalp.

I take a big breath and jump up to the window, shotgun ready. Lupercio aims the bottom of the machete handle directly at my head. I cover his face with the barrel and pull the trigger.

He seems to accelerate into something red. His face ripples and he lifts from the boom and rolls off it.

I watch him drop through the sky, machete pinwheeling beside him, all the way to the Lincoln.

He hits the roof with a loud, slightly muffled crack. His head bounces just once, quickly. The machete clangs to the asphalt beside the car and rocks tip to handle, handle to tip quicker and quicker, then settles and stops. The roof metal cradles Lupercio. He's still as a dropped sandbag.

I'm expecting him to pop up and come after me with his machete but I know he won't.

I stand for a while in the cab, staring down, reviewing my reasons. My heart feels harder. I understand that an invisible but permanent stain has settled inside me and it will be there until I join Lupercio in the Great Whatever. I see that I have failed to find a diplomatic solution, but the harder I try to figure out what it might have been, the louder I hear these three words: *he deserved it*. He has paid his price and I will pay mine and you will pay yours.

I've never killed a person before.

I leave the crane running, take my shotgun and satchel and climb from the cab. There are two more shells in the magazine of the 12-gauge.

I walk slowly past the Lincoln, not too

close, shotgun off safe and pointed at the lifeless man on the roof. There's a small chance of explosion but the car wasn't running when it hit and they built those old Lincolns with good fuel shut-off systems.

In Phillip's office I turn on the parking lot lights that he had left black for me. Then I go to the bathroom and strip off the wig to look at my head in the mirror. There's a small rip just down from the point of my crown but it doesn't look too bad. My new blond hair is marbled with red and I dab it dry with paper towels. It burns. Maybe Allison's wig slowed down the BB. I walk back outside.

It takes me a few minutes to get up my nerve but finally I lean the shotgun against the parking lot fence, march over to the Lincoln and pull Lupercio off the roof. I have to stand on the door frame and pull on his arm and push off with one foot in order to move him. I jump back and he lands on the asphalt with a splat.

He's close enough to the open rear driver's side door that I can crawl into the seat, get on my knees and pull his head and shoulders inside. Then I get out and go around and push him farther onto the seat but by the time I get back inside he's slumped back to the asphalt. This goes for on a minute or two. There's blood fucking everywhere. I'm sobbing quietly.

Finally I get a rope from the toolshed and tie it around Lupercio's chest, under his arms. Dragging him into the backseat of his Lincoln is the single most difficult physical thing I've ever done with the exception of giving birth. I throw the machete in after him. I vomit in the darkness over by the fence.

Back in the crane I fire up the electromagnet again and lift the Lincoln onto the tow truck that Phillip left for me. I line up my crushed prize with the big flatbed of the tow truck and set it down with a heavy clunk. Then I shut down the crane, look again at the shot holes in the Plexiglas and wipe the stream of blood from my chin. I'll owe Phillip for the damage.

Down by the tow truck I take from my satchel the digital camera I stole from Office Depot. I put on my wig and mask. Then I set the trigger delay on the camera, balance it on the roof of a totaled Buick and take Allison's picture in front of the wrecked Lincoln. It takes me eight shots to get two good ones, where I look victorious and you can really tell what I'm standing in front of, and there's nothing in the frame that might identify Superior Wrecking & Salvage. I get two shots of Lupercio. I shoot thirty seconds of video, too.

When I'm done I stash the mask in my satchel. I drive the tow truck half a mile down the access road and make a left that leads out to a rock quarry. The night is cool and I can smell standing water. Ahead of me a pit pool glistens flat and shiny as a mirror. I dump the Lincoln.

Fifty minutes later I'm back at the Sunset Tower.

35

The next evening on TV Hood saw the pictures and video of Allison Murrieta posing with the death car. She sat astride the heap with her knees up and her boot heels hooked into the wreckage, braced on her hands like a cowgirl on a corral. There was smeared blood on the tip of her chin.

Dave Boyer explained that the images he was about to show would be accompanied by a scrambled voice-over supplied by Allison earlier in the day. The voice sounded to Hood just like the one that Boyer had played for the cops at the task force meeting seventeen days ago:

"Hi, Dave, Allison Murrieta here. I'm sure you have the video clip and images I made up for you and I hope you have it on-screen. So your viewers know, Lupercio Maygar is dead in this car. I'm sorry the police couldn't find him first but they've had ten years to do it. This man murdered two brothers down in

Valley Center, and those two cops in Bakersfield. Frankly, I'd had enough of him. This city doesn't need him. Now Suzanne the schoolteacher can go back to work without being hunted down by a killer. And by the way, sorry to the surfer in Huntington Beach — hope your ear is okay, honey. It was an accident! Get tubed and *vaya con Dios!*"

Earlier in the day Hood had seen Boyer hustling down a headquarters hallway toward the sheriff's office. With him were an assistant sheriff, Wyte, two lieutenants and Marlon. Hood was not asked to attend, but Marlon briefed him afterward. He told Hood to watch Boyer's news show that night and to expect a call when the Allison story was over.

After a commercial for sleeping pills, Boyer was back with video links to three guests — a UCLA law school professor named Mark Tice, UCI professor of social ecology Kimber Wells and *Los Angeles Times* media reporter Josh Steiner.

Hood picked at a burrito from the corner taquería as he watched the experts.

BOYER: "Professor Tice, give us a briefing here — what exactly are we looking at in legal terms?"

TICE: "The first thing I noticed was that the woman — whoever she is — does not

440

admit to anything criminal. I'd say she's looking ahead to her day in court. Incidentally, counting the killings that this woman alluded to, Lupercio Maygar was suspected in *sixteen* Southland murders but never charged."

BOYER: "Professor Wells, just how possible is it that this woman is a direct descendant of the notorious outlaw Joaquin Murrieta?"

WELLS: "Virtually impossible, Dave. We're not even sure that the legend of Joaquin Murrieta is based on a true character. True charac*ters,* more likely."

BOYER: "But, men being men and outlaws being —"

WELLS: "Right, Dave. If there was a Joaquin Murrieta — and some historians say there were actually three 'Joaquins' hunted down by lawmen — then he certainly could have helped conceive a child."

BOYER: "If she's not a descendant of Joaquin Murrieta, then who is she, Professor Wells?"

WELLS: "I think she may be coopting that legend to fuel her alter ego and help justify her actions. It's also possible that she's very ill. Schizophrenia with a delusional subset and episodic violence. I'm no psychia—"

BOYER: "Josh Steiner, what's your take on this?"

STEINER: "I don't know who she is, but people are fascinated by her. She's had a hundred inches of ink here in the *Times*. She's racked up almost three hours of television coverage over the last three months — that's right here in a tough media market. She's gotten the cover of both the L.A. and Orange County weeklies, scores of write-ups and pictures in community newspapers, half a page in *People* and a fat paragraph, with picture, in *Time*. We're getting letters about her every day. Personally, as I go about my everyday living, guess what people are talking about? Allison Murrieta, that's who. After this thing with Lupercio Maygar, we'll see Allison get even hotter."

BOYER: "What are people saying, Josh?"

STEINER: "Most people love her. She's half Catwoman and half Robin Hood. She's a superhero with a 'tude. She's mysterious. She's beautiful —"

BOYER: "Well, I see *you* love her —"

STEINER: "She donates to charity! But you know what people really love? This woman takes the *victimization* that happens in our fear-driven, consumer lifestyle, and she turns it into *power.* If you ask a hundred people if they've ever wanted to express their frustration by swift, decisive action, every last one will say yes. Allison Murrieta turns

442

anger and frustration into something dramatic, she *expresses* it."

TICE: "She expresses it through criminal violence, Josh. We've seen her commit felonies on TV. That's a real gun she brandishes — just ask Trent Brown, the surfer she refers to. These are real crimes against real people and real property. I did some rough calculations earlier today. Based on her robberies caught on camera, and the cars she's allegedly stolen at gunpoint, *not counting* the vigilante murder of Lupercio Maygar — if Allison was convicted and given *minimum recommended sentences,* she'd be looking at one hundred and sixty years in prison."

BOYER: "If she doesn't stop robbing and stealing, do you think Allison's going to hurt or kill someone innocent, someone who just happens to be out picking up some KFC for the family?"

WELLS: "It's inevitable that —"

TICE: "I agree with Kimber."

STEINER: "Absolutely. That's one of the reasons people are so fascinated by her."

BOYER: "Will she stop?

TICE: "I hope so."

WELLS: "She enjoys it too much."

STEINER: "She won't stop. She loves the action and the attention. I guarantee you that she's watching us right now. She thrives on us just like we thrive on her."

BOYER: "Mark Tice of UCLA School of Law, you said that Lupercio Maygar was suspected of *sixteen* murders right here in Southern California. Is what happened to him justice?"

TICE: "Of course not. There's no process. It's the worst kind of vigilante action."

STEINER: "Which is interesting, because ninety percent of the letters and calls we get about Allison are positive. People *like* her."

WELLS: "That's why we have a rich history of outlaw lore in this country. People crave stories. People crave heroes. And villains. Remember the old saying, *When the facts become legend, print the legend.*"

BOYER: "Interesting. The teacher that Allison mentioned, Suzanne Jones, was nearly a victim of Lupercio Maygar. She had apparently witnessed a crime that he committed. Now she's free to come out of hiding and return to her family and to work. Any thoughts on that?"

WELLS: "Allison is coopting Suzanne just like she coopted Joaquin. She's justifying herself."

STEINER: "Sure. Good deeds make good legends."

BOYER: "When someone finally lifts that mask from Allison Murrieta's face, who are we going to see? If she isn't Joaquin Murrieta's great-great-great-great-great-great-granddaughter, who *is* she?"

TICE: "I won't speculate, Dave."

WELLS: "An out-of-work actress."

STEINER: "An employee of one of the franchises she loves to stick up."

BOYER: "Quickly, now — guess her age."

STEINER: "Late twenties."

WELLS: "Mid-thirties."

TICE: "Old enough to stand trial as an adult."

BOYER: "Wig or no wig?"

WELLS: "I think wig because —"

STEINER: "It's her hair."

TICE: "It looks real to me."

BOYER: "We're out of time. Thank you all. I see the phones are really ringing now. Call back later, folks, we'll be taking calls on our ten o'clock hour. We want to know what you think. Thanks to our guests."

Hood finished off the cold burrito and Marlon called.

"Where's Jones?"

"I don't know where she is, sir. I haven't talked to her in two days."

"Do you have a number for her?"

"Not a current one, no."

"I want to bring her in, ask her some questions about Allison Murrieta. This whole

445

thing has gotten out of hand. You'll help with that?"

"Of course I'll help."

"I'll take some uniforms and collect her myself. I can keep you out of it."

"No, sir. It was my idea that she's Murrieta. I'll face up to that."

"Make it happen."

"I'll do my best."

Forty minutes later the phone rang again.

"Hello, Charles Robert."

"You okay?"

"I'm perfect. Merle's at the House of Blues. I got tickets at will call."

"Pick you up or meet you there?"

"I'm outside your apartment in a rented Cadillac STS. It's black on black and the leather's smooth as your cheeks after a shave, Charlie. I kid you not."

It took Hood a moment to figure how she'd gotten his home address. He looked out the window and saw the car. "You looked in my wallet at the restaurant."

"I confess."

"You saw the news?"

"Did I ever. I've been with my boys almost two whole days. Right now I'm the happiest woman on earth. I'm celebrating and I'm going to listen to Merle and drink. I rented the car, bought a new blue blouse and some tight black jeans for you. Tomorrow we're all moving back home and things are getting back to normal. Except Ernest and I will have separate quarters from now on. He's cool with that. I start school Monday. Can you hurry?"

"I need five minutes. Come on up."

"We'd never get to the House of Blues."

Five minutes later Hood came down. Before getting into the STS, he went to the driver's side window and gave her his best traitor's kiss.

Merle Haggard looked seventy years old and too mean to die, which Hood figured was pretty much what Merle was. His voice was clear and honest, and his band played the sad old songs with the same lightness and good cheer that Hood had always loved.

Suzanne was beautiful, though Hood missed her brown waves. The new blouse was silk, sleeveless, cobalt blue. She wore a beat-up denim jacket over it and it looked right. She drank four whiskey sours fast then went to seltzer with lime. She kept the beat with a boot toe on the floor and a hand high on Hood's thigh under the table.

She leaned back and caught his eye, smiling big and innocent, and Hood marveled at all she had accomplished in the last days, in the last months, in her short life.

Hood listened to Merle's stories of heartbreak and drinking and poverty and prison, and he thought of being young in Bakersfield and how those songs had nudged him toward the right side of the law. The loneliness in them had hit him hardest — the aloneness of the drinker who calls the bar his home, or the con walking to his execution, or the released inmate who can't get away from his past. Now Hood realized that the songs were also about Suzanne Jones and Allison Murrieta and all people who chase their own histories to the edge of their own cliffs. He saw that stories like these get told over and over because they apply to so many of us, only the names of the characters changing with time.

"You look thoughtful, Charlie."

"Every once in a while one sneaks in."

She held his gaze. "I thought about what you said the other morning when I was up in the tree. About us meeting when we were real young, both getting our pictures taken for the newspaper. When you said it I thought it was an unglamorous proposition but I came to like it. Very down-home. Two kids, they fall in love and ride off together. Exactly *not* what Merle sings about."

"I never thought glamorously. It's a fault."

"Don't act so humble, Charlie. You're not that great. Indira Gandhi said that but I can't remember about whom."

Hood smiled back but felt a strong sorrow.

A little past midnight he and Suzanne came through the exit. The night was damp and warm, and Marlon and two deputies were waiting.

36

They worked it out so Hood would drive her in the STS to the Marina del Rey safe house. The safe house was Hood's idea — a courtesy to Suzanne, who would be recognized by Sheriff's deputies and reporters if they talked at headquarters. This was not an arrest. It was not an interview, not an interrogation.

Susan stared straight ahead and said nothing.

"They want to ask you about Allison," said Hood.

She continued staring through the windshield.

Hood followed Marlon's plainwrap for the freeway. The Sheriff's cruiser had fallen in behind him.

"I know you're her," he said. "I know you'll hate me for what I've done, but I didn't betray you to gain something for myself. I did it because Allison is going to get you killed.

I love you and I'm sorry."

"You *love* me? What does that matter? You just accused me of murder and armed robbery. I want my lawyer."

"You're not under arrest."

She was on her phone before Hood made the freeway. She turned to the window and spoke quietly, hung up, then resumed her wordless surveillance through the windshield. Five minutes later Hood heard a ringtone — the whinny of a horse — and Suzanne again turned away from him.

Hood caught a few phrases:

"L.A. Sheriff's . . ."

". . . asinine thing I've ever . . ."

"Allison Murrieta, the . . ."

". . . hilarious someday . . ."

". . . right now, a safe house in Marina del Rey, on Bora Bora . . ."

She punched off with a flourish and flung the phone back into her bag.

"I'm starved. Hit the Jack on Lincoln, will ya? I'll spring for all you miserable cops, don't worry."

Hood saw through this as a stall for Suzanne's lawyer, but he did it anyway.

The late night line for the drive-through window was long, but Suzanne didn't say a word. She leaned over and glared at him and ordered four kid's meals and one adult combo. Then she sat back, dug into her bag and tossed a twenty onto Hood's lap.

"Thank you."

"Fuck off, Charlie."

As soon as they walked into the safe house, Suzanne brushed past Marlon and the two deputies and locked herself in the bathroom. Hood remembered that the window in it was high and small.

He set the food on the dinette table. He heard the bathroom fan go on.

Marlon and the deputies sat at the table. Hood stood beside it, utterly at a loss.

Suzanne came out looking at her watch. "Eat up, children."

She didn't look at Hood as she took the adult bag to the couch, dropped it on the coffee table before her and sat.

"You can ask your questions while I eat."

"I take it Charlie has filled you in," said Marlon. He gave Hood a sharp look.

"Get to the point if you have one," said Suzanne.

"I just have a couple of simple questions. One is, have you ever met this Allison Murrieta?"

"No comment."

"Seen her on TV?"

"Of course."

Suzanne shook her head and bit a French

fry in half and leveled her gaze on Hood. He was surprised at the voltage of her anger.

Marlon waited with a hopeful look on his face. "You might not know this, but to some people, Allison Murrieta looks like you. You with a wig. Maybe it's ridiculous to think that you're *her*. But when a really unusual idea like that gets under my skin, it's like a splinter I can't get out. It bothers me."

Suzanne took a bite of a sandwich, looked at Marlon. "I'm so glad you're bothered."

"Ms. Jones, what do you make of that resemblance?"

"Not one thing."

"But you do see it?"

"Don't try to lead me. You can't."

"If you can tell me where you were last night, we're pretty much done here."

"It's none of your business. Where were you?"

Marlon opened his kid's meal bag and looked in. "Home. The truth is usually simple."

Hood heard something outside and the doorbell rang. He opened the door and a small, stout woman held his look as she walked past him into the room. She wore yellow sweats and a yellow ball cap. He recognized her. Behind her came a large young man in a sharp black suit.

The men stood. She looked at them, and at Suzanne, then once more at Hood. The young man closed the door softly then stood with his back to it and his hands folded like a deacon waiting for the plate.

The small woman stepped forward and handed a card to Marlon.

"My name is Ruth Mayer. I am an attorney representing Suzanne Jones. Is she under arrest?"

"No, ma'am, she isn't," said Marlon. "We just had some simple questions for her and we were trying to get some simple answers. As a courtesy, we didn't want to bring her downtown."

"Suzanne will not speak to you now. I can be reached twenty-four hours a day at the number on that card and I will answer any and all questions on her behalf. If you choose to arrest her, we would appreciate a call twelve hours in advance. Suzanne promises not to leave the state of California for the next thirty days, except in the case of a family emergency. My client is an award-winning primary school teacher, and school starts next week — correct, Suzanne?"

"Yep."

"You should know that my client is an excellent teacher. My niece had her for eighth-grade history."

The young man held open the door.

"Good night, gentlemen," said Mayer. "Suzie, come with me. Jason, the door."

But Marlon stepped ahead of them and asked Jason to move his hands away from the door. When he let go, Marlon kicked it shut with a slam and turned back to the room.

"Okay, we'll do it your way. Ms. Jones is under arrest for grand theft auto unless she can explain that STS downstairs. The valet at the Ivy surrendered the keys to it at gunpoint this afternoon. To Allison Murrieta."

"Don't *say* anything, Suzie," snapped the lawyer. "Not one word."

Marlon Mirandized her, and one of the uniforms cuffed her wrists behind her back.

Suzanne looked through Hood.

The lawyer told her she'd be free by late Monday morning.

37

At nine Monday morning Ernest delivers ten grand cash to a bondsman for a hundred-thousand-dollar bail bond. The judge accepts Ruth's argument that as a mother and a teacher with no criminal record I pose little flight risk, but she points out that allegedly there was a gun involved. I've been in jail fifty-six hours and my clothes are wrinkled, my hair smells of weak shampoo and my attitude is bad. But the hole in the top of my scalp itches, healing up nicely.

At eleven fifteen Ruth and Jason the hunk and I walk out of the jail into the hot Los Angeles morning. There are more cameras and reporters than I've seen since O.J. Ruth's office has called every reporter she knows, and many that she doesn't. I'm beginning to understand how celebrities feel and I like it.

Bradley and Jordan walk beside me, Ernest trails, and I carry baby Kenny, who smiles and bubbles and grunts.

Ruth has given Fox News the privilege of hosting me in return for their airing her full statement, so we make our way through the booms and mikes and the cables and the cameras and the shouted questions bouncing off us like hailstones. There's a Fox uplink van with a podium and microphone set up directly in front of the Fox News logo.

Ruth steps onto the plastic milk case that Jason has set behind the podium. Ruth is five feet tall, in shoes. She angles the mike and waits for the reporters to quiet down.

"When I first visited the Franklin middle school classroom of Suzanne Jones two years ago, I didn't imagine that I'd be defending her from the most egregious, false criminal charges that I, in thirty years of practicing law in this city, have ever seen. Now I have that dubious honor. Last night L.A. Sheriff's deputies arrested Suzanne on suspicion of stealing, *at gunpoint* yesterday evening, a car from Ivy restaurant. There were two witnesses to this theft. Both witnesses recognized *and identified* the armed robber as Allison Murrieta. Allison Murrieta, as you know, is a colorful local criminal to whom Suzanne bears little resemblance. In the Sheriff's Department's haste to arrest Allison Murrieta, they've spun their wheel of fortune and the needle has landed on

Suzanne Jones — mother of three, award-winning schoolteacher in L.A. Unified, a former teacher of the year. I've seen bad arrests, but this is the first-place winner. I'm sure the district attorney won't file on this, but if he does, we look very forward to our day in court. But why should you believe me? Use your own eyes and explain to me why the L.A. Sheriff's can't tell a brunette from a blonde, or a dangerous felon from a fine and decent citizen. Suzanne, come up here."

I step over to the mike still holding Kenny. My arms are getting tired and I realize I'm out of shape for holding him, and what a poor mother I've been the last few weeks. I've always loved lugging around my children.

I keep my head high and look out at the crowd. "This is all a big misunderstanding but thanks for being interested and coming out. Jail is a rotten place, so don't get falsely arrested on a Friday night 'cause they won't let you out until Monday. I can't talk about the case because Ruth will kill me but I'm sure they'll just drop it when they learn the facts. I'm so relieved that I can go back to my family and my job. I don't have to run anymore. These last few weeks have been a nightmare for me and my family. I never knew how richly blessed my life was until it was almost taken away."

I manage a tired smile as I hold up Kenny for a moment then step away from the podium.

Ruth hops back onto the milk crate for questions.

After lunch we go to Ruth's office in Century City. We're twelve stories up, receiving steaming triple espressos produced by an elaborate copper machine in Ruth's suite and served by one of her secretaries. The suite is cream-colored everything, except her desk, which looks like Honduran mahogany, and the art on the wall, which are silk screens from Warhol's animal series and some very nice Hockney lithographs. There's a glass table with magazines on it and on top is this week's *People* with Allison's masked face on the cover.

When the secretary leaves, Ruth sighs deeply, punches a remote control to open a window and takes a pack of cigarettes from her desk. She offers me one but I decline.

She sits behind the desk, looking hard at me. She's still looking hard at me as she lights her smoke with one of those long windproof fireplace lighters that is basically a flamethrower. She sets the lighter on the desk, slides a yellow notepad over and takes a pencil from a thick glass holder. Beside the pencils is a small box that looks like a speaker, and she turns it on. The smoke drifts into the box.

"Talk to me, Suzanne."

"Where do I start?"

"With why you drove a stolen car to a Merle Haggard show."

"Fastest way to get there?"

"Suzanne."

"Ruth — relax. This is all simpler than it looks."

I sit back in my chair and watch her smoke rise and dip. I look her straight in the eyes.

"About two weeks ago I got a call from a woman claiming to be Allison Murrieta. I have no idea how she got my number. It was the day after the Sheriffs plastered my face all over the TV, telling everyone that Lupercio Maygar was after me. She had seen all that and she said she wasn't going to, and I quote, *let that vicious thug kill you.* I told her I could handle my own problems and she laughed. She asked me if I needed anything — a car, some cash for living on the run, maybe a good gun. I said I didn't need anything, though I did make a crack about a Cadillac STS being the car I'd most like. I'm a car girl."

Ruth exhales hugely, more smoke than you'd think a small woman could get inside her. The smoke lingers upward then changes its mind and hurries down into the box. She steadies the yellow pad with her cigarette hand, writes something with the other, fixes me again with her clear brown eyes.

"Of course I figured it was a hoax," I said. "A few days later she called again. Same voice. It was evening. The night before, the real Allison Murrieta had robbed a Kentucky Fried Chicken, and the night before that, a Burger King. She talked about them, about this old guy who had some kind of seizure at the BK, and her gun going off accidentally. She had details you wouldn't have gotten off the news clips of those robberies. You know, stuff you'd have to be there to know — what the old man's wife did, and what the surfers smelled like, how when she's wearing that mask it cuts down her peripheral vision which really bugs her but she has to have it and the crystal — she said it's a Swarovski — adds a little bit of class. She made the mask herself, she said."

Ruth doesn't write much. I blather and she studies me and scribbles something, then she studies me some more.

"Why did she call?"

The espresso is extremely good. It makes

me want to stand up and run around, maybe pull a gun and rob someone, just for the pure joyful rush of it. But I sit still and answer.

"Same reason, I guess — she wanted to know if there was anything I needed. I said no. She said if she knew where I was she might be able to provide some 'meaningful security' for me. I refused to tell her where I was. I think she wanted to tell someone about the crimes she committed. So, she talked."

Ruth scribbles, underlines something. "Then?"

"She called me again a day or so later. Said she wanted to know how I was doing. I was wishing she wouldn't call anymore but I was also kind of getting to like her. She said she had a feel for Lupercio, thought she'd catch up with him soon. I said, what — you're not *looking* for him are you? And she laughed and said, *You're damned right I am.* She said I'd enjoy my freedom even more when I got it back again. Said she had a kick-ass eighth-grade history teacher and loved him. Then she hung up."

"Did she scramble her voice?" said Ruth.

"No. It was natural. A woman's voice, no accent that I could tell. A mature voice, but not an old one. Smooth, calm."

"Good. Go on."

"The day after Lupercio got smashed up in his car, I left the hotel late afternoon —"

"What hotel?"

"The Sunset Tower — to buy a few things then go see Ernest and the boys. They were down in Huntington Beach. I bought a blouse and jeans at a boutique on Sunset. When I came out, Allison Murrieta was leaning up against my Sentra."

Ruth looks up from her pad. She opens a drawer and slaps a green glass ashtray to the desktop. "Describe her."

"I had no idea who she was. Five feet five or six, one-thirty. Curvy but stout. She wears a wig for the robberies. Her real hair is short, straight and has a red henna job. Her eyes are brown. Good skin. On TV, the mask makes her face look wide, but her face really is wide. She has high cheekbones and pretty lips and chin. She's attractive. Sexy attractive, not girl-next-door attractive. She was wearing a workout suit and athletic shoes. She had a leather satchel over her shoulder. I can tell you I could see her every day, talk to her all the time, and not see Allison Murrieta in her — they look so little alike."

Ruth stares at me. The pencil is poised but unmoving.

"She said, 'I'm Allison. Get in. Let's talk.' She flashed that little white gun. I'd never had a gun brandished at me and it's a very chilling thing. I wondered if she was going to do something violent and flamboyant to me, but I kept thinking that I was better PR for her alive than shot up. Anyway, I had my key out so I opened the driver's door and hit the unlock. We sat in the car for a few minutes. She was wearing the new Tommy Hilfiger scent. She told me that she'd seen Lupercio the night before, crushed to death in a car. She didn't say she'd done it, but it was implied. She seemed unfazed. She said I could go back to my family, go back to work. She took a plastic Blockbuster bag out of the satchel and handed it to me. I looked in — it was heavy with bills and some change. I gave it back. I told her I didn't need it, didn't want it."

"How much was there?"

"Maybe a thousand. I really just glanced at it. She put it back in the satchel and said, 'Suzanne, you can say no to money but I know you can't say no to *that*.' She nodded at this Caddy STS parked right next to me. It was black and beautiful. I remembered that joke I made to her the first time we talked and I thought me and my big mouth. 'Drive it tonight,' she said. 'Go out and celebrate. You deserve to. It's not stolen, it's borrowed. Leave it with the Tower valet when you're

464

done with it and I'll take care of the rest. I'll make sure this pathetic heap gets back to your hotel.' She called my Sentra a *pathetic heap.*"

"And what did you do?"

"Ruth, I thought about it. I loved the STS, I'll confess to that. But I also saw that Allison really wanted me to take it. I wondered if it was just to make her more colorful, make her seem more like Robin Hood. If it was something she'd tell the press about, and exploit. I also believed that it was a borrowed car, because I figured if she'd stolen it, she'd be proud, right? But mainly, I felt that if I turned the car down she'd feel disrespected and then get angry. I thought of the gun. There was an underlying threat from the gun — at least in my mind. So I agreed to take the car."

She grinds out the butt in the green ashtray, getting every last little ember.

"You were afraid to defy her?"

"Yes."

"Afraid of the gun?"

"Who wouldn't be?"

"Why didn't you report this to the police?"

"Later, I almost did. I had my cell phone in my hand to make the call. But Allison Murrieta hadn't harmed me. In fact, she had rid me of a killer who was on my tail. She had allowed me to get back to my family and my job. I realized that with one call I could probably have the police staking out the Sunset Tower when she drove the Sentra back there. I couldn't do that to her. At least, I didn't. On some level I felt like I owed her something. On another, I was afraid of her. And I also . . . well, I wanted to touch her fame for a short time, to be a part of it. It's been exhilarating for me."

Ruth puts the ashtray back in her desk, dead butt and all. "Suzanne, are you telling me the truth?"

"Whole, and nothing but."

"Would you be willing to testify on your own behalf, if this were to go to trial?"

"Yes."

"Suzanne, I've seen elaborate alibis hold up under cross-examination, but not many."

"The truth is easy to tell. I'll stand by it, Ruth."

Ruth nods, drops the pencil to the pad and sits back. "This won't get that far, Suzanne. I've got an appointment with the DA in about an hour. I'll outline for him what we talked about. I expect the charges to be dropped by the end of the workday."

I sigh and look down.

"Do you want to bring a civil suit for

wrongful arrest? You could win a pretty nice judgment for the damage to your reputation, the jail time, the usual inconvenience and stress. I'd demand a million dollars and you'd get maybe one-quarter of that."

"No, thank you."

"Good. Your decision not to press a civil case will be a large motivator for the DA to fold up and go home."

"Yes."

Ruth's secretary came in just then, set a sheaf of papers in front of Ruth, smiled at me and walked back out.

"Here's a contract, with a substantial fee adjustment because you're a schoolteacher and I like you."

"Thank you."

"You won't see the inside of a courtroom on this matter again."

"I really do truly thank you."

"Tell me about the deputy. Hood."

I haven't said one word to her about Hood. So I tell her. Basically the truth. Pretty much all of it. She listens without interrupting. She makes no notes. She looks down at her hands.

"I had a guy like that once," says Ruth. "Forty years ago. Haven't seen him since. I think of him often. I dream about him. In my dreams he's never aged, and neither have

I. I also love my husband."

"I know the feeling."

I see that Ruth is thinking about him. She comes out of it.

"Was he suspicious about the car?"

"I told him I rented it."

Ruth eyes me in a way that makes me glad she's on my side. Very glad.

"In your presence, did Allison wipe her fingerprints off the interior of your Sentra?"

This is a fastball but I pull it.

"Yes. She had a box of wet wipes in her satchel."

"Good. Because the DA might try to get fancy on us, say all the prints in the Cadillac are yours."

"Well, some of them are. And Hood's."

"If she wiped down the Sentra, then she would have wiped down the Caddy, too."

"I would think."

"So your prints are in both cars and hers are in neither."

"I don't know what she did in the Caddy."

"No, how could you?"

38

I spend the rest of the day with my boys and Ernest, moving back into our home down in Valley Center. It's blazing hot but the sky is clear and the air is clean and I feel a great relief spreading through me as I look out at my home and the barn and the big oak tree and the pond.

Bradley boards and Jordan fishes. I love the sound of the skateboard wheels on the wooden half pipe and I love the sight of Jordan out there trying to fool the crafty bass that live in the cattails near the pond's south edge. Baby Kenny rides Ernest's broad shoulders, his tiny hands clamped to his father's ears.

The dogs bound around the property, repissing on things and fruitlessly chasing the rabbits and ground squirrels and bullfrogs.

Ernest is very quiet as always, but I can see the hurt in his face since I told him about the new arrangement here. It'll be tough for a while. I don't doubt for a second that Ernest will find suitable female company — he's got the look and the talk when he needs it. I won't let him brood. I've gotten to know some of the single women down here. They're country craftsman types — horse people and farmers and makers of things — and they like Ernest's broad-backed humility and good humor. I may try to nudge one or two his way. No matter what I'm doing with whom, I'm going to keep Ernest in my life and in Kenny's life as much as Ernest wants to be. We need him. We need all the fathers we can get.

Bradley's father, of course, cut out after I shot him. I've told him a thousand times that he's welcome around here. He comes around now and then but he acts like a dog that's been kicked too hard too often. His wife is bitterly ugly which pleases me. He is now a man almost completely devoid of everything I was once attracted to. He still has good teeth.

Sometimes it's hard to understand why his son is a prince. Even at sixteen Bradley is wise, charming, articulate, acutely aware of others and the world around him, mentally incisive, athletically gifted, physically beautiful, flawlessly polite and agonizingly shy. He tested at 160 on the Stanford-Binet IQ test they gave him this year. The results embarrassed him. He's pushing six feet tall already and still growing. They call him Radley on the varsity football team, where he started at wide receiver and safety last year as a sophomore. He hits extremely hard. His freshman English teacher called me to say he was the most talented writer she'd ever had, and you know how much I value the opinions of teachers. On the downside, he bores easily and has a genuine appetite for risk and danger. He has little if any sense of his own mortality. But with his black hair to his shoulders and his chocolate eyes and his silly goatee he looks like a god-in-training, a poet-warrior, a hero. I'll take some of the credit for that but I think history is more responsible for Bradley than any of us are. Now I sound like my mom.

So I look at Bradley out the window and I know it's time for me to have the talk with him. The truth of me and Jack and Joaquin, of the old clothes and the Cahuilla arrow and the head preserved in alcohol out in the barn. The truth of Allison Murrieta and the diamonds and Lupercio and Harold and Gerald and the cops in Bakersfield. The truth of Hood, who knows a small part of this.

Is it Bradley's truth, too?

471

You can see the pickle I'm in. Few mothers on earth would send their son into the world as an outlaw, even the world's most handsome and potentially successful. But if Bradley is who I think he is, he suspects already. He's seen me the same way Hood and my mother have seen me, and although Bradley hasn't quite put it all together, he might. The truth can make us free but it can also lead us to prison or get us killed.

I may say nothing to Bradley and let him figure it out or not. In spite of the long reach of history, there is plenty of free choice to be had: I didn't have to carry Bradley to term but I chose to, and I didn't have to kill Lupercio but I did.

But without my great-uncle Jack I would not have found the beginnings of my story, and without me Bradley might never find his. Send him into the world without the truth of who he is? I don't know. Maybe an absence of truth would be the most valuable gift I could ever give him — a chilling notion.

Jordan's dad is dead of cancer and that's a shame. Great guy. Ernest means a lot to Jordan although there is an empty and yearning place in the heart of a boy whose father has died. Jordan told me that he was very impressed by the calm and bravery of

Deputy Hood because he fought in Iraq.

When Jordan asks if he'll see Hood again, I tell him I'm not sure.

To be honest I can't blame Hood for what he did. I said some ugly things to him but that was just anger and humiliation. Allison may well be the death of me, and for Hood to have seen me in her puts him on a different plane than other people. My mother told me that someone would see that Allison was me, or that I was Allison, and that person would have a special connection to me. My mother has a strangely fated but romantic view of things — half Mexican folktale and half paperback bodice-ripper. I don't know how romantic it is, but Hood was the one who made the connection. He *saw.* And boy, did I see him.

But as soon as Hood saw, he was really stuck because he's a cop and it's his job to put people like me behind bars. The fact that I was, and still am, abundantly hot for him only made matters worse. I played him like a good guitar. Talk about star-crossed.

I don't see a way to keep Hood. The DA might drop the charges against me but Hood won't. I might be able to persuade him into an occasional sexual escapade but that would be small potatoes to us now. There for a while, when he was having me and knowing who I was, it was hard on Hood's soul. I weakened him. I think he's stronger now that I know he knows. The spell is broken. I really wish I could cast it again but Hood has that thing inside, the simple Man Thing that you just can't get around. He *let* me around it while he made up his mind what to do with me. But I can't get around it without his permission. And I don't think I'll get that again.

If Allison vanished, never to return, Hood might accommodate me. Might not. I think it would stick in his craw forever if he let a car-thieving armed robber who committed murder go free on his watch. Hood's not wired to let that happen. And Allison isn't going to vanish, because I need her. I'm not wired to let *that* happen.

There are three things I want to square with Hood.

One is that secret of his, from Iraq. He never told me what happened there but I know it's something he believes he did wrong and it haunts him. I think it hurts him to keep it inside. A *gusano*. I want to know so I can bear a little of it for him, my contribution to the war.

Second, I'd like to say good-bye to Hood with my whole body and heart, a true extravaganza — you know, the kind of good-bye where you're making love and crying at the same time and what you feel is the sweetest love there is because you know you'll probably never see that person again. I don't know if he'd allow that. I think I can seduce him one more time. I'll certainly try. Maybe that would be a good time for him to reveal his war ghosts to me.

Third is the necklace I had made for him, that elegant H of diamonds. Guess I'll have to keep it to myself for a while, which is too bad because I know he'd love it.

Then there's the problem of Guy, that spooky bastard with the fancy computers who was helping Lupercio find me so he could kill me and take my diamonds. My source inside the LASD has come through for me. Guy is actually Captain Reginald Wyte — one of Hood's superiors. As I suspected. And thanks to the little GPU that I shoplifted from the Sports Authority not long ago, I know exactly where to find this hideous man who is a buyer and seller of all things, an employer of murderers, and a law enforcement officer.

I'm going to fix his wagon like I did Lupercio's and I want Hood to know why.

Of course I can't tell him.

If I tell Hood what I know about Wyte and how I know it, I may as well drive to his apartment in Silver Lake, sit down on his couch and put on my own handcuffs. Actually that could be a lot of fun, but enough.

I know how to handle Wyte. But I don't know how to tell Hood about him.

I stand in the kitchen with the windows open and the AC on, trying to get the house aired out and cooled down. I look out at the boys and Ernest all doing what they love to do. I have their diamond jewelry in my satchel, which I picked up from Quang the day I evened my score with Lupercio. While my sons and Ernest are outside, I get the gifts. Before setting the black boxes on their bed pillows, I peek into each one. Few things in life have struck me as this beautiful.

I'm very happy and content and I tell myself to enjoy it because it never lasts long.

A couple hours later Ruth calls: charges dropped.

"But the heat's not off, Suzanne," she says. "They'll keep looking and digging."

"They can knock themselves out."

"Strive to be a model citizen for a while."

"Easy. I've got history to teach."

"Shifting gears, I've had fourteen people call my office about you — print, television and radio. Film and book agents. Producers. Some of these people are serious and big,

Suzanne. Interested?"

"Of course."

"It will be a little like selling your soul."

"I can't wait to get started."

"You would have no privacy for a month, maybe two."

"I can make some interview time. Only the really important stuff."

"Let me try to establish some kind of priorities, thin out the field. There will be more inquiries, believe me. I may need to sell myself into some of this. You can't buy publicity like this. It's priceless."

"Cut right in."

Ruth went quiet for a beat. "It's nice getting to know you a little better, Suzanne. If the media or the cops harass you, call me immediately. Don't talk to anybody but through me. Anything you say to them now reduces the value of what you say later. I told the DA you were not interested in a wrongful arrest suit, but reminded him that people change their minds. When Ruth Mayer says wrongful arrest, people listen."

"You've got big feet, Ruth."

"They're size four."

By nine o'clock we've had dinner and teamed up on the dishes and we're watching TV just like a regular family. I've answered six calls on the home phone and screened six others. All media, except for Betty Little Chief welcoming us back. I don't know how the reporters and producers come up with unlisted numbers so fast.

My cell throbs against my waist and I take it outside.

"Hello. It's Guy."

"I thought you'd call sooner."

"You've been a bit busy. Ruth Mayer is terrific but I hope I never need her."

"I have unpleasant memories of you."

"Mine aren't pleasant either."

Silence then.

"I made some mistakes," he says.

"Lupercio got what he deserved."

"I agree absolutely. I failed to understand you. But now I do. We're alike. We're gifted. Trust can make us wealthy."

"You already said all that."

"But now I know your secret. In my opinion you are a criminal genius. Allison — I want to work with you."

"I don't know what you're talking about."

"Of course you do. Laura. Suzanne. Allison. It doesn't matter what you call yourself."

I'd like to say: *It's a big city. Let's go our own ways. We're free and prosperous and it can't get much better.*

But my position is precarious — I'm a budding celebrity schoolteacher who tried to sell stolen diamonds. If Wyte finds out that I know who he really is, he'll kill me. Without question. He doesn't have the stones to do it himself but he can find another Lupercio. There's always another Lupercio. My ignorance, in his eyes, is what makes him want to work with me, and what keeps me alive.

I look inside at Jordan's face flickering in the TV light and I see the potential cost of doing business with this man.

"I've thought about this a lot," he says. "And I have a very interesting proposal for you. Name the time and place. No Angel and no Rorke. Just us. I have a way for you to achieve everything you desire. Bring the diamonds and I'll give you your price. It will get us off on the right footing. Forty-five grand is nothing compared to what fortune will come later."

"The L.A. River," I say. "Midnight tomorrow. First Street Viaduct, down at the water."

"It's September. There is no water."

"There's always a little. Stand out in the open where I can see you."

39

The night is starless and a half moon resting on its back dangles light over the river. I trot across the railroad tracks and the gravel crunches under my feet. The power lines above me buzz as I stop beneath concrete stanchions acrawl with graffiti vibrating green and red and yellow and blue even in the darkness. I stand and watch. A man waits at the bottom of the channel, downriver. I scan the banks of the channel and the walls of the bridge and the deep-cut shadows beneath the caissons, but I see no one else. I sidestep down the gently angled side of the viaduct.

At first it looks empty. But as I jump from the steep side to the flat bottom of the channel I see a faint gray ribbon winding toward the ocean. It's no more than a stream and almost invisible as it reflects the featureless sky above.

The man is wearing a Dodgers warm-up

jacket. His hands are in the pockets. He studies me as I approach. He has the big torso and short legs of Wyte. I've got my Colt Gold Cup .45 in my right hand, out where he can see it. My left hand is empty and down at my side, and Cañonita is in the left pocket of my coat.

"Suzanne."

"Guy."

"That's a big gun."

"Yes, it is."

"I brought high hopes to this meeting. I'm unarmed."

"Take your hands out slowly."

"Of course. I like your new haircut."

"Thank you."

Wyte slips his hands out, turns his palms toward me, lowers them. "This is going to be a challenge, trying to make a legitimate business proposition at gunpoint."

I lower the .45. "Why's that?"

"It suggests a lack of trust. But that will change. A year from now we'll be sitting across from each other at the Peninsula, say, or the Edison, sipping single malts and toasting our many successes. I believe in that future. Tonight we're going to begin something unique, enduring and shamelessly profitable. Do you have a vision of your life at forty years old?"

"By then I want a big solid house, piles of money in the bank, acreage, my boys and a drawbridge."

"Crocodiles in the moat?"

"Very large ones."

"You can have them, and more. Suzanne, I can sell everything you can acquire. *Everything.* I've never once paid anyone over thirty-five percent of what I earn but I'll make you an equal partner — fifty percent each. You've shown determination and courage. There's nothing I respect more than respect."

Wyte studies me. "I'm getting top, top dollar for all things American. Even our enemies love our cars and trucks and light planes and boats. They love our guns and ammo and our copper wire and our sheet metal and our cigarettes and porn. I've got arrangements within the Ports of Long Beach and Los Angeles that afford me virtually unlimited use of containers — unopened and uninspected except for random radiation scans. Which is fine because we have no intention of exporting nuclear devices unless, of course, you think you can steal one."

Wyte is smiling. It's a dry, big-toothed smile but even at night I can see the twinkle in his eyes.

"Suzanne, listen. Because of my connections I know where all this product *is*. I know who has it and how they protect it. I have security information on harbors, ports, marinas, railway and bus stations, airports and hundreds of Los Angeles County institutions. Hundreds. Consider: when a beautiful new shipment of Mercedes-Benz automobiles comes in by rail this Friday, I know when the yard security will be lax and where the fence can be breached. Or, as we've seen, when an unfortunate diamond broker tries to pay off his gambling debts in stones, I know when and where it's going to happen. You might not ever like me, but you'll love my information."

He stops and lifts his nose to the breeze.

"How can you know all that?"

"It's what I do. I work hard at it."

"The merchant of menace."

Wyte sighs and lifts his chin but I can't tell if he's sniffing the breeze again or showing me disappointment.

"Why me?" I ask.

He takes a deep breath and lets it out slowly. He looks up, maybe at the power lines throbbing overhead, maybe at the recumbent moon. When he looks back at me there's a different glimmer in his eyes, something wild.

"Because you are youth. You are health

and strength. You can do things I can only dream of. You can do things *you* haven't dreamed of, yet. Suzanne, listen. You have to let go of Allison, quit the fast-food stick-ups and the publicity. The risk is much too high for the reward. Find a new way to taste your own adrenaline. Don't contribute to charities — create one of your *own,* a tax-free shrine to comfort the afflicted and coddle your soul. You must steal more cars. You must also steal motorcycles and personal watercraft. You must graduate to higher-cost items, such as light airplanes and motor yachts. These require more planning and less luck. Let Allison go into history beside her great-great-great whatever he was. Secure her legend by allowing her to vanish. If Allison is never heard from again, she'll be talked and written about for decades. Maybe longer. The cover of *People* magazine — that's a triumph — what more can Allison want? You must continue to be an award-winning schoolteacher and a terrific mom. They'll want you to go on television to tell the story of your relationship with the outlaw Allison, the killing of Lupercio, your wrongful arrest. This is the real mask that hides you. Let them worship the silent Allison Murrieta. The most powerful stories are told in whispers."

I hear what I think is a grocery cart rattling down the channel behind me. Wyte looks past me but I can't tell if he's curious or expectant. I aim the Colt at his chest, step back and turn my head. The cart glistens dully toward me, more sound than sight. The wheels clatter on the concrete and the loosely jointed steel shivers and clanks.

Wyte's chest reappears atop my gun sight. "I'll put my hands up if you'd like."

This is exactly what he'd do if he had a handgun holstered under his coat and behind his neck.

"Don't move."

He watches the cart.

I turn again for a look at the pusher: a man, hooded in a dark sweatshirt, baggy pants. He's a hundred feet away. The cart is filled with what looks like grocery bags. It veers left then right as if it has its own mind, and I figure the guy is drunk or acting that way. I look back at Wyte. Hands still up, good boy. I slide my left hand into my jacket pocket.

With the Colt still aimed at Wyte I step back from Cart Man's path so I can see both of them with a minimal turn of head.

"He's a bum," says Wyte.

When Cart Man is fifty feet away I can see he's a black guy. Maybe Rorke. The cart veers and shakes and rattles.

"Don't move," I say to Wyte.

"Move where?" he asks.

Cart Man at thirty feet is still lost inside his hood. The cart makes a racket. At twenty feet it veers right. Cart Man appears to be fighting a bad wheel but he looks at me.

I draw Cañonita at him and he stops. "Hands up, Rorke. Let go of the fucking cart. Now."

I see the whites of his eyes. He takes his hands off the handle and raises them high. The cart starts to roll toward the water, the back end coming around and one front wheel buckling over and over. It picks up speed. I can see it's going to hit the water about the time it tips over. So Cart Man makes a move for it.

"Daz all my stuff. Everthin."

"FREEZE!"

I look at Wyte but he hasn't budged. Cart Man actually does freeze, like a kid in a game, one foot in the air and both hands extended toward the cart. I've got Cañonita trained on his dark sweatshirt. The cart rolls into an even tighter turn and goes into the river. But the water stops it. It doesn't tip over. When I turn back to Wyte I can hear the water lapping against the steel.

"Take off that hood then put your hands

back up," I say to Cart Man.

"But I'm gonna fall."

"Then put down your foot."

He lowers his foot to the concrete, then slowly pulls back the hood and I see his matted hair, his sunken eyes, the dark patches of beard. I know that Wyte could employ more than one black man but I also know this guy isn't one of them. I can smell him. I pocket Cañonita.

"Get your cart and get out of here," I say.

"Yes, ma'am. You sure got the guns."

He looks at Wyte for the first time, then back at me, then pulls the hood back up and follows his cart into the river. He's ankle deep when he gets to it. He pulls it out by its front end, leaning back to use his weight. He gets it clear of the water and grabs the handles and looks back once at me then pushes hard into a wobbling walk-run as the lame cart starts veering again.

Wyte looks at me smugly. "Think about my proposal. Take all the time you need. You can use my condo in Maui for a week while you consider. Take your family. Or stay at my home in Mammoth — view of the Sherwins, sunny and light."

"Nothing in Mexico?"

"I own a *casita* in Puerto Vallarta, but

I'm very sorry it's occupied now. Close friends."

I feel the weight of the Colt that I've got aimed at Wyte's chest. Easy shot. It would make me and my family safer. But I can't kill him when the scale in my soul says he doesn't deserve to die.

"My answer is no."

He cocks his head like a dog toward a distant bark. "No? But why?"

"I have enough bosses. I only do what I do for me. That's my final answer."

"I respect it."

"Slowly take off your jacket and turn around."

He does. It's noticeably heavier in the pockets than it should be. He holds it in his left hand as he turns away from me. No back rig. His right hand is still empty and in the open. He looks over his shoulder at me.

I come up behind him, stepping loudly so he knows where I am.

"I have the diamonds," I say.

"Jacket," he says. "All three pockets. Forty-five grand takes up some space."

"Throw the coat away from you, to your left."

It lands on the channel bottom with a puff of dust. I keep the gun on Wyte as I step to it. The four-by-six manila clasp envelope in the left pocket is taut with used hundred-dollar bills. So is the envelope on the right. And the envelope in the buttoned inside pocket. Two go into my coat pocket and the other into the waistband of my jeans.

From my own jacket I take the twenty-carat parcel of near colorless SI2-clarity round-cut parking lot gravel and toss it on the ground up ahead of him where he can see it.

"You have my number," he says, looking over his shoulder again.

"Stand right there until I make the railroad tracks."

"I believe you'll call me."

"Believe what you want. Turn back around and stay that way."

I climb the embankment and jog along the river. The graffiti on the concrete caissons glows softly in the darkness. The last I see of Guy he's standing down there by the little trickle of the water.

I hop the tracks, cut through the side streets and head for my car, cradled in the night.

I'm just about to put the car key in the door when I hear the sound of a double-action revolver being cocked.

"Don't move," says the voice behind me. "Do not move. Do not turn around."

"I'm LAPD, dumbass."

"There's a problem with your product, Suzanne. It's the wrong kind of rock."

I hear motion behind me then I feel cold steel against the back of my skull.

"To your knees, hands on the ground. Now."

I do as he says. Rorke. I can smell him, that get-laid cologne he wears. The gun leaves my head. He quickly removes the bulky envelopes. I hear the rattle of a plastic bag.

"Look straight ahead. Do not move."

The gun pokes the back of my head again. Rorke palms my ass. I feel the bag of money, looped over his wrist, nudging the back of my thigh.

"Sweet."

I hear footsteps, long and padded, then nothing but the high-voltage thrum in the power lines and the cars out on First Street.

40

I'm back at Franklin Intermediate on Wednesday, a week before the students arrive. It's good to see the other teachers, meet the new ones, drink a cup of the bad coffee in the lounge. The teachers are fascinated by what I've been through — my brush with Allison Murrieta, my bad arrest. But they're cool about it, too. They cut me a slightly wider swath than usual and I like it.

Even my principal, a hazy and short-tempered alcoholic, seems slightly respectful. He says he likes me with the cropped blond hair, which I take differently than liking the hairstyle. He is an odd man, a bachelor, and he keeps his job because no one can anticipate him.

I've got my old classroom back, and I like it. I hang my matted copies of the Preamble and the Declaration of Independence and the Gettysburg Address up on the walls.

I set up my 9/11 display, which is mostly

before and after photographs of the World Trade Center. I bought them right there in 2004 when I was one of the teacher-chaperones for an L.A. Unified eighth-grade pilgrimage to Ground Zero. Some of my students wept as they read the posted notes saying good-bye to loved ones in the rubble. It made me proud that they could feel beyond themselves.

I also set up my usual display on the history of baseball in America, since September is the playoffs and lead-up to the World Series. I'll show the students part of Ken Burns's PBS documentary, though to be frank, eighth-graders are more into hoops and extreme sports than guys spitting tobacco juice on the dugout floor. And black-and-white footage tends to put them to sleep.

Luckily, Franklin is a closed and fenced campus and all visitors have to come and go through the office. The office secretary is Wanda and she can be very unwelcoming. By the end of my first Thursday she's turned away four TV news crews, the *Los Angeles Times,* KNX and KFWB radio and a free-lancer hoping to land a *Good Housekeeping* assignment. I'm willing to be temporarily famous but you can't have reporters drop-ping in on you whenever they want. Ruth is arranging the really big stuff anyway.

By Friday morning the classroom is ready but I still have meetings with the principal and the district and the PTA and the school board and even an LAPD presentation here on gang activity and what to do about it. They claim these meetings are necessary but they're agonizing beyond description. I wear my sunglasses and stare out the windows and think of Hood under me on the cushions at the Persian restaurant or sprawled on the bed in the Hotel Laguna looking out at the ocean and muttering something about his world being turned upside down. On a notepad I make a short list of the new cars I'd like to boost, which includes the new Chevrolet Silverado with the six-liter V-8 and 10,500-pound towing capacity, Porsche's naturally aspirated 415-hp GT3 and a Shelby GT-500, which is only a Mustang but with five hundred horses it's the fastest pony — 155 mph — ever built. There are others.

After the last exhausting presentation by an L.A. Unified risk management team — *your best defense against on-site accidents is AWARENESS* — I make it to my car and screech out of the lot before any reporters spot me.

It's ninety-two degrees out. My AC needs a freon charge. Driving the Sentra to and from work every day is spiritual punishment for me but that's the way it'll be for the next nine months. On my salary I can't show up at Franklin Intermediate in a Maybach. The Friday traffic on the surface streets is awful. It takes twenty minutes to go three blocks. Ahead I can see the freeway overpass and it is clogged with cars that do not move.

I can't do it.

I have my needs.

I call home and tell Ernest I'm staying up in L.A. for the night.

I do an hour of hapkido with Quinn downtown, trying to focus but still a little uptight, a little distracted by the last week. I imagine Guy receiving every punch and kick. I'm furious at him for stealing my money but I haven't figured out how to get it back. Yet. Quinn kicks my ass and sends me out with a throbbing shin, sore ribs and a ringing in my head where he caught me with an elbow. Of course I had my headgear on and my mouthpiece in, but I actually felt my brain hit my skull. Quinn sat me in lotus position and worked my neck and temples until my focus came back, pointing out to me that it won't go down like this on the street.

I check into the Mondrian on Sunset and call Hood.

"Charlie." There's a pause. I figure there might be a few of them.

"Hi, Suzanne."

"How much do you miss me?"

"More than a little."

"Catch any bad guys?"

"Only you."

"You've got me all wrong, Charlie."

"Okay."

"Okay?"

"They kicked me off homicide. I'm back on patrol until I get auto theft. So if Allison keeps up her high jinks I might get a shot at her."

"I hope you don't mean with a gun."

"No, I mean give her a shot at due process and getting her life back together."

"What makes you think she needs to get her life back together?"

"She needs her life period."

"She does take some risks."

"If you just came in and spilled it, hired Ruth to represent you, you might do pretty well."

"I'm innocent."

Hood is silent.

"What if Allison disappeared?" I ask.

Another pause. The money pause.

"I wondered about that," he says.

"Say she went away, Charlie. Adios. The public wonders, then they get interested in someone else. You spend some time with me and the boys. Come down to Valley Center on weekends and holidays — you'll love it there. We have a pond with bass and the neighbors have horses we can ride, just like you used to do in Bakersfield. Ernest is going to be okay with how things are. I'm going to set him up with a dressage rider who needs to experience a real ride. So here's the deal, Charlie: the deputy and the teacher, who met by chance on the night of one of L.A.'s worst crimes, fall in love."

Hood chuckles. "Yeah. I thought of all that. Except the dressage rider."

"What do you think?"

"I won't do it."

"Why not?"

"It has to do with what I believe in."

"Tell me what you believe in."

"I'd like to."

"Can I come over?"

Hood's apartment in Silver Lake is like Hood: tall and narrow and neat. It's an older place, with wainscoting, wall cornices and a high, stamped aluminum ceiling. The furniture looks cheap and new. He's got a few books and a bunch of music and Ansel Adams pictures on the walls.

He follows my eye and says that's Yosemite in winter and I try very hard not to but I step across the room and put my arms around him. Next thing I'm on the floor looking up at Hood's face above me haloed by the ceiling lamp. His expression is serious. We're slightly slower about it than before, there's some acknowledgment in it, some awareness of a shared history, and it's good, fantastically good.

Later he brings a bottle of wine and two glasses back to the bedroom. I pull up with the sheet around me and he tells me about the Iraqi man and his three boys shot to death by seven soldiers and Lenny Overbrook trying to take the blame for all of them, just like they told him to. Hood was a NCIS detective and it was his job to figure out what happened, but he was also right there after this shoot-out and he saw six guys running away and this simpleton Lenny wiping down a Russian gun after putting it on the dead Iraqi's lap. And it came down to Lenny's word that he'd shot up these four men himself, against Hood's that he saw six more running away from the house, but Hood couldn't ID anybody. So he could either take Lenny's mostly false confession and send him to prison for four murders he couldn't have committed, or he could let four innocent people get murdered and watch everyone walk away from it. He set the kid free and tried to keep the case open but he got no cooperation up the chain of command and when his tour was done he came home. A sniper's bullet hit a wall right next to him one day, broad daylight in a controlled zone, and Hood wasn't sure if it was an Iraqi or a fellow soldier. Hood tells me that that bullet revealed a truth about himself that he wasn't prepared to face — that he was feared and hated. I think the idea that his own men wanted him dead broke part of his heart, though he didn't use those words. He couldn't sleep and he couldn't eat and by the time he got back to Pendleton he weighed fifteen pounds less than at the start of his second tour, and he was pretty much skin and bones even then.

When Hood is done with the story, or I think he's done with it, he takes a Bible from the drawer of his nightstand and opens it up where there's a folded piece of paper to hold the place and I figure it's time for Psalms or maybe Job, but he hands me the paper and sets the Bible down.

I unfold it and he explains it's a list that Lenny gave him of the six others — names and ranks all written out in handwriting that quite frankly looks like a third-grader in a hurry.

"I think about that piece of paper sometimes," says Hood. "Some days I think I'll call the navy and tell them what I've learned. Other days, not."

"Let it go, Hood. You did the right thing. Our soldiers should never have been there in the first place."

"That's not the point."

"It's the whole point — it should never have happened."

"All that matters is what happens. I never thought we should have gone in there either but rules don't get suspended because of what you think. Murder is the same thing in Anbar as it is in L.A. I know those soldiers were furious and scared. You can't even believe the pressure that builds up. You're surrounded by betrayal and ugliness and hatred. The heat and the dust and the blood. It gets into you and you have to do something. For those guys, the four dead Iraqis were that something."

"That's why you did the right thing, Charlie. Those soldiers were put into an unwinnable situation and they did the best they could. Your letting them go is your part, Hood. It's your duty and you're guilty of doing it, just like they are. It's the guilt that earns your forgiveness."

He looks at me. "No. If you make murder okay you make everything okay. And you tilt the world to an angle where you can't build anything. Nothing."

"You are not God and you are not your own judge."

"I am very much my own judge, Suzanne."

Hood refolds the list of names and sets it back in his Bible. I watch his upper body, the indentation of his backbone and the rounded straps of muscle that run alongside it. He's got a cool mole and I touch it.

He turns off the light and gets into bed beside me and pulls the sheet up and we're alone in the near darkness. His voice is just a whisper.

"I'm sorry," says Hood.

I know there's no reason to argue with him. Or to deny what he knows. He has seen me. *Seen.* Hood is Hood and he's got the Man Thing. Nothing sneaky about him. It's my turn to whisper now but the words sound so loud to me.

"You can't prove anything. And your sheriff buddies can't. And the DA can't."

His heart beats faster and harder. I set my cheek against his chest. "Suzanne, there's guys like Lenny and guys better than Lenny getting killed every day. While you boost cars and stick up minimum wage workers. That's disrespect."

"The war used up all your forgiveness?"

"It used up all my something."

Hood's heart is going strong. I put my nose next to his ear, the same place I put it down in Valley Center.

It's an empty feeling when your love isn't enough. It's supposed to be but sometimes it's not. I know that Hood's past has shaped him, and that my past has shaped me. These are powerful things. You can enlist in them or rebel against them but in your heart you always know the truth of who you are and you cannot escape it.

I begin to dress in the darkness. I can see Hood's eyes shining down there, stars in the universe. There have been many needs inside me, some all self and others not all self. Some that take, some that honor and make strength, some simple and some imponderable. But not like this. This is his, mine and ours.

"Charlie."

"Yes."

"It's Wyte."

"I thought so. Talk to me."

I tell him almost everything I know — the building in Long Beach with the swank computers, Wyte's arrangements with the ports, Rorke, Wyte's offer of partnership. He says nothing while I talk.

"It's all in the notebook in my purse," I say. "His address in Long Beach, a phone number. Descriptions of his place, every detail I can remember, which is a lot. I'm going to leave it on the counter out there. It's more than enough to get you started. And, Charlie, Wyte doesn't know that I know. You can surprise him."

"Did you sell him the diamonds?"

"Not exactly."

I'm finished dressing. Seems like with Hood I'm always dressing and undressing.

There's a moment in the near dark when I can just barely make out his shape. I know he's watching me. I can see the glimmer in his eyes. They look like lights across a vast ocean.

"Good-bye, Charlie. I'm leaving something for you. I'll put it on top of the notebook."

"Vaya con Dios, Suzanne."

41

Hood got back his old Region II patrol shift. It felt right to be in the summer-weight cotton-poly uniform and the law enforcement Ford. He had failed homicide and he felt shame but some relief. Maybe someday he'd get another shot. His thoughts were often of Suzanne Jones and Reginald Wyte, and his dreams were haunted by them.

Rolling through his first September night back on patrol, Hood had the repeating thought that he was alone in L.A. and far removed from the powers that shaped it but nonetheless entrusted with this small piece.

On his third night out Hood was up in Vernon when Marlon radioed him. "Charlie, Allison Murrieta just stuck up the Lynwood Denny's on Long Beach Boulevard. Shots fired. I'm on my way."

Hood hit his siren and running lights and made the scene in twelve minutes. Gunning the Ford down Long Beach Boulevard, he saw three cruisers jammed at crazy angles outside the restaurant, their lights pulsing yellow and red in the darkness, and the bristling silhouettes of armed officers moving like figures in firelight. A helicopter already hovered in the sky above.

Two deputies stood guard at the entrance. Hood saw blood on the ground and bullet holes in the windows. Through the shattered glass he saw that two other deputies had witnesses corralled in a rear section and they were letting some of the diners exit by the back door.

In the lobby by the cash register a young South Side Compton Crip gesticulated elaborately before two more patrol deputies and three of his homies. Hood could hear some of his words through the shut glass doors, and he could hear the wail of sirens in the distance.

"The bitch has me dead but she don't pull . . ."

"Murrieta was robbing the place and the Crip shot her," said one of the deputies, nodding toward the lobby without looking. "Someone said her gun jammed. She ran into the parking lot, through the bushes."

Hood made his way across the lot then through a wilted hedge of hibiscus to the poorly lit street. Three more cruisers and a paramedic unit were parked at the end of a cul-de-sac ahead of him. He ran down a narrow, dislocated sidewalk, past the old cars and the beaten houses and the people inside their heavy screen doors or standing in their yards.

"That Allison in there at Rachman's?"

"That's Allison, shot up and bleeding."

"You go get her, cowboy. You rescue old Rachman!"

Hood bent low and joined the deputies behind the forward car. Cruz, the patrol sergeant, squatted with a megaphone in one hand. A big deputy peered over the hood of the car cradling a combat shotgun in one arm. Three other deputies steadied their sidearms on the roofs of their units, feet spread for balance and heads still.

"She's got an old man hostage," said Cruz. "She shot at us a few minutes ago. SWAT and the negotiators are on the way."

"Give me the megaphone," said Hood.

To his surprise the sergeant gave it up. Hood stood and looked at the house. It was square and plain, with a dirt front yard and a "For Sale" sign and simple iron grates over the windows and curtains behind them. The lights were faint inside.

"Allison, it's Charlie," he blared. "Charlie Hood. I'm going to come talk to you. If you want a hostage, use me. I'm coming now."

He tossed the megaphone to Cruz and walked toward the house with his hands up and open. He heard the sirens getting louder and the voices behind him.

"The man's goin' in. He is actually goin' into Rachman's!"

"Get her, cowboy!"

"Take that mask off her! Rescue Rachman!"

Hood knocked on the door. He heard voices. A moment later the door cracked open and Hood found himself looking up at a large black face.

"She said let you in. But I ain't sure."

"Open the door. You're free to go."

"She needs help."

"Go."

"Deputy, you can't throw me out of my own house."

He turned and walked away, and Hood followed him inside and shut the door. He was taller than Hood by a head and almost twice as thick.

"It's the teacher," Rachman said. "Crazy. The teacher is Allison. That's something. But she won't let the paramedics in. I can't talk any sense into her."

Suzanne lay on her back on the living room sofa. She was wrapped in what looked like bedsheets and a brightly colored purple-

and-blue afghan. Her wig and gun and mask were on the floor beside her. Her face was pale and he heard her teeth chattering and saw the rapid rise and fall of the covers that she had pulled up tight to her chin. Her knuckles were hard and white.

"Charlie."

"Don't talk — listen. The medics can keep you from dying, Suzanne, but I can't."

She shivered and coughed red. Hood touched her forehead, which was cool and damp. When he'd worked the covers free of her grip, he lifted them and saw the blood and smelled it.

"I'm getting the medics, Suzanne."

"Okay."

Hood slid the derringer far under the couch, then crossed the room and threw open the front door. He called out from the porch. Rachman joined him, waving them in.

Back inside, Hood knelt beside her. He took Suzanne's hand. Her fingers were strong and her nails dug into him and her voice was thin and wet.

"Like your diamonds, Charlie?"

"They're beautiful."

"It took that kid forever to get his gun up. I just couldn't shoot him."

"That's okay, Suzanne."

"Bradley's age."

"You did the right thing."

"Tell the boys I love them."

"You can tell them that yourself."

"This isn't right. So much to do. So much you don't know."

"Right now you think about good things, and you keep breathing in and out. You're going to be okay, Suzanne. They're almost here. These guys are good."

Hood leaned over her and put his face next to hers, felt the coolness of her skin against his, smelled the faint aroma of her perfume and the strong metallic odor of the life draining out of her.

"Oh, I like you," she whispered.

"I love you. Be strong."

He heard Rachman's voice, then the deputy with the shotgun burst into the house, then more uniforms with their weapons drawn. Last were two firemen carrying medical equipment, and two paramedics angling a backboard through the doorway.

Suzanne coughed again. Hood rose up, and he felt her nails digging deeper into his hand.

"Call me later," she said.

She looked at the men then back at Hood. Her throat rattled and the light retreated from her eyes and her face relaxed.

"I will."

He stared at her a moment. The paramedics pushed Hood aside, and threw back the covers and lifted Suzanne to the floor. One of them strapped an Ambu bag to her head then started an IV in each arm. A fireman cut away her blouse and pressed a big defibrillator patch to her chest while the other started CPR. A moment later the EKG monitor showed only a small, occasional blip.

"She's in PEA," said one of the medics. "Epinephrine and atropine, run the IVs wide open. I'm going to needle her."

He stabbed a large IV needle between her ribs. Hood heard the trapped air hissing out but the EKG line had gone flat.

He turned away.

A minute later he stopped for Marlon on the front walkway. "Suzanne was Murrieta. A kid shot her."

Marlon nodded.

"I'll notify her family," Hood said. "If that's okay with you."

"It's okay. I'm sorry, Charlie. I know she meant something to you."

"Her gun is under the couch."

Back at the Denny's Hood talked to the shooter for a few minutes, found out his gang name was Kick because he took kung fu once, and his gun was a .38-caliber. A South Side Crip. Kick asked about the reward and Hood told him there was no reward and Kick said too bad, his mama needed money for an operation. Hood had no idea what they'd do with him — just carrying a concealed piece was a crime, and it was probably stolen property anyway — but when a woman in a mask is brandishing her own handgun, you've got a good start on self-defense.

He walked back through the parking lot and down the cul-de-sac. He lingered outside the house until the coroner's team wheeled her out, wondering how to tell Ernest and the boys.

Two hours later when he pulled up, Ernest was standing on the Valley Center porch in the glow of a yellow bug light with a mug of coffee in his hand and the dogs alert at his feet.

42

The next afternoon Hood stood in the Valley Center barn while the sunlight slanted through the old boards and the pigeons cooed up in the eaves.

He felt that he owed Suzanne a good-faith search for the head and effects of Joaquin Murrieta, though he knew what he would find. Two hours in the house had yielded nothing and neither had the garage. The barn would be Joaquin's last stand.

Ernest and the boys were up in L.A. Hood had explained that an autopsy was required by law after violent death, and Ernest and the boys had left at first light, wanting to be closer to her.

Hood understood. In his imagination he sheltered her body from the terrible saws and blades used for autopsy.

Ernest had wept openly when Hood told him — he'd known something was wrong.

Ernest had told Bradley and Jordan himself. A few hours later, when they left, Hood saw in Bradley a withering rage that reminded him of Suzanne on the night he betrayed her into arrest. Bradley was taller and fuller than Hood had remembered and there was something both controlled and wild in him.

Hood listened to the pigeons.

He looked down at the unmistakable stain left by Harold and Gerald Little Chief.

All this for forty-five thousand dollars' worth of diamonds.

He sized up the big industrial shelves along one side of the building, the way they were filled with clear stacking plastic boxes, each labeled. She could hide things in plain sight, thought Hood, but it wasn't likely.

Still, he carried over an extension ladder and searched the highest and most remote boxes. Old children's clothing. Years of Mexican TV soap opera magazines, some of them with her mother on the cover. Old quilts and comforters redolent of naphthalene. He sneezed from the dust as he slid them back into place, moved the ladder, then opened more.

He poked through the cardboard boxes behind the bicycles, but they were all filled with outgrown toys. He walked the perimeter of the barn tapping for a false wall but found none.

Ditto the floor for some kind of basement, but the concrete slab was continuous and gave up nothing.

Suzanne would be laughing, wouldn't she?

He sat on a hay bale and looked through the open door at the bright barnyard and the towering oak in which she had sat waiting for Lupercio.

The sun is coming up over the hills and colors are starting to form.

No more hills for you, he thought, no colors. He felt the diamond H against his chest.

Hood had never lost a lover to death before. His feelings were deep and clear — sorrow, regret, blame, anger, helplessness — all taking their separate turns to advance and retreat and then advance again, holding hands in varying combinations. But the most powerful feeling of all was one without a name and therefore unspeakable — a recognition of having lost forever someone singular and irreplaceable and beyond valuation.

There was a recently added bathroom built into one corner of the old barn, and Hood used it and drank from the tap and splashed water in his face and looked up at the too-noisy ceiling fan before he pulled the chain to turn it off.

He saw the access hatch. He walked out of the bathroom and across the barn enough to get a good perspective, and when he turned, he saw what he thought he might: the roof of the bathroom was a good seven feet higher than its ceiling. An attic.

He stood on his toes and popped the hatch and slid it under the insulation and away from the opening. He pushed on the insulation. He got a stepladder this time and stood on the first step, moving the sheets of batting to the side. The layers of it were neat, and the paper backing was in nearly perfect shape, and Hood could tell that it had been placed there to suggest that the space was dead, insulation only, without further utility. Maybe it was. It took him a while to make an opening for himself.

When he was finally able to stand and pull the chain for the ceiling light, the white walls of the attic came to life and Hood found himself facing a simple wooden picnic table. It was covered by a thin woven blanket beneath which Hood could see the shapes of things.

He ran his hands over the shapes, dubious but imagining.

Then like a magician he took up the corners of one end and lifted the blanket high and slowly, moving in small side steps to reveal the illusion beneath.

He dropped the blanket just beyond the edge of the table and it landed in a quiet puff of dust.

The head sat in a jar of vague yellow liquid, skin gray and eyes closed. Peaceful. Bald. The black hair was long and formed a loose bedding at the bottom. The neck was severed cleanly. Beside the jar was a lariat. Beside that was an oily red bandana, which Hood moved aside to see the Colt single-action revolver. An old handmade arrow with a small obsidian head lay in front of two topless, rough-hewn wooden boxes. In one was a nameless leather-bound book sitting atop a stack of carefully folded but very old clothes. In another were newspapers and photographs and a nearly empty bandoleer.

He sat down with his back to the wall and closed his eyes.

An hour later he covered the artifacts with the blanket and carefully replaced the insulation and finally slid the access cover back into place.

He was shouldering the stepladder from the bathroom back into the barn when Bradley appeared at the open door then stepped inside.

"What are you doing?"

"I didn't hear you drive up."

"They made us view her on a TV screen. I insisted that we see the actual body. There was an argument but I stayed patient and they let us."

"I'm sorry, Bradley."

"I asked you what you're doing."

"Looking for stolen property."

"Find any?"

"None at all."

"What's the stepladder for?"

Hood looked at the boy, then at the stacked boxes he'd been through earlier. He saw the illogic of using a stepladder to reach the high boxes and knew that Bradley saw it, too.

"I need the extension ladder," said Hood.

Bradley glanced toward the bathroom then gave Hood a hard stare that looked very much like his mother's.

Hood saw his choices — either show Bradley the truth of his blood history, or show him nothing and let that truth either expire or be discovered later.

"I'll help investigate," said the boy.

"I can't let you," said Hood. "There's a chain of evidence you need for court, and if it's compromised by a citizen the case can be ruined."

"Even the son of the accused?"

"Especially."

"Then I'll watch."

"I'll check a few of those boxes up there, then I'm done."

"No stolen property so far?"

"None that I can see."

Hood traded ladders then started up on top again and checked through different boxes. The pigeons watched him, heads down and cocked in curiosity. Bradley sat on the hay bale where Hood had sat.

"How old are you?"

"Almost seventeen."

"Still thinking LAPD?"

"That's a long time away."

"You just started your junior year?"

"Yeah, but I'll be done with all my solids at the end of it. I'll have sixteen college units by the end of my senior year, something like that."

"You should go to college."

"What's the minimum age for the Sheriff's?"

"They want twenty-one, with a couple years of college."

"But what's the minimum age?"

"Nineteen and a half, and they'll swear you for duty at twenty. It's a good gig, Bradley. It keeps you fit and the people are mostly good and you can hang it up after twenty years with some nice bennies."

"Have you killed anybody?"

"No."

"Want to?"

"I used to want to make a really great shot that saved a life. Most young deputies imagine that. Not anymore. I've seen enough blood."

"A gangbanger. My age."

"Yeah."

"Kick."

"That's his gang name."

"I know what it is. You talk to him?"

Hood nodded. "Not a whole lot there to talk to if you know what I mean."

"They going to charge him with murder?"

"I don't know. The DA decides that."

"I always knew she was hiding something."

"That doesn't surprise me."

"She was her but not her. Joaquin Murrieta was a real outlaw. They cut off his head and put it in a jar and showed it for money. It wasn't unusual. They decapitated dead suspects back then because there was no refrigeration and the heads were easy to identify. He was twenty-three, barely old enough to be a deputy. She told me about him when I was a kid. I never knew she wanted to be like him. Maybe that was my fault. Maybe I should have seen that in her."

"There's no way you could have seen it, Bradley."

The boy glanced toward the bathroom but said nothing.

Hood looked down at him, sitting on the hay bale. "If you want a recommendation to the L.A. Sheriff's, I'll make it when the time comes. With your grades, Bradley, and the college units, and those athletic skills of yours — you'll get in."

Bradley shrugged. "I'll think about it. Maybe as a deputy I'd run across Kick someday. And I could draw my sidearm and blow his fucking heart out his back."

"You could."

He shrugged again. "You were in love with her, weren't you?"

"Yes."

"I was, too. I thought she was the most beautiful woman I'd ever seen or ever would see. Everything I did was for her. Just a common Oedipal thing. I knew I'd outgrow it like most boys do."

"Bradley?"

"What."

"Go to college."

43

The memorial service was up in Bakersfield in an old cemetery that sheltered sixteen of Suzanne's relatives. There were news crews all over the place, allowed in by Madeline so her daughter could make history instead of only teach it. The casket was open, and at a good moment Madeline fainted into Bradley's arms. The cameramen scrambled and shot. When it was his turn, Hood could hardly stand to look.

The day was clear, with an east wind that carried an infernal heat, and Hood stood graveside with the mourners in the insufficient shade of a pepper tree. Suzanne was buried above her great-uncle Jack, with an empty plot on either side of her for Madeline and her grandmother.

Hood went over and stood with Ernest and the boys when it was over. They talked for a minute while the mourners went back to their cars and the gravedigger waited patiently atop his front loader.

On his way back up the hill to his car, Hood decided for probably the one hundredth time that he'd show and tell Bradley everything he knew about his mother. But two steps later he decided for the one hundredth time to let the boy find his own way through life.

He visited friends and stayed in a Bakersfield motel that night. He got drunk and slept poorly but rose early for the drive.

At eleven A.M. Hood was admitted into a fourth-floor room of the Manhattan Beach Marriott Hotel, hung over but ready to face internal affairs. Three of the four men he'd never seen before. Two were scruffy and didn't look like cops. Another looked like a TV version of the driven prosecutor. One was an assistant sheriff, clearly unhappy about this.

On the coffee table were two digital recorders. Beside it was a small video camera on a black tripod.

Hood sat on a floral rattan sofa and looked through the window to the warm, hazy sky. He was exhausted by his own betrayals.

One of the scruffy cops turned on the voice recorders and the lawyer fixed the camera on Hood then in a strong clear voice established the place and time and players.

"Deputy Hood, tell us about Wyte," he said cheerfully.

44

Two days later Hood again let himself into the Valley Center barn. Bradley was due in half an hour. He had agreed to be on time for what Hood promised would be an important meeting.

Hood got the stepladder and slid open the bathroom attic hatch, careful not to tear up the insulation.

When he turned on the light, he saw that the blanket was thrown to the floor and everything was gone. Everything gone but the blanket and the table.

He climbed back down and settled the access cover into place and took the ladder back where it belonged.

Outside in the barnyard he looked out at the massive old oak tree and the pond and the dirt road that separated the property from Betty Little Chief's.

He sat on a bench in the shade of the barn and tried to figure out what would happen next, knowing he had little say in it now.

Then up the dirt road came Bradley's green 1970 Cyclone GT, slowly but thunderously, the dust rising behind the fat back tires and the Glasspaks spitting up dirt. It made a deliberate turn at the pond, and Hood heard the snarl of the 351 Cleveland in first.

Behind it was a low-slung Honda Accord, and behind the Honda was a cobalt blue Mitsubishi Lancer, and behind that was an old red-and-white two-tone F-150 agleam within the swirling dust.

The Cyclone rumbled along and came to a stop twenty feet from Hood. Bradley was at the wheel and the backseats were piled high with luggage and boxes. The other cars idled in a loose line behind the Cyclone, exhaust stirring the road dust. Two of the other drivers were young men, genuinely tough-looking. Hood couldn't see much of the truck driver.

The driver's side window went down, and Bradley looked at Hood from behind dark sunglasses.

"Looks like you're moving out, Bradley."

"That's because I am."

"You going to just drop everything, or finish up school and sports?"

"More or less."

"Where you going?"

Bradley shook his head. "Places."

"Take off those glasses, Bradley."

Bradley hesitated then pushed his sun-glasses up into his long black hair. "I knew you'd been up there. You didn't put the insulation back right. Sorry I had to spoil your surprise."

"I thought you might do this. I don't know what your mother wanted for you, but I've thought about it a lot. I decided the right thing was to tell you, show you those things in the attic, let you take it from there."

"She tried to tell me a couple of times. She never quite got the words out. But really, how hard was it to find that stuff? I had years."

Hood looked back at the other cars then at Bradley again. These guys looked too young to be outlaws, but he knew they weren't too young.

"The trouble is, you'll get shot down and you'll be dead forever," he said. "It happened to Joaquin and Suzanne and it'll happen to you."

"Do you feel obligated to say that?"

"Only because it's true."

"Well, Hood, thanks for the counsel."

"You can do better, Bradley. The whole world is out there. You can be whatever you want."

"I'm already what I want."

Hood didn't answer. The driver in the Honda gunned his engine, then the Lancer and the pickup truck followed suit. Bradley answered with some throttle of his own, checking his buddies in his sideview mirror.

"It's a waste of your life and you'll regret it."

"I like you, Hood, but you old guys don't know shit."

"Are you going track down Kick?"

"Wouldn't you?"

"Don't try it in my jurisdiction."

Bradley lowered his sunglasses. Then he reached into the passenger seat and brushed aside a leather jacket and lifted the jar containing Joaquin's head. For a moment he held it up in front of his face. The head shifted slowly and the hair lilted and the surface vibrated with the car engine. Then Bradley put it back on the seat and covered it with the jacket. He looked at Hood and nodded and gunned the engine.

Then the Cyclone trundled around the oak tree, spit some dirt and rocks against the old trunk and lumbered back down the road the way it had come.

Bradley's gang followed, engines growling, the first two drivers giving Hood their best killah stares as their cars eased past him.

The truck came last and paused, and Hood saw that the driver was a girl, red-haired and beautiful.

She studied Hood for a moment with an expression beyond her years, then the truck accelerated around the oak tree and down the road.

45

Hood sat on the dais in Captain Wyte's fortress in Long Beach. The room was dark except for scattered indicator lights in red and blue, some blinking and some not. Outside the great cranes of the Port of Long Beach hovered over the containers and the powerful lights made the port look as if it were the most important place in all the night.

He heard the elevator moan. His Glock sat on the table next to one of Wyte's custom computers, a brushed aluminum masterpiece that shivered with subtle colors even in the near darkness of the room.

Hood heard the elevator come to a stop, then the door slide open. Wyte stepped from the lighted box, a leather briefcase in one hand and a bottle-sized brown paper bag in the other.

He went to the wall and turned on the lights low, then adjusted them lower. He had taken just two steps toward Hood when he realized he was being watched and he tried to not react. Hood placed his hand on his pistol as he spoke.

"I've got a weapon in my hand, Captain."

Wyte stopped and looked up at him.

"This is private property and you are trespassing."

"You're a sworn peace officer. Within the Sheriff's Department you have fewer rights than a convicted rapist."

"You've been talking to IA."

"I have."

Wyte nodded to the space around him. "All of this can and will be explained. I look forward to it."

"Me, too."

"Suzanne started you down this path, no doubt. Something about a computer in the safe house, right?"

Hood shrugged.

"Charlie, she should never have gone after blood diamonds."

"You shouldn't have either. All those lives for forty-five grand? What a fuckin' waste."

"You have no idea of the truth."

"I know a lie when I hear it."

"Why are you here, Charlie?"

"Just to see the look on your face."

"Let's talk."

"Let's."

"Drink?"

"First, say hello to some friends of mine."

One of the IA pack turned up the lights and the others emerged from their respective corners and shadows. Wyte broke for the elevator, but one of the scruffy undercovers shot him straight in the chest with a Taser. Wyte flew backward with a scream and crashed to the floor. The briefcase went one way and the bottle went the other, exploding when it hit. It looked to Hood as if Wyte had been struck by lightning. The cops disarmed him and cuffed him and dragged him upright and dumped him onto the leather sofa below the dais that Suzanne had described to Hood.

Hood stood and holstered his sidearm, went down the stairs then through a side door.

A short hallway led to another room, a windowless, high-ceilinged warehouse filled with neat rows of industrial shelving nearly twenty feet high. Hood saw the big rolling platform ladders like in a home improvement store. Hundreds of televisions, DVD players, computers and peripherals, telephones, faxes, stereo equipment, cameras, musical instruments, coffeemakers, toys — all new and still in their boxes. Near the big roll-up door in the back he saw the pallets heaped with cases of liquor and wine and beer and soft drinks and candy, wrapped in heavy translucent packing plastic. Pallets of tile and car wheels and cigarettes. Pallets of porno magazines and service china and sprinkler heads and hand tools and ready-to-assemble bicycles and swimming pool chlorine and extra virgin olive oil. Bins of granite and marble and electrical cable and shiny new copper pipe.

Hood shook his head and walked back out to where the cops were interviewing Wyte. He walked past them looking at no one, took the elevator down and drove home.

Two mornings later he walked into the Navy Criminal Investigation Service headquarters on Camp Pendleton with Lenny's list in his pocket. It weighed a thousand pounds.

Lenny walked in behind him, buzz-cut and ramrod straight, the familiar inexplicable light in his eyes.

46

Hood sat on a rock on the bank of the Merced River in Yosemite and tied a fly on for his father. It was early and they were alone. The morning was cool and quiet, and Douglas seemed uninterested in the skills he had mastered and taught to his son and then lost, all within his lifetime.

Hood finished the knot and watched his father stare out at this new old river. Beyond it the hills were thick with conifers and the sky was a pale blue and there was a plume of smoke from a distant fire.

"We may as well start with a caddis," said Hood.

"By all means."

"Thanks for coming out here with me."

"I don't see any reason to stay more than just a few minutes."

"All right."

They waded into the cold water. Hood pointed to a riffle upstream of them, possibly the same riffle that Douglas had pointed out to him when they first fished this stretch twenty years ago. Hood understood that the saying about something going past in the blink of an eye can be literal, not just figurative.

Hood stepped back to give his father room to cast, the water powerful against his legs. Douglas held his old handmade rod in the air with his right hand and some slack line in his left. The fly was in the water, skittering in place on the surface at the end of its downstream tether. Beyond this basic posture for casting Douglas appeared flummoxed and looked at his son.

Hood waded up behind him and took his father's hands and started the old motion that Douglas had shown him, the rod tip held high and the wrist firm and the elbow forming a fulcrum and the left hand feeding line or hauling it tight. It was an easy rhythm, and up this close Hood could smell his father's aging body and the aftershave he'd used his whole life, and he could feel the loose coolness of his skin and the lightness of his bones and the reluctant machinery of his joints.

Douglas shrugged him off with an obscenity and Hood waded toward the bank so he could watch.

His father looked at him, then took up the cast again, and Hood watched the white fly line loop back and forth overhead in increasing lengths until it shot forward straight and settled and a silky filament unfurled at the last instant, placing the tiny fly at the head of the riffle.

His father mended the line then smiled at Hood with joy and the memory of joy.

Standing where this river briefly intersected time, Hood believed that all on Earth was forgiven.

He smiled back.

AUTHOR'S NOTE

History reached out and clenched me as I sat in my fourth-grade class, reading about the great outlaw Joaquin Murrieta. He was allegedly bloodthirsty, and an accomplished horse thief, gambler and killer. Joaquin's picture made him look certifiably crazy. There were rumors he gave some of his loot to the poor. We crew-cut 1960s fourth graders were supposed to be fascinated by the California missions built by the Spanish, but in my young and impatient mind the missions were stone-cold adobe boredom compared to dashing Joaquin.

Many years later, when I went to write *L.A. Outlaws,* I set out to do some more serious research on Joaquin. But I found that the harder I pressed for the truth of his life, the more quickly the "facts" were either complicated, changed, or sometimes simply made to vanish.

His date and place of birth are disputed.

The spelling of his name is disputed.

Some say he was forced into a life of violence by the rape of his young wife, Rosa; others say this was legend only.

But this much is agreed: The outlaw Joaquin Murrieta was shot down and beheaded in 1853, and such was his notoriety that the head — preserved in a jar of alcohol — was exhibited on tour. It cost a buck to see it. It was possibly lost in the great San Francisco earthquake of 1906.

So, the Joaquin you read about in *L.A. Outlaws* was very much a real man.

In *L.A. Outlaws* I've compiled the Joaquin myths and added a huge fiction: the existence of his great-great-great-great-great-great granddaughter, Allison Murrieta.

If you want to read more about Joaquin, you can hit the library, the Internet or a good bookstore. I've written a piece on him at www.tjeffersonparker.com.

If you want to read about Allison — his beautiful, brave, audacious outlaw descendant — read the novel you've got in your hands.

It's all the stuff of legend.

T. Jefferson Parker
Fallbrook, California
2008

ACKNOWLEDGMENTS

I'd like to thank Steve and Pam Cardamenis for all of their help with the diamonds.

And Dr. Kurt Popke and Noah Byrne for knowing how to save a life.

I thank John Austin and Dave Bridgman, brothers of the badge, for their expertise on fast cars and hot guns.

Thanks to Ken Wilson for the early read.

And once again, thanks to researcher Sherry Merryman, SuperSleuth, unlocker of secrets.

My humble thanks to all of you.

T. Jefferson Parker

ABOUT THE AUTHOR

T. Jefferson Parker is the bestselling author of fourteen previous novels, including *Storm Runners* and *The Fallen*. Alongside Dick Francis and James Lee Burke, Parker is one of only three writers to be awarded the Edgar Award for Best Novel more than once. Parker lives with his family in Southern California.

3/09